BY MONICA MURPHY

ONE WEEK GIRLFRIEND SERIES
One Week Girlfriend
Second Chance Boyfriend
Three Broken Promises
Drew + Fable Forever (e-Original Novella)
Four Years Later

THE FOWLER SISTERS SERIES
Owning Violet

Owning
Violet

Owning Violet

A Novel

Monica Murphy

BANTAM BOOKS TRADE PAPERBACKS
NEW YORK

A Bantam Books Trade Paperback Original

Copyright © 2014 by Monica Murphy
Excerpt from *Stealing Rose* by Monica Murphy copyright © 2015 by Monica Murphy

Published in the United States by Bantam Books, an imprint of Random House, a division of Random House LLC, a Penguin Random House Company, New York.

BANTAM BOOKS and the HOUSE colophon are registered trademarks of Random House LLC.

This book contains an excerpt from the forthcoming book *Stealing Rose* by Monica Murphy. This excerpt has been set for this edition only and may not reflect the final content of the forthcoming edition.

ISBN 978-0-553-39326-2
eBook ISBN 978-0-553-39327-9

Printed in the United States of America on acid-free paper

www.bantamdell.com

9876543

Book design by Karin Batten

To my critique partner, my friend, my secret wifey, Katy Evans, for encouraging me throughout the writing of this book, for the cover quote, and for claiming Ryder as her own. I couldn't do this without you, Katy! Love you!

But then she looks at you, and in you
there is sun, there is love, there is life.

—FELLINI

Owning
Violet

Chapter One

Violet

Tonight, my life is going to change.

In preparation for it, I spent all day at the spa. Treated myself to a facial, massage, wax, mani, and pedi. My skin is smooth, my face is clear, my fingers and toes are painted a perfect demure pink. My muscles are relaxed and loose, but my brain . . .

My brain is jumpy. My stomach is a mess of nerves. My outward appearance is the exact opposite of my inside because so much is on the line. Everything I've strived toward these last few years is coming to the final pinnacle tonight.

Finally.

I found a dress to wear for this special moment a few days ago at Barneys, one I knew Zachary would approve of. A navy-blue sheath, it hits just above the knee and skims over my curves, subtly sexy because he doesn't like anything overt. Obvious.

Meaning he hates everything my older sister wears, does, says. He doesn't much approve of the way my blunt baby sister acts, either.

But that's fine. He's going to ask me to marry him tonight. Not Lily or Rose.

Me.

There's nothing obvious about me. I'm the epitome of understated. I would make the perfect politician's wife. Standing behind my man, offering my never-ending support all while wearing the pleasant smile I've mastered over the years. There have been a few slipups in the past. I struggled once. Fought for my life, really, and survived.

My father and grandmother like to pretend none of that ever happened. Zachary doesn't even know about it. It's a moment in time—before I met him—the family prefers to sweep under the rug.

It's so ugly, Violet, Father told me once. *Wouldn't you rather forget?*

So I try. For the family.

Zachary arrives at my apartment right on time because heaven forbid he's ever late. One of the many qualities I admire about him. He's punctual, thoughtful, efficient, handsome, and smart. So incredibly smart. Some call him conniving. Others call him cutthroat. Rumors swirl that there are other women. I'm not stupid. I have my suspicions. They might have even been confirmed once or twice. But when we're engaged, when we're married . . .

That will change. It has to.

Zachary and I have a perfect relationship. The sort of relationship I'd dreamed of since I was a little girl. One that Lily mocks constantly, but what does she know about love?

Sex and addiction and getting into trouble, she knows plenty. But love? I don't think she's had a real relationship in her life.

I have. Boyfriends throughout junior high and high school, then my one very serious boyfriend in college. The one I'd originally thought I might marry. The one I gave my virginity to midway through freshman year. I'd been a real holdout, one of the last remaining virgins among my friends.

He dumped me the beginning of our sophomore year. Right after everything . . . happened. The incident, I like to call it. The thing no one likes to talk about. So I don't talk about it either.

After the breakup, I remained single. Tried my best to rise

above everything that happened by focusing on finishing school and then on my career, my legacy at Fleur Cosmetics.

I might have quietly fallen apart for a short period of time that not many know about. We kept it secret. Father didn't want any more public humiliations. We lost Mom so long ago and he always said I was the most like her. Delicate but determined. Smart but not always practical.

I lived up to his expectations for a brief, not-so-shining moment. I needed therapy. I needed medication. More than anything, I needed to be numb. *Craved* being numb. Feeling emotions only hurt, and I was so tired of hurting.

But eventually I knew I needed to learn how to cope on my own.

Father let me return to work after my brief stint away. And when Zachary Lawrence started working for the company two years ago, getting to know him, I was soon interested. And so was he. I could tell. I didn't care if at first he talked to me only because I was the CEO's daughter. I flirted. I wanted his attention.

And I eventually got it. Got *him*.

I knew dating someone I worked with wasn't the smartest move, but I couldn't help it. Where else can I meet a man of such good quality? Someone I can trust? I have trust issues. No surprise, considering what I've been through.

While my father calls most of the shots, the company really is a family business. Both Rose and I work there. Even my grandmother still comes in and consults, though she's now eighty-five and mostly retired.

She loves Fleur Cosmetics and Fragrance. My grandma *is* Fleur Cosmetics and Fragrance. She started the brand. It was her face that appeared in the magazine advertisements and billboards for so many years. Dahlia Fowler is a legend in the cosmetics industry.

And despite my weaknesses and my father's once complete lack of faith in me, I desperately want to follow in her footsteps.

With Zachary by my side, of course, considering he works in the brand marketing department and has higher aspirations. The two of us could take Fleur to the next level. I know it. He knows it.

Together, we're a force to be reckoned with. And once we're married . . .

"You're lost in thought."

Zachary's deep voice washes over me and I blink, realize that he's watching me. His brows are furrowed and his mouth is turned down. He looks concerned.

"I'm fine." I smile, hope lighting within me when I see the worry etched all over his handsome features slowly disappear. His blue eyes twinkle as he reaches across the table and takes my hand, grasping my fingers tightly.

"I have something I want to discuss with you," he says in that low, reassuring way of his.

My smile grows and I nod, squeezing his fingers. "Now?"

"Yes." He takes a deep breath and lets go of my hand. *Odd.* "I've known about this for a while and it's . . . taken everything within me to work up the courage to tell you."

Oh. How sweet. He's nervous about proposing. Zachary's always so confident about everything—I'm surprised. "Go ahead and just say it, Zachary. I'm fairly sure it will all work out in the end."

"I agree. Your father said the same thing."

My heart skips a beat. He spoke with Father. This is serious. This is exactly what I've been waiting for all this time. I can't believe it. My fingers are literally trembling in anticipation of the ring he's about to slip on my finger. I wonder how big it is. I don't like gaudy jewelry. Neither does Zachary. Understated, refined—that's more our style. Perhaps he spoke with Grandma and she gave him her engagement ring, though rightfully that should go to Lily since she's oldest . . .

". . . so he's asked me to test out the new position in London and see if I'd be a good fit. And I said yes."

Wait. What? "P-position? In London? What are you talking about?" I clear my throat, proud that I keep my voice level. I didn't want to make a scene in the middle of one of the most elegant restaurants in all of Manhattan. I could hear my father's voice now.

Violet, that just wouldn't do.

"Your father is sending me to the London office, just on a temporary basis. They've created a new position there since growth in the UK and Europe has been so strong the last couple of years. I'll be trying out the new chief brand and marketing director position both in London and Paris. It's a tremendous opportunity, Violet. One I couldn't turn down. This promotion could change everything." The pointed look Zachary gives me says he's made his choice and there's no chance I can talk him out of it.

"But . . . Wait a minute." I shake my head, a huff of fake laughter falling from my lips. He can't be serious. That's what he wanted to tell me? About a possible promotion? To London? "What about . . ."

"Us?" he finishes for me with that rueful, charming smile. The one that says he knows he's a little bit in trouble but somehow he'll talk himself out of it. As usual. "I won't be gone for long, only a few months. Hey, I bet you could fly over for a weekend. Come to London or even better, Paris. We can explore the cities together."

No offer to take me with him to live there—not that I'd go, especially since it's temporary. But it could turn permanent and he might end up staying. We don't know.

Would I leave to be with Zachary? Only if he promised that we would be married—and he vowed his complete fidelity. I feel safe here. Everything I know, my family, my friends, my career, is here. In New York. Not London or Paris. And what about the ring? The proposal?

It sounds terrible in my own head, but I expected that. A beautiful diamond solitaire ring accompanied by an offer of marriage, along with Zachary's promise of undying love and faithfulness to me. A girl can tolerate only so much and I know it's stupid, but . . . I love him.

I do.

Disappointment threatens to wash over me, but I hold it at bay. I have to.

"I think I know what you were hoping for," he says softly. "But what sort of marriage could we start if we're on two different continents? It wouldn't be fair to either of us. We're still young, darling, especially you. We have plenty of time."

"We've already been together almost two years . . ." My voice drifts and I drop my head, blinking my eyes shut for an agonizingly long moment before I open them again. I refuse to cry. I am twenty-three years old. I refuse to bawl like a little girl.

"And maybe we'll have another year, maybe two years, like this, but I promise, I will marry you." My heart leaps at his words. "I swear. I just—I need this. This promotion is important to me and I'm not the only one your father is considering. I'm a front-runner, but still, there are no guarantees. For you, it's different. This is your family. They'll give you whatever you want," Zachary says, irritation making his voice scratchy. Does he even register the change in tone? "But for me? I have to work at it. Constantly."

I stiffen my spine, offended by his words. They make it sound like I'm some sort of spoiled brat who gets whatever she wants whenever she wants. "I've worked very hard at Fleur since I was in my early teens," I say in protest. "You know this."

He waves a hand, whether dismissing his words or mine, I'm not exactly sure. "You know what I mean. Just . . . let me have this. I'm not a selfish man but I've worked damn hard for this career, Vi." I hate it when he calls me Vi and he knows it. "I'm almost thirty years old. The time for me to do this is now. Before I marry you and we have children and I won't be able to ever leave."

The way he said that makes me think he would feel like he's stuck with the wife and children. In other words, with *me* and our future children. Why am I letting this bother me? Am I being too sensitive? What he's saying makes sense. He needs to push forward with his career. I understand that. But I need to push forward with my career as well. And my life. My personal life, with marriage and children and . . .

My voice is hesitant as I say, "I could ask my father to step in and offer you a promotion here—"

"No. I refuse to take that sort of handout. I will earn this promotion," he says vehemently. "I want to do this. I would never hold *you* back, you know."

"That's not fair," I murmur, my gaze locking with his. A mixture of anger and sadness fills me, but he doesn't appear sad at all. No, he looks excited. Like this is exactly what he wants. What he needs.

Does this mean I'm not what he wants? What he needs?

"It's the truth," he says simply. "And you know it."

He never told me he was interviewing for the position. And this sort of thing goes on for weeks. Sometimes months. My father didn't tell me either, and that hurts because he knew what was happening yet never gave me a warning. More than anything, though, I hate that Zachary has kept this secret from me.

Makes me wonder if he's kept any other secrets.

Don't fool yourself. He's kept plenty of secrets from you. Why do you put up with him?

I swear my sister's voice is berating me in my head. I can just see Lily's smug expression, telling me she knew it all along. Zachary Lawrence doesn't deserve me. She's said that time and again. So has Rose.

I'm starting to wonder if they're right.

A woman's husky laugh draws my attention and I glance at a table a few feet away, recognition making my stomach sour. *God,* of course he's here. A million restaurants in all of Manhattan and he'd have to show up in this one. The mysterious, arrogant Ryder McKay, fellow corporate employee of Fleur Cosmetics.

Ryder's with . . . of course, Pilar Vasquez, his former boss, his supposed lover, girlfriend, whatever he might call her. Their relationship is strange, to say the least.

Strange because Pilar doesn't talk about it and Ryder definitely doesn't talk about it either. No one's sure exactly what happens between them, but everyone would love to know.

Not that *I* want to know. Or really care. His arrogance, the look on his handsome face, the way he strides around the building as if he's the king of all he sees, drives me crazy.

If all goes as planned, that right will eventually go to Zachary someday. He is without a doubt the future CEO of Fleur.

Or me. I could be the CEO. Grandma has said that more than once. If I had half of her confidence, I could conquer the world.

All I know is that Ryder McKay is definitely not on par with Zachary and all of his experience. He's worked at Fleur a bit longer than Zachary, a little over two years. He came to the company via Pilar, who got him a position since she worked with him at her previous employer. Somehow, he's gotten into the good graces of practically every executive who works at Fleur. His charm is dangerous, and I can reluctantly admit he's a valued employee.

Which makes him lethal. And I refuse to fall for him. Zachary hates his guts. Something about Ryder rubs me the wrong way.

Ignoring the disgust curling through my blood, I try my best to keep my attention on Zachary, trying to ignore that the life I'd planned is falling apart in front of my eyes. But Zachary's phone rings, and he takes the call without asking if I mind. Like I don't matter, and I hate that. I hate even more that he turns away so he can murmur into the phone without me hearing.

More secrets. It's probably a woman. That I sit here and tolerate his behavior makes me want to smack him.

Or smack myself.

I'm at a loss. I don't know what to do, how to act, and I can't help my gaze from drifting to where Ryder sits. He's disgustingly gorgeous in a charcoal-gray suit and a crisp white shirt, though he's sans tie and a few buttons are undone at the neck, revealing the sexy column of his throat. His dark brown hair is in slight disarray, as if he's run his fingers through it countless times, and the entire look gives him a rakish air. One that says he doesn't care what people think of him while he sits in a restaurant that caters to some of the richest people in all of Manhattan.

That is the exact sort of attitude Ryder McKay always seems to have and I find it infuriating. Not that I have to deal with him, not much. He was promoted to associate director of package development a few months ago, a position I now can't help but wonder why Zachary didn't apply for, though it would have been more of a lateral move, not necessarily a step up. It would have kept him in New York, though.

Unless Zachary had no desire to stay in New York . . .

I stare harder, wishing I could listen in on Ryder's conversation with Pilar, but I can't hear a thing. His face is shrouded in shadows, the candle flickering in the deep red votive that sits in the middle of the table casting it in golden light. He's very attractive, I can reluctantly admit. Flashing a wicked smile at Pilar, he lets forth a glorious, downright filthy-sounding laugh that sends a spark of heat zipping over my skin.

Only because it sounds so devastatingly wrong and shockingly dirty, not because I have any sort of interest in him. He's too quiet, too mysterious, too . . . dark and full of secrets. That wicked smile is still curving his lush lips as he reaches across the table and takes Pilar's hand, bringing it to his mouth to kiss.

I watch, transfixed, as Pilar laughs, her voice raspy as she seemingly admonishes him. He merely shakes his head in return and drops her hand, his gaze going to mine for the briefest second and then lingering.

I'm caught. Snared in his intense gaze and for a long, charge-filled bundle of seconds, I return his stare. Recognition flares in his eyes and I quickly look away, my cheeks heating, and I'm thankful the lighting is dim so he can't tell. He thinks nothing of me, I'm sure. I'm barely a blip on his radar, and that's just the way I like it. I don't want his attention.

His type of attention . . . scares me.

Glancing across the table, I wave my hand in front of Zachary's face but he doesn't see me. I hiss out his name, earning a hard glare from him before he turns away.

A sigh wants to escape and I stifle it, chancing a glance in Ryder's direction again to find him still watching me. And he doesn't look away, either. His smile softens and he leans back in his chair. He positively reeks of a man who knows just how to please a woman—a man who has no qualms about flirting with one woman while sitting at a table with another.

I remind myself that I can't stand him. I hate his cocky behavior. His confidence is galling and Zachary can't stand him. I should be disgusted that he's looking at me in such a blatant manner, but . . . I'm morbidly fascinated.

What's it like to think that way? To feel that way? Pilar seems absolutely thrilled to be with him, which only confirms that something is going on between those two. And I wouldn't doubt he'd try and touch her in some inappropriate manner if he hasn't done so already. She probably wouldn't protest, either. She's an eager climber who has no problems stepping on people to get what she wants, both professionally and socially.

They look like they're enjoying their evening, though.

Whereas I'm tense and upset at Zachary's seeming rejection, they're laughing and carrying on as if they have zero worries.

Funny, I can't help but think how lucky Pilar is. To be lost in the pleasure of Ryder's wicked company while I'm lost to my own turbulent emotions at the thought of Zachary leaving me. Of being alone.

Again.

Tearing my gaze away from Ryder McKay, I focus on Zachary, who's off his cell phone and watching me with an expectant expression on his face. "Now, where were we?" he asks, looking genuinely confused. How could he forget that he'd just delivered such life-altering news?

"You were telling me about your possible new promotion." I hold in a breath, count to three, and then let it out in a soft exhale. "I'm happy for you," I finally say, forcing myself to smile. But it doesn't feel genuine. My lips tremble at the corners and I let the smile fall away. "Congratulations, Zachary."

"I knew you'd understand. You always understand. Everything." He reaches across the table and grasps my hand again, giving it a gentle squeeze. "If I get the position, I don't see myself staying in London beyond two years. We can make it work, can't we, darling?"

"Of course we can," I whisper. But I'm not sure. Two years with Zachary in another country, meeting numerous women? Most likely *bedding* numerous women?

For all I know, this could be the beginning of the end.

Chapter Two

Ryder

"I'm going to seduce Violet Fowler." I keep my gaze locked on the very woman I'm referring to, enraptured with the way she tucks a wayward strand of glossy brown hair behind her ear, her pretty smile directed at that asshole boyfriend of hers.

I fucking hate Zachary Lawrence. And I fucking want his girlfriend.

Which, of course, gets my mind churning with ideas. Not a one of them good.

"Absolutely not."

I jerk my gaze away from Violet and stare incredulously at my former boss and occasional lover. "What did you just say?"

"Please. You heard me." She scowls, her blood-red lips forming into an obvious pout. Even angry, she's strikingly beautiful. Her exotic features help Pilar stand out among any crowd. "Why in the world would you want to even *touch* Violet, let alone fuck her? She's so incredibly boring."

She sounds jealous. Not that I'd ever say that. Pilar has extra-sharp claws and she's not afraid to use them. "That's what's so intriguing about her." I have the distinct feeling that in the hands of the right man, Violet Fowler would be anything but boring.

"You just want her because you can't have her. Typical

male." Pilar waves a hand dismissively. "Can't we talk about something else?"

"Fine." I stare at her, knowing she has information I want. It's the reason I asked her to go to dinner with me tonight. "Tell me about Zachary."

Pilar's lips curl into a cat-got-the-mouse smile. Now I was talking her language. "What do you want to know?" She sounds bored but she loves this. I can tell from the glittering of her golden-brown eyes that she's far from bored.

"I heard they're sending him to London," I say.

"Yes, they are."

"To do some sort of temporary tryout for the global marketing director position that was just created," I continue.

"Yes. It's an excellent opportunity. One that many would want." She looks so damn pleased with herself, saying that. She knows my blood is boiling.

And I feel like I'm about to burst. "Right. Like me. *I* want that job." So bad I can almost fucking taste it. I'm damn good at what I do. I've risen among the ranks within Fleur at surprising speed.

She rolls her eyes. "You haven't earned it."

"I work my ass off. I've earned it far more than fucking Lawrence. He gets the chance because of who his girlfriend is." I can't even say his first name. I hate how he insists everyone call him *Zachary*. It makes him sound like a complete pussy. *Pompous asshole.* "I told Fowler."

Pilar frowns, her eyes dimming. The excited sparkle is gone just like that. "Told him what?"

"That I want the position."

She looks shocked. *Good.* It's rare when anyone can surprise her. "And what did he say?"

" 'Prove yourself, son.' And that's a direct quote." I lean across the table, my gaze locked with Pilar's. "So that's what I plan on doing."

A perfectly arched eyebrow rises. "How? By getting into Violet's granny panties? Please. That little prude won't let you even look at her. How do you think you're going to get your dirty paws on her pristine body?"

I hadn't thought that through yet. But it doesn't matter. Once I focus on something, I always get what I want. At least now I do. When I was a kid, hell no. I begged. I stole. I fucked to get what I wanted. My past, though, just made me tougher. More determined.

And for whatever reason, just looking at Violet Fowler sitting there in her pretty little dress with her pretty little body, tolerating that asshole Lawrence while he ignores her and chats on the phone . . . makes me want to jump her. Show her what a real man could do for her.

I'd probably scare the shit out of her. Hell, I might enjoy scaring the shit out of her.

Clearly, I'm a twisted fuck.

"If her asshole boyfriend is leaving her behind, I'm sure I can figure something out." I shrug. "She'll be alone and vulnerable. Missing Lawrence. I can step in and ease her pain."

"Ballsy, aren't you?" Pilar murmurs. "And what about me? Am I supposed to sit by without protest while you're out fucking another woman?"

"You have before. Plenty of times. Not like we're committed." Our relationship isn't what I would call conventional. Our ties are there, but we're not forever bound to each other. Pilar is a user.

So am I. It's why we work so well together, both personally and professionally.

Lately, though, I've felt conflicted. I know I'm ready to end the sexual relationship with Pilar, but we have a history. She's the only woman who ever took care of me, so I take care of her.

My mom disappeared when I was little and I don't remember her. Dad was a semi-presence in my life until I was around fifteen, but he was never a real parent. More like a roommate. A man who brought whores around and passed me my first drink when I was barely twelve. A real stellar example of what a parent should be.

When Pilar walked into my life, took one look at me and decided I would become her personal little project, I was relieved. Fucking thankful.

I was nothing more than a stupid, dirty street kid, nineteen and with a minor drug problem, no job, and no place to live, when we first met. I slept on a park bench at night and hung out in Starbucks all day. At least it was warm. I could afford a tall coffee and a free glass of water. I nursed that shit all damn day. I didn't care.

Pilar entered that Starbucks like she owned the place every single morning. Sometimes I saw her, sometimes I didn't. One morning in particular, I caught her eye and she surveyed me like I was a bug under a microscope. She came closer to where I sat, peering at me. She's older, beautiful, and radiates so much confidence that I was caught. Hell, I *wanted* to be caught.

She brought me home to clean me up. Her apartment was like a palace. Clean, with new furniture and food in the refrigerator and a toilet that flushed, with a shower that had hot running water and soft towels, a warm bed to sleep in at night. I was in heaven.

When she said she could get me a job where she worked as her assistant, I said yes. That job was more than anyone had ever given me before. The meals she provided? I ate more than I'd ever eaten in my entire fucking life. The first night I stayed with her, I threw up, I ate so much goddamn food. I remember thinking what a waste as I bent over the toilet and puked my guts out.

Nobody had ever wanted me. Nobody had ever given two shits about me. When no one has ever given you anything, not one thing in your life, and then someone comes along and gives you not only what you need, but what you want . . . you never forget it. What Pilar and I share, it's not what I would call good.

But it's more than I ever thought I'd be getting.

That she was interested in me had blown my mind. Made me want to work harder for her, prove that I could actually amount to something. She rewarded me, too. First with sex, and eventually with job opportunities, and I've proven my worth. Even though I don't work directly under her anymore, supposedly I still owe her.

I'm ready, though, to have my debt paid in full.

"I won't sit by and let you screw around with *her*. Have you lost your mind? Do you really believe by getting Violet Fowler in your bed, you'll automatically get a promotion? Forrest Fowler is extremely protective of his daughters, you know. He'd probably chop your dick off if he found out you fucked his little girl," Pilar points out. "Especially since she's the damaged one of the bunch."

The CEO of Fleur is overly protective of his two youngest daughters. The oldest one—Lily—is a walking disaster. A sexy one, too, who spent most of her time at parties half naked and drunk, gaining constant coverage on shitty gossip sites.

Violet is the restrained, fragile one. Rumor is she'd been admitted to a psych ward at one point. That their mother offed herself when the girls were young and Violet's just like her. Vulnerable. Unstable.

A mess.

She's the perfect victim. I could scoop her up and spit her out, no problem.

"I want to get in her good graces," I say, because what the hell else can I say? I know Violet Fowler doesn't give a shit about me. That I caught her staring at me a few minutes ago had surprised the hell out of me. "Besides, haven't you always wanted to fuck around with Lawrence?"

The mock surprise on Pilar's face is telling. "I've found him . . . scrumptious. On occasion."

Scrumptious. The word in reference to Zachary Lawrence grates. The guy is an arrogant prick. It takes everything I have to restrain the frown that wants to appear. "So help me out here. Wrap your lips around Lawrence's dick, take a few pictures, somehow get them to Violet, and then she'll break it off with him. I'll console her, look like a superhero, and Fowler will have no choice but to give the promotion to me." It sounds like a shitty plan and I prefer to earn my promotions the old-fashioned way—doing a damn good job—but I'm pissed. I'd love nothing more than to snatch that job right out of Lawrence's hands.

Snatch the promotion and his beautiful girlfriend, all at once.

"It's not that simple, darling. Zachary is leaving for London. Remember?"

"Not for another week or two. That's plenty of time for you to set your sights on him and fuck him over." She moves quickly when she wants. So do I.

Pilar smiles and tilts her head back to let out a throaty laugh. One she's honed to perfection over the years. Not one thing Pilar does is spontaneous. She's calculated down to the very finest detail. "Aren't you the naughty one, suggesting I nail Zachary Lawrence to help you get ahead in the company? What do I get out of it?"

"Sex with Lawrence?"

She smirks. "Not good enough. I want more."

I decide to distract her by changing the subject. "Speaking of that jackass, he's sitting over there right now having dinner with Violet." He's such a smarmy asshole. He knows how to put on the charm and most everyone at Fleur is completely enamored with him, but I see through the façade. I've lived enough, especially during the first nineteen years of my life on the streets, to recognize some real bullshit and know that what Lawrence is dishing out is top-of-the-line B.S.

"I saw them already." Pilar schools her expression, grabbing her wineglass and bringing it to her lips so she can take a sip before she responds. "Such luck, that we chose the same restaurant tonight. I assume he's telling her that he's leaving."

Good riddance. I won't miss the guy, though I'm sure ninety-five percent of the staff is ready to throw him a huge going-away party. I bet he's fucked about ninety-five percent of the female staff, too, what with the way he loves to chase a skirt.

More than once I've heard that Violet knows about Lawrence's extracurricular activities but chooses to turn a blind eye. Why she tolerates him I have no clue.

Pilar sighs when I say nothing, propping her elbow on the edge of the table and resting her chin on her hand, looking like a wistful teenage girl. "He shall be missed by all."

"Not by me," I mutter.

She laughs. "You're just jealous."

"Of Lawrence? Hell no." I shake my head. "He's an asshole."

"A charming asshole who has everything you could ever want." The look on Pilar's face tells me she thinks she knows all. "Admit it. You're jealous. He's your direct competition."

I shrug. He's the closest thing to competition I have when it comes to work. I started at Fleur about six months before he did. We've both moved up the ranks, at right about the same speed, though he's outpaced me recently. I blame it on his relationship with Violet.

It doesn't matter what anyone says. The man is banging the owner's daughter. There has to be some advantage in there someplace.

"Tell me what you want, Pilar." I say, wanting to refocus. *Needing* to refocus. I have to come up with a new plan. After speaking with Forrest Fowler earlier, letting him know that I want the position Lawrence is temporarily taking over, I want my chance.

I *deserve* a chance. So I need to use every advantage I can get.

She sobers, her expression thoughtful as she taps a blood-red fingernail against her pursed lips before she snaps her fingers and points her index finger at me. "I know. I want Violet gone."

Now it's my turn to raise my eyebrows. "Gone?"

"Mmm-hmm." Pilar nods and drops her hand to the table, her fingers clutching the edge. "Zachary has something you want? Well, Violet has something I want."

"And what's that?"

"Power," she says simply.

No shit. "She's a Fowler. Of course she has power."

"Yes, but if she's gone, that's one less Fowler I have to deal with, hmmm? And Violet is so determined to follow in her grandmother's footsteps. Certainly more determined than Rose is." Pilar smiles, her lids lowering. "You destroy Violet, she'll crumble like she has before. Then . . . she's gone."

Unease slips down my spine at Pilar's suggestion. Yeah, we've played these sorts of games before, but she's never asked me to *destroy* someone, particularly someone as delicate as Violet.

"You've already admitted you want to fuck around with Violet, right? Once Zachary's gone, you'll get the promotion and move to London and Violet will be left behind to pick up the pieces. She'll fall completely apart, disappear, and I'll step in and take over." Pilar leans back in her chair, contemplating what she just said. "I personally think it's a brilliant idea."

It's a fucking *dangerous* idea. One that makes me feel uncomfortable, not that I'd ever tell Pilar that. She'd use it against me.

I let my gaze slide toward Violet, watching as she perches on the edge of her seat, those wide, velvety brown eyes taking in everything that asshole Lawrence has to say. My skin tightens as I imagine her looking at me like that. Like I hung the moon and stars and everything in between, all of it just for her.

Yeah, I've fantasized about her. More than once. Who wouldn't? Sometimes even when I'm fucking Pilar, I've imagined

Violet in her place. Pictured her beneath me, all that long, silky dark hair spread across my pillow, her cheeks glowing, that velvet gaze stuck on me. Only me. There's just something about her shy, reserved personality that drives me out of my fucking mind. That makes me want to drive *her* out of her fucking mind.

With my cock imbedded deep inside her tight little body.

"I don't know. This idea comes with zero guarantees," I finally say with a quick shake of my head. One wrong move and we could both be fired. I can't afford to screw around. I need to focus. I need to get away from Pilar once and for all and get her to back off.

I need to grow the fuck up and do something with my life. I'm tired of dealing with distractions. But sick as it is, Pilar is all I have. There's no family, no real close friends. It's hard to let her go.

And she knows it.

"Just when I was ready to agree with your plan, you act like this. You're no fun." Pilar mock pouts. "You've become awfully serious lately."

"I have to be. Look, Pilar." I lean across the table, wanting her to see just how damn serious I am. "I can't afford to fuck around anymore. I want that promotion. I want the fuck out of here. We start pulling too many people into this and actually . . . *hurt* someone, the CEO's daughter for Christ's sake—it's too damn risky."

"Oh, it'll be fun. And like you care about Violet's feelings. When has she ever done anything for you? She usually looks at you like you're a piece of dirty, sticky gum on the bottom of her shoe."

Pilar's probably right. Doesn't matter, though. I may be a user, but the idea of pushing Violet over the edge doesn't sit well.

Guess I have some morals after all.

"I don't know . . ." I start, but she cuts me off.

"Please. You can't do this for me?" She waves a hand, dismissing my words. Since when did this plan turn into *her* project? "After I took you in. Gave you a job when you had nothing. You'd be dead if it weren't for me."

Fuck. I know. She's told me often enough.

"You owe me," Pilar continues. "I loaned you money."

"I paid you back, didn't I?" *Freaking tenfold,* I want to add but don't.

"I saved your life," she reiterates. "Come on. I think your idea sounds fun. Everyone gets what they want."

Fun. The idea is much more than just fun. "Meaning me and you," I say.

"Darling, we are the only ones who count in this world. If we can't look after each other, then no one else will." She reaches across the table and settles her hand on top of mine. "Come on, my darling, sweet boy. Do this for me—do this for *you*—and we can ensure each other's climb at Fleur. I guarantee it."

How the hell can she guarantee anything? I'm not the same gullible kid I was when she first found me. "Knock it off, Pilar," I mutter, sliding my hand from beneath hers.

I swear I feel Violet's eyes on me, watching me. Judging me. *Little prude.* She probably thinks I'm a complete jackass, when she's the one inviting the biggest asshole on the planet into her bed every night.

Makes me wonder how she is in bed. Uptight? Prim and closed off? Lawrence probably has to pry her thighs open with a crowbar to get in there and then she dissolves into tears every time they have sex.

Sounds like a nightmare to me.

Yet I'm *still* hard as a rock just thinking about it.

Which means . . . I should do this. *Fuck it.* What have I got to lose? And if it all comes together as planned, I have everything to gain. Everything.

"If I do this . . ." I start, lowering my voice. The excitement that flares in Pilar's eyes fuels my own. "If I fuck her . . . play with her for a while, we have to be discreet. Meaning you have to keep quiet."

Pilar nods, her eyes going wide. "I can do that."

"You fuck Lawrence and cause them to break up, but don't make a huge scene. Then we get him the hell out of Fleur," I say, laying it all out. "I console Violet, we become closer. I prove to her father that I'm perfect for the London job and he has no choice but to promote me. I leave Violet behind, devastated that I broke up with her so harshly, and then she'll need to—go away for a while to recover. That's when you slide in and take over her responsibilities."

"Sounds perfect," she croons, her hand covering mine once more, her foot sliding along my leg. My cock twitches to life, both from Pilar's actions and the challenge of the hunt, the chance at the prize.

Fucking Violet Fowler and getting a promotion in London, away from Pilar? I couldn't ask for anything better.

"After her, this is it, though. No more games. We remain friends only, Pilar. That's all," I add.

The smile on Pilar's face diminishes, but I can still see the glow in her eyes. She loves it when I talk like this because she thinks I don't mean it. This time, though, I do. "Fine. Whatever you want, darling. It'll be fun. We can compare notes."

I don't say a word as she scoots her chair closer to mine, her hand gripping my shoulder as her gaze goes to my lap. "You know, you can act like I'm the one who selected Violet as your latest conquest, but remember it was *your* idea. I suspect you've wanted her for a while," she whispers, reaching out to settle her hand on my dick. "So pretend all you want that hard-on of yours isn't for her."

I take a deep breath, tell myself to remain calm. "It isn't. It's all for you," I lie smoothly. My life is fucking chaos. I don't need Pilar making it more of a mess than it already is and she knows how. That's the scary part. "So you'll start in on Lawrence tomorrow?"

She arches a perfectly sculpted brow, removing her hand. I swear my cock breathes a sigh of relief. "And you'll start in on Violet?"

"Yes." I take a deep breath, pushing aside the uneasy feeling that wants to take over. "But then . . . like I said, that's it. We're done. I go my way and you go yours. My debt to you is paid in full."

"All right." The smile returns, darker this time, her eyes lit with an unfamiliar fire that makes me wary. "Then we'd better make this interesting, shouldn't we?"

"As interesting as we fucking can." I shift in my seat and her hand falls away from me, thank Christ.

My gaze wanders yet again to Violet and Zachary's table, but they're gone. They've just left, Zachary heading toward the entrance of the restaurant, Violet going in the opposite direction, most likely to the restroom.

"I should go after her," I suggest, never taking my eyes off of her. *God,* she's beautiful. I want her.

Though I shouldn't.

"Yes, you should. Now shoo." She waves her hands, as if she's a mama duck pushing me out of the nest for the very last time. "Work your McKay magic all over her and I'll go find Zachary."

Without another word, I stand and wind my way through the tables, following the path Violet just took. It'll be a game. A little fun. How long will it take to make her fall for me?

I've done it before and I can do it again. I know how to play the game. Be what she wants me to be. I'm a chameleon. Been told that since I was a kid. "Adaptable" is a much nicer way to put it.

A phony. A fake is the more honest term for what I do. I own every title. After all . . .

I'm practically a professional.

Chapter Three

Violet

I LIED WHEN I TOLD ZACHARY I WASN'T UPSET ABOUT HIS LEAVing but I put on a brave face, something I've become exceptional at doing. Just when I believe things are going my way, news is delivered that's like a punch to my stomach. But I'm a survivor, not weak, or at least so I've been told again and again. Now it's all about my game face. That's what Father calls it.

Like life is one big game. Who thinks like that? Who actually *lives* like that?

Just as the waiter took away our plates, Zachary told me he would drop me off at my apartment. "Too much to do," he murmured with that reassuring smile of his pasted on his face. So phony. Why do I believe his lies? Am I that insecure? "My only chance to start packing is at night, after work. I leave in less than two weeks. You understand, don't you, sweetheart?"

Of course I understand. I'm the perfect girlfriend who stands by her man and lets him do whatever he wants. Including letting him leave her while he attempts to take on a new and glamorous job in another country. He'll most likely go find a new and glamorous woman, too.

He's done it before . . . though never out of the country. So that'll be a new adventure for him. One I'm supposed to ignore and pretend doesn't exist.

The telltale stinging in my eyes lets me know I need to get out of there so I can be alone. Zachary would be embarrassed if I cried. He'd probably tell Father, and I can't . . . I can't let him know that I'm upset. I'm fine. I'm composed. I'm happy.

I'm perfect.

So when the tiny imperfection tries to slip through in the form of tears, I excuse myself and go to the bathroom. Hide away in a stall so no one can see me as I lean against the wall with my face buried in my hands, the tears streaming freely down my cheeks. I only allow myself approximately ninety seconds of crying, though. Any more and my cheeks would turn ruddy, my eyes bloodshot. Zachary would know what I was doing.

And I can't have that.

I keep Visine in my purse for moments like this and after I exit the stall, I go to the row of sinks to wash my hands and assess myself in the mirror. I look . . . like I've been crying. My cheeks are a little rosy, my eyes damp and with a tinge of pink. I dry my hands and reach into my purse, grabbing the eye drops so I can take care of the problem. I'm always ready for any situation. My sisters love it. They make fun of all the things I have in my bag, but I like to be prepared.

The drops go in easily and I blink, then grab a tissue and dab at my eyes. My skin is still flushed, so I splash cold water on my face and dry off, then grab my Fleur Cosmetics Perfect Pressed Powder and dab at my cheeks, taking the redness out. A slick of Lickable Lip Gloss in Macadamia Nut on my lips and I finally look presentable, ready to face the world. Face Zachary.

Despite my anger, I know I need to cherish these last few days with him before he leaves, but my stomach hurts when I think about how he and Father kept this from me when I could have known weeks ago. I could have prepared myself. Instead, he blindsided me.

Get over it. Be strong. You can go on without him. This is temporary. It's not like he broke up with you. All sorts of couples manage through a long-distance relationship.

They do. I can. Zachary loves me in his own special way. He needs me, but he also needs to do this to further his career. Otherwise, he'll resent me forever.

Taking a deep breath, I slip my Chanel bag over my shoulder and exit the bathroom, stopping short when I see a man standing in the darkened hallway, almost as if he was waiting for me. His face is in shadows but I recognize his build, the way he holds himself. Confident, with that arrogant tilt of his head and those incredibly broad shoulders.

It's Ryder McKay.

"Well, well, well. Violet Fowler, how are you this evening?" His rumbly deep voice washes over me as he steps out of the shadows, tall and imposing and handsome as sin.

I take a step back, not wanting him in my personal space, but he invades it anyway. "Mr. McKay," I say politely, not daring to call him by his first name. That would imply I know him, that we're friends or at the very least friendly coworkers, and we're neither of those things. He may work at Fleur, but I rarely speak to him. I don't have to, and besides . . .

There's something about all that edgy darkness and how it radiates from him. He demands attention without saying a word, and there's an air of danger that surrounds him, that ensnares me despite my reluctance to be near him. The innate sexuality that he represents . . . it scares me.

He scares me.

"I've worked at Fleur long enough for you to call me Ryder, don't you think?" He pauses for a heavy beat and the air seems to fill with electricity as I wait for him to speak. "You don't mind that I call you Violet, do you?"

He somehow makes my name sound like a sexual promise. I take another step back and my butt hits the wall. He smiles, and I know *he* knows I've realized I'm trapped. "Of course you can call me Violet," I say, thankful my voice isn't shaking. I have no idea what to say to him, how to act. "Did you have a nice dinner?"

He grins. "Why yes, I did, thank you for asking. The view was spectacular." His gaze slides down the length of me, taking me all in. My breasts, my stomach, my hips, my legs, lingering on my feet before moving back up, his gaze once more on mine. "The food was good, too."

My checks heat, but it's not from the leftover tears. It's the way he looks at me, his gaze so bold, like he wants to devour me. His mention of the view is in reference to me. As if he's somehow attracted to *me*.

I don't believe it. He's just trying to unnerve me with his not-so-subtle flirting. And it's working.

"How's Zachary?" Ryder asks when I still haven't answered.

I jolt, giving myself a little shake. *Zachary*. I need to remember that my boyfriend is outside waiting for the car. Waiting for me. "Fine," I say as I step away from the wall. But that only brings me closer to Ryder and he doesn't budge. I can smell him. His scent is as dark and alluring as he is. "I should go. He's waiting—"

"I hear he's leaving for London." The expression on Ryder's handsome face is all polite sympathy, but with a hint of mockery in his dark blue eyes. He doesn't like Zachary and the feeling is mutual. Zachary complains about him all the time. I'm sure Ryder's thrilled that Zachary is leaving. "Trying out for a promotion, correct? I'm sure you're proud of him."

Proud of him? I should be. And seriously, did everyone know this bit of news but me? "H-how did you hear?" I press my lips together, angry that I let the little stutter slip. I need to remain composed, especially in the face of this particular man.

He's a shark. I know he takes advantage of the weak and gobbles them up. I've heard the stories. And those stories are more than half the reason Father is so pleased that he works at Fleur. Father admires a shark. It's why he loves Zachary so

much, too, though Zachary is much smoother in his . . . predatory approach to business.

"My dinner partner told me the good news." He inclines his
head when he notes my confusion. "I'm here with Pilar."

"Oh." Pilar. How could I forget? His relationship, his usual
aloofness—it's all such a mystery. Hardly anyone knows much
about him, but they all want to learn more. At the moment,
though, he's being downright friendly with me.

"Yes." He smiles, and it's so dazzling I feel like I'm momentarily blinded. "Oh."

"How is Pilar?" I ask, being polite when I realize he seems to
be waiting for a response. He still hasn't moved out of my way
and I inhale discreetly, taking in his sharp, masculine scent. I let
my gaze linger on him for a long moment as he looks down at
the floor, as if he's savoring a personal joke. His eyelashes are
long and thick, casting shadows upon his cheekbones, and my
belly flutters when he glances up, his intense gaze meeting mine.

"She's well. Up to her usual tricks." The smile that curls the
corners of his lips tells me he is in on the joke and I am definitely
not. "I should probably go check on her."

"Where is she?"

"She's waiting at the front for her car. We rode together." His
smile grows. "I wanted to come back here and check on you."

I frown. "Check on me?"

He shrugs those impossibly broad shoulders encased in fine
Italian charcoal wool. "You seemed upset."

Really? Does that mean Zachary noticed, too? He never said
anything to me. I practically broke down in front of him at our
table and he never uttered a word of concern.

"From the way you leapt up from the table, I had a feeling
that Zachary just delivered the news." Ryder takes another step
forward, reaching out to settle his big hand on my upper arm,
giving it a brief, somewhat innocent squeeze.

My reaction to his touch is anything but innocent. That

squeeze swims through my blood, settling like a pulse between my legs.

"We're fine. Really." I step out of his touch, then move to the side so I can get past him. I hurry down the hall, as far away from Ryder as I can get, when he speaks.

"And you? Are *you* fine, Violet?"

I pause and close my eyes, fighting the tears that threaten yet again. What's wrong with me? Why do I want to cry at something stupid Ryder McKay just said? It makes no sense. My reaction to this man makes absolutely zero sense.

"I'm perfect." I turn to find him watching me, his hands slipped into his trouser pockets, his legs spread in a typical masculine stance.

"Yes," he says, his gaze roaming over me yet again. I'm tempted to fidget but keep myself still. "You are." He looks like a warrior ready to stand down against the enemy, tall and powerful with an arrogant curl to his upper lip, his eyes glittering in the dim light.

"Thank you for your concern," I add, frowning at my ridiculous graciousness. I need to walk away. His presence completely throws me.

"Anytime. Always so polite, aren't you," he murmurs, his voice drifting toward me, soft and sexy. "I hate to see such a beautiful woman so upset."

My knees wobble at his casual compliment. When was the last time Zachary said something like that to me? Called me beautiful? Such a simple word, but it carries so much power. "You flatter me," I murmur in return.

"I speak the truth." He steps forward, drawing close once more. "May I escort you outside?"

Ryder offers his arm and I have no choice but to accept. As he said, I am always, above anything else, polite. So I slip my arm through his, around his elbow, and he leads me through the restaurant toward the entrance. I try to ignore the hummingbirds fluttering their wings within my belly. Try to ignore the heat that radiates off him, inviting me to snuggle closer.

I smile, barely able to hold back the laugh that wants to escape. *Snuggle* is not a word I would use when talking about Ryder. I'm sure no woman has ever wanted to merely *snuggle* with him. He's far too intimidating.

"You're laughing," he says, his lips at my ear as he bends his head toward mine. A shiver moves through me when I feel his warm breath caress my skin. "Do you find me that amusing?"

The man notices everything. It's rather unnerving. "I wasn't laughing," I counter. "Just smiling at someone I know."

"Mmm-hmm." That low hum rumbles from his chest, the sound knowing. As if he's confident he's caught me in a lie.

Which he has.

Ryder opens the door for me and I step out into the bitter-cold air. Zachary is standing on the curb in front of our car, Pilar standing in front of him, her hand on his chest as they both laugh.

My blood runs cold and I stop in my tracks, watching them. Ryder stops as well, never letting me go and not saying a word either. I curl my fingers around his rock-hard biceps, momentarily distracted as I tilt my head to look at his arm. The man must work out obsessively to have muscles like that.

I wonder what his skin feels like. Bare and smooth and hot . . .

"Violet!" Zachary strides toward me, his eyes flashing as he takes in me standing beside Ryder. "There you are. I was worried you'd fallen in."

I grimace. Such a crass remark. I can't believe he said that in front of Pilar and Ryder. He never talks like that. "I'm fine." I smile and lift my chin. "I ran into Ryder on my way out and we were talking."

The anger simmering in Zachary's gaze is undeniable. *Good.* He should know I'm not thrilled that Pilar has her hands on him either. She's standing beside him, her dark red lips curved into a closed-mouth smile, looking awfully pleased with herself. "I didn't realize you two were so close," Zachary says, his voice sharp, his gaze assessing.

"Someone needs to take care of her now that you'll be gone, don't you think, Lawrence?" Ryder chuckles.

I immediately release my hold on Ryder's arm, shocked at his words. The fire in Zachary's gaze rises and I go to him, sliding my arm around his waist and giving him a squeeze. "Ignore him," I whisper, placing my hand on Zachary's cheek when he continues to stare at Ryder like he wants to murder him where he stands. "Please."

Zachary breathes deep, his chest rising against mine, his expression contrite. "You're right. I'm sorry." He glances up, glaring at Ryder again. "See you both tomorrow?"

Pilar murmurs a goodbye, though Ryder says nothing. Zachary opens the door for me and I slide into the car, Zachary following in after me. Just as he pulls the door shut, I hear Ryder's voice, clear above the usual city noise.

"See you tomorrow, Violet."

He doesn't bother mentioning Zachary. It's as if he's completely focused on me.

And that makes me fairly sure Ryder is quite possibly the last person I want to see tomorrow.

"TELL ME." I KEEP MY GAZE FOCUSED FIRMLY ON MY MONITOR so my sister won't suspect I'm up to anything. I'm on a research hunt and I want no one to suspect a thing. "What do you know about Ryder McKay?"

Rose laughs. "I know he's sexy as hell."

My head whips in her direction so fast I swear I just threw out my neck. I rub the back of it, wincing. "What do you mean? Do you have a crush on him?"

Rose laughs even harder, the little witch. "What woman that works here doesn't? Not that he notices any of us. He's too focused on his work. Or he's spending time with Pilar Vasquez." She grimaces. "*There's* a relationship I don't really understand."

"Agreed." I can't get him out of my mind. I tossed and turned last night, my mind racing. Why had he been so nice to me? What had he meant by that remark he made to Zachary? And why did Pilar have her hands all over Zachary's chest?

Such a strange night. One I can't help but reexamine and try to take apart. But every time I try to put it back together, the pieces don't fit.

"I've heard he's very driven," Rose says, interrupting my thoughts. "He's determined to succeed at Fleur, which I'm sure Daddy loves."

"He does love it. He approves of Ryder's tactics. Father has lavished praise on him to me more than once." Only Rose would get away with calling our father Daddy. I don't think I've ever called him that. He's Father to me. Not even Dad.

Our relationship has always been more on the formal side.

"I'm surprised he hasn't tried to match me up with him," Rose continues, turning her head so she's gazing out the window. "Like he matched you up with Zachary."

"He didn't match us up," I argue, offended that she would even suggest it. She knows the truth behind the start of our relationship. "I chased after Zachary." I took one look at him and knew he would be perfect. Father encouraged our relationship, I won't deny that, but it was no predestined match.

"Whatever you say." Rose shrugs and turns her attention upon me. She's the astute one. The savvy one. Nothing much gets past my baby sister. "Why are you asking about Ryder anyway?"

My mind blanks as I try my best to act like it's nothing when it's so something. A very big something I discovered when I went over my schedule with my assistant earlier this morning. "I've been working on a project and just realized I'm going to be in constant contact with him over the next few months. I want to know what I'm dealing with." Not necessarily a lie. I'd been in a meeting earlier this morning, discussing the new line we're creating under my name. We've come to the point where design needs to be involved, and Ryder is the associate director of packaging.

"Packaging?" Ah, Rose the mind reader. "I've heard he's very good in whatever position he's put in. You haven't met with him yet?"

"I scheduled a meeting later this afternoon." The timing of this meeting is a little odd. It almost feels . . . planned. How, I'm not sure, but everything's falling into place quite nicely.

I don't mention to Rose the strange encounter last night. I don't want to. Zachary had been angry the entire ride back to my apartment, sitting silently beside me, stewing over what I haven't a clue. He brushed a distracted kiss upon my cheek when we arrived at my building and I climbed out of the car, hurt that he didn't even bother to tell me he loved me.

Sometimes, I can't help but wonder if he really does. But then I tell myself my insecurities are showing and I push the worry aside. I'm good at that.

Quite good.

"I've spoken to Ryder a few times, but nothing major. He's quite the charmer. And like I mentioned, Daddy seems enamored with him." Rose rolls her eyes. She's been on the outs with Father lately, and so has Lily. Our oldest sister is banned from working at Fleur. Father cast her out, tired of her sullying the family name and cheapening Fleur's brand with her constant antics and partying.

His words, not mine.

"So if Father approves, you don't?" I ask.

"If he's anything like Daddy, then yes. I will automatically hate Ryder McKay. It doesn't matter how nice he is to me." Rose smiles, her golden eyes twinkling. She has the face of an angel, but it's countered with that devilish glint in her gaze. With her mesmerizing eyes, round face, rosebud lips, and long, golden-brown hair with perfect blond highlights, she's stunning. Twenty-one and confident, she holds the same position as I do at Fleur, consultant at large. It's a lofty position, one all three of us were given since we're the daughters of Forrest Fowler.

Rose and I have earned that position, though, what with the many hours of work we've put in over the years. I may have had a minor setback with my epic nervous breakdown, but once I returned, I threw myself into my work, wanting to prove myself. *Needing* to prove myself.

Eager to do this job, take care of this legacy that's been so graciously handed to me.

"I should ask Grandma," I say, grabbing my cell when it buzzes, hopeful it's Zachary. But it's a message from Lily, asking if I could call her later tonight. My stomach flips as I type back a yes in response.

My sister is . . . troubled. And I don't know how to help her. None of us really do.

"Oh, I'm sure if Dahlia has met him, she will definitely have an opinion." Rose grins and stands. She came into my office a while ago just to chat, which turned into a twenty-minute session talking about Zachary leaving. Rose doesn't much approve of my boyfriend either.

Rose really doesn't approve of much of anything.

"I'll talk to her later, after the meeting." I want to form my own opinion about Ryder's work and abilities. I know how he affects me on a personal level and the most polite way I can phrase it is, he makes me very . . . uncomfortable.

If that translates at work, too? Then we're in trouble.

"I'm sure he'll come up with a brilliant idea for your packaging. Maybe you should request that he lead the project," Rose says.

"Let's not get ahead of ourselves. He has to prove himself first," I murmur, glancing at my schedule on the monitor. Just seeing that meeting listed makes my stomach jump. That I'll have to face him again after last night worries me. I'll need to put my bravest face on so he doesn't see how much he unnerves me.

I can't let him get the upper hand.

"I don't doubt for a minute he'll prove himself. Like I said, he's very good at what he does," Rose says.

Ugh. The way she says it almost sounds . . . sexual. Of course, that could be my own overly active imagination pinning sexual connotations on everything in regards to Ryder.

Very unfair of me.

"Hmm. I suppose I'll find out." I tap my finger against my cell screen, surprised when a new text comes over and it's from Zachary.

We'll meet for lunch.

Frowning, I grab my phone and quickly type. I hate how he doesn't ask. He always just assumes I'm sitting around waiting for him.

Sorry, I have plans.

Another lie, which niggles at me. I'd rather sit at my desk, eat a sandwich, and prepare for the packaging meeting than watch Zachary eat and worry over what he thinks of me.

"I should go. I have a conference call in fifteen." I glance up as Rose smiles down at me. "Make sure and tell me how your meeting with Ryder goes."

"You should sit in on it with me," I say distractedly, staring at my phone screen, nervously waiting for a response from Zachary. He doesn't like it when I refuse him.

"If you want me to, I totally can. Just let me know when."

"Two o'clock? Does that work for you?" I ask.

"Definitely." She nods. "I'll see you then."

" 'Bye," I say as Rose leaves, but I don't pay any attention. Too busy watching as Zachary types his response.

I can't see you tonight. I have plans too.

Is this his way of getting back at me? He's done this before when we've been in disagreement over something. Almost like he's withholding his company from me. Like I'm supposed to fall apart and not know what to do without Zachary by my side.

Which isn't too far off from the truth.

My fingers hover over the keyboard for agonizing seconds before I finally type.

Maybe another time then.

Closing my eyes, I let my phone fall to my desk with a clatter. I don't want to play games. I don't want to avoid Zachary, either, but something isn't right between us. I thought I'd been very accepting of his news, but maybe he thinks I'm upset. I am, but I'd never let on. I'm a good enough actress that I can always pull through.

But maybe he saw through the cracks in my veneer. Maybe I shouldn't have lied and said I had plans. I hate lying. Lies only lead to trouble.

His answer is immediate.

Dinner tomorrow night?

I chew on my lip, wishing I could just say yes like normal and carry on with my day. Instead I'm mulling over every little thing. Analyzing his behavior and mine, wondering why I can't stop thinking about Ryder McKay calling me beautiful, flashing that gorgeous smile at me that made me feel weak in the knees.

Thinking of it, remembering, I *still* feel weak.

Pushing all thoughts of Ryder out of my brain, I finally answer Zachary.

Dinner sounds perfect.

Chapter Four

Ryder

THIS IS GOING TO BE TOO FUCKING EASY.

I couldn't believe my luck when I checked my schedule after I first came in. Right there in black and white, a meeting with Violet at two p.m.

After more than two years at Fleur rarely encountering her, I set my sights on her and within twenty-four hours of doing so, I'm going to be in a meeting with her. Working with her closely on a project—*her* project.

She's falling right into my trap, and Pilar and I have barely put this plan into action.

Slipping out of my office, I pull the door shut behind me and wander down the hall toward the elevator, nodding as I pass people, trying to withhold the yawn that wants to burst out of me. I'm on my third cup of coffee of the day and I still feel tired. Hell, Pilar commented on it first thing this morning, noting the bags under my eyes. Someone suggested the new cool eye mask Fleur had just launched and next thing I knew, I was lying on the couch in my office, wearing a gel eye mask and feeling like a jackass. It did help, though.

Ah, the perks of working at a cosmetics company. If any of the kids I grew up with could see me now, they'd probably kick my ass. Hell, sometimes I want to kick my own ass.

Despite the mask and the endless cups of coffee, I'm still tired. I couldn't sleep last night. Pilar tried to get me to come back to her place, but I declined. She is the last thing I need right now. She would have pumped me for details about my talk with Violet and then demand that I fuck her.

That's a firm hell no. Not with my head filled with thoughts of Violet.

I'd gone home, taken a shower, and crawled into bed completely naked, my skin still damp, my thoughts hot. Closed my eyes and imagined Violet in bed with me. Pressing my lips against her soft, fragrant skin, tasting her. Kissing her. Consuming her. Stroking her everywhere, my hand between her legs, discovering that she's hot and wet, just for me. *Only* for me.

Thinking of her like that had left me painfully hard. I'd jerked off to flashes of Violet in my mind. Naked and on her knees in front of me, her perfect pink lips wrapped around my cock, my hands fisted in her hair as I held her still and thrust deep. Deeper . . .

Damn. I could get hard all over again just thinking about it.

"Where are you off to?"

I push the up button next to the elevator and turn to find Pilar standing in front of me, her hands resting on her hips, skeptical gaze resting on me. "Meeting upstairs."

That damn perfect eyebrow of hers rises. "With whom?"

Should I tell her? She'll find out anyway, so why bother hiding it? Hunting season is open and she's locked and loaded. So am I. "My department." I pause. "And Violet."

The smirk that crosses her face is full of triumph. "Why you wicked, wicked boy. You certainly move fast, don't you?"

"I only learn from the best." I shrug, not bothering to tell her it's a legitimate meeting. She laughs as she steps closer to me.

"Are you going to give me all the details later?" she practically purrs, drawing her perfectly manicured nails across my shoulder. "You look delicious in this suit. It fits you so well. Prada?"

"Gucci." The door slides open and I step away from Pilar's touch and into the elevator. "I'll text you when I'm finished."

"Oh, yes. Please do," she calls as I press the number-twenty button. Violet's floor. "Give me all the lurid details, my darling. Every single one."

I turn to face Pilar, remaining stone-faced as the doors slowly shut with a soft swooshing sound. She'll understand. She knows it's my game face. My hunter face. I'm analyzing, mentally preparing myself, wondering exactly what sort of lion's den I'm about to step into.

But Violet Fowler is no lion. I doubt she'll give us much shit this first meeting, since it's all about ideas and concept. She's more like a soft, sweet little kitten. A fuzzy little ball of fluff who'll hopefully want to play with me and eventually beg for my attention. Who'll preen and rub against my leg and hope for more of what only I can give her.

Soon. I can't get ahead of myself. First I need to earn her trust. Pilar needs to get her mouth around Lawrence's dick. None of this is going to be easy, especially with the short amount of time we have to work with.

It makes it that much more challenging, though. And I love a challenge, especially when the reward is so delicious.

The elevator doors open and I exit, turning right and heading toward the conference room where our meeting is being held. I'm ten minutes early; I always am, and this gives me time to absorb the power I feel radiating in the air. The executive floor has a more hushed quality to it, an elegant, almost refined air compared to the kinetic energy on my floor. I can almost smell the money as I wander by the offices outfitted with custom desks that cost twenty thousand dollars and views of the city most executives would kill to have.

This is what I want someday. Power. Money. The confidence that nothing can break me down. And I want to earn it on my own, not ride Pilar's coattails to an executive position at Fleur or maybe some other cosmetics company. Considering I'm an associate director, the experience I've gained in this position could take me practically anywhere.

But the more I think about it, the more I realize I don't want to go anywhere else. I want to stay with Fleur. I'm damn good at what I do, which still surprises me. Who knew a loser kid from the streets could clean up nice and know how to sell cosmetics? Definitely not me.

What I really want is the job that Lawrence is this close to getting. I want the hell out of here, away from Pilar and everything else. A fresh start sounds like a fucking dream.

A dream I'm determined to make my reality.

I slow my steps, admiring each office as I pass. The conference room is at the end of the hall and Violet's office is nearby. Last door on the left, and that door is currently open. I pause at the edge of the mostly glass wall that fronts her office, peeking around the corner to find her sitting behind her desk. She's staring at her computer screen, a dreamy expression on her beautiful face as she runs her fingers absently along the side of her bared neck. Her index finger slides up, gently playing with the diamond stud in her ear, and I'm as hard as the stone she touches. Just like that. The very last thing I need is to walk into a meeting with a tent in the front of my trousers.

Fuck.

Taking a deep breath, I tell myself to get my shit together. All I did was watch her touch her fucking earring. Big deal. I've seen better. I've watched all sorts of depraved things happen in front of me while bored out of my skull. I've lived far too much, seen far too much, to think there's even a hint of innocence inside me.

Not even close. My soul is hard. As hard as that damned diamond Violet is touching. Hard and black and ugly, and crazy fucker that I am, I revel in the blackness. The darkness. Pilar has told me more than once that sometimes I scare her.

Good. I should scare her. I may be the smooth businessman at work but during my off time, I can relax. Can become more my true self. Underneath the expensive suit and high-end watch is a man who could have easily become a hardened fucking criminal in and out of jail. Hell, I've been in jail. More than once.

But I'd been a juvenile and my record is sealed. *Thank Christ.*

If Violet knew about my past, she'd probably freak. She's one giant ball of insecurities. Something happened to her, something no one really talks about that sent her spiraling out of control. Daddy locked her up at the most expensive and discreet mental health facility money could buy. She came out a few months later refreshed and medicated, back at work at Fleur and leaving every employee she worked with full of envy. Supposedly, they hate her.

At least, that's the story Pilar told me on the drive home from the restaurant last night.

Blood thrumming with anticipation, I stroll past Violet's window, pausing at her open door and knocking before I enter. I don't bother waiting for her to acknowledge me; I just stride inside, stopping short in front of her desk when I get a good look at her.

And just about have a heart attack.

Jesus, what is she wearing? A sleek black dress that hugs her breasts and reveals her slender arms, with her long dark hair up, exposing her neck, wavy tendrils brushing against her skin. The look is simple but effective.

As in, one look at her and I'm immediately hungry for more. More skin, more Violet, more everything.

"Ryder." She blinks up at me, those big brown eyes wide and full of shock. "Wh-what are you doing here?"

"We have a meeting in . . ." I check my Rolex, then return my gaze to hers. "Five minutes. Remember?" I remain standing, my gaze dropping to the neckline of her dress. It gapes slightly at the front, allowing me a glimpse of shadowy cleavage, and I catch sight of the sheer white lace bra covering her full, tempting breasts.

I immediately break out in a sweat.

Her glossy peach-colored lips part as she stares at me. Hell, I'm going to fantasize later about my dick sticky with peach gloss—I can just see it. She gives herself a little shake. Like she's just as entranced as I am. *Interesting.* "Of course I remember. I was just about to head to the conference room."

"Same here. I'll go with you." I don't bother asking, because I'm not about to give her the opportunity to refuse me.

"I was waiting for my sister. She's going to sit in on the meeting, too." Violet nibbles her lower lip, her teeth sinking into peachy lush flesh, and *holy fuck,* who knew that sort of innocent look could be so sexy?

"I don't mind waiting for Rose." I've spoken with her before. She's friendlier than Violet, much more open. "If you don't."

Violet tilts her head back, contemplating me, and I realize what a power position I have over her. She's seated; she's the one behind the twenty-thousand-dollar desk. Truly, she's the one with the power over me, career-wise.

But towering over her, I know that in this moment I'm all that she sees, all that she hears. And I fucking love it.

"No. I don't mind." She busies herself, gathering a notepad and a pen, grabbing her cell phone and setting it on top so everything is in a nice, neat pile. Her office is clean, not a hint of clutter to be found anywhere, and I bet where she lives is the same way.

Clearly this is a woman who needs some messing up so she can get a little dirty. Have some excitement in her life for once. I get the feeling she's orderly to a fault.

That sounds infinitely boring.

"She should be here any second," Violet says when I remain quiet, as if she's desperate to fill the silence.

Watching her, seeing her hesitate, feeling the discomfort radiate off of her in near visible waves, I'm even more confident my plan will work. She's so vulnerable, so unsure, such a damn easy mark. And she's beautiful. Fucking beautiful, with a scent that drives me wild.

I can smell her now, and I want to inhale her like a drug. I hear her shift in her seat, see her lick her already glossy upper lip, and my cock hardens. What would she do if I pulled her out of her chair, spread her out on top of her desk, and fucked her right here? Anyone could pass by and see us, but we'd be too overcome with lust to care . . .

Damn. I rub my hand across the back of my neck, tearing my gaze away from her. She's fucking tempting. This is the most excited I've been about a woman in a while. I make her uncomfortable, though. I sensed that last night and I'm sensing it again. Right now. I need to try and put her at ease, but . . .

Either I can use that edgy discomfort to my advantage or I can throw it all out in the open and see how she reacts.

I let my gaze return to her, tracking her every movement, remaining locked on her fingers as she tucks a stray strand of hair behind her ear and fidgets uneasily. I'd like to be those fingers. Touching her, learning how soft her skin really is. "You want me to leave, don't you," I say, because that's completely logical.

Her gaze flashes to mine. She looks miserably guilty. "Not at all."

"Because I make you uncomfortable." I pause, waiting for an answer, but she says nothing. "I don't want to upset you, Violet," I lie.

But I like affecting her. It turns me on.

Her eyes now flash with a new emotion. Amusement. "I'm not a delicate flower who needs coddling, Ryder." She checks her phone, huffs out a sound of irritation, and stands, gathering her things and pressing them to her chest. "We don't have time to wait for Rose. Let's go."

Well, well, well. A show of a personality. I like it.

I fall into step beside her as she strides the short distance down the hall to the conference room. I hurry ahead of her at the last moment, holding the door open, and she strides in before me, murmuring her thanks. I let my gaze fall to her ass, appreciating the way it shifts and moves beneath the fabric of her dress. The simple black heels she wears are really nothing close to simple, considering that recognizable red I see flash as she walks.

Christian Louboutins. I know because Pilar says she feels sexy when she wears them, and so she wears them all the damn time. I swear the man designs shoes so that women feel sexy and men want their women wearing Louboutins and nothing else when they fuck them.

"Is this everyone from your team? Are they ready?" She waves at the two men and two women sitting at the table waiting for us before she turns to face me, determination written all over her pretty face. I nod in response, immediately impressed.

"Good." She strides to the head of the table and pulls out a chair, settling in with a polite smile on her face. "Ready whenever you are, Mr. McKay."

So we're back to the formalities. Well, two can play at this. "Can't wait to discuss your new project, Violet." I settle in at the other end of the table, thankful we're not in one of the bigger conference rooms. Otherwise, we'd be shouting at one another.

Her gaze flickers at my saying her name but other than that, no reaction. "As you know, I've been working on creating my own cosmetics line. Something similar to what my grandmother did when she first started Fleur."

"Yes, we're all aware. I hope you don't mind, though, that we didn't bring any initial concepts to you." I glance around the table at the other members of my packaging team. "We wanted to hear what you are looking for first. Best to come in with no preconceived notions, don't you think?"

"I do." She nods, looking pleased. "The line will be small. Sold at only the most high-end stores in a limited-edition run. We'll be using only the finest quality pigments and ingredients. I'm a big believer in saturated color. The cosmetics will be natural but vibrant."

Violet has turned into the efficient businesswoman. She's hot in this mode. "What sort of packaging were you looking for?" I pull out my iPhone, ready to take a few notes, knowing that everyone else at this table is taking notes, too, and would give me theirs. I prefer to listen. Absorb.

Observe.

"I was talking about it with Rose earlier and we both agreed it's imperative to get the packaging just right. It will make or break the success of the line, you know," she continues, sending me a pointed look.

I sit up straighter. No chance am I going to disappoint her with this. "Packaging is definitely important, I agree."

"Definitely. It has to grab the customer's eye. It has to feel rich and elegant, glossy and perfect in their hands. And that's what I want. Glossy perfection." She tilts her chin up, those dark, fathomless brown eyes meeting mine. I'd call her lips glossy perfection, but I don't think she'd appreciate hearing it. "Those are the two key words. Plus I want something sexy, sophisticated. Rich. It needs to say 'exclusive' without screaming it."

"So nothing too obvious." I type hurriedly in the notes section on my phone, listing her key words.

"Exactly." She glances up when the door opens, and I turn to see Rose hurrying in. She settles in a seat close to mine, sending me a smile before she looks at her sister.

"Sorry I'm late. I had another meeting," Rose explains. "It just let out."

"We were talking about glossy perfection," Violet tells her.

"Right!" Rose turns to me, a thoughtful expression on her pretty face. She's as stunning as her sister, but I find Violet infinitely more attractive. "You know, kind of like Violet's lips. Did you happen to notice them today?"

I swallow hard. Damn Rose Fowler for bringing up her sister's sexy-as-hell peach-glossed lips! "I didn't," I lie smoothly.

"Hmm, well, I think even the color is perfect. It would coordinate well with Fleur's current palette." Rose waves a hand toward her sister and I lift my gaze, meeting Violet's across the table.

She's blushing, licking her glossed lips and making me fucking crazy. "What's the name?" I ask.

"What?" Violet blinks, reminding me of a trapped animal about to face her doom.

"Of the lip gloss you're wearing." I smile blandly.

"Oh. It's called Peachy Pie. Part of the Lickable line." She blushes more and I'm captivated. I have never in my life encountered a woman so shy, so unsure of herself and her sexuality. Businesswise, she seems on it. Yet even a hint of flirtation comes into the conversation and she's a bashful schoolgirl, completely unaware of her power.

The contradiction is arousing. And if we're going to sit around and talk about lickable lips and peach pie for the entire meeting . . .

I'm fucking done for.

Chapter Five

Violet

"HE'S NOT ACTING RIGHT."

"Does he ever act right?" Rose asks with an evil laugh, but I ignore her. All I can focus on is Zachary and the way he's ignoring me. Instead of spending time with me like he usually does, he's allowing Pilar to run her hands all over him. She flashes him simpering glances what feels like every two seconds and that fake trill of a laugh, which grates on my nerves every time I hear it.

We didn't go to dinner alone tonight as we'd originally planned. Instead we're at an industry cocktail party along with various people from Fleur Cosmetics. I didn't want to go. Tried my best to beg off, but Zachary wouldn't hear of it. He's in full-blown suck-up mode at the moment, ready to do whatever it takes to please Father and any of the other executives paying attention to him so he can secure that job promotion in London.

It doesn't matter if I'm left alone in the process. It doesn't seem to matter either that we're together yet he allows Pilar to hang all over him. I've never doubted our relationship more than I do at this particular moment.

Ever.

"We were supposed to go to dinner by ourselves," I tell Rose as we stand on the opposite side of the room from where Zachary is. I'm watching him, sipping my glass of wine distractedly. "I forgot about this stupid party and so did he, but we thought we'd make the best of it. Put in an appearance and leave—those were his exact words." I slowly shake my head, remembering how earnest he'd seemed. How he promised we wouldn't linger long. What a lie. He came here to see Pilar, not to spend any time with me. "We came together, but the moment we entered the doors he took off. Hasn't spoken to me since, and we've been here over an hour."

"Are you saying he ditched you?" Rose sounds shocked, though with a hint of sarcasm.

I nod and sip from my wineglass again, surprised to find it empty. I drank that faster than I thought. My head is feeling lighter than usual, too. "Can you believe it?"

"No, I honestly can't. He's always so attentive. Sometimes *too* attentive." Rose rolls her eyes.

"Not tonight," I mutter, feeling a little looser. Must be the wine. When one of the wait staff suddenly appears, I reach out and grab a fresh glass, leaving my empty one on his tray. "Thank you," I say, beaming at him. He smiles and nearly trips over his own feet.

"What's up with you?" Rose asks the moment the waiter leaves, sounding incredulous. "You're being weird."

"How am I being weird?" I drink more wine, enjoying the buzz of the alcohol as it courses through my veins and how it heats my skin. My hair is down, the dress I'm wearing is black and sleeveless, with delicate sheer lace along the shoulders and stretched across the bodice. I have on the highest, shiniest black heels I can muster, the skirt of my dress hits mid-thigh, and maybe it's the outfit mixed with the wine, but . . .

I felt pretty, confident, as I prepared for the evening earlier. The day had been positive from the start. I gathered a collection of inspirational photos and sent them to Ryder so he and his team understood my vision. Lily and I met for lunch, and for once she wasn't drunk by noon or being followed by endless paparazzi. We had a positive, sober conversation. I'd been excited about tonight despite usually dreading these sorts of events.

My excitement withered up and died the moment I realized just how disinterested Zachary was, particularly in me. I don't understand his hot-and-cold moods. I never have.

"I don't know. Griping about Zachary—and you never complain about him. Drinking wine like it's water when you have a one drink maximum at these wretchedly awful parties, and usually just drink club soda. And you flirted with that waiter," Rose says pointedly.

"I did not."

"Did so. You smiled at him and almost sent him sprawling."

"So?" I'm oddly pleased that I could send someone sprawling. "Smiling at a stranger. Is that a crime?"

"When you're usually too worried and fidgety over what other people think of you, yes. It's a crime for you, Violet Fowler." Rose slowly shakes her head, surveying the quietly murmuring crowd before us. "God, this is awful. You, on the other hand, feel like a breath of fresh air."

"I'm not acting different." Fine. I *am* acting different. I'm frustrated with my boyfriend's behavior. If he doesn't care about me, then why should I care about him?

I can't even believe I'm thinking like this.

"You are, but whatever. I'm going to enjoy it. Ply you with more wine and hope you make a spectacle." Rose starts laughing when I shoot her a deathly glare.

"Stop," I tell her firmly, going into big-sister mode. "There will be no spectacles made tonight, especially by me."

Rose lets out an exaggerated sigh. "Well, isn't that a shame?"

"What, you want me to make a fool of myself? Become sloppy drunk and get all crazy like Lily?" I continue drinking because it's calming my frazzled nerves. Not because I want to act the fool. Hearing Pilar laugh, watching as Zachary leans into her and whispers in her ear, is making me upset. But I refuse to confront him. What good would that do me? I'd end up ashamed in the morning. Zachary would make me feel guilty for causing a scene.

I'd rather pretend it's not happening, no matter how hard that is.

"You shouldn't knock her," Rose says quietly. "She's trying."

I immediately feel awful. Using my older sister as a punching bag is not my normal style. "I know she is. I had lunch with her today, remember?" I polish off the rest of my glass of wine and snatch Rose's glass from her hand. She stares at me, her eyes wide, mouth open in shock, and I shrug, not bothering to acknowledge what I just did.

"He's an ass," Rose mutters under her breath, and I know exactly who she's talking about. In fact, I agree. Not that I'm going to say anything.

Ignoring her, I sip from my pilfered glass, purposely keeping my gaze averted from Zachary. Watching him with Pilar only makes me angry. And I don't feel like being angry tonight. Or upset. Or jealous. Or any of those other, horrible, self-defeating emotions I'm so used to dealing with.

There's a bit of freedom in not worrying what your boyfriend thinks about you as you drink yourself into oblivion. I should remember that. Revel in it.

Soon you'll be able to revel in that particular feeling all the time. Especially once Zachary is in London and realizes he doesn't want to be with you any longer.

I shove the nagging voice in my head firmly to the side.

"Oh my, look who's heading in our direction," Rose murmurs, giving me just enough warning to glance up and see Ryder McKay coming toward us, devastatingly handsome in a dark suit and tie, his hair in casual disarray, his eyes filled with a predatory gleam that's directed toward me.

And me only.

"Ladies." He stops in front of us, blocking my view of Zachary with Pilar completely, which is probably a good thing. "You're both looking especially beautiful this evening."

"Charming as ever, aren't you, Ryder?" Rose laughs when he offers her a quick wink and jealousy rises within me, dark and ugly. *Ridiculous.* I'm with Zachary, no matter how much he's behaving like a bad boyfriend at this particular moment. It shouldn't matter to me if Rose and Ryder flirt. Father would love it. He's trying his best to create a monopoly within the company. Since he feels like he's already lost Lily completely, he's trying his best to steer both Rose and me toward what he believes are the right choices.

And Ryder McKay, with his obvious ambition and how quickly he's moved up the ranks at Fleur, is the perfect choice for Rose. Just like Zachary was the perfect choice for me.

"Always," Ryder says, his dark gaze sliding to mine and staying there. I stare back, bringing the wineglass up to my lips and swallowing the rest quickly. Was that my third? Or my fourth? I blink slowly, my head swimming for the briefest moment, and I purse my lips, blowing out a shuddery breath. His smile falters and he takes a step closer, his head tilted toward me as he lowers his voice to ask, "Are you all right?"

Startled, I blink up at him a few more times before I answer, "Yes. I'm fine. Why do you ask?"

"You're not a big drinker." It's a statement, not a question.

"And you know this because?"

His smile returns, softer this time, and I find myself helplessly entranced. "You might not think I've paid much attention, but I know a lot about you, Violet."

Alarm races through me at his words, leaving my skin chilled, and I look to my sister for support. But Rose is gone; I catch a glimpse of her retreating back as she moves into the crowd in the center of the room, her arm raised in greeting at someone she must know. Leaving me all alone.

With Ryder.

"I know you're cautious. That you keep yourself under tight control whether at work or at social events such as this one." He glances around before returning his attention to me. He leans in my direction and lowers his voice, almost as if we're sharing intimate secrets and having a private discussion no one else is allowed to hear. "I know you're not a big drinker and you don't like it when Lawrence drinks too much. Which isn't often, and you're thankful for that."

I part my lips, ready to say something to defend myself, to defend Zachary, but Ryder cuts me off.

"I know you tend to dress conservatively and the dress you have on tonight does cover you well. But it also just happens to be the sexiest damn thing I've ever seen you wear." His gaze drops to my chest and I glance down as well, noticing how sheer the lace bodice is, how the tops of my breasts are on display. My skin warms at his blatant perusal. "The excessive drinking tipped me. You seem a little . . . off." He reaches out and touches my arm lightly. "I'm concerned. Is something upsetting you?"

"Why do you care?" I ask incredulously. I have no idea why he would. We've never really spoken beyond formal niceties in the past. Now we're working together, had one official meeting so far, and he's suddenly concerned? Oh, and we run into each other at a restaurant and now he's my old friend? It makes no sense.

"I'm upset, too, you know," he says, his voice so low it's my turn to lean into him to hear what he says next. "How obvious they're being together."

Realization dawns and I take a step around him, his hand falling away from me. I stare at Zachary and Pilar across the room, all the air escaping my lungs at what I see. She's got her hand on his arm and he's bent forward a bit, so that she can whisper directly in his ear. Her splayed hand slides upward to rest on his shoulder, giving him a squeeze before she steps away.

Anger burns inside of me. It tears at my gut, making my head spin. How dare he let her hang all over him. How dare he make such a fool of me in public.

Lifting my chin, I keep my voice even and say, "It's probably nothing." I don't take my gaze from them, though. It's as if I can't look away.

"It doesn't appear to be nothing," Ryder drawls.

I turn on him, my voice tight, my emotions barely reined in. I blame the alcohol for eliminating my normally cool head. I also blame Zachary for being so blatantly, arrogantly *stupid*. "Stop trying to cause trouble."

Ryder steps away from me as if I offended him. And maybe I did, but for once in my life, I really don't care. "I'm not the one causing trouble, Violet. They are."

I return my attention to Zachary and Pilar. Big mistake. They're talking and laughing as if they're together. Another couple approaches them. I recognize the woman, a well-respected beauty editor with one of the top fashion magazines. Zachary introduces Pilar to the editor, and the calculating gleam in Pilar's eyes is noticeable as she shakes the woman's hand.

Doesn't he realize she's just using him? Of course, he could be doing the same . . .

"I can't watch this anymore. I've seen enough." I turn on my heel and start walking, not sure where I'm going, what I'm doing, what I'm even thinking. My mind is on fast forward, flipping through the endless possibilities, the scenarios that could play out tonight. I don't know what to do, what to say, how to act.

All I know is that I need to get away from Zachary. Get away from Pilar and Ryder and . . . all of them.

I can't take it.

"Violet, wait." I hear Ryder's deep voice call after me but I don't stop. His request actually makes me move faster as I stride through the crowd, not paying attention when someone calls my name, when another person waves. I don't care. I just want to leave, to get some fresh air and clear my head. Right now it's a jumble of confusion, of liquor, of arousal and irritation and hate and need.

I spot the double doors that lead outside and I rush toward them, pushing both of them open so I walk through the center as they swing wide. I take in deep, gulping breaths of air as the cool spring night hits me. A few people are mingling outside and I glance around. Despite my irritation, I'm impressed with the lit rectangular pool in the center, the giant pots of overflowing colorful mixed flowers scattered about. It's a gorgeous night, a gorgeous location, and I can't believe the majority of us were stuck inside when we all could be out here, admiring the night sky, all the lit buildings, feel the refreshing breeze blow across our skin.

"Violet." I feel a warm hand clamp my shoulder, strong, assured fingers burning into my skin, and I close my eyes. His thumb traces the strap of my dress, slips beneath it for the briefest moment, and I hold my breath. Hating myself for wishing he would touch me more . . . but then his hand drops away and I'm left feeling more alone, more despondent than ever.

"Please leave me alone," I whisper harshly, not caring in the least if I'm offending him. I blame the alcohol. I'm usually so careful with my words, with my behavior. But Ryder? He struts around the building without a care, so really, why should I worry?

"I upset you." Ryder's deep voice washes over me and I brace myself, not wanting to feel a thing except anger or irritation. But I feel something . . . different. Never, ever before has a man's voice twisted me up inside and made me yearn. "I didn't mean to do that. I'm just . . ."

"You're just what?" I ask, my voice small, my back still to him. I can't face him. I'm afraid I'll stare into his eyes and drink in all of those handsome, perfectly masculine features and do something stupid. Like throw myself at him. Beg him to take me out of here and make me forget.

Warmth suffuses my body and I release another shuddery breath. This is definitely the wine talking.

"Jealous. Worried." Another pause, this one heavy with unspoken tension. "Pilar and I . . . we have an unusual relationship."

"Really." A snort escapes me and I slap my hand over my mouth, embarrassed. I shouldn't have reacted. I hate that I did.

"It sounds ridiculous, I know. But she helped me when I was at my lowest point and I feel like I still owe her. We've had plenty of . . . understandings in the past, but she *knows* how I feel about Lawrence."

I finally risk turning around, angry because I already know how he's going to answer my question. "And how do you feel about Zachary?"

His lips thin and his nostrils flare the slightest bit. Even angry, he's devastatingly gorgeous. "Isn't it obvious?"

Three words, so simple yet filled with passion. And not the good kind of passion, either. Hateful, deep, and abiding, that's how they sound. Why he dislikes Zachary I'm not sure. They're business rivals, but there's so much hate, and it's not one-sided. "But why?"

"He's a conniving, underhanded asshole." I glance down to see Ryder clenching his hands into fists. "I know he's your fiancé, but I can't help the way I feel. We've been in competition against each other for two years and he's done some pretty underhanded things to me. My opinion of him is tainted by our work history."

"He's not my fiancé," I say.

Ryder frowns. "What?"

"Zachary. We're not engaged." I don't know if we're ever going to get engaged, but I don't tell Ryder that.

"Of course. I'm not surprised." He's practically fuming, he seems so mad, and I can't help the tendrils of pleasure that curl through me at his words. "I can't say I'm not glad he's such a stupid fuck. And why would an intelligent woman like you waste so much time with that asshole?" He studies me, his anger fading into confusion. "What's even more puzzling is why are you still talking to me?"

My heart kicks up speed at the way he's staring at me. "Wh-what do you mean?"

He moves closer, intimidatingly so. I feel trapped. "We both know who I am. What I'm like."

I don't really know much about him at all, but I don't argue. "Really. So tell me, what are you like?"

He smiles, and something deep within me begins to throb. "Wouldn't you like to know?"

Frightened by the intensity in his eyes, the double meaning in his words, I walk away from Ryder without a backward glance, heading toward the railing so I can see the view of the city more clearly. Leaning against the metal bars that separate me from certain death, I tilt my head back and close my eyes, relishing the rush of the wind. It's stronger here, closer to the edge. I can't remember the last time I stood close to the edge, either figuratively or literally.

Of course, Ryder follows me. He's like a wild dog and I believe I've become his favorite bone. What a gruesome thought. "Are you upset over Lawrence wanting to go to London while you want marriage?"

I hesitate. This conversation has become personal fast. I shouldn't open up to him. Ryder McKay seems the type that would use my words against me to his advantage. "I don't know if I want marriage. Not yet, anyway. But a commitment would go a long way in showing that he's . . ." *Invested.* Why am I telling him this? "Not that it's any of your business," I add.

"You're one hundred percent right. It is none of my business.

But I had hoped we could at least become . . . allies, Violet. We're going to be working together very closely over the next few months." I turn to find him watching me carefully, his arm overlapping the metal bar, the breeze tossing his hair carelessly about his head. It's a good look for him. The elegant suit, that unruly mess of hair blowing, his gorgeous face, and all that pent-up anger still hanging onto him. Very sexy, dark, and dangerous. I've never been attracted to dark and dangerous. I dealt with that enough in my past. Fought against it and won.

So why am I suddenly drawn to this man? And why does it feel like he's also drawn to me?

"I don't dislike you," I say. "We can have a professional relationship."

"But what about what's happening now?" The pointed look he gives me is filled with unspoken meaning. Meaning I'm not sure I want to decipher.

I go ahead and try, even though I'm nervous. "What exactly are you referring to?"

"You know what I'm talking about, Violet." His eyes never leave mine. "There's more between Pilar and Lawrence. You know there is." A pause, and his gaze darkens, if that's possible. "And you know there's something going on between you and me."

Chapter Six

Ryder

THE PLAN CAME TOGETHER FASTER THAN I THOUGHT. CONSIDER-
ing we don't have much time before Lawrence leaves for his test
run in London, this is a good thing. Pilar has already worked her
magic. Lawrence is practically mauling her in public, he's so in
lust with her. She told me they kissed last night in the office
when everyone had left and she had her hand on his dick within
seconds.

But that's all she told me, the conniving little witch. I know
there must be more. Funny how she's always digging at me for
information but has become oddly tight-lipped when it comes to
that utter douche in a suit.

I don't fucking get it. Not that I'm giving her much information in return. Not that I even *have* that much information to
give her. I attended the meeting with Violet. Stopped by her office this morning with the excuse that I wanted to go over a few
things regarding plans for the packaging but she blew me off,
saying she had a meeting to go to and she was already late.

She flew out of her office within seconds of my arrival, keeping her head down so we couldn't make eye contact. *Weird.* I got
the sense that I still make her uncomfortable, which is going to
be a giant obstacle if she doesn't get over that.

Besides, women don't blow me off, even for business matters. Arrogant but true.

I knew tonight was my best chance to truly start working on her, getting into her head and filling it with doubt regarding her boyfriend and Pilar. Pilar and I had discussed it but hadn't come up with a plan prior to arriving. Hell, we arrived separately because I knew that if something went down tonight, I wouldn't want to leave with Pilar.

It wouldn't look right, not when I'm the one who's supposed to be hurting and pissed at her.

I hadn't bargained on Violet looking so heartbreakingly beautiful, though, which was a mistake on my part. When I first saw her, she took my breath away, and I didn't think that was possible, I'm such a callous asshole. But that dress, the way it reveals her creamy, smooth skin but not too much. A hint of sexiness mixed with those big, velvety eyes full of pain and wariness. She doesn't trust me. Smart girl.

She shouldn't.

"You believe Pilar and Zachary are . . ." She screwed up her mouth, those pouty, delectable lips covered in scarlet-red lipstick. "Involved?"

"There's a flirtation there. There has been for a while." I step closer to her, our shoulders brushing. She's still shorter than me, but the heels she has on tonight are incredibly high and incredibly hot. All that restrained elegance she wears as some sort of costume hides a very sexy woman just lingering beneath. "Did you see the way she clings to him?"

Violet averts her head, a little sound escaping her that reminds me of a wounded animal. I've pushed her too far. She'll probably cry and fall apart, and then what am I supposed to do? Cry along with her? I'm supposedly as wronged as she is in this situation.

"This isn't the first time," she says, her voice cold yet steady.

Shock races through me. *Well, there's a twist.* I've heard murmurings of Lawrence's indiscretions in the past, but I've had no real confirmation.

I decide to play dumb. "Are you referring to Lawrence and Pilar?"

"Please." She waves a hand, dismissing my suggestion. "Well, maybe they have; I don't know. I wouldn't put it past him. But I do know for a fact that Zachary has been—unfaithful to me in the past."

So she *is* aware. The revelation blows my mind. "Yet you stay with him."

She stares at me with that pretty red mouth turned down. "We've been together a long time. We make a good team." Her voice is flat. She sounds like a robot. Like someone fed her that information and she's just regurgitating it.

"I'm sure he agrees," I say dryly. "He does whatever he wants and you put up with him. It's a great deal."

Violet narrows her eyes. Anger flashes in their depths, brief but intense. I touched a nerve. "You have no room to judge, considering your very—what did you call it? Your *unusual* relationship with Pilar? No one has any clue what to call you two. Are you together? Are you just friends? Is she your boss and your lover? Or just your boss?" She glances around guiltily. I'm sure she realized her voice rose with all of those interesting questions. It went to show that she thought about me. Wondered about Pilar and me, and what we mean to each other. I can't deny that pleases me.

"Forget my questions," she says hurriedly. "What you do during your private time is none of my business."

"For one thing, Pilar isn't my boss any longer and she hasn't been for a while," I say. The blush on Violet's cheeks is unmistakable. "And two, yes, we have been . . . involved. Sexually." We tease each other still. But she's been feeding her needs elsewhere and I'm not sure with whom. Not that I really care, since I've sought others to satisfy my needs as well.

"Please. I don't need any more details." Violet shakes her head, holding up a hand, but I don't want to stop. I may as well stem her curiosity.

"It is what it is. There's no clear definition. We're both fairly open about it." I shrug. I can never explain my relationship with Pilar properly because I barely understand it myself. "I don't want to defend it and I'm guessing you don't want to defend yours, either, so we'll just leave our relationship statuses alone."

She stares at me for a long, quiet moment, her eyes focused solely on me. I take the opportunity to drink her in, study her every feature. The delicately pointed nose, the high cheekbones, those big, dark brown eyes. Her skin is flawless. Her lips the perfect red pout. So fucking beautiful it hurts.

"Thank you," she finally murmurs, ever polite, always proper. "I can't begin to explain to people why I put up with certain things, especially to my sisters and particularly Rose. They can't understand if they've never been in my position, you know?"

I do know. More than she might realize. If I could, I would have shed Pilar long ago. But I owe her my success. At least, she tells me that constantly. Still, I figure that by now I've finally proved my worth, but according to Pilar, I'm moving up at Fleur because of her influence. Not because I've done a good job.

You hear that enough from a person who's taken care of you better than anyone else in your life and you start to believe it.

My cell buzzes and I pull it out of my pocket, checking as discreetly as possible to see who the text is from.

Pilar.

You should stop by the bathrooms with your new little friend and see what's happening. It's rather . . . jaw dropping.

Christ. The woman moves way too fast for me. I can only guess by her reference that she's already got Lawrence's dick in her mouth. I'm fucking impressed.

And disgusted, though I have no room to judge. I'm afraid this won't be easy, dealing with Violet. She's a delicate little flower. Discovering Pilar and her fiancé—or boyfriend, or whatever he wants to call himself—together has the power to destroy her. She could crumble into tiny pieces, fall into a fit of rage, cry buckets of tears. I have no idea.

I don't like that. I've dealt with enough unknowns in my life. When it comes to this scheme, I want to be in control. I need to. Pilar is trying to take that control away from me.

Deleting the message, I turn to look at Violet and find her staring at the city spread out before us, the wind blowing through her lustrous dark hair, her red, red lips pursed into a delectable pout. She appears contemplative. But I see the wrinkle in her brows, the tightness in her jaw. She's upset.

"We should go inside," I say gently, touching her forearm, streaking my thumb across her baby-soft skin slowly, just once. A tremble moves through her, subtle but there, and she lifts her gaze to mine. "Lawrence is probably looking for you," I tell her, feeling like a liar the moment the words fall from my lips.

She laughs, but there's no humor in it. "I'm sure he's not, but thank you for your feigned concern."

"Violet," I murmur, but she says nothing, just pushes away from the railing, away from me, and starts toward the door.

I let her walk ahead of me, my mind feeling as if it's on speed, rushing through the endless possibilities of what might happen next. A few minutes alone with her and I should be feeling on top of the world. It's all going according to plan, even if the plan was placed on fast forward and is skipping through all the relevant scenes. Instead of triumph, guilt slips through my veins, turning my blood cold. This woman has been made a victim by her asshole boyfriend time and again. Why is she so blind to his faults? Why has she let him continue to cheat on her? It makes no sense.

But it's not my concern. It's not as if I have any concern for anyone but myself. She's exactly the same way. It's all about appearances for her. I need to remember she's nothing but a rich bitch who can have whatever and whomever she wants. Not my problem that she chooses to stay with an utter asshole who loves nothing more than cheating on his beautiful girlfriend. She's smart, successful, beautiful, and worth an absolute fortune. Yet he's never satisfied.

Again, I can relate, though I'm loath to admit that I can relate to Zachary fucking Lawrence. But that incessant need is always clawing at my gut, reminding me that I must strive for more. I want to rise above it all, show everyone who I am and what I can do. At least I don't have a girlfriend on my arm who I'm pretending I love just to get ahead.

Clearly, Zachary Lawrence wins the Asshole of the Year award, not me. Though I'm close.

After what I plan on doing to Violet, I'll probably surpass him.

"Thank you again for tolerating me," Violet says from over her shoulder as I reach out to open the door for her. Tolerate her. She's hilarious. I'd give anything to show her what a hardship it would be to *tolerate* her.

By stripping her out of that dress. Seeing what she has on beneath it. Then proceeding to kiss her all over that sexy body . . .

"Always a pleasure, Violet," I say, smiling at her as I pull open the door.

We reenter the building at the exact time Lawrence and Pilar emerge from the hallway that leads to the bathrooms. The two of them appear disheveled, especially Lawrence. His hair looks like her fingers just ran through it repeatedly, his tie is askew, and his pants are wrinkled. Pilar's lipstick is completely gone, her mouth swollen, and the triumphant smile she's wearing says it all.

That must've been some quick blow job.

"Funny running into you here." Pilar sounds as if she's ready to burst into laughter. At least Lawrence has the decency to appear contrite. And guilty as fuck. "And what are you two doing?"

"I could ask you the same thing," Violet says, charging toward Lawrence like she wants to head butt him. Instead she reaches out and shoves at his chest, sending him jerking backward. "What exactly did you do, Zachary? Sneak off and fuck her in the bathroom? Or was it just a quick blow job in a hallway? I know that's your usual style."

Whoa. That was completely unexpected. "Violet . . ." I start, but I'm cut off.

"Stop it, Violet," Lawrence says, angrily spitting out her name like it's a curse. "Don't make a scene."

"Why not? For once in my life, I'd absolutely *love* to make a scene." She shoves at him again, a little harder this time, but he's prepared for the blow and stands his ground. "I can only take so much, Zachary. You really believe I'd turn a blind eye when you screw around with someone we work with in public? Someone I'd have to face day in and day out while you're off in London having the time of your life, proving yourself to Daddy and propositioning every female you meet?"

"You have before, darling, so why change now?" Pilar drawls, and I send her a warning look.

"This isn't your argument. Stay out of it," I murmur under my breath. *Jesus,* she has some nerve. She needs to keep her mouth shut.

And I'm completely fascinated with Violet's behavior. Who knew she was so fiery? We could blame the wine, and I'm guessing that's a contributing factor, but when someone drinks, the truth usually comes out.

And the truth is that Violet Fowler has a backbone. It might be buried deep, but it's definitely in there.

"Why *should* I stay out of it? Let's be very real here. You're going to accuse us of any wrongdoing, but you're the ones sneaking back inside with each other. And I'm positive the two of you have been up to no good," Pilar says, the disgust in her voice abundantly clear. "When are you up to *any* good, Ryder? What dirty trick do you have up your sleeve now? Remember, I know who you are. What you like."

I'm stunned. She's practically calling me out, as if she had no part whatsoever in our little plan. What's her real motive here? She's making me sound as slimy as Lawrence and I fucking can't stand it.

Reaching out, I grab hold of Pilar's arm, clamping my fingers tight. "We were outside talking," I stress as I lower my mouth closer to her ear. "What the *fuck* are you doing?"

She ignores my question and doesn't say a word, pulling herself out of my grip and rubbing her arm as if I hurt her. And this bitch likes it when I hurt her. I've done it enough in the past.

"Let's go." Lawrence brushes right past me, sending me a furious glare before he takes hold of Violet's wrist, gripping it like a manacle, and starts to escort her back into the party. But she shakes out of his grasp, stepping away from him and nearly backing into me.

"Don't touch me."

He turns to face her. "We're leaving. Now."

Violet shakes her head. "No. You're not calling the shots any longer. We're through, Zachary. I can't live like this. You don't really want to be with me. You want what my name can give you, what my father can give you, but you don't love me. You just love what I represent."

Lawrence stares at her, breathing so heavily I can hear him. "We're not having this discussion here. Not now," he whispers, his voice almost a hiss. "We're leaving, Violet. We'll go back to your place and talk about this. Privately."

"I'm not leaving with you. You're not coming over." She crosses her arms in front of her, plumping up her breasts, which I can see through the lace front of her dress. She's furious, her cheeks are a flaming pink and her eyes blaze with unrestrained anger and hurt, but she won't back down. It's Lawrence who finally gives in first.

"This isn't over," he says, pointing at her accusingly. "We'll discuss this tomorrow when you're rational and actually sober."

"I feel more rational now than I ever have before. Funny, how a couple of glasses of wine and the truth can make everything clear. And trust me, there's nothing left to discuss." Her voice is cold, her expression defiant. "You can go to London free of me. I'm sure that's what you secretly wanted, right? You just didn't know how to break it to me? Didn't want my father upset with you?"

He says nothing. There's nothing to say, since I'm assuming Violet's words hit pretty close to the truth. Lawrence merely turns and strides away without a backward glance, heading back into the cocktail party. Pilar sends me a triumphant smile before she chases after him, her heels clicking loudly on the tiled floor.

Leaving me alone with Violet.

"Well." She drops her arms to her sides and releases a shuddery breath, turning to face me. "That was unexpected."

"Very," I agree.

She rubs a hand across her forehead. "I'm sorry you had to witness that."

"I'm sorry you had to go through it," I automatically say, frowning. I don't apologize to anyone. So why her?

"It needed to be done. It should've happened long ago." She shrugs, and I swear I can see her sadness settle over her like a heavy blanket. "I should find Rose. I'm sure she'll come home with me."

I'm about to offer to escort her home but I clamp my lips shut, deciding against it. I can't push too hard too soon. I need to process what unfolded, anyway. Figure out a new plan of attack. I still can't believe what just happened. We broke the two of them up much faster than I thought we could. It was easy.

Almost too easy.

"Wasn't it amazing? She was so incredibly angry. I didn't know stupid Violet Fowler could act so . . . unhinged." Pilar clasps her hands together. "Did you see her face? Wish I would've had a camera to capture it. Talk about shock. I'm surprised she didn't faint."

I'd come home from the party less than an hour after the confrontation, planning to head straight to bed. But when I opened my door, I found Pilar sitting on the couch, curled up in one of my old T-shirts and nothing else. She seemed edgy, excited, almost manic.

There went my peaceful night.

"I couldn't miss it. I was there, too, you know," I remind her. Violet had been beautiful despite the anger, the pain, and the sadness.

"He was an incredibly easy mark." When I meet her gaze questioningly, she waves her fingers at me. "Zachary, darling. He caved like a cheap suitcase. Isn't that how the saying goes?" She taps her index finger against her pursed lips before shaking her head. "It doesn't matter. All that matters is that it's done. The power couple is no more. He'll chase after me until he leaves for London. Then it's over and we'll both get what we want."

I'm not so sure about that. "Ever think he could be pissed at you for what happened?" *I* would be. Fucking around with Pilar ruined his good thing. Who knew how old man Fowler would feel when he realized Lawrence and his daughter broke up, especially if he discovered the details of how it happened? And did this put Pilar in jeopardy?

"I spoke to him. Remember?" She gives a dismissive laugh. "I ran after him like the grieving, how-can-I-make-everything-better mistress. He said he wasn't angry with me or that we were caught. He just wasn't pleased with how it ended, with an argument near the bathrooms during a cocktail party. He thought that was rather . . . cheap."

Jesus. Only Zachary Lawrence would care about appearances during a nasty public breakup. He should be thankful no one else caught them. What the hell's wrong with this dude? "You're lucky, then. If I were him, I'd hate your guts for destroying my sure thing."

"Please. He's so over that sure thing. There are plenty of others, trust me. She's nothing. *Nothing.*" Pilar shakes her head. "You don't have to go through the torture of pursuing her any longer, you lucky, lucky man."

"What do you mean?"

"I mean that it's over. Done with. I'd needed you to distract her while I went to work on Zachary, but he fell for my—*charms* much faster than I anticipated. It's not necessary for you to try and hook Violet any longer," Pilar explains before examining her nails.

Damn it. I want to pursue this, pursue Violet and get her naked, now more than ever. I'd been looking forward to seducing her just for the challenge of it all. "This was part of the game, Pilar. You would get Lawrence, I would get Violet, and then I'd dump her. Get her out of your way so you can pursue . . . whatever it is you're so intent on pursuing."

"The game changed, darling." Her attention is still zeroed in on her stupid nails. "So let's move on, shall we?"

"It's changed for you, but it hasn't changed for me. You got what you wanted." Realization slowly dawns. *Fuck this,* now I'm getting pissed. "You're jealous. You don't want me anywhere near Violet, but it's okay for you to fuck around with Lawrence."

"How could I be jealous of that weak little girl? Please." She makes a dismissive noise. "She wouldn't know how to satisfy a man like you if she tried."

"A man like me," I say, my voice flat.

"Oh, don't play dumb. You know what I mean." She drops her hand and stares at me as that familiar lusty hunger fills her golden eyes. "You like it hard. And dirty, and sometimes a little mean, and even a little . . . painful. Can you imagine Violet splayed out on your bed begging you to fuck her?"

Fuck yes, I could. "You gave me a challenge. I'm going to meet it."

"So you're only doing this to please me?" Pilar asks hopefully.

"This isn't about you." I pause. It's about me wanting Violet. Wanting what Zachary Lawrence just lost. "You go do what you need to do and I'll do the same," I tell her.

The crestfallen expression on Pilar's face says it all. I completely disappointed her. "So you're shutting me out."

"I have to," I stress. No way do I want her involved in my pursuit of Violet. I never did. "We get sloppy, she catches on. We keep our distance from each other; you keep up your game with Lawrence and I'll take care of Violet." I'll wear her down eventually. I know I can.

"Meaning you'll eventually destroy her?" Pilar asks.

Sighing, I scrub a hand across my face. "Why are you so hell-bent on *destroying* her? What did she ever do to you?"

"She was born a Fowler. Just because she's blood doesn't mean she deserves the position and authority that she has at Fleur. It's infuriating." Pilar scowls. "She's teetering on the edge, though. I can sense it. Ending it with Zachary will push her harder. If you're determined to do this, then fine. You toying with her will send her straight over. She'll spiral out of control and someone will need to replace her. That will be me."

"Rather certain in your abilities, aren't you?"

"Oh darling." The smile she flashes at me is fucking scary in its intensity. "You have no idea."

Chapter Seven

Violet

AS I EXIT THE ELEVATOR I NOTICE THE STRANGE LOOKS, THE CU-
rious murmurings, though they're trying their best to be discreet. I nod and smile hello at those brave enough to face me
head on, hoping that the Fleur employees I encounter are talking
about me because I rarely make an appearance on this floor. Not
because they've all somehow found out that my now ex-
boyfriend let the barracuda of Fleur suck his dick last night
while at a cocktail party. In a hallway. By the bathrooms.

God, it sounds so vile, so tawdry. My skin crawls just thinking about it.

Oh, and yes. *Suck* his *dick*. I'm not the type to say such . . .
vulgar things, but I'm calling a spade a spade. I'm owning what
happened last night because I'm not at fault. I'm not the one
who pushed him into the arms of another woman. He's actually
used that excuse before and I've fallen for it.

Who's the real fool in this situation? Me. And I'm sick of it.
Zachary is a despicable human being who's cheated on me for
the very last time.

I smile politely at the receptionist as she greets me with a
cheerful good morning, then turn right and start heading down
the hall. I lift my chin with feigned determination while deep
within, nerves dance inside my stomach. This needs to be done

and it's best if I get it over with first thing. Rose told me I should just do it via email, but I insisted that telling him in person would have more impact.

I'm starting to think I should have listened to Rose after all.

Smoothing my hands down the front of my vivid red dress—purposely chosen because I feel so bold wearing it—I straighten my shoulders and pause at the slightly closed door, knocking twice before I peek my head inside. "May I come in?"

Ryder McKay stands behind his desk looking like a ruthless, commanding king, his hands propped against the edge as he surveys the various photos and paperwork spread all over the top. He lifts his head, his stark blue gaze meeting mine, and for a moment all I see is ice. His gaze is impenetrable. A little bit mean.

But then the ice melts and he smiles slowly, the crinkles that form around his eyes charming and telling me that he does smile more often than it might seem, which somehow reassures me.

"Violet. What a pleasant surprise." He stretches to his full height and waves a hand at me. "Close the door."

"Oh." I jump a little, running my fingertips over my hair, which I pulled into a no-nonsense, sleek ponytail, as I turn to look at the door. "Um, what I want to talk about won't take long, I promise."

"But you want privacy, I assume?" His delectably deep voice washes over me and I repress the shiver that wants to overtake me at his words. He can make "privacy" sound like a dirty sexual act he wants to perform on me and me alone. I glance over my shoulder to find his head tilted, his gaze seemingly locked on my backside. "Shut the door, Violet."

His demand tells me I shouldn't argue, so I don't. I go to the door, the plush rug I walk across softening my steps so that I don't even hear the click of my heels, and I very carefully close it all the way. The firm click sounds loud in the otherwise silent room, indicating I'm alone with him. There are no exposed glass windows on this floor. Everything's encased and closed off, so no one knows I'm in this office by myself with Ryder. Excitement buzzes along my skin like a shock wave and I tell myself this is no big deal. It's just Ryder.

But there is nothing casual about this man. I'm drawn to him like those stupid moths drawn to a flame. The ones that get closer and closer until their wings sizzle and their bodies smoke. When it's over, they fall to the ground like burned little crisps.

I turn to face him, leaning against the door, suddenly needing the space between us so he doesn't get the wrong idea of why I'm here. Or I don't get the wrong reason as to why I'm here. The last thing I want is to get burned.

"Is everything all right?" He rounds the desk and comes to stop in front of it, leaning against the center. Clasping his hands in front of him, he holds them loosely together, drawing my attention. He has large hands. Long arms. A broad chest and shoulders. His expression is neutral, though just as handsome as usual. "I know the last time I saw you, you were quite upset."

Oh, leave it to Ryder to get right to the point. He minces no words, this man.

"I wanted to . . . thank you for last night," I start, hating the hesitation, the nervous shake in my voice.

He frowns, looking confused. "Thank me for what?"

"For not making what happened between Zachary and me any worse." The ranting voicemails and crazy text messages Zachary had barraged my phone with long into the night had left me shaken. I'd hardly slept and was buzzing from the Venti dark roast I gulped down before I even arrived at work. "You were very calm, and I appreciate that."

"You were the one who was not so calm. A rather impressive show of anger you offered us, Violet." The little smile that curls his lips makes my heart flutter. I like it when he says my name and he does it quite often. He makes it sound like an endearment. *Ridiculous.* "Are you feeling better this morning?"

"Not really. But I'll get through it." I shake my head, ignoring the look of concern on his handsome face. "I just . . . I wanted to ask you a favor."

"What sort of favor?"

"I was hoping that I could ask for your agreement to remain silent in regard to what happened last night." My request sounds completely convoluted. I wouldn't be surprised if he told me to screw off and get out of his office. Not that he ever would, but . . . I am making a complete muck of this. I know it.

"You're asking for my silence," he says softly.

I nod and press my lips together. I don't want to say anything more for fear I'll sound like a complete idiot.

He watches me, his gaze roving over my body in such a languid manner my skin heats, everything within me coming alive. My breath stalls in my throat as I wait for his answer and when he finally lifts his gaze to mine once more, I feel dizzy. Like I'm still drunk on too many glasses of wine.

"Your dress matches my tie," he says, throwing me off kilter with his change of subject.

"What?" I take a few steps toward him, squinting as I stare at his broad chest. The solid red tie he wears is almost an exact match. "Oh. Yes. You're right."

"Like we planned it."

"You didn't get the memo?" I smile. I can't help myself. I should be feeling down and out, crying into my bowl of Cheerios this morning over the loss of my boyfriend, but I'm not.

I'm excited to be in this man's presence, as crazy as it seems. The way he looks at me, he makes me feel incredibly aware that I'm a woman.

"I must've missed that one." His answering smile is brief and dazzling. "You look beautiful. Like you could grab Lawrence by the balls and wrench them off cleanly, all while you have a giant smile on your face."

I burst out laughing at the image. It's crude but empowering. "Hopefully he'll stay away from me today."

"If he's smart he will." Ryder's smile fades. "I can keep quiet, Violet. But I'm going to have to ask you for a favor in return."

"All right." Curiosity runs through me as I wait for his response. I'm thinking he likes to do this. The pausing, the calculated, well-thought-out statements he makes. He enjoys the anticipation and I've come to a new appreciation for it myself, especially when he's the one who's delivering it.

"Come to dinner with me tonight."

My mouth drops open and I start to utter my protest, but he holds his hand up, halting me.

"A working dinner," he reassures me. "I have some ideas I want to share with you in regard to the new line. I've gathered a lot of images these last few days and I think the team and I have come up with something amazing."

Why am I disappointed that he wants this to be a business meeting only? What in the world is wrong with me? I'm supposed to be heartbroken over Zachary. I should still be in love with him and not wanting to be with anyone else. I don't want to go to dinner with Ryder and talk about business. "Can't you show me your ideas in our next meeting? We could reschedule if you'd like. I have some free time in the afternoon most of this week."

He slowly shakes his head. "Some of the suggestions we've come up with are . . . a little out there. Rather than embarrass my team if you flat out reject their ideas, I thought it would be good if we met prior and I could show you what we've come up with so far."

I'm intrigued despite my wariness. He knows I'm curious about anything that has to do with my project. My baby. "Tonight?" My voice is squeaky and I clear my throat.

"Unless you already have plans." He keeps his eyes locked on me. As if nothing else matters. I can almost believe that, too. "Do you?"

I did. Before I ended everything with Zachary. "No, I don't."

"Perfect." He smiles. "I'll arrange everything and email you all the details before lunch."

"All right. Sounds good." I turn and start toward the door, eager to get away yet reluctant to leave. He makes me uncomfortable. I can't quite put my finger on exactly how or why, but there it is.

"Violet?"

I wait until I reach the door before I face him once more, reaching out my hand to rest it on the handle. "Yes?"

"Wear the red dress tonight." He smiles, looking slightly devilish as he lets that wicked gaze roam over me yet again. "I like you in red." There's an undercurrent to his request. An unspoken meaning, as if he's demanding I wear red to please him and no one else.

I'm so startled by his request I can't answer him. Instead, I push open the door and practically run down the hall back to the elevator. Back to the safety of my floor and my office, back to normalcy and away from those lusty thoughts that swirl within me every time I'm close to Ryder.

But his words echo in my head for the rest of the morning and I find myself restlessly checking my in-box again and again, hitting refresh so many times I start to annoy myself. The fear that nags at me won't let up. What if he forgets? What if he has to cancel? What if he's changed his mind and decides he doesn't want to see me tonight after all?

And why do I want to see him again so badly?

I remember how he touched me last night when he followed me outside. When he rested his hand on my shoulder, his warm fingers slipping just beneath the lacy strap of my dress. My skin tingles just thinking about it, and I wonder what it would feel like if he touched me with more purpose. If he sunk his hands into my hair and held me still, his mouth descending upon mine. I have no doubt he's an expert kisser. A master at seduction. He's so tall and muscular, I can only imagine what his body must be like. Not that Zachary has a bad one, but he's a little soft in spots. It comes with the desk job, and considering Ryder has one, too . . . but from what I can tell there's nothing soft on that man's body whatsoever. Except, perhaps, his hair.

Oh, and his lips.

A shiver moves down my spine at the thought.

An email comes through and I see the familiar name. I click on it eagerly, my heart hammering in anticipation of what it might say. I should be doing a thousand and one things at the moment and instead I'm waiting for emails like a silly teenager waiting for her boyfriend to call.

Clearly I've lost my mind. And I can't blame it on the alcohol any longer. I may be hung over, but I am stone-cold sober.

> Violet,
> I've made arrangements for us to have dinner at Harper's at seven o'clock. I hope this works for your schedule and isn't too early. I know you like to stay late at the office on Wednesday nights, so I tried to accommodate you as best I could.

I sink my teeth into my lower lip, my gaze snagged on the last sentence I read. Had Zachary ever tried to accommodate me in any way?

That would be a no.

I figured we could just ride over together. I've arranged for a car. Unless you wanted to go home first,
which I completely understand. Let me know.
Best,
Ryder

I should make him wait. I should get on that phone call I've
been meaning to make for the last few days. Fill out the boring
paperwork Rose left me with last Friday that I still haven't done.
   Instead, I hit REPLY and immediately type out my response.

Dear Ryder,
That sounds perfect. I haven't tried Harper's but I've
heard it's delicious. And hopefully on a Wednesday
night it will be quiet enough that we'll be able to
discuss the project freely without disturbing anyone.
I look forward to our meeting.
Thank you,
Violet

I hit SEND before I can second-guess myself on what I said,
but of course, I second-guess myself. Is it wrong that I said
Harper's was delicious? Or that I hoped it was quiet enough?
Did I sound like I was implying anything? *God*, I'm being ri-
diculous. Absolutely ridiculous—
   His reply hits my in-box so quickly it shocks me.

I arranged for us to have a private room so we won't
disturb anyone. I hope you don't mind. I wanted your
undivided attention while I talk to you.

Oh. Swallowing hard, I hit REPLY.

If that's what you want, then you'll have it.

I let my finger hover over the mouse for one beat. Two. Before I finally close my eyes and hit SEND.

That's what I want more than anything.
Looking forward to tonight.
R.

The pleasure that blooms within me makes me smile and I cover my face with my hands, shaking my head. I feel like an alien has taken over my body and is making me say these things, think these things. I have never in my life sent any sort of innuendo-filled email to anyone, not even Zachary. A few moments with Ryder and I act like I want him to jump me.

I sort of *do* want him to jump me.

Dropping my hands from my face, I reach out and pick up the phone, dialing Rose's extension. She answers on the first ring with a hurried hello, sounding completely distracted.

"I know I just broke up with Zachary . . ." I pause, and Rose butts in before I can say another word.

"If you're telling me you're taking him back I will hang up on you. Right. Now. And I won't talk to you again, either. I don't care if we're sisters. I don't care if we work together. I won't let you go back to that tool," Rose says, sounding fierce, in her typical defensive *I will kill anyone who hurts you* sisterly way.

"No. No. Don't worry about that." I pause, suddenly feeling scared to say anything about Ryder to Rose. She'll tell me I'm crazy. Warn me that I'm rushing into something I probably can't handle. He's too much for me. I know it. I think he knows it, too. But that's not stopping him.

And it's not stopping me either.

"Really?" Rose asks cautiously.

I can't tell her. Not yet. I should keep this my little secret for a while longer. It hasn't even been twenty-four hours since Zachary and I split and I'm already thinking of someone else. Rose will freak. Or think I'm having a mental breakdown. "I just wanted to let you know that I'm sticking to it. I won't take him back."

"No matter how hard he tries to win you over?" Rose sounds skeptical, not that I can blame her. I've given in before, though we've never really split up, so this is a new development in our history.

"No matter how hard he tries," I promise. "Not that he'll try. He's leaving in less than two weeks. It's temporary, but I'm assuming Father will give him this promotion. He'll move on. *I'll* move on. It's over."

"If you say so. I think the idiot will realize what he's lost and come back begging."

I laugh. *God,* I hope not. He is the last thing I want to deal with. I'm so over him. "I doubt it."

"I'm so proud of you. You sound so strong, so sure of yourself," Rose murmurs. "You can do this. I know you can."

"I know I can, too." I do. And I think using Ryder as the perfect distraction will help.

Or hurt. I can't tell yet.

But that doesn't scare me enough to stop me.

Chapter Eight

Ryder

ANTICIPATION HUMS THROUGH MY VEINS AS I WATCH VIOLET exit the building, that sexy-as-fuck dress she's wearing standing out amidst the sea of black and navy and gray that passes by between us. I'm standing on the edge of the sidewalk waiting for her and it's getting colder by the minute. No one can count on spring in New York. One day—yesterday—it was a perfect high of seventy-five degrees. Today's high was sixty and the temperature is dropping at a rapid rate. Violet is wearing the short-sleeved dress with no coat or sweater, a black Chanel bag slung over her shoulder, her hair still as sleek and perfect as it was when I saw her first thing this morning, and all I can think is how vivid she is. How startlingly beautiful and perfect.

And how badly I want to mess her up. Tug the band out of her hair and watch as those long, dark waves fall around her face. Place my lips on the spot where her pulse throbs at the base of her neck and suck there. Nibble her skin. Lick her. Learn her taste. Let my hands wander, memorizing every curve . . .

She catches sight of me and the shy smile that lights up her face sends a buzz of awareness straight through me. She pushes her way through the crowd until she's standing directly in front of me, the scent of her, the heat of her lithe body despite the cold surrounding me, drawing me in. Her lipstick is as red as her dress, reminding me of the shade she wore last night, and I have the sudden urge to kiss it right off of her. Smear it, get it on my lips, let her mark me.

If I have my way, I will definitely mark *her*. In primitive, sexual ways that she'll keep hidden beneath her clothes. I'll know those marks are there, though.

I swipe a hand across the back of my tense neck. *Jesus,* something about this woman fills me with confusing, possessive thoughts. Thoughts I don't normally have. I don't care about anyone but myself. I've had to be this way. It's the only way I survived when I was growing up. I raised myself for the most part.

"Sorry to keep you waiting," she says, sounding breathless. Can't help but wonder if she'd sound that breathless just after I make her come. "I had a last-minute call and it took longer than I expected."

"It's fine." She's five minutes late, tops. No big deal. Funny how she acts like she's committed an unforgivable sin. "I haven't been waiting long."

"Good." The relieved smile she sends me makes my own lips curve without thought. "Are you ready?"

"Absolutely." I take her elbow and steer her to the car, opening the door for her so she can climb inside. I let my gaze drop to her ass, watching the way the thin red material hugs her curves, and I quell the lust that rises within me as best I can.

But it's difficult. Having her close, all of my senses focused on her and no one else, I feel almost overwhelmed—or more like a beast ready to rut. Not the usual experience I have when in the presence of a beautiful woman. They're the ones who slobber all over *me,* not the other way around.

I climb into the backseat of the car behind her and pull the door shut, indicating to the driver that he should get going. We have less than fifteen minutes to get to our destination in time for our reservation and there's no way we'll make it. They won't give up our spot, though. I guaranteed the small private room for Violet and me with my credit card. We'll be alone all night. I'll start working my magic on her the minute we're behind closed doors and she'll be ready and willing within the next few days, if not by the end of the night.

I'm that confident in my abilities.

"I can't wait to see your ideas," she says, her voice holding a tremor of excitement. She curls her hands together in her lap, her body angled toward mine. "I've been looking forward to this dinner all day."

Her admission surprises me. Violet's usually so reserved, holding her feelings, her opinions, close to her chest. But I think back on those emails we exchanged earlier. I read more into them and I think she did, too. I was taking a risk, sending her innuendo-filled emails. Not that I meant to at first. And given that she dumped Lawrence only last night, I'm surprised by her behavior.

But as I also observed last night, there's more to Violet than meets the eye. I think she's offering me a glimpse beneath all of those layers she keeps so carefully hidden. Makes me eager for her to reveal even more.

Much more.

"So have I," I murmur, wishing I could reach across the center console and grab her hand. I'd probably shock the shit out of her if I settled her palm on my growing dick. Would she jerk her hand away, or curl her fingers around my cock and stroke me straight into oblivion?

I'm guessing the former. I'd bet good money she's never given a hand job to Lawrence in a car. Maybe she's never given him a hand job *anywhere*. I have no idea. Just thinking about her sex life with that asshole makes me want to punch his face in.

Grimacing, I stare out the window at the passing buildings,

the sounds of the always noisy city soothing me. Reminding me of who I am and where I came from. Focusing on Lawrence gets me nowhere. Pilar would call this absurd feeling taking over me jealousy.

For once, I'd have to agree with her.

"Did you bring the photos?" Violet asks hopefully, pulling me from my thoughts.

"I did." I point at the briefcase resting near my feet. Though this plan was partially calculated to help me get Violet completely alone, I'm also going to show her the inspirational photos my team and I found. Images that capture the idea behind Violet's new cosmetics line and what she hopes it will represent to her buyers.

I just hope she likes what we've come up with.

"I spoke with Zachary," she says out of nowhere, her voice hushed, her eyes huge. The lights from outside shine into the backseat, casting us both in shadow, but I can see that pretty face, those big, sad eyes. "He's very angry with me."

"He's angry with *you*?" The nerve of this dickhead. He blows my mind. "Isn't *he* the one we caught with Pilar?"

"He said it wasn't what we thought. That they just . . ." Her voice trails off and she turns toward the door, staring out the window. "That they only kissed. Nothing else."

If she really believes that, I have more problems than I thought. "Can I be completely open with you, Violet?"

She whips her head around, her gaze meeting mine once more. "Of course."

"If he said they were only kissing, as in Pilar was kissing his *dick,* then yes, go ahead and believe him." I don't mince words and I can tell I shocked the hell out of her. I didn't think those gorgeous brown eyes could get any larger. "Don't fall for his lies. You're too good for him."

She clears her throat. "He also told me that if I had any interest in you, I'm crazy. That the only reason you would want to spend any time with me beyond work is because you want to use me to get ahead."

He should know, considering that's exactly what Lawrence did to her. "He makes you sound like a silly little girl who can't think on her own."

Violet's quiet for a moment, as if she's absorbing what I said. "You're right. He does." She stares straight ahead, her jaw tight, her lips thin. I can see the delicate line of her throat as she swallows and I want to rain kisses on the fragile skin there. Whisper exactly what I want to do to her in her ear.

Jesus, I have it bad.

"Don't you want to prove him wrong, then?" I ask.

"How?" She tilts her head, her ponytail slipping over her shoulder. It rubs against the fabric of her dress, all that shiny, silky hair beckoning me, making my fingers itch to touch it.

"Instead of always being the one who gets used, I think you should do the using." I have no idea where I'm going with this, but from the way her interest perks up, I keep going. "So maybe you should go ahead and use me."

Her mouth drops open for the briefest moment before she snaps her lips shut. "What do you mean, I should use you? How? And why would you want to be used?"

Everything's clicking into place, piece by piece. I feel like I'm on some sort of high, the type I usually only get at work, when I'm putting together a presentation and I know I fucking nailed it. It's the same sort of high I used to get when I was young and living on the streets, scheming to find my next meal, my next hit, my next fuck.

"Your ex hates my guts. And I'm not a fan of him either." Deciding the hell with it, I reach out and take her hand, interlacing her fingers with mine so our palms are pressed close together. I swear I can feel her heart beating through her fingers and I match my breathing to the increasing rhythm, wanting to both calm and excite her. "If he knew the two of us had become involved, it would drive him crazy." And maybe distract him enough that he would fail miserably in his new temporary position.

She blinks at me, looking a little interested but a little lost, too. The attraction is there between us. I know she must feel it. But is that enough to get her to make such a daring move? "I think you're attracted to me," I whisper, letting my gaze drop to her lips. She darts her tongue out, wetting all that slick red flesh, and I want to groan. Want to lean in and kiss her fucking senseless, but I control myself. "And I am definitely interested in you."

"You are?" She shakes her head, a little sigh escaping her. "Please. This is crazy." Her fingers tighten on mine the slightest bit. "I hardly know you. You're involved with someone else. I broke up with Zachary only last night when a few days ago, I thought he was going to ask me to marry him. I *wanted* to marry him."

I push through the anger that clouds my brain. What a waste it would have been, Violet marrying Zachary. He would have made her life miserable. "I know. I agree with you—it's totally fucking crazy." Her eyes widen at my word choice. There's the slightest thrill in shocking her. I feel like everyone tiptoes around her, but why, I'm not sure. She's always had this fragile air around her. I'm starting to think she's not the one who's behind that, though. "Let's see where tonight takes us."

"T-tonight?" Her voice trembles and she's breathing shallowly—I can see the rapid rise and fall of her breasts.

"We'll treat it as part business, part pleasure." Clutching her hand tight, I lean in and press my lips to her forehead, letting them linger before I slowly pull away from her. "It'll be . . . interesting. Don't you think?"

Those luminous dark eyes stare at me like I have two heads. I've totally turned her world upside down. Only fair, because she's done the same to me. She's all I've thought about for days.

"I think it's a huge risk," she says softly. "I've heard the rumors about you."

I frown and release my grip on her hand, settling back in my seat. I swear disappointment flashes across her face, but I can't be too sure. "What sort of rumors?" *Jesus,* this is the longest car ride of my life. And where she's taking this conversation isn't making me all that comfortable.

She shrugs. "That you and Pilar have engaged in some kinky sex games. That you can't let her go no matter how hard you try. That you'll have sex with anyone in a skirt and walk away from them afterward without a care. Zachary says you're the most despicable human being on this planet."

All of it true. Every last bit. And *her* skirt in particular is arousing me at the moment. "Love how much he insults me when we're actually very similar," I murmur, puzzling over her words and how I'm going to defend myself.

"I told him none of it mattered," she continues, surprising me. "That I didn't care about your personal life. We're involved professionally but that's it. And if something happens between us it's none of his concern. I refuse to let him control my emotions and make me feel bad that I gave up my doormat ways and kicked him out of my life."

Violet's backbone is making an appearance again. "You did the right thing, ending it with him."

She smiles faintly. "You'd say that no matter what. I think your words were . . . *hmmm* . . . that you hate him?"

"You're right. I do hate him. I also hate what he's done to you." I'm going to hate what I plan on doing to her, too.

"What I'm really trying to say is I don't know if I want to take the risk and . . . 'use' you." She lifts her eyebrows, almost as if she's daring me to argue with her. "I think you might be a bad idea."

"I am a terrible idea." This is the last warning she'll get. I'm being one hundred percent honest with her here. I'm the worst idea out there, especially for Violet. My plans for her won't end pretty. But if it gets me what I want, then I'm going to take the chance. She'll recover.

Eventually.

Laughter escapes her at my candidness. "You aren't one for holding back, are you?"

"No." I shake my head. "What you see is what you get."

Her eyes light up with unmistakable arousal. "I like what I see." Now it's my turn to be the one who's shocked.

"You already know I like what I see." My gaze drops to the V of her neckline, how low it dips, offering me a glimpse of her cleavage. All that smooth, creamy skin on display is the most powerful drug to an addict like me. I want to touch her so bad it's damn near killing me. "That dress you're wearing is driving me crazy."

"Does that mean you like it?" She glances down at herself, then lifts her head, amusement etched all over her face. I have no answer for her but I think she can tell. "It's like armor. I felt so brave today wearing it. Facing you this morning. Facing Zachary this afternoon. The meeting I had, that I feared would go terribly, ended up being successful. And now . . . with you again. More armor."

"You feel the need to protect yourself against me?" Smart girl. She impresses me every time I talk to her, I swear.

Not a good thing either, admiring her. I need to remember she's nothing. Nothing to me.

If I keep telling myself that, maybe I'll convince myself it's the truth.

She nods, her full lips pursed in amusement. "Tonight is going to be torturous. I can tell."

"Torturous how?" I can think of many ways I can torture her. Every one of them would bring her agonizing pleasure . . .

"You like to make people wait for things, me especially. I think you enjoy the anticipation. All that longing, waiting to see something, taste something, watch something."

Ah fuck. This conversation is turning into a sexual one. Usually I don't mind. Typically I'm the instigator. But the last thing I need is to get all riled up with Violet and then be left hanging, unable to do anything about it while we walk into a restaurant and have to make nice.

I'm no longer in the mood to make nice. I'd rather lift up the fabric of her dress and fuck her in the backseat of this stupid car.

The stupid car comes to a halt, jerking us both in our seats, and then the driver is climbing out, going around the front of it so he can open Violet's door first. She thanks him profusely, which makes him act the fool, and he nearly slams the skirt of her dress in the door. Then he's opening my door, all stern and expressionless, nodding at me when I start to stuff a twenty-dollar bill in the front pocket of his shirt.

"Stop ogling her like you want to lick her from head to toe or I'll crush your nose in with my fist," I tell him pleasantly, slapping his chest after I shove the twenty in his pocket. "Got that?"

"Sir, yes sir." The driver practically snaps to attention and I send him one last menacing glare, taking hold of Violet's arm as I guide her into the restaurant.

"What was that about?" she murmurs questioningly after I open the door for her.

"Don't worry about it," I reassure her with a quick shake of my head.

The restaurant is huge; it had once been a warehouse that was recently converted and they played up all the exposed pipe, beams, and brick walls as part of the theme. I'd come here often enough when it first opened that I became friendly with the manager, who explained to me the theme behind the restaurant, the menu, and the drinks at the bar. Casual but elegant comfort food, with a sort of old-fashioned speakeasy vibe—that's what the owner had been going for.

I think he pretty much nailed it.

"Ooh, I love what they've done with this place," Violet says as she takes it all in before turning to smile at me. "I've heard the food is excellent."

"It is." I lead her to the front podium and offer up my name to the woman who's standing behind it. Her eyes light up with interest and she grabs some menus, then asks us to follow her. We do so, me placing my hand on the small of Violet's back, pressing my fingers into her skin. She doesn't say a word, doesn't tense up, doesn't relax, but I can tell she's hyperaware of my presence. She seems slightly on edge and I like it.

Hell, I revel in it.

The hostess leads us to the back of the restaurant, to a wall that has four thick wooden doors lining it, all of them closed. "Number three is your room for the evening," she says as she leads us to the second door, resting her hand on the handle. "Please let me know if you need anything else. Your server should be right with you."

She pushes open the door and we both walk inside, the hostess flashing a friendly smile at us before she pulls the door shut behind her. The space is cool and quiet, and the giant rustic wood table that sits in the center of the room could fit at least twenty people around it.

"We could have a conference here and your entire team would fit comfortably," Violet marvels as she walks toward the table, resting her hands on the back of one of the chairs.

"Yes." I approach, stopping just behind her, so close I can breathe in her deliciously addictive scent. "But I'd much rather be with you tonight. Alone."

She says nothing, merely stares at me from over her shoulder, those velvety eyes drinking me in. I can't tell if she likes what she sees or if she hates me. I can't get a read on her and that drives me insane. I can read people. That ability alone has got me far, both when I was a punk kid and now in my career.

But Violet? I can't get a solid read on her and I don't get why.

Chapter Nine

Violet

THROUGHOUT DINNER RYDER WAS A PERFECT GENTLEMAN. HE made polite conversation, keeping any overtly sexual undertones out of it. Oh, he flirted. He flashed the occasional smile that made me a little dizzy. He plied me with plenty of wine, too, and I wondered if that was because he saw how I reacted at the party last night. Fueled by my anger, fueled by the alcohol, ready to do battle with Zachary.

I still can't believe I behaved that way. If Father had seen me like that, he would have been mortified. Rose was still upset that she hadn't been able to witness me raging at my jerk of an ex.

Typical.

I couldn't help but think as the dinner went on and Ryder was so polite, so subtly charming, that he was like some sort of predatory animal lying in wait. Calculating his next move, soothing me, tricking me into believing all was well. And then he'd strike. Capture me completely and take me as his willing victim.

And I feel willing, as wrong as I know it is. I want him. It's wrong, but I do.

"The inspiration file." He pulls it from out of nowhere, though I knew he'd brought his briefcase in with him. I take the file, our fingertips brushing, the jolt his touch elicits every single time surging through me. "Take a look. Tell me what you think."

His tone is casual but beneath it I hear the edge, though I can't quite decipher it. Is he nervous? Prepared for me to challenge his team's choices? Afraid I might hate everything I see?

My fingers shake as I slowly open the file, my breath catching in my throat when I see the first image. It's of a woman with long, dark hair, her head thrown back, her eyes not quite closed, deep red lips parted. Her hand rests at her neck, her arm between her bared breasts. The photo is sensual, not sleazy, but the woman definitely appears as if she's in the throes of passion.

I flip it over, refusing to look at Ryder, to let him know that I'm already off center and I've only looked at one image.

The next photo is of a stack of French *macarons,* each one a distinct, vibrant color. The image, each delicate cookie, is beautiful in its simplicity.

I scan over each photo carefully, surprised at how different they all are yet still somehow work together. One is a photo of a sky and a woman's hands rising toward it, a delicate, bright orange butterfly resting on the tips of her fingers. A bouquet of colorful wildflowers is in one image; a stark green field with a single sunflower growing in the center, rising toward the sun, in another.

It's the last photo that gets me. A couple wrapped around each other, staring at each other. The woman is heartbreakingly beautiful, her dark brown eyes sad, her bold pink lips parted. The man has his hands on her, one gripping her face, the other holding her backside, his gaze intense on her face, their foreheads pressed together. They're completely focused on each other and I can feel the connection between them.

I stare at the image for so long, the silence between us grows heavy. Unspoken words and thoughts float in the air and as time ticks on, I'm afraid to look up and meet Ryder's gaze.

The photo speaks to me and I can't explain why. The man . . .

it's as though he owns that woman. That she's everything to him and he doesn't want to let her go. She looks as if she's fighting a war within herself. Or maybe a war with the man and the passion that he feels for her. She wants it, needs what he can give her, but she's also fearful of him, of what he represents. All while he looks like he just wants to possess her in any way he can.

"She reminded me of you," Ryder says, his deep, rumbling voice startling me. I glance up to find him watching me, his eyes fiery, his expression somber.

"How?" I ask in a whisper.

"She looks like you. The dark hair, the dark eyes, and her sad expression. She looks frightened."

"He looks like he wants to own her."

"Doesn't every man want to own a beautiful woman? Or at the very least, take care of her?" He doesn't smile, doesn't so much as blink, and I return his gaze, feeling ensnared.

Trapped.

"You make her sound like a possession." And I sound like a breathless fool.

A wolfish smile appears and I know I should be frightened. His entire demeanor has changed. The polite business associate is gone. "Is there anything wrong with a man wanting to possess a woman?"

"Yes, if he's controlling."

"But what if she likes it? What if she wants to be possessed?" He's trying to push me and I'm not sure why. "I would never want any man to possess me."

The smile fades and his eyes darken. "Then you haven't met the right man yet."

I have no answer for him. Instead I slap the folder closed and push it across the table toward him. "I like the photos."

He lifts a brow. "Really?"

Why does he sound surprised? And why does that irritate me? "They're very colorful and sophisticated and . . . sexy."

"That's the idea we were hoping to go with. Not just for packaging, but with advertising as well. I know that's not our portion of the campaign," he says quickly, cutting me off before I can correct him. "But it all comes together, you know? It needs to fit cohesively. And I keep thinking about what Rose said in our first meeting. Glossy perfection."

I press my lips together, remembering that Rose had been referring to my lips. "I like those words."

"I do, too." His gaze drops to my mouth and lingers there. "Glossy, vivid, colorful perfection. Those are the words we tossed around a few days ago as we cultivated these particular images out of the hundreds we'd gathered."

"Hundreds?"

"This project is important to you, right? And to Fleur. We're taking it very seriously," he says, his tone full of reassurance. "We want your new line to have the right message, to capture the right audience. Don't you agree?"

"Of course I agree. And I like the direction you're taking. I can see me taking these images to marketing." I flip open the file again and thumb through each photo, my gaze snagging again on the final image. The way the man's hand grips the woman's backside so tightly, his fingers are making indents through the fabric of her skirt. And the fabric is gathered between his fingers, exposing her thigh.

My heartbeat slows and a throb starts low in my body, vibrating just beneath my skin. He's exposing her. Possessing her but willing to put her on display, and there's something so inherently sexy in the image, I can't help but wonder what it would feel like. To have a man touch me like that.

To have the man I'm sitting across from touch me like that.

"I'm glad you like it." At his low spoken words I jerk my gaze up to his. "Perhaps we should leave?"

"Oh." I swallow hard, trying my best to ignore the disappointment that rings through me. *This was a business dinner, you ninny. Of course he doesn't want to continue this further. It doesn't matter that he told you to use him. He was just testing you. And you fell for it.* "All right."

I say nothing else. Just grab my purse and follow Ryder out of the room, into the mostly empty restaurant. His long-legged stride takes him far ahead of me and I admire his walk, the broad expanse of his shoulders and back, the way he carries himself. I can't help but compare him to Zachary, who was always moving briskly, ever eager to get to the next thing.

Ryder moves with such an easy grace, it's almost . . . lazy. As if he has all the time in the world, yet he still moves just as fast, just like Zachary. There's an urgency beneath Zachary that's almost frantic at times. Ryder isn't like that at all. There's nothing frantic about the man.

Well, there *is* the frantic sensation he gives me every time he's near . . .

He waits for me by the double doors as I approach him, sucking in a sharp breath when he touches my lower back and guides me outside. The car is waiting for us, as if he snapped his fingers and it magically appeared, and he opens the door for me, giving me a gentle push to help me slide inside. I do as he silently bids, my imagination running wild as I watch him enter the car behind me.

What would it be like to be possessed by him? Was he serious in his offer to let me . . . use him? That entire conversation on the drive over had been strange. Stranger still was the normal way we interacted at dinner. He confuses me. Sends mixed messages, when he would be the last person I'd think would do something like that.

The car pulls away from the curb and into slow-moving traffic. Ryder says nothing and neither do I, but I'm achingly aware of his nearness. I study his hands, which are braced on his knees. The wide sprawl of his long fingers, the way he flexes them every few seconds, then grips his knees once more. He seems tense. I can practically feel the emotion roll off his body. I don't know what to say, what to do, how to act . . .

"Violet." His quiet murmur of my name allows me to look at him straight in the eyes and see his solemn expression. "I want to apologize."

I frown. "For what?"

"For making you uncomfortable. For offering myself up to be—used by you." He chuckles and shakes his head. "Ridiculous, right? And extremely unprofessional of me. I should've never said those things to you."

For whatever reason, I can't form words. And there's a huge lump in my throat, making it impossible to swallow.

"Our relationship depends on this project. I can't go fucking it up by propositioning you," he continues, tossing out the profanity like it's no big deal. I'm just . . . not used to it. Zachary watched what he said around me. Father isn't one to curse. Lily can trash talk with the best of them, but she rarely does it around me. "And I probably shouldn't have used that particular word, right?"

Still I say nothing. I can't. It's as if my tongue is stuck. My thoughts. My words. My . . . oh God, my *everything* is just stalled. I recognize what I'm feeling and though I want to deny it, I *need* to deny it, I can't.

I'm disappointed. Disappointed that he's being a gentleman. Disappointed that he doesn't want me to use him. What's wrong with me? Why should I be disappointed? I should be glad he took back the offer. Thankful he's trying to be a decent man.

Instead I feel let down that I've somehow lost the chance to be possessed by this man. Owned by him . . .

"I hope you understand that I got caught up in my—dislike for your ex," Ryder continues, oblivious to my tumultuous thoughts. "In my blind need for seeking revenge against him, I offered myself up to you in the process, and that's just not . . . right."

I clear my throat. Avert my head so I'm staring out the window and not looking at Ryder. I don't think I can face him at this moment. I don't want to. I'm afraid I'll do something insane like beg him to touch me. And I can't do that. Not after he just took back his earlier intriguing offer.

"Violet?" He touches me, his fingers settling on my arm, pressing into my flesh for the briefest moment before he lets go. "Did you hear what I said?"

I nod but don't dare face him. Not yet. "I did."

"I've made you uncomfortable."

Leaning my forehead against the cold glass of the window, I close my eyes. "No." The disappointment that tinges my voice is obvious even to my ears. "Maybe . . . maybe I wanted to take you up on your offer."

The silence that follows my words is deafening. I feel him next to me, can hear him shift in his seat, exhale a low breath, thread his fingers through his hair. I can also watch him in the reflection of the window and I see him do all of those things. The struggle he's having with himself. What to say, what to do, how to react. Does he ever feel uncomfortable? It's a normal occurrence for me, but is it for him?

"You don't mean it," he finally says.

I face him once more. He looks conflicted. But there's no disguising his hungry gaze and how it roams all over me, from my head to my legs and everywhere in between. A surge of power rushes through me and I lean toward him, the cool air nipping at my skin, making my nipples harden beneath the thin, sheer material of my bra. "I know what I want." My voice is surprisingly firm and it echoes in the interior of the car. I'm thankful for the glass partition separating us and the driver. No way would I have said this with an audience.

Ryder studies my chest—most likely my hard nipples—as he speaks. "So what is it?"

The moment of truth. I can either be a coward and say nothing or be brave and tell him. "I want . . . to do something with no worries or repercussions."

His gaze lifts to meet mine but he remains silent.

I lick my lips, forcing the nerves clawing within me to settle. "I want to know what it's like to be selfish."

He lifts a brow. "I'm an expert at that."

His confession makes me laugh and he smiles in return. "Then maybe you could teach me."

"Teach you how to be selfish?"

I lean into him, rest my hand on his shoulder and place my lips at his ear. I'm shaking, I'm so nervous, but I have to do this. I *want* to do this. Perhaps the wine at dinner is assisting me, but I need this. "Teach me how to give myself up to the pleasure and worry about everything else later," I murmur close to his ear.

Ryder turns to look at me, his mouth so close to mine I can practically taste him. I stare into his eyes, see the blue shot with little flecks of gold, the thick black fringe of eyelashes, the faint scar along the bridge of his nose. I want to ask him how he got it. I want to tell him every woman in America would kill to have eyelashes as thick as his.

But I say nothing. Those thoughts are meaningless anyway.

"You want me to teach you how to be selfish when it comes to . . . sex?" He tilts his head, his mouth coming dangerously close to mine, and I fight the urge to press my lips against his. The anticipation is agonizing.

A delicious kind of agony, but agonizing nevertheless.

"Yes," I whisper, hating the way my voice trembles. Hating how badly I want him to kiss me. Have I ever felt like this with another man? Zachary and I had such . . . clean sex. Not messy, not loud and sweaty and passionate. I would find my satisfaction—mostly—and he would always find his, but it was never overwhelming, all-consuming.

Ryder hasn't even kissed me yet and I'm feeling all of those things.

"Half the thrill is in waiting," he whispers in return, his lips moving against mine with those last two words before he moves away from me, settling back in his seat.

I drop my hand from where I gripped his shoulder, mourning the loss of his nearness. "I don't believe you. You don't seem like the sort of man who likes waiting."

"Depends on the woman," he says. And then he's touching me, his hand is cupping my cheek, his face is in mine, his body blocking out all available light until he's everything I see and feel and touch. "And you are definitely worth waiting for."

I part my lips to protest, to tell him I don't want him to wait, but then his mouth is on mine, silencing me. Taking from me . . . everything I have to give.

The kiss isn't gentle. It isn't a sweet exploration or a tentative question. His kiss takes. Takes and takes, and I do nothing but give willingly. His tongue thrusts into my mouth and I whimper. His fingers tighten in my hair, destroying my ponytail, and I reach for him, curling my arm around his neck, plunging my hand into the soft hair at the back of his head. His scent, his heat wraps all around me, consumes me, lights me up and sets me on fire.

All in the space of approximately two minutes.

Not that I'm counting the seconds, but *my God*. The rustle of clothing, the frantic breaths, the thrust of tongues and the whimper that escapes me when he breaks the kiss first . . .

I've never experienced anything like this.

I'm clutching his tie like a lifeline and he glances down with an amused expression, reaching up to slowly disengage my fingers from the fine red silk. "Sorry," I whisper, my cheeks going hot. He must think I'm a little fool while he's the experienced, take-charge man.

But he doesn't laugh, doesn't chastise me for crushing his tie. He slips his strong fingers beneath my chin and tilts my face up so I have no choice but to look him in the eye.

"Don't be sorry," he murmurs, the aroused glow in his gaze making me weak. "I like that you were overcome so quickly."

I lower my gaze and he pushes beneath my chin, forcing me to look at him again. "Don't be shy, either," he says, his voice a soft but firm command. "Not with me, Violet. Not if we're really going to do this."

"And what are we doing?" I almost wish I hadn't asked, but I need to know what his definition of "this" is between us before we take it any further.

"Getting to know each other?"

I slowly shake my head. "That's not enough," I whisper. Well. Really, he's not *saying* enough. There's a difference.

Not really.

"A friendship with benefits?"

"I'm not even looking for that," I tell him honestly.

"Now who's being the forthright one?" He strokes my chin with his thumb, a soft sweep across my skin that sends a flurry of tingles all over me. "A quick fuck?"

The throb between my legs at his words surprises me and I release a shuddering breath. "A little more?"

His chuckle is the sexiest thing I've ever heard. "Many quick fucks. Is that what you're looking for, Violet? For us to become lovers?"

"Do we need to define it?"

"Everyone needs a set of guidelines," he muses. "Even the rule breakers."

"I've never really been a rule breaker before," I admit.

"I know." He leans in and drops a firm, breath-stealing kiss to my lips. "So let me teach you how to play."

His choice of words, the gravelly sound of his voice, all of it hints at something wicked. Forbidden. Secret. When have I ever indulged in something like that?

Never. And that scares me. Tempts me. Makes me want to forget all reason and righteousness and just . . . do it.

"We can't tell anyone." The words rush out of me so fast his hand drops from my chin and he moves away from me. I'm afraid I offended him. "I mean . . . this is our secret, right? It's just a temporary thing. No one else needs to know about it."

"Of course." He nods, running his hand over his hair, then across his front, over his crumpled tie. Remorse hits me at how I destroyed it. I had no idea my grip could be so strong.

Ryder McKay is making me realize a lot of things I never knew about myself.

We don't say anything the rest of the ride back to my building. There's just this tense silence that fills me with unease and arousal all at once. I shift in my seat and cross my legs, trying my best to stop the ache between my thighs as I resume my study of the city passing by. I have no idea what just happened. No idea what to think of it. I press my lips together and taste him, relive the precise moment of when he first put his mouth on mine. That startling, first electric contact. The feel of his fingers in my hair, gripping and pulling, his tongue sliding against mine . . .

"Tomorrow. We'll meet?"

I realize the car has stopped and I see my building through the window, the familiar doorman standing out front, his arms crossed behind his back as he waits. He doesn't know I'm in the car or he'd rush forward and open the door for me.

"When?" I ask quietly. "What time?"

"For lunch. At noon. My office?"

"Your office?" I finally turn to look at him. "There's not a restaurant you prefer?"

"A secret, remember? And my office has solid walls." He smiles, reaching out and drawing his finger across my lower lip. "Wear something sexy."

"To work?" I'm shocked by his request.

And aroused.

"Beneath the clothes, Violet. Wear your armor." He smiles. "And then wear a little something that will slay me underneath it."

Chapter Ten

Ryder

I HAVEN'T FELT SUCH ANTICIPATION FOR SOMETHING LIKE THIS in a long time, if ever. I couldn't sleep for shit. I'd gone straight home and jacked off in the shower to thoughts of Violet. Asking me to give her pleasure in that achingly sweet voice. The taste of her lips, the scent of her, the sensation of her tongue against mine . . .

I'd come all over my hand in seconds.

This morning I had an early meeting and fucked off mentally during the entire thing. Waste of my time and everyone else's. The conference call I had at nine thirty? I can't even remember what was said. Now I sit holed up in my office until noon, avoiding everyone I can for fear I'll say something stupid or worse, go up to Violet's floor and stare at her through the window of her office, my hands pressed against the glass. Hell, with the way I'm feeling, I'd probably press my fucking drooling face against the glass, too.

Then she'd just consider me a stalker and file a restraining order against me. Or worse, have me fired.

A package arrived for me at approximately ten thirty, someone from reception delivering it with a cheery smile and flirtatious wink as she handed it over. I scowled at her and set it on my desk, staring at the long, narrow plain brown box, curiosity filling me. There's no return address, no business listed, just my name scrawled across the back of a small, cream-colored envelope that's taped to the center of the box.

Carefully I pry the envelope from the box and turn it over, pulling the tiny card out of it. It's covered in the most beautiful handwriting I've ever seen and I stare at it for a moment, recognizing that writing before I even see who signed it.

To replace the one I ruined last evening.
Yours,
V

My lips curl into a tiny smile, and I pop the lid off the box and push the layers of tissue away to find a gorgeous red tie nestled within. I run my fingers over the fabric, impressed with the quality but not surprised.

Violet Fowler never does anything half-assed or cheap. That includes asking someone to indulge in a secret affair.

I pull the tie out of the box and admire it, the subtle pattern that runs through the fabric, the brutally red color. It's the shade of victory, of blood, of death and triumph and sex and lust.

I'm feeling all of those things. I can imagine taking this tie and wrapping it around Violet's wrists, binding them tight. So she can't touch me, can't do anything but let me pleasure her.

My cock comes to full attention at the image.

Should I wait to thank her properly when she finally makes her way to my office in less than two hours? Or should I thank her now?

Reaching for the phone, I dial her extension and wait for her to answer, my fingers never straying from the tie.

"Good morning, this is Violet."

She sounds cheerful but brisk and efficient. A contradiction as usual. "Good morning," I say in reply, not bothering to identify myself.

There's a moment of silence before she finally speaks. "Hello." Her voice warms. "How are you?"

"I'm fine. Better since I received my gift." I pause, wondering what I can say to her without sounding like a lecherous ass. *May I tie you up so I can go down on you and bring you to orgasm with my tongue?* Better yet, *Let me bind your wrists behind your back and push you to your knees while I push my cock into your mouth . . .*

"Do you like it?" she asks shyly.

"I love it. Thank you."

"I felt bad. For what I-I did to your tie last night." She sounds so unsure of herself, it just about kills me. Does she have any idea how sexy she is? All that innocent vulnerability is an incredible turn-on.

Most would say because I'm going to take advantage of her. That's why I find her naivety so freaking sexy. She's easy pickings.

They would be right.

"I didn't mind," I reassure her. And it's no lie. The crumpled tie can be fixed. Nothing a good dry cleaner can't tackle. "But I like this one, too."

"I'm glad." She lowers her voice. "We're still on for noon?"

She sounds excited. And I feel victorious. This is just too easy. "Yes." I don't say another word. I'm in the mood to hear her squirm.

"Are we going to have . . . a heavy lunch?"

Is she speaking in code? "I was thinking more along the lines of an . . . appetizer."

"Oh." She takes a deep, shaky breath. She's already aroused. By the time noon rolls around and she shows up, she'll be primed. "That sounds . . . good."

"It'll be more than good." I glance up at the sound of a knock on my door, dropping the box under my desk and the tie into my lap when I see Pilar standing in the doorway. "Sorry to cut this short, but someone's at my door."

"I'll see you soon." Violet hangs up before I can say another word and I settle the phone back in the receiver, offering Pilar a polite smile.

"What brings you here?"

"What sort of greeting is that?" She strides into the room, the scent of her strong perfume following her like a cloud. Her bold choice in dress, in hair and makeup and scent, fits her. It's all a part of her personality, her own brand, she's told me more than once. She wants to be memorable, and she most definitely is.

I sometimes wonder, though, where the realness is. Who is Pilar really?

"I figured you'd be off toying with Lawrence's affections," I say, regretting it immediately. I sound like a sullen, jealous idiot.

"Oh please. I can play with both of my boys." She smiles winningly and settles herself in one of the chairs across from my desk. "I wanted to talk to you. I've heard rumors."

I'm instantly wary. "What sort of rumors?"

"That you went to dinner with Violet last night." She makes a *tsk*ing noise, shaking her head. "I thought you were giving up that part of the game."

"You wanted me to give it up," I point out. "I never agreed."

"You should. It's pointless, what you're doing. She's a little nothing." She flicks her fingers, as if she could dismiss Violet from the room, from my thoughts. "You're wasting your time."

"You already told me that. Numerous times." I level her with my most intense stare. "But I'm going to do what I want."

"And what is that? Violet?"

"Does it really matter? You've changed the rules of the original game. I'm going to do my own thing and you'll do yours." We each want a different outcome. She, for whatever twisted reason, wants to take Violet out and I want to take Violet to bed.

She pushes her lips into an exaggerated pout. "I miss you, Ryder. It's not the same."

I want to roll my eyes but restrain myself. "It all went down only two nights ago, Pilar. You act like we haven't talked in months."

"It feels like it." She shrugs, turning toward the window that faces downtown. "I'm afraid you won't care about me anymore when you fall for Violet."

"Who says I'm going to fall for her? And I will always care about you. You know this," I reassure her. I sound like I'm on repeat, saying the same thing to her over and over again. I've said the same words so many times, they're starting to mean nothing.

"You'll fall for her. Every man seems to fall for her. I don't understand why. She's nothing special. Just some weak, stupid little girl who can barely hold her shit together. The other one is too tough to make up for that disgustingly beautiful face of hers, and the oldest one is a complete whorish mess." Pilar leans forward so she's perched on the edge of her seat. "The Fowler sisters are falling apart. Their grandmother and their father will see eventually, and maybe then they'll let an outsider come in to run the company."

"I'm assuming you believe you're the perfect person to do that?" Now I do roll my eyes. "Give me a break, Pilar. If that ever happens, we're still a long way out. Focus on doing what you can here and then move on to another cosmetics company. Or a fashion house. Something bigger and better than this."

She reaches out and punches the edge of my desk with her fist, her face full of fury. "I want this company," she says through clenched teeth. "This is what matters to me. Fleur. Nothing else. That they continue to practice such blatant nepotism when those two girls can barely keep their shit together is beyond me."

I glance at the screen of my desktop, see that I have a new email. From Violet. I tune out Pilar as she continues her diatribe and read what Violet wrote.

> Dear Ryder,
> I hope you didn't think me rude with the way our phone call ended. It's been bothering me and I hate to imagine you being offended over my hanging up on you. You mentioned someone had come into your office. Well, someone had come into mine, too.
> If that hadn't happened, who knows where our conversation could've taken us? Somewhere exciting, I'm thinking. But of course, having these sorts of conversations via the company phone or company email isn't the smartest route, correct?
> So here's my cell number: (212) 555-2624. You can send yours if you want. In fact, I would love it if you did. That way if I need anything from you . . . in regard to the new project . . . you're merely a text away.
> I'm looking forward to our lunch meeting. I know you'll show me plenty of new ideas that will keep me begging for more.
> Yours,
> V

". . . and I'm not going to bother giving you any more details because you'll just end up jealous. You're a complete asshole when you're jealous, you know."

I blink Pilar into focus, trying my best to remember what she just said, but there's no use. I'm still mulling over Violet's email. The subtle innuendo wrapped up in a perfect, politely worded package. For once I'd love to see the woman say something blatantly dirty. "What?" I ask blankly.

Pilar is staring at me as if she wants to smack me across the face. Can't say that I blame her, especially when all I can think of is the way Violet signs off her emails. I like the use of "yours." It's cute and perhaps even a submissive gesture. As if she really wants to be mine.

I'm probably reading too much into it, but the word choice is sexy as fuck, even if she didn't mean it to be that way.

"You're not even paying attention. Too wrapped up in thoughts of what? Fucking around with Violet? I'm sure she'll be *delightful*." Pilar stands and approaches my desk, then leans over the edge of it. "You're playing with fire, Big Daddy. And you're going to go up in flames if you don't stay focused and on the ball."

"I'm one hundred percent focused," I tell her assuredly. On Violet, most definitely. On whatever crap Pilar is feeding me?

Not at all.

"Just not on me." She gives me another pout, but I don't even blink an eye. It means nothing anyway. She's just trying to get under my skin.

"You have Lawrence to distract you," I tell her. "You don't need me. Enjoy him these next few days. Fuck his brains out and then drill him for information. He'll give in to you while in that post-orgasmic glow. I know how you operate."

She smiles at me, the very picture of peaceful and serene. What a pack of lies. Inside that devious head of hers she's trying to come up with a new way to fuck everyone over. Including me. "I could have the best of both worlds if you weren't so jealous."

"Sorry, not going to let you touch me after you just had your hands all over Lawrence's dick." A man can only tolerate so much.

"Disgusting pig." Pilar stands to her full height, snarling at me. "You're all the same. The minute another man shows a hint of interest, you're casting me off. Learn to live with it, darling. I'm fucking Zachary Lawrence."

"Really? Well, learn to live with *this, Pilar.*" I cup my hands together and lean forward, my elbows propped on the top of my desk. "I'm fucking Violet Fowler."

"In your dreams," she returns.

"It's going to happen."

"How? That girl is as tight as a virgin kept under lock and key. And closed off like a little ice queen, too. Zachary told me she's a terrible lay."

More like he's an awful, selfish asshole who didn't know how to meet Violet's needs. "I'll find out if that's true or not on my own terms, thank you very much."

"God." She's leaving. *Thank Christ.* "You don't listen to me. Fine, have fun fucking around with your little boring baby. Can't wait to see how she puts the spark in your eyes while I'm off getting fucked like crazy every chance I can get."

I ignore what she said, which I know will drive her crazier than if I acknowledged it and continued the fight. "We'll talk later," I say to her as she leaves and she gives me the finger before flouncing out the door.

"Maybe I never want to talk to you again. Ever think about that, asshole?" she calls from the hallway.

Huh. That went terribly. I rub my hand over my jaw, hoping like hell not too many people heard that send-off. Not that we haven't argued like this before around the halls of Fleur, but it's been a while. I take my job seriously. I'm trying to look like I can keep this together. Like I'm worthy of the London position—or one similar—just like Lawrence is. The only reason that asshole got the offer was for being involved with Violet. It gave him the in to old man Fowler. The in that I would fucking love to have.

Well. He isn't with Violet any longer. I'm about to be. Secretly, but still. Soon we'll be out in the open. Soon I can cozy up to Forrest Fowler. Get into that man's back pocket so he'll really see what an asset I am to the company. That's what I want.

And that's what I'll damn well get.

Chapter Eleven

Violet

I TAP MY FOOT AGAINST THE FLOOR OF THE CROWDED ELEVA-tor, my gaze locked on the numbers above the door. The count-down takes forever and I suck in a loud breath, drawing the attention of more than a few of my fellow Fleur employees in the elevator with me.

They're all on their lunch break, ready to get out of the eleva-tor and make their escape. So am I. But I'm not hungry. At least, not for food.

The elevator slows and then stops, the doors sliding open with a smooth whoosh. I push through the crowd and exit, no-ticing a few murmurings from the people within, probably won-dering what I'm doing on the tenth floor when most are on their lunch hour.

I don't care what they say. What they think. I already have an excuse prepared if anyone asks. It's a lunch meeting with Ryder, the head of packaging. We're both so busy that our jam-packed schedules only allowed us to meet at noon. It's normal. I've had multiple business meetings over lunch. This is nothing new.

But it *is* new, what we're really doing. I've never had a lunch . . . rendezvous. A nooner. An affair. Dalliance. Whatever sordid word you want to call it.

Coming to a halt in front of the tenth-floor reception desk—which is abandoned, thank goodness—I rest my hand on my chest, feel my crazily beating heart beneath my palm. Maybe I shouldn't go through with this. I broke up with Zachary only a few days ago. He stopped me in front of my office first thing this morning, trying to get me to talk to him, go have coffee with him, something, anything for a bit of time alone with me.

I told him no. Had been so proud of my firm refusal of him, too. I'd seen Rose lingering in the background, offering me a thumbs-up when Zachary walked away. The surge of pride that had flowed through me felt good. Felt right. I was taking command of my life, my emotions, my needs, for once. Zachary didn't fit into that anymore. Had he ever? It had always been about him, our relationship. It centered on his wants and needs. Never mine.

I'd been on such a high, I'd gone right into my office and started the online search for the perfect red tie. Something gloriously sophisticated and expensive and sexy and elegant. I clicked on my favorite store sites until I finally found the one I knew he would love. And I loved it, too.

When he called me and thanked me in that deep, sexy voice of his, I'd wanted to melt.

My cell dings that I have a text message and I pull it out of my purse to find a number I don't recognize, along with a simple message.

I see you.

Glancing around, I see that no one else is nearby. The offices appear mostly empty. The entire floor has a hushed quality to it that I almost find unnerving.

Or maybe that's just me, completely unnerved and worried about what I'm about to do.

My phone beeps again.

You're late.

And then there's another message.

We only have fifty minutes to indulge in our appetizer lunch. I suggest you head over to my office now.

The pleasure that blooms across my chest at the texts from Ryder makes me rush down the hall only to find him already standing there, leaning against the wall opposite his office, his arms folded across his chest, his biceps straining the fabric of his snowy white shirt. He must have taken off his jacket; he's clad in only the shirt, black trousers, and a silvery gray tie. His hair is in the usual tousle, his eyes glittering as I come closer.

"You made it," he says when I stop just in front of him.

"Sorry I'm late." I swallow away the nerves as best I can, hating how jittery I sound. "It's been crazy this morning."

"Same with me." He grabs hold of my elbow and leads me into his office, closing and locking the door behind us. The click of the lock is loud in the silence and my gaze roams over the interior of the room, noticing that the red tie is sitting in its box on top of his desk.

"Do you really like it?" I ask when I turn to him, adding when I see his confused frown, "The tie?"

The slow smile that crosses his handsome face makes my insides tremble. "Oh yes, very much." He takes a step closer to me, reaching out to drift his fingers down the length of my arm. "Almost as much as this dress you're wearing."

The dress is simple, in a subtle black-and-white patterned fabric that fits me well but isn't too terribly sexy. I feel confident in it, though. Another suit of armor for me to wear. "Th-thank you," I whisper, overwhelmed by the sensations his fingers on my skin pull from me. He entangles his fingers with mine and jerks me to him, our bodies colliding, fitting against each other when he slips his other arm around my waist.

"Don't be nervous," he whispers just before he dips his head and presses his warm, damp lips to the side of my neck. I tilt my head back and close my eyes, resting my hands blindly on the solid wall of his chest. "We'll take this slow. An appetizer, re- member?"

I want to laugh at our silly choice of words. I want to moan when his lips blaze a trail across my skin. My fingers curl into the fabric of his shirt as I anchor myself to him. He slips his hand down my back until he's gripping my butt and he hauls me into him. I can already feel him, big and thick. He's hard. Hard for me.

I can't believe I can make a man like him react like this. That he wants me. *Me*. Most of the women who work at Fleur find him to be a mystery they can't figure out. But hopefully he'll let me in.

"What do you want, Violet?" he asks when he lifts his head, his hazy blue eyes meeting mine. I part my lips, ready to say I have no idea, but he takes advantage, kissing me before I can say a word.

And what a kiss it is. Again there's no gentleness, no sweet exploration. He plunders my mouth with his tongue, twisting it around mine in a rhythm I can only imagine he would use while he thrusts inside my body. I can do nothing but respond, my eager hands roaming all over his chest, clutching his shoulders as I move into him. As if I want to become a part of him.

"Well?" he asks seconds, minutes later. His breathing is harsh, his shirt a wrinkled mess from my seeking hands. I keep this up and I'll ruin all of his clothes. "What do you want from me?"

I stare up at him, at a loss for words. How can I express to him exactly what I want when I hardly know myself? I'm scared to say it. Embarrassed, too. I've never spoken freely about sex. That's more Lily's style. Which is silly because I'm a grown woman with needs and wants, just like everyone else. I've been with other men. I've had orgasms, plenty of them. Brought on by myself, by a vibrator, by a man. Mostly brought on by my- self . . .

"Do you want me to touch you?" He presses his lips to my

forehead, his hand still gripping my backside. "Do you want me to make you come?" he whispers against my skin.

Oh God. Everything inside me goes hot and loose and I nod, keeping my eyes tightly closed. "Yes," I say shakily.

He moves away from me, and the loss of his heat, his strength, makes my eyes pop open. "Strip," he commands, his tone firm.

I gape at him. "What?"

"Take off your clothes, Violet." He smiles, his gaze roving over me, hungry and unfettered. "At least the dress. For now."

No man has ever demanded that I strip in front of him. Usually they undress me. Or it's a hurried frenzy of pulling off clothes in bed, in the dark, whatever, eager to get naked quick.

So this feels . . . odd. As if I'm putting myself on display for him.

Which I am.

I'm wearing a wrap dress—a purposeful decision since I knew what was going to happen today—and I reach for the knot at my waist and slowly pull it free. The fabric gapes with the movement and I undo the tie completely so that the dress falls open, revealing slivers of my skin. My breasts, my belly, my legs.

Ryder never takes his gaze away from me. He leans against the edge of his desk, his arms crossed in front of his chest again, his head bent to the side. Observing me like he's studying a science project.

I shrug the dress off my shoulders and it falls into a heap at my feet. I not only chose the dress for today, but also my lingerie. He'd asked for something sexy and I hope I delivered.

Pray that I delivered.

His gaze lights up as it skims over me and rests on my chest. "Nice bra."

I glance down. My breasts strain against the thin fabric, cream silk trimmed with black lace, my nipples hard and poking against the lace. The panties match, cut in a bikini style that covers more than reveals. I feel sexy every time I wear the set, which isn't often. I bought them on a whim while out shopping with my sisters. Lily convinced Rose and me to buy something frilly and indulgent. Not for the men in our lives, Lily had said, giving me a pointed look because I was the only one who had a serious boyfriend. But for us.

I wore the set a few times. Once when I had a particularly difficult meeting and I'd needed to feel confident in my femininity when facing a bunch of old men who don't necessarily understand the cosmetics industry. Another time I wore it for a date with Zachary. He hadn't even noticed, hadn't even complimented my choice in lingerie. Did we even have sex that night?

I'm not sure. I don't remember. How sad is that?

So I shoved the bra-and-panty set into the back of my dresser drawer, forgotten. Until I had a minor panic attack last night over what I should wear for Ryder. He wanted something sexy, something that would slay him . . .

"Take it off."

I blink him into focus. "What?"

"Your bra." He waves a hand at me. "Take it off, Violet."

My fingers shaking, I reach behind me to undo the clip on my bra. I fumble with it, feeling many times the fool as he levels me with that cool, noncommittal stare. He appears completely unfazed by my standing in front of him almost naked. But I can feel his eyes on me. Lingering and hot, almost like a physical caress.

"My panties next?" I ask, letting the bra dangle from my fingertips before I drop it onto the floor.

"Yeah." His voice is faint and he clears his throat. Another tell that he's not as unaffected as he appears.

A tiny surge of power runs through me and I take a few steps toward him, so close I can smell his cologne, see the way his lids lower over his eyes as he not-so-discreetly drinks me in. "Do you want to help me?"

He slowly shakes his head. "You seem perfectly capable of undressing yourself."

How could I forget he likes the anticipation? I hook my fingers into the waistband of my panties and slowly slide the thin fabric past my hips, down my thighs, until they fall to my feet. Carefully I step out of them and stand tall, completely naked save for my favorite black Louboutins.

"Sit on the couch," he says the moment my gaze meets his again. "Now."

I turn and go to the small couch that sits in the corner of his office. It's more the size of a love seat and a deep, velvety blue color, reminding me of a dark twilight sky. I perch on the edge of it, watching as he goes to his desk and plucks the tie I gave him from the box, holding it stretched out between his hands before he approaches.

Nerves flutter in my belly when he stops directly in front of me. I lift my head, my gaze meeting his for a brief moment before I let it drop to the slash of red he holds in both hands. Fear trickles through me, icy cold, and I wonder what he wants to do to me with that tie.

"We only have forty minutes," he murmurs, twisting either end of the tie around his fingers. Back and forth, winding the fabric up before letting it unfurl. I watch, mesmerized by his long fingers, the crimson silk so vivid against his skin. "Think that's enough time for me to make you come?"

I nod shakily, excitement and fear taking away my voice.

"I know for some women it takes . . . time. They need the buildup. The foreplay. I enjoy that, too, but with our limited schedule . . ." He lets the tie unfurl completely from one hand, so that the fabric drops like a flag of red surrender in front of my face. "Would you let me tie you up, Violet? So I can do whatever I want to you?"

My mouth is dry. My brain is . . . completely empty, save for one stark image. Me sprawled on the couch, Ryder's big body between my legs, the tie wrapped around my hands. "Is th-that what you want?"

He shakes his head, his expression grim, though I swear there's a light sheen of perspiration on his forehead. I'm glad to see it, because so far there have been minimal clues that he's even affected by me. "It doesn't matter what I want. What do *you* want?"

I lick my lips, searching for an answer. The thought of being tied up, unable to stop him from doing whatever he wants, both excites and terrifies me. I want to say yes. The practical side of me is screaming no, but . . .

"Tell me." He caresses my cheek with his fingertips and I lean into his hand, closing my eyes. His touch is so gentle but his words are so stern. "Do you trust me?"

I open my eyes and stare up at him. "*No*. I don't know." It's true. Can I really trust him? What if he uses this moment, this affair, against me? I'm putting everything at risk, especially my reputation.

And to me and my family and our business, my reputation *is* everything.

He smiles. "Good answer. You shouldn't trust me. Not completely. But I can promise that I won't hurt you. That's not my intention here. You can put a stop to this at any time. This is all for you."

All for me? No man has put my pleasure ahead of his before. But doesn't Ryder want anything out of it? He's talking as if this is some great sacrifice. "I understand," I say with a small nod.

"Good. Now." He pauses. "May I tie you up? Just your wrists."

Another small nod and a shaky sigh. "O-okay."

He reaches for my hands and lifts them above my head. "Lie back," he urges softly and I do as he commands, my arms resting on the edge of the back of the couch. He steps close, his chest brushing against my face as he wraps the red silk around my wrists once, twice, three times before tying the fabric into a knot. "This is loose enough that if you really struggled, you could break free. Or just tell me to stop and I will."

I test the knots, jerking my wrists against the binding fabric. My butt is sunk into the cushion and my legs are slightly spread, heels braced flat on the floor. Ryder steps away, his eyes roving over me, from my arms bound above my head down to my chest, my breasts pushing upward because of the position I'm in. His gaze drops farther, to the spot between my legs, and he smiles.

"Spread your legs open."

I do as he asks, my shoes sliding across the floor. I can feel myself. I'm wet. So wet and aching for him, I feel light-headed. Like I could faint.

And then he's right there in front of me, his mouth taking mine hungrily, his hand pressed against my right breast, cupping my flesh, his thumb circling my nipple. I lift into him, a moan breaking free as his tongue finds mine. His hands are every-where, his mouth like a drug that I can't get enough of. I lift my arms, a frustrated whimper escaping me when I realize I can't touch him, and he pulls away from me, shaking his head.

"Leave your arms above your head," he warns and I do as he asks, my head going back when he rains kisses along my jaw, my throat, my chest. Drawing closer and closer to my breasts until I'm squirming beneath him, wanting his mouth on my nipple, sucking it deep.

But he teases me, as if he knows exactly what I want, and instead gives me something else. He blazes a path with his mouth between my breasts, along the underside of first one breast, then the other. I'm trembling, my breaths coming in short puffs as he tortures me endlessly with his mouth. He licks my skin with his warm, velvety tongue and when he finally takes a quick swipe at my nipple, I cry out.

"Sshh," he murmurs against my skin, just before he draws my nipple between his lips and sucks it deep.

I buck against him, closing my eyes and then immediately opening them again. I don't want to miss a thing. Don't want to miss the sight of Ryder's head bent over my chest, his tongue circling my hard, wet nipple, his hand sliding down, down, down, until he's gripping the inside of my thigh and pushing my legs apart even farther.

He pulls away and kneels in front of me, his hands on the inside of my thighs, his gaze locked in between my legs. I watch him watch me, my chest rising and falling, my skin on fire, my entire body aching for more. It's all happening so fast and I feel like I could come apart at any moment. Just having his eyes on me, his fingers curling into the sensitive skin of my inner thighs, is almost enough to make me come apart.

"Beautiful," he murmurs. "And so wet."

I should be mortified that he's studying me so intently, but I secretly love it. Wish I could spread my legs farther to let him see more, all of me. He grazes his fingers over my trimmed pubic hair and I flinch. His fingers fall lower, tracing my skin with a feather-light touch. Searching my folds, streaking across my clit, sliding back down to trace every single part of me . . .

"Could I make you come with just my fingers?" It's almost as if he's talking to himself. "Or would you like my mouth on you, too?"

Oh God, he's trying to kill me in the absolute best way. "Your mouth," I whisper.

His eyes meet mine, full of wicked intent. "Yeah?"

I nod, pressing my legs in so my thighs bracket his hips. "Please."

The sly smile that spreads across his face tells me he likes this. Making me beg. "Just my lips?" He drops the softest, briefest kiss on the very top of my pubic bone. "Or my tongue, too?"

"All of it," I say on a gasp, wishing I could grip his head with my hands and push his face into me. I'm on the edge, on the verge of falling completely apart, and he's teasing me.

Always teasing me. Testing me.

As if he knows I'm so close, he doesn't bother with words any longer. He puts his mouth on me, licking and sucking, his tongue searching my folds as he pushes his finger inside me. I whimper, tossing my head back and forth against the edge of the couch, my gaze never leaving the sight of Ryder devouring me. Another finger joins the first one and he's pumping them inside my welcoming body, his lips attached to my clit, his hot mouth driving me to the brink.

I still watch, lost to the sensation, to the sight of this gorgeous man bringing me so much pleasure. He runs his free hand up my thigh, over my hip, my waist, to caress my breast and I arch into his touch. He opens his eyes, brilliant blue locked directly on me, and he lifts his mouth from my body, his lips damp and swollen.

"You like to watch."

I don't bother denying it. "I like watching you."

"You are a complete surprise." He dips his head, runs his tongue along the length of me, making me cry out. He pinches my nipple, as if that might shut me up, but the sharp taste of pain with my pleasure only makes me moan louder. "People might hear you, Violet," he chastises.

"I don't care," I huff out, my body starting to quake. I'm almost there. So close and I close my eyes, unable to fight my body any longer. I want it. I need to come. I feel like I'm going to explode.

He rests his hand directly over my mouth, muffling my whimpers, and I open my eyes to find him still looking at me. "I like seeing you like this. All naked and wet and shivering, completely at my mercy."

Oh God. He's trying to devastate me with words. And when his lips latch onto my clit and he sucks, his tongue teasing, that's all it takes for me to fall completely apart. I moan against his hand, push my hips up as the intense orgasm rushes over me, sweeping through my body until I'm left a shaky, exhausted mess.

Ryder kisses one hip bone, then the other. Sweet, simple little kisses that melt me further. He rears up to his feet and reaches for my bound hands, undoing the tie, then rubs my wrist. The muscles in my arms shake from being in the same position for so long and I let them fall to my sides, then stretch them out in front of me.

I don't know what to say, how to act. I've never let a man bring me to orgasm on his couch in his office before, let alone while being tied up. I've never done *anything* like this at work. Or at home, or anywhere really.

"Twenty minutes." He backs away from the couch and checks his watch on his wrist, then smiles down at me. He looks very pleased with himself. "Which means we have another twenty minutes to kill. Unless you've . . . had enough?"

Chapter Twelve

Ryder

I CAN STILL TASTE HER ON MY TONGUE, STICKY SWEET ON MY lips and chin. Never in a million years did I think I could get Violet Fowler on my couch in my office, naked with her wrists bound, my face between her legs tonguing that pretty pink pussy until she came all over my lips.

Yeah. Hottest fucking experience I've had in a long time, if ever.

She's still naked, save for the sexy black shoes. Her skin is flushed. Her breathing is labored and her full breasts move with her every shaky exhale, her rosy nipples still standing at full attention.

Not really a surprise, because I figured she was hiding that smoking-hot body beneath the clothes, but *damn*. The woman is gorgeous. Absolute perfection. And the way she responded to me, the sounds she made . . .

"Come here," she whispers, her voice gone husky with arousal.

I'm not that far from her so I take a few steps closer, startled when she reaches for my belt and tugs me forward. Her face is practically on my dick and it swells painfully, demanding satisfaction.

He's always been a greedy bastard.

"Twenty minutes is a long time," she says as she starts to tug my shirt out from my pants. "It's your turn."

I'm so shocked that she's undressing me, it takes a full minute for me to realize what she's saying. I try to step out of her reach but she has a firm hold on my belt, undoing the buckle with a few quick flicks of her fingers. My cock strains against my boxer briefs, ready for her attention, and within seconds she has the button undone and the zipper down, her slender fingers stroking, fondling my cock without bothering to take off my underwear.

"Violet . . ." I'm protesting but I don't know why. I definitely don't want her to stop. And it's erotic as hell, watching her sit in front of me naked while I'm mostly clothed, Violet's hand in my pants. If she doesn't stop, I might embarrass myself and come in my briefs.

She tilts her head back, all that long, dark hair spilling over her shoulders, down her naked back. She's beautiful like this, her hand wrapped around my cock, her lips parted, eyes smoldering. She's enjoying this. A lot.

"Take me out," I tell her. Her hand stills. "Take my cock out."

Without a word she jerks my underwear down and pulls out my cock, wrapping her fingers around me tight. I press my lips together, fascinated with the sight of her fingers on my erection, stroking, teasing, her thumb swirling around the head. She leans forward the slightest bit and drops a single kiss on the very tip. I grunt at the touch of her pouty mouth, let out a hissing breath when she takes me between her lips and sucks.

And then it just gets worse. Or better. Not sure which way to look at it because with her lips on my cock, it's pure agony. Exquisite torture. She grips the base and licks the entire length, swirling her tongue around the head before she draws me completely into her mouth. I stand there on shaky legs, fascinated with the magnificence of her lips and tongue, surprised at her expert blow-job skills.

Because holy hell, is Violet Fowler giving me one hell of a blow job.

I drop my hand on top of her head, thread my fingers into her hair and push it back. She glances up at me, her mouth full of cock, her big brown eyes wide and seeking approval. She pulls away as I settle my other hand on the side of her head so I'm gripping her, holding her. Wishing I could fuck her face and come down her throat, but I hold myself in check because she's needing some sort of approval. I can sense it.

"So fucking good," I murmur, letting her hear the satisfaction in my voice. Her eyes light with desire. Not only does she like to watch, this girl likes words, too. "Don't stop, baby. Make me come."

A hum of satisfaction escapes her as she slides me back into her mouth and I thrust my hips, needing more. She takes it, tilting her head back, her eyes falling closed as she licks and sucks me straight into oblivion. I pump in and out of her mouth, groaning when she sucks the head of my cock so tight her cheeks hollow out. I feel the tingle at the base of my spine, my brain going fuzzy as the sensation hurtles up through my body.

"I'm gonna come," I warn her but she doesn't move away. Hell, I think she takes me even farther, and that's it. I'm coming with a groan and a shudder, my entire body heaving as I bend over her, her hair tangled around my fingers as I pull it. She whimpers but takes it all like a pro, swallowing as I jerk and shudder into her mouth.

Jesus. How long did that take? Not even five minutes? Any other moment I would've been embarrassed. I like to take my time and prolong things. Hell, even Violet has me all figured out in that respect.

But one touch of her lips on my dick and all I could think about was coming and how long I could hold off before I lost it.

Without a word I stuff my still hard dick back into my pants and zip up, tucking in my shirt as best I can. She remains seated on the couch, looking the tiniest bit uncomfortable as she dabs at her lips with her fingers, then wipes at her cheek.

I hold both my hands out to her, and she takes them so I can pull her into a standing position. With the heels on she's tall, but not as tall as me. I duck to look into her eyes, reading that nervous expression on her face as the look of someone who thinks she just royally fucked up.

"Amazing." I kiss her. A long, tongue-tangled kiss that has her sagging into me, all that pretty bared skin molded against my body. I wrap my arms around her tiny waist and hold her close, my hands caressing the smooth, plump skin of her ass as I kiss her thoroughly. I can taste myself on her lips, taste her there, too, and my cock springs to life, ready for more action. "I think we might have a few minutes to spare."

She laughs, a soft huff of sound that breathes over my lips. "I'd better go clean up first. I'm sure I look a mess."

"You're beautiful." I kiss her again. "And naked."

Unbelievably, she blushes. "I should get dressed."

Violet reluctantly withdraws from my arms and goes to the spot where her underwear and dress lie on the floor. With hurried, efficient movements she puts on her bra, then grabs her dress, pulling it on over her shoulders and wrapping the tie at her waist. She's about to reach for her underwear when my cell starts ringing from where it sits on top of my desk.

She freezes, her gaze going wide. "Who could that be?"

Anyone. But I don't answer her. Instead, I dash over to my desk to see who's calling me. And I don't like the answer.

Fucking Pilar.

"No one," I tell Violet, hitting the ignore button and slipping the phone into my pants pocket. I turn to her, smiling. "Now, where were we?"

"We were getting me dressed so I can go back to work." She runs her hands down the front of her dress, then over her hair. She isn't as sleek and perfect as usual and I like it. Makes her appear more human, with the messed-up hair and the dreamy expression on her face. Her lips are swollen and the surge of pleasure that runs through me is potent. Undeniable. She looks that way because of me. And I feel like some sort of caveman who wants to tell the world I'm the asshole who put that just-fucked look on her face.

"I'm going to go . . . wash up," she murmurs when I don't say anything.

The phone starts to ring again but I ignore it. I refuse to take a call from Pilar. Not here, not now. "I should probably do the same." I hate to take away the evidence of what happened between us, but I have a meeting later this afternoon. And it wouldn't do for me to walk in with Violet Fowler's come all over my lips and chin.

Though I love the image. It would be my little secret. No one would know . . .

There's a knock on the door, startling us both. Violet stares at me, her expression panicked when we hear whoever's on the other side rattling the door handle, trying to get in.

Shit.

"Who could that be?" she whispers.

"I don't know." But I do. I think I do. It has to be Pilar.

"Just a minute," I call out as I reach for Violet so I can fix her hair, but she bats my hand away. Instead I run my finger along her lower lip. That is one hell of a sexy lip. "You ready?"

She nods but remains quiet.

"Whoever it is, act casual. Pretend we were just having a business lunch," I tell her. "Nothing else."

"Right. Of course." She nods, sounding like a robot. A bland smile appears on her face. "Let's do this."

I bend over and grab Violet's discarded panties from where she left them on the floor, shoving them in my pocket. I go to the door, running my hands through my hair in a wasted attempt to tame it. I can smell Violet on my fingers and I sniff the air, hoping the room doesn't smell like sex.

Christ. This can't be good.

Slowly I undo the lock and open the door, not surprised at all to find Pilar standing in front of me. "What the hell are you doing?" she asks before I can even greet her.

"Hello to you, too," I say, holding the door firm when she tries to barge in. "Can I help you?"

"Let me in. We need to talk."

I step into the hallway and close the door behind me. "You can't just force your way inside my office, Pilar. What's wrong with you?"

"Who's in there with you? Tell me! Is it Violet?" Her eyes are wide and wild-looking and her cheeks are red.

"Christ, keep your voice down." I lower mine and keep it level, hoping to force her into calm. "We're having a meeting while it's quiet. Talking about our ideas for packaging."

"You're a goddamn liar," Pilar accuses, stabbing a pointed fingernail into my chest. "Did you fuck her in there, Ryder? Make her scream your name?"

It's eerie how close she is to the truth. Makes me wonder if she has spies. Cameras. Is she constantly watching me? "Like I said, we're in a meeting, Pilar. I suggest you keep your accusations to yourself."

As if on cue my office door opens and Violet appears, looking calm and serene as usual. Her dress is straight, there's fresh lipstick coating that glorious mouth, and not a hair is out of place. The girl is good, I'll give her that. "Oh, Pilar." She smiles that bland, phony smile. "I didn't know it was you knocking and rattling the doorknob. I was on the phone." Violet turns to me, her expression neutral as she says, "Thank you again for meeting with me, Ryder. Looking forward to what your team puts together next."

"I agree," I say with a solemn nod. I can feel a smile tease the corners of my mouth but I don't let it spring free. I'm afraid Pilar will catch on to our ruse. "Let's meet again soon, all right?"

Her smile grows faintly, a spark of happiness lighting up her eyes. "Sounds good."

Violet walks away without another word, her hips swaying as she hurries down the hall toward the bank of elevators. I admire her form, reliving that moment when I had my mouth on her clit and my fingers buried inside her body, the way her breath caught just before she came all over my lips. Pilar banishes the pleasant memory with a low curse and a hard fist to my upper arm.

"Meeting, my ass. You're training her to be as shady as you, asshole," Pilar mutters.

"Not true." I rub my arm, impressed with the strength behind her punch. "It's just difficult for you to wrap your head around the idea of a man and a woman who work together meeting solely for business purposes."

Her eyes narrow into slits and she screws her mouth up into an angry scowl. "Prick."

"Bitch," I say pleasantly in return.

"God." She tosses her head back and stalks away from me, heading down the hall in the opposite direction of Violet. Why, I'm not sure, considering Pilar's office isn't even on this floor, but I don't care. I'm thankful the craziness left so I can make my escape into my office. I stride inside and shut and lock the door, leaning against it with a relieved exhale.

I can smell her. Violet. The scent of her perfume and skin lingers in the air, also with the faint musky scent of sex. Closing my eyes, I let the back of my head thunk against the wood as everything that just happened sinks in.

Fucking crazy. More like fucking crazy *amazing*. The taste of her, her lips, watching her drag her tongue along my cock . . .

Jesus, that had been hot.

My phone buzzes in my pocket and I pull it out, reluctant to see who the text is from. Knowing Pilar she's around the corner from my office, furiously typing away every bad name she can think to call me.

But it's from Violet.

Sorry I had to leave in such a rush.

I smile. Always polite.

Is Pilar still there with you?

No. I'm alone, thank God.

She seemed angry.

She'll get over it.

No reply for a while, so I push away from the door and settle in behind my desk, determined to get my mind off Violet and focus on the work that still needs to be done. I have a meeting to prepare for. Emails to answer. A few phone calls to make.

But then my phone buzzes again and I practically leap for it to see Violet's response.

I still can't believe what we did.

Frowning, I start to type.

In a good way or a bad way?

Good.

I smile. Then immediately frown. I need to stop acting like a lovesick fool. I'm above this. I'm just using her. This is all fun and games until someone gets hurt.

And that someone will be Violet.

My cell rings and I pick it up, answering before the second ring can sound. The sound of Violet's voice twists up my insides.

"Tomorrow is the opening of the collaborative," she murmurs.

"I know." The executives at Fleur put together a small collaboration between the company and a handful of up-and-coming bridal designers. The project has been in the works for almost two years and is only now being revealed.

"Are you going?"

"I am." I pause, savoring the sound of her breathing. *Pathetic.* "Are you?"

"Of course. My sister is going, too."

"Rose?"

"Lily."

Ah. The hot-mess Fowler sister. "That ought to be interesting."

She ignores my jab. "I'd like to . . . get together with you tomorrow evening. Sometime during the party. What do you think?"

What do I think? I'd give up a hell yeah, but I need to show some sort of restraint. "Is Violet interested in being a bad girl, sneaking off with me at the party?"

"I just . . . I know I'm going to need something to take the edge off." Her voice falters over the last few words and I savor that sound. Savor the idea of her seeking me out in the middle of a party, needing me to get her off.

One encounter and she already needs me. I love this.

I lean back in my seat and turn toward the window, staring at the city spread out before me. I'm feeling good. On top of the damn world. I have Violet Fowler in the palm of my hands. And I'm not about to let her go. "So an orgasm would help with that?"

She releases a shuddering breath. "Maybe."

Ah, now she's playing coy. "That could be arranged."

"Good." Her voice firms. "See you tomorrow night, then?"

"Yes. And Violet."

"Hmm?"

"Don't wear any panties. Tomorrow." I let the words linger in the air for a moment. "I prefer easy access."

She hangs up on me without another word, making me smile.

Making me anticipate tomorrow. Far more than I want to admit.

Chapter Thirteen

Violet

A FEW DAYS AGO, BEING IN A ROOM FILLED WITH BEAUTIFUL models wearing gorgeous wedding gowns would have made me incredibly depressed. Sad. Frustrated that Zachary still hadn't asked me to marry him. Irritated that everyone around me would be thinking the same thing.

But now, I couldn't care less. Yes, I'm admiring the gowns. It's a varied collection of frothy and fairy tale-like to sleek and sophisticated. Every single model's face is stunning, and that's because they're all wearing Fleur cosmetics. I'm proud of our latest collaboration, something Fleur is known for in the beauty industry. The party so far is a huge success, professionally because the buzz is so positive and personally because I've managed to avoid Zachary the entire evening.

He has Pilar to distract him so for once, I'm actually thankful for her presence. Doesn't mean I like her, though. Oh, no. I can't stand the woman. How proprietarily she'd treated Ryder yesterday when she pounded on his door. Disrupting what had been the most scandalous yet sexiest lunch of my entire life.

My skin flushes hot just thinking about it. About him.

I haven't seen much of Ryder since our lunch and that's probably best. I need the distance. It's a reminder that what we're engaging in isn't a relationship. Not even what I would define as dating. We're fooling around secretively. I'm letting him tie me up and go down on me in his office. Talk about sordid. I should be ashamed of myself.

But I'm not. In fact, I can't wait to do it again.

"God, this is boring."

I turn to see that Lily is standing beside me, clutching an ever-present cocktail in her hand, with a detached expression on her otherwise gorgeous face. I'm envious of both of my sisters' good looks. I always feel like I got the short end of the stick with my boring brown hair and eyes. Whereas Lily has all of this wavy, golden-brown hair that she on occasion colors bright blond, though currently it's the most natural I've seen it in a long time. And then there's angel-faced Rose, who everyone thinks looks like she walked straight out of a Botticelli painting.

I've always felt like I couldn't measure up.

"It's not that bad," I chastise. I'm always chastising her. But she's always complaining, so I have to say something to make her stop. Sometimes I feel like her mother. I'm sure she just adores that.

It's nice having her here tonight. She's been talking to Father lately, trying to get back into his good graces. Rose is out of town so he decided Lily could come in her place, all contingent on her behaving properly—his words.

Meaning he needs me to babysit my big sister and make sure she doesn't do anything outrageous. Not that he asked me to, but I know what's expected.

"It's dreadful." She sips from her glass, her hazel eyes scanning the room. "All of these pretty girls in wedding dresses. Makes me want to break into hives."

"What do you mean?"

"I'm allergic to weddings. Marriage." She mock shivers. "It's the devil's work."

She thinks everything that's traditional and normal is the devil's work. She'd rather have four men on a string and endless parties to go to every night than one steady guy to spend quiet evenings with at home. She used to have a drug problem. I sometimes wonder if she still does.

"Not everyone is like you," I tell her. "There's nothing wrong with marriage. It's just that so many people go into it not knowing what to expect. Or not knowing exactly who they're married to, you know?"

"Hmm, like you would've been if you'd married that asshole you were dating?"

I gape at my older sister, wondering how she heard about it. We talked maybe a week ago, right before Zachary and I split.

She shrugs when I don't say anything. "Rose told me. So did Daddy."

God. She calls him Daddy, too. Why am I the only one who has a problem with that? With him? I haven't talked to him in a while. He never even called me to express his opinion over my breakup with Zachary. Which is so unlike him. He's usually meddling in my business, especially when it comes to Zachary. "I don't even know how he found out."

"Zachary came to him, of course." Lily rolls her eyes, then drains the rest of her glass, jiggling the ice that's left inside it. I continue to gape at her. I can't *believe* Zachary went to my father. But then again, I can. "He wanted Daddy to talk to you and convince you that staying with him was the best thing."

I let out a little snort that makes Lily laugh. "He actually told you that?"

"Rose filled me in on that part." Lily patted my arm. "You did good, dumping that guy. He was never good enough for you."

I absorb her words, wondering how much I really believe in them. Zachary Lawrence looks fabulous on paper. Any woman would want him, including me at one point. I put up with a ton of his crap, including his chronic cheating. Oh, he hid it well at first and I was clueless. But with confidence comes arrogance and eventually the man became sloppy, leaving clues every-where. I just turned a blind eye to it all.

Eventually, this made me feel like a doormat and I had no one to blame but myself. I was a pathetic, useless doormat of a woman and I hated it. Still don't quite understand how I dealt with him for so long.

But there are some things we just can't question, not while we're still too close to them.

"I need to focus on work," I tell Lily firmly. "And me." I think of Ryder. How he'd brought me to orgasm so easily yester-day afternoon. My skin heats at the memories and I scan the room yet again, searching for him. I know he said he'd be here and I believe him, but I haven't spotted him yet.

"Yes, you do. But you need to have a little fun, too." Lily flashes one of those knock-you-out-and-leave-you-flat smiles that she has patented. She really knows how to turn it on and look like the good-time party girl. I wonder if it's exhausting keeping up that sort of pace. I know my diligent *I want to in-herit Fleur, so I must work twelve-hour days* pace is starting to wear on me, so I can only imagine.

"I know how to have fun," I say, my mind still filled with images of Ryder. *Talk about fun . . .*

"I mean *real* fun. Not sitting at home eating your favorite takeout after a hard day's work and watching your saved-up Bravo shows on the DVR." It's as if she peeked inside my brain. "That's not fun. That's boring. And you, Vi, are anything but boring."

Lily is the only human on this planet allowed to call me Vi without my getting mad at her. God, I really hate that nickname. "I know how to indulge myself. If I like to eat my favorite take-out and watch Bravo shows, what's wrong with that?"

"Everything." Lily glances around as if she's looking for something. Or someone. Knowing her, it's probably both. "I'm going to grab another drink from the bar. You want one?"

"No, thank you. I'm fine," I murmur, vowing to not make a fool of myself again by drinking too much. I need to keep a level head. I'm already edgy enough, knowing that Ryder is around here. Somewhere.

I remember his demand that I not wear any panties and I did just that. It feels strange, wearing nothing underneath my dress when usually the barest I go is a skimpy thong. And I only do that so I won't have visible panty lines, not because I want to please my man . . .

The dress is a pale, pale pink and the skirt is short, hitting me above the knee, and flares out. I'm not wearing a bra either, since the dress has a deep V in both the front and the back. I wore my hair up as well, so I'm feeling exposed. Or more like extremely naked.

And the tiniest bit hopeful. Will Ryder like my dress? My hair? The fact that I followed his orders? No man has given me orders before. It felt odd, doing something at his command. Like I'm his little pet and he owns me. Not that Ryder McKay wants to own me . . .

"You look beautiful tonight."

At the sound of the man's voice I turn, breaking into a smile at who I expect to see standing before me. But it's not who I thought . . . it's someone else, and he makes my smile fall and my scowl form in a matter of seconds. "What do you want?"

Zachary takes a step toward me and pauses, most likely because he can see I'm shooting imaginary daggers at him with my eyes. "I just wanted to say hello."

I tilt my chin up, wishing like crazy Lily were with me. It would be so much easier to face him with someone by my side. And knowing my sister, she'd probably tell him to kiss her ass. "Hello." My voice is like ice, and hopefully he'll get the hint. That I want to freeze him out.

"I miss you, Violet." His admission is quiet and sounds so sincere. I've heard him say things like this before, in that same tone of voice. Time and again, and I always fell for it. Above all else, I always believed him.

Not this time, though. Not ever again.

"Where's Pilar? I know she's eager to keep you company." I can't hide the contempt in my voice. I hate her. And she's insinuating herself so completely into my life, it makes me uncomfortable.

Not that it matters to her. Or to Zachary.

He makes a face at my words and my tone. As usual, he looks perfect. Wearing one of his elegant suits with not a wrinkle in sight, every single hair in place and that bland expression on his face. No one else in the room would know we're having a private discussion in such a public place. "She means nothing to me, Violet. You know this."

"How am I supposed to know, Zachary? It's not like you told me. At least with this one, you keep seeing her. That says to me she actually might mean something." My heart cracks a little at my words. I'm over him. I *need* to be over him. It's going to take time, though. Losing myself in the rush of a passionate secret affair could help.

But maybe not enough. *God,* I don't know.

I'm so confused.

"The only woman I've ever loved is you." His voice is hushed and I swear I hear a faint tremor. I won't fall for his words. His lies. I can't. He's hurt me too much. Violated my trust in him too many times.

"I'm not sure you know how to love." I swallow hard, past the shaking in my own voice. I hate showing even a hint of vulnerability to him. I don't want him to think he has any sort of hold over me.

As usual, Zachary ignores what I say. Heaven forbid he should react to my insult. "Don't let it end like this, Violet. We need each other. I need you more than you'll ever know," he implores.

"What? You need me so you can get ahead in the company? You seem to do a fine job of it all on your own. Sucking up to my father for the potential London promotion? Nice work on that one." I take a drink from my wineglass, telling myself to keep my patience. It wouldn't do for us to start arguing, though I think we're halfway there already. Not that Zachary and I ever argued. We're too polite for that.

"I deserve that. You're right. I've behaved badly during our relationship and for that, I'm sorry. I'm sure you think I've— used you. I regret many of the choices I've made, Violet, but I've never regretted *you*." He takes a step toward me and I step back. "Can't you give me another chance? I know I messed up. I was angry that you were always so consumed with your work, even when I told you that I'm leaving you for London in a few weeks."

I gape at him. I always made time for him. *Always*.

"And then you started spending time with McKay. It threw me. I didn't know what you were up to." He runs a hand through his hair, then immediately pushes it back into place. "Pilar filled my head with a bunch of lies and I overreacted."

A bunch of lies? What could she have told him? "Overreacted how? By letting her put her mouth on your penis?"

He looks shocked. *Good*. I'm feeling a little shocked by this entire conversation, too. "What I did with her doesn't matter. I *love* you. I don't want to lose you."

This is the last thing I need to deal with tonight. "It's over, Zachary. I don't know why you think otherwise or why you believe you can change my mind, but you need to stop," I tell him firmly.

"You can't just cut me off. We have a history. A shared past together. We planned on running this company someday, side by side. What about those plans?" he asks indignantly.

"They're over. You ruined them a long time ago." I start to walk away but he darts out, grabbing my arm and stopping me.

"You're being ridiculous." He thrusts his face in mine and I recoil, fear trickling down my spine. I've never seen him so angry. "We *belong* together, Violet. You know this." His tone is low and downright menacing. I can almost believe he's threatening me.

"Let her go, Lawrence."

We both turn at the same time to find Ryder standing there, watching us with a furious scowl marring his otherwise handsome face, his legs braced wide apart and his hands stuffed inside his trouser pockets. My heart races at seeing him, at the fierce way he's staring down Zachary, looking absolutely in command in his dark suit, his hair a delicious mess and that cold, dark stare.

"Get the fuck out of here," Zachary snarls, his teeth clenched. I gasp at his choice of words. This is a man who rarely says anything bad. "We're having a private discussion."

"Fuck you. Stop pushing her around, asshole. She's not with you anymore, or did you forget that?" The mocking tone in Ryder's voice sends about a thousand different shades of red flashing across Zachary's face. He's so furious he's practically vibrating with the emotion.

"Stay out of my business," Zachary fumes just as I jerk out of his hold and go over to stand by Ryder's side. I can tell the gesture alone surprises him. Hurts him. Infuriates him.

For the first time since I laid eyes on him, I don't care what he thinks about me. I'm done being the pretty toy he puts up on the shelf and admires from afar while he's off playing with his other dolls.

"I'm not your business any longer, Zachary," I tell him, stiffening when I feel Ryder's hand rest at the small of my back. He's putting on some sort of unified front for Zachary and I'm not sure if I want him to. "There's nothing left for us to discuss."

"Violet . . ."

"Not here," I say, interrupting him. "Stop. Go. Before you make a fool of yourself."

He glares at us both, his gaze going from me to Ryder and back to me. I stiffen my shoulders and lift my chin, hoping I look strong when I feel anything but.

"We'll talk later," he mutters before he walks away.

"The guy can't take a hint," Ryder says the moment Zachary is out of earshot, streaking his thumb across the center of my back, making me shiver.

I step away from him, uncomfortable. "You shouldn't have butt in."

He cocks a brow. "You looked like you needed a helping hand."

"It was fine. I'm capable of having a civil conversation with my ex." I release a shuddering breath, hating how everything tightens inside of me at the mention of the word *ex*. Am I regretting my decision? I just . . . I don't know what I want anymore. I feel completely out of control.

And I don't like it.

"You might be, but I'm not so sure about Lawrence." Ryder takes a step toward me and I back up, feeling cornered. Feeling . . . trapped.

And angry. Why do all the men in my life try to push me around? "I don't need you to come to my rescue."

He smiles, but it looks more like he's baring his teeth. "Looked like it to me."

I cross my arms in front of my chest. "I don't need you interfering in my personal business." I sound like a shrew but I really don't care. I'm mad. Mad at Zachary, mad at Ryder . . . I'm being completely irrational, but my life has become tumultuous at best or an absolute tornado at worst.

He takes another step toward me, his expression menacing, eyes dark as he watches me. I step back, my butt hitting the wall, and I drop my arms, bracing my hands flat. "He had his hands on you." He's now so close his leg brushes the skirt of my dress. "He was yelling at you."

"He wasn't."

"Why are you defending him? He's fucking Pilar," he says harshly.

Hearing him say it like that . . . sounds so sordid. And makes me feel bad because I'm doing the same exact thing with him. "And I'm fucking around with you. What's the difference?"

He raises his brows, looking almost amused at what I said. "Right. You're not with him anymore. You're with me."

"We're not together." He touches my cheek, drifts his fingers across my skin so lightly I shiver. "It happened once."

"And it was amazing."

I shrug, trying to ignore the husky reverence in his voice. It doesn't matter what he thinks. We probably shouldn't be doing this. Any of this. I think I'm in over my head. No. Not think . . . I *know* I'm in over my head. "It shouldn't happen again," I whisper as he leans in, his nose brushing against the side of my face.

"Oh, it's going to," he whispers, his lips moving against my cheek. "You want it to. I bet if I slipped my hand beneath your dress I'd find you bare. Just like I asked."

I close my eyes, praying that no one will find us here. Yes, we've maneuvered ourselves somehow into a darker corner of the party, but still. We're not in complete hiding.

"And I bet if I slipped my fingers between your legs, I'd find you wet," he continues, his velvety, deep voice weaving some sort of seductive spell on me. I'm almost tempted to dare him to see if I'm as wet as he imagines. "I bet I could make you come in seconds."

A huff of surprised laughter escapes me. "Rather confident in your abilities, aren't you?"

"Just remembering how I had you coming all over my face the last time I saw you."

My entire body goes weak at his words. I open my eyes to find him tracing his finger along the plunging neckline of my dress, teasing at the sensitive skin between my breasts. "We shouldn't be having this conversation here," I protest breathlessly.

He smiles. "Let's take it elsewhere, then."

"Ryder . . ."

"Violet," he mimics, slipping his finger beneath the fabric and touching my breast. "Your skin is so damn soft."

My eyes fall shut when he strokes my nipple. "Please. Stop," I murmur.

In an instant his hand is gone and his body heat disappears. Opening my eyes, I find he's stepped completely away from me, his hands stuffed into his pockets once more, his expression neutral. Almost as bland as Zachary's.

I hate it. Hate having him that far away from me. Hate even more the turbulent emotions swirling within me. I want him. I don't. I like him, but not really. He's so closed off most of the time. Treats life like it's one big joke.

Sexually we share a strong connection. One I can't deny. One I want to explore further.

But I would be stupid to even attempt it. Ryder McKay scares me.

"Don't give me that sad little look, Violet." He sounds cold, distant. Dismissive. "If you say no, I'm not about to push myself on you."

I part my lips to say something but before I can, he walks away.

Chapter Fourteen

Ryder

"I CAN FEEL THE SEXUAL FRUSTRATION POURING OFF OF YOU IN waves. Already frustrated, hmm? I told you she was an ice queen."

I ignore Pilar and down my drink, setting the glass on the cocktail table beside me, the ice rattling with the force. "Fuck off," I mutter.

"Oh dear, you *are* in a mood. What happened? Is she going to take Zachary back after all?" She scowls. "I certainly hope not. That means I'll have to take drastic measures, and that is the last thing I want to do," Pilar says drolly.

Meaning she would love to take drastic measures. Anything she can do to decimate Violet. "Leave it alone."

"Hmm, I don't like this. You're being so mysterious. I hate it when you do that, you know? I always have. I don't know near enough about you. And I've told you everything about me," she says.

There are some things no one needs to know about my past, especially Pilar. She'd probably use any and all knowledge against me. "I didn't think you were coming tonight." I turn to face her, wishing like hell she wasn't here. Same with that dick-bag Zachary Lawrence. They cast a dark shadow on everything I try and do with Violet. For Violet.

To Violet.

Pilar shrugs her bare shoulders. She's wearing a long column of a dress, strapless and black, stark among the pretty women dressed in pastels tonight. Her hair is slicked back off her face and her lips are the trademark bold red. As usual, she wants to stand out.

And she's succeeded.

"Ah, I've been laying low." A lie. Pilar doesn't know how to lay low. "Zachary is in a mood, too. I saw him talking with Violet. She worked him into a froth."

"He did the same to her." I clamp my lips shut. Why the hell did I say that? Violet had been visibly upset and angry when I found them arguing. Hell, he was touching her, and the wave of fury that bled through me made me want to fuck him up. As in make him bleed. I could have taken him. Easily. He's a wimpy, pampered asshole and I'm a former street kid–slash–drug addict.

I'm just real good at pretending to be a pampered asshole like Lawrence.

After getting rid of him, I tried to calm Violet down, but she was pissed. More at Lawrence, I'm sure, but she took it out on me. Hell, seeing her so worked up had aroused me, sick fuck that I am. I'd been ready to take her right there, not giving a damn who saw us together. But when she asked me to stop, that was it. I had to walk away.

No way could she ever accuse me of pushing myself on her. In this weird little game I'm playing, she calls all the shots—at least when it comes to if and when we have sex.

Hell, if we'll ever have sex. One taste and I crave her like an addict. Not good.

"So protective," Pilar murmurs, her lips curving into a knowing smile. "Just fuck her and get it over with. Once you realize what a horrible lay she is, then you'll be done with her."

Anger makes my voice tight. "What? You have personal experience in fucking Violet?"

Pilar laughs so loud she draws the attention of more than a few guests at the party. "Please. Like the little prude would swing that way."

That's it. I'm done standing around pretending I want to listen to Pilar go on about Violet. I don't even want to be at this stupid party full of wedding dresses and greedy brides-to-be. I only came here to see Violet.

And she's pissed at me. So I blew that all to hell.

"Quit insulting her," I toss over my shoulder as I make my escape, pushing my way through the crowd. It's mostly full of young, beautiful women tonight and normally, I'd be in heaven. Flirting my way through all of them, zeroing in on the most responsive—and receptive—one.

Not tonight, though. I don't notice any of them, even when they flash me flirtatious looks and welcoming smiles. I'm intent on finding Violet so I can talk to her again. Look at her. Smell her.

Touch her.

I spot her quickly, standing with her older sister, Lily, the two of them in what looks like an intense conversation. They're standing close, their heads bent toward each other, Violet listening while Lily does all the talking, gesturing wide with her arms. Violet just nods, staring at the ground, looking sad.

I hate seeing her like that. But even in her sadness, she's beautiful. I know everyone says Lily is the prettiest Fowler sister. The sexiest.

But I disagree. I only have eyes for Violet.

Suddenly she looks up, as if she can feel me staring at her. Her gaze locks with mine, those dark, dark eyes looking right through me. Lily's still talking and Violet reaches out, resting her hand on her sister's forearm. She never takes her eyes off me as she speaks, then Lily turns, looking at me as well.

I don't move. I don't look away, even when I start to feel uncomfortable at being under the scrutiny of two Fowler sisters.

And then she's walking toward me. The sister I want. The sister I can't seem to get enough of. She stops just in front of me and tilts her head back, steely determination in every move she makes.

"I took out my anger at Zachary on you and I shouldn't have. I'm sorry."

I slip my hands into my pockets so I won't reach for her and pull her to me. The urge to shove my fingers into her hair and ruin that perfect updo she's got going on nearly overwhelms me. "You're forgiven."

A smile plays at the corners of her pretty pink lips. "I didn't mean it when I said I wanted you to stop."

I clench my hands into fists, still keeping them in my pockets. "What did you mean, then?"

"I don't know." She shrugs. "This entire . . . situation confuses me."

That makes two of us.

"It scares me, too," she admits softly.

Ah hell. She talks like that, looks like that, and all I want to do is reassure her that everything's going to be just fine. Even if I don't believe it.

Because I don't. Saying that to her would be a lie. I have no idea what's going to happen.

"Come with me," I say.

"I can't just leave."

"Yeah, you can." I reach out and place my hand on her arm, but she jerks out of my touch. "Come on, Violet."

She frowns. "Where are we going?"

I shake my head, irritated with her, my reaction to her, all of it. This was supposed to be easy, taking advantage of Violet. Instead, it's turning into something far more complex than I thought. "Don't ask questions."

"Don't boss me around." She crosses her arms in front of her chest, plumping her breasts. They look ready to pop out of that low-cut dress she's wearing and I step closer, shielding her from anyone else's view.

"I thought you liked it when I bossed you around," I murmur, drawing my finger along her exposed collarbone.

She swats my hand away. "Don't say things like that. Not here."

"Right. That's why you need to come with me." I touch her again, tracing the bodice of her dress, my finger dipping low, lower, almost touching her breasts. She goes completely still and I lift my gaze to hers. "I won't take up too much of your time." I don't bother hiding my snide tone. I'm frustrated and I don't care who knows it, least of all Violet.

The surge of triumph that flows through me at the disappointed look flashing across her face shouldn't matter, though it does. The small confirmation that she wants me like I want her fuels me.

And I need it.

Without a word, I take her hand and lead her out of the cavernous room, my fingers laced with hers. She follows behind me silently as I pull her through the crowd, noting Lawrence as we pass by him. He looks fucking furious and I feel victorious. If he only knew what I have planned for his ex-girlfriend . . .

"Ryder," Violet protests when I push open the double doors leading to the lobby of the building. I ignore her, glancing first left, then right, where I spot a door that leads to I-don't-know-where.

I decide to check it out and see where it takes us.

"What are you doing?" she asks. I can hear the fear and irritation in her voice. Again, I ignore her, and I test the door handle to find it unlocked. I peer inside to find a supply closet and I tug Violet in after me, shutting the door so we're shrouded in complete darkness.

I can't see her, but I can feel her. Smell her. I press her back against the door, rubbing against her since there's not much room. She grips my shoulders at the same moment I grab her head with both hands to keep her still. "What do you *think* I'm doing?" I murmur just before I kiss her.

She sags against the door, sags against me, and I let one of my hands fall to her side, squeezing her hip with firm fingers. A little moan sounds from her, vibrates through me, and I deepen the kiss, my tongue sweeping her mouth, searching, circling hers. The dress she's wearing is sexy as fuck, giving me easy access. I tug aside the front of it, pushing one wide strap off her shoulder and baring her breast.

It's so damn dark and I wish I could see her, but I can't. Her lush flesh fills my palm and I tease her nipple with my index finger, circling it again and again, feeling the bit of flesh tighten further with my attention. "You want me. Don't deny it," I murmur, and she doesn't protest.

She whispers my name against my lips as I pull away from her, bending over her chest so I can draw her nipple into my mouth. I feel frantic, on edge, the need to touch her, please her, completely taking over me. I savor the taste of her sweet, hard flesh, sucking deep. I slip my hand beneath the other side of her dress, my fingers covering her breast. I pinch her nipple, twist it the slightest bit so she cries out, and I want to laugh. Want to shout in triumph because I know this girl . . . this prim, perfect girl, likes it when I'm a little rough.

And the poor thing has no idea what I'm capable of.

I skim my hand down her side, along the dip of her waist, the gentle curve of her hip. The fabric of her dress is smooth and soft, almost as soft as her skin, and my fingers get lost in the folds of her skirt before I shove my hand beneath it. I lift the fabric up to skim my hand along the outside of her thigh and bare hip, finding that she's not wearing any panties, just like I asked her.

"Fuck," I choke out as I caress her hip bone, then slide my hand down. Farther . . .

"I did as you asked," she murmurs as she shifts beneath my hand, spreading her legs.

Giving me better access.

So I take it. I cup her between her thighs, feel the heat of her scald my palm. She thrusts against my hand as I draw it up, teasing the very seam of her with my index finger, dipping in and lightly caressing her hot, wet folds. She's on fire for me, her moans growing louder with my every touch, and I kiss her to shut her up, loving how noisy she is. Dying to get her alone so she can be as loud as she wants for me and no one can hear us.

She lifts her leg and wraps it around my hip, opening herself up to me even more. I break our kiss and thrust my finger deep inside her pussy, fuck her with one finger, then two, and she's grinding against my hand, murmuring nonsensical words. I wish I could see her, stare into those pretty eyes, watch her face as I make her come apart.

Hell. I feel like *I* could come apart. With her like this, I feel as if I could spiral out of control at any moment. All I want is her. All I can think about is fucking her. Making her mine. Owning her.

Jesus. I need to get a grip.

She's clutching at me, her hands having slid to my chest, fingers grasping at my shirt. The girl seems hell-bent on ruining my clothes. I can feel her nails scratching against my skin, the desperate seeking of her orgasm obvious. She's close. So damn close, and I just need to push her over that edge.

I decide to toy with her instead.

"You want me to stop?" My fingers still within her body and she gasps, her breaths coming fast, the sound harsh in the otherwise quiet of the closet.

"N-no." She reaches for my face, her fingers tentative on my jaw before they find my cheek, and then her lips are seeking mine. I let her take over, my fingers still inside her pussy as she kisses me desperately, her tongue licking, her hips moving against my hand as I slowly start to push my finger inside her welcoming heat once more. "Please," she whispers, her voice shaky. "I need it."

"You need *it* or do you need *me*?" I ask, my voice harsh as I still my fingers again. A whimper escapes her as she rolls her hips just as I withdraw my hand from her body and reach up, touching her lips. "Tell me, Violet."

Her hot breath bathes my damp fingers as she parts her lips and starts to speak haltingly. "I-I need you."

"Open your mouth. Taste yourself," I tell her and she does, sucking my fingers, her lips tight, her tongue swirling. My cock is rock hard, knowing I have sweet little Violet Fowler licking at my fingers after I had them buried inside her.

She's sexy as hell. After all the talk I've heard about her being an ice queen, uptight, a horrible lay, I'm thinking they were wrong.

Or she was just with the wrong man, which doesn't surprise me.

"Say my name, Violet," I urge her as I withdraw my fingers from her mouth.

"Ryder," she whispers.

"Ask me to make you come," I demand.

"Make me come," she says breathlessly. "Please?"

Hearing her say my name, making her beg, and not being able to see her heightens the vulnerability, the need in her trembling voice. I touch her, slide my fingers back inside her body and brush my thumb against her clit, her sharp gasp urging me on, making me touch her there again. And again. "You like that?"

"Yes," she moans as I press my lips against her throat and kiss her there. Lick and nip at her sensitive skin while I plunge my fingers deep inside her pussy, circling her clit with my thumb over and over. "Feels so good."

Pleasure rushes through me and I lift my head, brushing my

lips against hers. "You're close, aren't you?" I can feel the way her body tenses against mine, her hand gripping my shoulder tight. Her clit swells against my thumb and I press it, my fingers buried deep as I devour her mouth with my own.

She falls apart within seconds, a little cry sounding from her that I swallow as I feel her inner walls contract around my fingers. Her entire body shakes as I slow my thrusts, my thumb still tight against her clit until she finally sags against me completely, overcome by her orgasm.

I press a kiss to her forehead, ignoring the wave of tenderness that I feel for her. I just made her come with my fingers in a dark closet while a party is happening in the room next to us. This isn't a moment for tender, sweet feelings.

This is straight fucking around and making Violet Fowler addicted to me.

"That was . . ." She releases a shuddery breath. "Oh my God."

Her praise isn't necessary. It's making me uncomfortable and I'm thankful for the darkness so I can hide from it. What the fuck did we just do? It's like I see her and all I want to do is tear her clothes off. My thoughts are consumed with her. I don't even remember why I'm pursuing her in the first place beyond my wanting her. There's another purpose, work-related, I know. But *hell*.

I can't worry about that. All I can think about is Violet. The taste of her, the sounds she makes, kissing her, touching her, being with her . . .

"If we had more time I'd make you suck my cock." My voice is harsh, but I don't care. I have to remember there's no place for emotion here. None.

A shuddery gasp escapes her but she doesn't say anything else.

Withdrawing my hand from her body, I push her skirt back

into place as best I can, considering I still can't really see. "But you need to get back out to your party."

"You . . . you're not going to join me?" She sounds sad and I almost fall for it.

Almost.

"You have your sister. And Lawrence is out there, too, begging you to come back to him." The words sound bitter and hell, I feel bitter saying them.

I need distance so I can gather my jumbled thoughts. I never wanted to give her any power. That was never part of my plan. I was going to own her, and I believe I'm almost there.

But I never counted on her trying to own *me*.

"I don't want Zachary." *I want you*. The unsaid words linger between us, heavy and foreboding, and suddenly I'm dying to get away from her. I haven't even fucked her properly yet beyond with my fingers and my mouth, and she's already twisting herself around me. Invading my thoughts at the oddest times. Making me seek her out when normally I'd be focused on something else. Anything else but Violet.

"You should go back out there." Unable to help it, I grab hold of her shoulders and lean in, dropping a chaste kiss on her forehead. She stills, I hear her breath leave her in a shaky exhale, and I immediately feel like an asshole.

"I want to see you again," she murmurs, her voice so low I almost don't hear her.

"Why?" My callousness knows no bounds. Pilar would be proud of me. Yet all I can feel is shame.

Shame at giving this woman so much pleasure and then treating her like shit, all in the space of about five minutes.

Violet remains quiet for so long I could almost believe she'd left. I start to say something but she moves just as I'm about to speak, wrenching the closet door open with a sharp turn of the handle, allowing a stream of light to hit us both. My gaze falls on her and my heart aches with how beautiful she looks. Everything perfect but her lipstick, which is completely gone thanks to me. Her mouth is swollen, her gaze full of hurt. Hurt I put there.

Pain I'm responsible for.

"I asked for this," she says quietly, perfectly composed as usual. "But maybe I'm not prepared for it."

I meet her gaze steadily, ignoring the panic that threatens me. Is she trying to end it already? Is this somehow my fault? And why do I even care?

"Are you saying you don't want to . . . pursue this any longer?" I ask, my voice cold. Hard.

"I don't know if I can," she admits.

"Then maybe you shouldn't," I say steadily, my thoughts anything but. *What the hell am I doing?* I don't want to end this.

But here I am, screwing it up.

She lifts her chin, defiance written all over her. I expect her to argue, to tell me to fuck off, but she doesn't say a word.

Violet slips out of the closet and walks away, never turning to look at me once.

I guess I deserve that.

Sticking my head out, I see the coast is clear and I exit the closet, shutting the door quietly behind me. I start toward where the party is being held, planning to check in real quick before I leave for the night, when I hear a throat clearing behind me.

And I turn to find Zachary Lawrence, the pompous asshole himself, standing there as if he was waiting for me.

"What the fuck do you want?" I ask, my tone ugly, my body tensing for a fight. Memories come back at me, one after another. I flash back to when I was a teenager and got jumped by punks that lived in my neighborhood, always looking for money, whatever I had that they could sell to score drugs. When I got older, I became the one who dealt drugs and they quit trying to beat the shit out of me—they bought from me instead.

Dad was gone. Mom didn't exist. I was on my own at fifteen.

I've dealt with plenty of drug-addicted assholes in my life who were full of adrenaline and knew how to fight. I could take on Lawrence, no problem.

"Leave Violet alone," he says through clenched teeth.

"She doesn't belong to you." I stride toward him, ready to shove my fist into his smug face, but I restrain myself.

"Yes. She does. I don't care what you two are doing—she's still mine." The heavy emphasis on the word *mine* makes me see red. But I refuse to lose my cool in front of this man. My enemy.

"Right. That's why she came all over my fingers not even five minutes ago," I say, feeling like a shit for taking it so low, but *damn it*. Just looking at him pisses me off.

His gaze narrows and his jaw tightens. *Good*. He *should* be pissed. I want him pissed. "She was in the closet with you." It's not a question.

I consider letting him smell my fingers, the ones still faintly sticky with Violet's come, but I don't. Instead I clutch them into a fist and bring it to my mouth, breathing deep. I can smell her, remember the way she came so easily just moments before. "Yeah. And I got her off, which is more than she can say about you."

His eyes flare with anger. *Good*. I'm ready to goad him some more. "You're just using her."

"And you weren't?"

Lawrence clenches his hands into fists, as if he wants to drive one of them into my face. I stand my ground, never backing down, wishing he would try and touch me. I'd beat the shit out of him.

And I think he knows it.

"She wouldn't slum with a piece of shit like you," he practically spits out.

"Oh yeah? I'll remember that the next time I go down on her in my office." I smile when he growls.

"I could make your life a living hell, you know," he says,

sounding smug. "One call to Forrest Fowler and I can have you fired."

"Go for it," I say, hoping he hears the warning in my voice. "You don't scare me."

"I should. You're nothing but an ass who fucks to get ahead."

"Says the pot to the kettle. What were you doing with Violet all this time? Fucking around on the side while pretending to be the perfect boyfriend. Staying on her good side so you could get this promotion to London." I laugh, but there's no amusement in it. "If anyone fucks to get ahead, it's you."

"I earned that promotion fair and square," he breathes.

"Don't think you fully earned it yet." I step so close to him my face is in his. I'm taller than him by an inch or two and I'm glad. I want this jackass to know I won't back down from him. No matter what.

"What? You think you can step in, get in Violet's panties, and then you'll have my job?" Lawrence laughs. "We'll see about that."

"Right. We *will* see." Now I remember why I'm using Violet. My greatest goal is to take everything this asshole has and make it mine. From his job to his woman, I want it. All of it.

Every last bit.

"She'll realize quick you're worthless," he says with a smile.

I return his smile. "Violet never protests when I have her spread out on my desk and my tongue in her—"

"Stop!" Violet miraculously appears and steps in between us, her beautiful face twisted in anger. *Damn it*, she probably heard every word. "Both of you."

"Violet. Darling." Lawrence reaches for her, his expression going from angry to beseeching in an instant. "I hope after hearing everything you realize what a scumbag McKay is."

"I think I'm starting to realize what scumbags the *both* of you are." She sends me a pointed look and I want to laugh. Cheer her on. I love it when she's feisty. I know she's pissed at me but when she shows this side, I can't help but be aroused. "Stop fighting over me like I'm a piece of property."

"Darling, please. Let me explain—"

"There's no need to explain, Zachary," she interrupts. "Clearly the two of you are having a *'my penis is bigger than yours'* competition. I'd suggest maybe you should quit while you're ahead."

Lawrence's mouth falls open and I snicker. She whirls around, glaring at me, her lips still bare from when I kissed her lipstick off just moments ago, a faint red mark on the side of her neck because I nibbled and sucked her flesh. Possessiveness rises within me and unable to stop myself, I reach out and touch the spot, my fingers gentle as I caress her. "Did I do that?" I ask, my voice low.

"Oh for Christ's sake," Lawrence mutters as she reaches up to touch her neck, her fingers colliding with mine.

"What is it?" I guide her hand to the spot and she touches it gingerly, pride swarming within me that I marked her. My feelings for her are so completely fucked up I can barely wrap my head around them. "My God, Ryder, did you give me a hickey?"

She sounds mildly horrified, but I don't really care.

Take that, Lawrence. Take fucking that.

Chapter Fifteen

Violet

"Rumor has it Zachary and Ryder McKay were fighting over you last night," Rose says as she enters my office.

Dread settles in my stomach, and I prop my elbows on my desk and cover my face with my hands. "Where did you hear that?" I ask, my voice muffled against my palms. It is far too early to deal with something like this. Of course, I've been dealing with it since the moment Ryder dragged me into that closet last night. Not that I fought him. Oh, no.

I went willingly and with no regret.

The things I said to him, the way he touched me, how he demanded I suck his fingers . . . my skin tingles just thinking about it. And that orgasm—it shook me to my very core. My legs were wobbly the rest of the night.

Needless to say, the moment in the closet and the argument afterward led to a restless—and unfortunately sleepless—night.

Rose settles into the seat across from my desk, looking far too chipper for me this morning. I wish I could hide, but if I can't deal with my sister, then who can I face? "The Fleur gossip mill is in full force today. You're the main topic of the morning. Well, you, Zachary, and Ryder. They're calling it a love triangle."

I drop my hands with a groan and slap them on top of my desk. "A *love triangle*? God. What exactly are they saying?"

"You sure you want to hear it?" The concern that crosses my sister's face surprises me. How bad is the gossip?

It can't be any worse than the truth.

"Tell me," I urge her, needing to know despite the worry that fills me.

"All right." Rose sighs and perches on the edge of the chair. "They're saying that Ryder and Zachary went at it after Zachary caught you and Ryder together, that you and Ryder were messing around in a closet. During the party. That they fought over you and you interrupted them, demanding they stop. That Ryder touched your neck and you let him and the two of you were making eyes at each other in front of Zachary even though you seemed pissed at the both of them at first." She ticks off each item like she's reading from a list. A really sordid, soap-opera-making list.

I swallow hard. "Is that all?" *Crap,* the gossip is scarily accurate.

"Yep." Rose nods with a little smile. She looks like she's almost . . . enjoying this? My sister is twisted. Both of them are. "So is it true? You were fooling around with Ryder McKay in a *closet*? What exactly were you doing in there with him, anyway?" She actually winks at me.

"It was nothing," I say dismissively, hoping Rose won't pursue it.

"Please. You don't go into a dark closet with a gorgeous man like Ryder and nothing happens." Rose studies me with her usual penetrating gaze, the smile falling from her face. "Did you do him?"

"*No.*" My cheeks heat and I curse yet again my tendency to blush. It's so embarrassing. Besides, I'm telling the truth. I didn't "do" him. He just got me off with his fingers.

Not like I can say that to Rose, though.

"Uh-huh." She doesn't believe me. Whatever. "Are you two seeing each other or what?"

"Not exactly . . ." My voice drifts and I frown. We were supposed to keep this secret and already people are talking about us. This is *so* not good.

"What the hell is that supposed to mean?"

"There's no way of defining what's happening between Ryder and me," I say airily. "So let's just drop this conversation."

"The very last thing I want to do is drop this conversation. This is the most fascinating thing that's happened to you in a long time." The grin that reappears on Rose's face seems as if it can't be contained. "You're fucking Ryder McKay, aren't you?"

"Rose!" I level her with the sternest look I can muster. Does she have to be so blunt? "Don't say such things."

"Why, because I'm cutting too close to the truth? My God, you just broke up with Zachary only a few days ago and now you're screwing around with Ryder. I'm so proud of you!"

"Proud of me?" I'm incredulous. More than anything, I'm embarrassed by this entire situation. I thought I had it in me to have a quick little affair. Ryder has always intrigued me, made me curious, and once Zachary and I were finished, I figured, what was the harm?

But a few stolen moments with him and I felt like I was in over my head. More like I *know* I'm in over my head. And the way we ended it last night . . .

I'm pretty sure we're finished before we'd hardly begun.

"You're taking charge of your life for once. I know you do it professionally, and that you've really come into your own here at Fleur over the last few years, but personally? You've let Zachary walk all over you." I open my mouth to protest, but Rose points her finger at me. "Don't deny it. You know it's true. He called all the shots and you let him."

I clamp my lips shut. She's right. I let Zachary take over our relationship completely. I was the meek little woman standing by her man. I thought it was what I should do, but I ended up letting Zachary take away whatever power I had left in me. So many things had happened to me that I didn't want to deal with, it was just easier to hand over the reins rather than take control.

Being with Ryder, sneaking around with him . . . he invigorates me. Fills me with a sense of self I don't remember ever having. Even after being so angry with him and Zachary over their pissing contest concerning me last night, I still don't regret what happened between us.

I secretly wish more would happen . . .

"So if having a fling with the hottest man who works here helps you recover from that disaster you called a relationship? Then I say more power to you. And to Ryder, too." Rose smiles and folds her hands in her lap, looking like the sweet little angel she is absolutely not.

"Yes, well, I think Father heard about the . . . confrontation. He's already asked me to stop by his office when I can. The sooner the better." It's barely eight o'clock and I already have to face him. I don't want to. It's bad enough discussing this with Rose. What am I going to say to my judgmental father who's probably horribly disappointed I split with Zachary in the first place?

I don't know. All I do know is that it's going to be a very long day.

"Violet. You're looking rather elegant this morning." Father greets me with a warm smile and I pause in the doorway of his office, wondering if he's trying to disarm me before he goes for the jugular with his disappointment over my behavior last night.

"Thank you," I say cautiously as I step into his office, walking across the soft, thick-as-a-cloud rug. The room is huge, nearly taking up the entire floor, and I remember how much I loved coming here when I was a little girl. The mini board table that was always covered with the latest Fleur cosmetics, how he would always let us play with them.

Now I'm inside this office filled with such fond childhood memories and all I want to do is escape.

"New dress?" he asks as I approach the giant desk he sits behind, looking as intimidating as ever.

I glance down at myself. The dress is white, short-sleeved, and fits me perfectly, the pencil skirt falling just above my knees. But what makes it special are the lace cutouts at the shoulders and around the waist, with matching ones on the back. It's elegant and sexy, not revealing at all, but with that hint of lace . . . it's very feminine.

I feel strong. Confident. More armor. I've needed lots of it lately, I suppose.

"Not really," I answer him as I settle in the overstuffed chair opposite his desk. I smooth the skirt over my legs, trying my best not to fidget. "I've worn it before." I hate the small talk. I wish he'd get to the true reason he called me here.

"Well, I like it," he says gruffly, leaning back in his chair so that it creaks. He has all the money in the world and he's had the same chair since I can remember. "How are you doing?"

I shrug, not sure if he's asking personally or professionally. "I'm fine. And you?"

"We're not talking about me." He waves a dismissive hand. "I'm boring. I want to know how *you* are. Are you dealing with Zachary's leaving okay?"

"Um . . ." I blink at him. How should I answer? How much does he know? "We've agreed it's best if we . . . split while he goes to London."

"Really?" He sounds surprised. I'm glad, since I was afraid he might have heard the rumors. "His time in London is temporary. I'm just trying him out for this position."

"Well, yes, but we both figured he has the job." Zachary is certainly counting on him having it.

"Don't assume anything. There are others I want to send over there as well."

"Like who?" I ask curiously.

"Like Ryder McKay."

I go still at first mention of his name. Hearing my father say it unnerves me. "You think he's qualified?"

"I know he is." He pauses, studying me. "And so are you."

If I was still before, now I'm completely frozen. "Wh-what did you say?"

"Aren't you interested in a promotion, Violet? You're capable of doing anything you set your mind to," he says casually. "You've impressed me these last two years. I think it would be smart to have you working in a variety of positions at Fleur for the next few years. You need to gain plenty of experience so that you can run the company properly someday."

His words are like a bomb detonating in my brain. He always acts so displeased with everything I do, everything I say. His disparaging comments had me questioning myself more times than I liked to count. And now he's saying, casually as he pleases, that I'll run the company someday? I think I'm in shock. "I don't think I'm ready to leave here yet, what with the launch of my new line coming up," I say carefully. I don't want him to think I don't want what he's offering, but I don't feel right in leaving yet, either.

"Understood." He gives me a firm nod. "Just know the offer still stands if you're interested."

"Oh, I'm interested." And I'm also completely blown away. Is this all he wanted to talk about? No mention of last night's party and the spectacle Zachary and Ryder made over me? No more questions regarding my relationship with Zachary? I can't believe it.

"I appreciate what you've said," I say. "That you believe I could . . . possibly run Fleur."

"If anyone can do it, it's you. I've been grooming you for it since you were a child." He rests his arms on his desk, clutching his hands together, all while I gape at him. This entire conversation has been surreal. "There's something else I need to tell you, Violet. Something you might find . . . unpleasant."

Ah, here it is. I'm almost relieved that he's about to deliver bad news. I didn't believe he called me in here just to lavish praise on me. That's not his style. "What is it?"

"I was contacted by my lawyer this morning," he says, his voice low, his expression grim. I feel my body sway at the mention of the word *lawyer* and I clutch the arm of the chair so tight my fingers hurt. "He notified me that Alan Brown is set to be released from prison in a few weeks."

The sway turns into a full body slump and I collapse against the back of the chair, my mind spinning. I haven't heard that name in so long I could almost forget the man existed.

Almost.

"I thought . . ." My voice drifts and I glance down, focus on my knees peering from beneath the hem of my white dress. I'm trembling and I grip my shaky knees, release a steadying breath, but it comes out like a stutter. *Stay strong, stay strong.* "I thought he had a twenty-year sentence to serve. It's barely been three years."

"His sentence was reduced. They let him out early." The disgust in Father's tone is clear. He hates this, probably as much as I do. "I didn't want you to find out in any other way, like reading something on the Internet or by a reporter contacting you. Or worse . . . someone from his family reaching out to you. Not that any of them will, but you know what I mean. I wanted to be the one who told you first."

"Thank you," I say with a short nod. The Browns are a family we grew up with. My sisters and I played with the Brown children. Went to school with them. My parents and the Browns were old, dear friends.

Until their son tried to attack me. Then the old family friendship was horribly splintered forever.

"No one will find out your connection to Alan Brown, Violet, especially considering you testified as Jane Doe during his trial. We took every precaution to protect your identity," he reassures me as he has before, countless times over the years. But we both know the truth. Anyone with decent research skills and access to Google could narrow it down and figure out that the college junior Alan Brown assaulted four years ago was me.

Little nineteen-year-old me. I fought him off and identified him to the police. My testimony got a dangerous man off the streets.

And now he's about to be set free.

"I'm not worried about the media. *He'll* find me," I whisper. "He knows exactly where to look."

I remember the cold stare he gave me as I testified on the witness stand during his trial. When I'd gone to college, Father encouraged me to look up Alan. He liked knowing Alan was there to protect me since I went to college not knowing another soul.

And at first it had been nice. He'd shown me around campus. He took me out to lunch and dinner, introduced me to his friends. But then he thought there was something more between us beyond friendship. When I rejected him, he became enraged.

He attacked me. Beat me up, punched me in the face with his fists again and again, tearing at my clothing. Somehow I fought him off with a ferociousness that still surprises me. He didn't get what he wanted, not from me.

Alan broke me, though. My family wanted the incident gone, swept under the rug, forgotten, especially Father and Grandma. It was too scandalous for the media to find out. It could have ruined the company image.

Instead, their dismissal of what happened almost ruined me. I no longer trusted anyone.

I put him in jail, though. The rage that had taken over his face when I described in court how I fought him, how I hurt him . . . it's something I'll never forget. But somehow, after the trial, all the fight was taken out of me, all of the strength and confidence that had once been a natural part of my personality for so long.

I only just now feel like I've gotten some of that strength and confidence back.

"He won't bother you, Violet," Father says firmly. "I promise."

When I meet his sincere gaze, I see that he means it. Believes it. But I don't know if I can.

Chapter Sixteen

Ryder

I WAIT JUST OUTSIDE VIOLET'S OFFICE, LEANING AGAINST THE wall across the hall from her door, my arms crossed in front of my chest, tapping my foot against the floor. I'm impatient as fuck, dying to see her, yet feeling cautious, too. She could tell me to get the hell out and I'd have no choice but to do what she says.

After all, she's my superior. And I had my fingers buried deep inside my superior's body last night, making her come in seconds. The memory fueled me for the rest of the night and through this morning. I keep finding myself jacking off to thoughts of her and I normally don't do that. If I want a woman, I have her. I use her and then I'm done.

Not Violet, though. I toy with her and end up unsatisfied instead. It's fucking torture. Not for her, since I've given her a couple of orgasms.

It's torturous for me.

The need to talk to her, look into her eyes, *hell,* tell her I'm sorry—and I never tell anyone I'm sorry, since I regret nothing —is damn near overwhelming.

Plus, we have a meeting scheduled later this afternoon. I thought it best that I approach her first and make sure we're on good terms. Where better to approach her than her office, with all those windows, where everyone can watch us and see that we're having a normal, work-related discussion?

Yeah, there are rumors that Violet's torn between two lovers or some such bullshit, but I know the truth. And so does she. So does that asshole Zachary Lawrence, who has to realize his chances with Violet have withered up and died.

I haven't spoken to Pilar at all. I don't know where she fits in all of this, but I can't worry about her right now. She might be pissed at me and keeping clear until the rumors die down.

That's not her normal style, though. She loves to gossip, except for when it's about her. Yet this little story might hit too close to home for her taste.

I hear the click of heels coming down the hallway and I glance up to find Violet approaching, looking fucking beautiful in a white dress that is far from virginal. *Jesus,* the clothes this woman wears tear me up inside. As she draws near, I see that there are little see-through lace inserts on each shoulder and around her waist, offering me a flash of skin. Yet there's nothing overtly sexual about Violet. She screams elegance.

And all I can think of is how fast it would take to get her out of that dress so I can put my mouth on her skin.

"Ryder," she says cautiously, stopping just in front of me. "What a surprise."

"Not a pleasant one, I assume?" I arch a brow, feeling a little testy having her in front of me looking perfect while I feel a mess. I slept like shit last night. Woke up late and haven't had anything to eat. I'm grumpy. Sexually frustrated.

And the cause of it all is standing before me, looking perfectly composed.

"Well, I'm not sure, after the words we had last night." She touches her neck, her fingers brushing over the very spot where I marked her. I see that it's faded to a light pink. If no one knew it was there, they wouldn't notice it.

But I notice. I put that mark on her, and the urge to do it again is strong. *Too* strong.

"I'm willing to forgive and forget if you are," I offer.

She studies me, then glances toward her office. "Would you like to come in and talk?"

"I would."

I follow behind her, my gaze dropping to her ass, watching it shift beneath the white fabric of her skirt as she walks. I had my hands all over that bare ass last night, gripped her flesh tight as I held her to me . . .

"We have a meeting scheduled at three, right?" she asks as she steps behind her desk and settles in the chair, scooting it close so she can access her computer.

"We do, yes. That's why I wanted to speak with you." I don't sit down, preferring to stand, hoping it gives me the advantage. "I wanted to make sure you were still okay with it."

"Okay with what?" She glances up at me, her delicate brows furrowed. Now that we're completely alone and I can study her unabashedly, I see the faint circles beneath her eyes, the weary way she's looking at me. She's tired, too.

Maybe last night's fiasco affected her as strongly as it affected me.

"Okay that I lead the meeting. If you're not comfortable with me being there . . ." I don't finish the sentence, anxious to see what she says.

"I have no problem with you being there, Ryder. It's our project that we're working on together. Plus, we're narrowing in closer on a decision. I need you in this meeting." She pauses, her gaze dropping to her desk. "I know how to separate my personal life from my professional," she admits softly.

"Good," I say. "The team is excited to show you what they've come up with."

The slight smile that curls her lips is like a punch to my gut.

"I can't wait to see what they come up with as well. They're very talented."

"So are you." She is. I respect her opinions, the way she thinks. She's not just a figurehead, as Pilar has said time and again. Violet cares about Fleur. It's her legacy and she treats it as such.

"Thank you," she murmurs.

I hesitate, not knowing what else to add, so I start for the door. "So I'll see you at three, then."

"Yes. Fine." I glance over my shoulder to see her lift her head, those big brown eyes meeting mine. Pausing, I turn to face her, waiting for her to say something else. Wanting to linger. Wanting to prolong my time with her.

This woman turns me into an idiot every time I'm in her presence. And I don't like it.

"Ryder." She murmurs my name, the sound of her voice sending a shock of lust through my veins. I take a step toward her desk, wishing we were back in my office because at least there, no one can see us. I'd give anything to throw her on top of that desk, shove her skirt up past her hips, rip her panties off, and fuck her. Hard. "I . . . I hate what happened last night."

I shake my head, shake out the lust-ridden thoughts. "What exactly are you referring to? What we did in the closet?"

"No." She tilts her head to the side, her cheeks going pink. That she blushes over this is adorable.

And I never think *any* woman is adorable.

"The fight between me and Lawrence, then," I say.

She gives me a look. A look that says I should have known better than to do that, and she's probably right. But she doesn't say a word, thank Christ. She's not my mama. Not that I know what it's like to have a mother in my life . . .

"You said some pretty awful things to him," she admonishes. "About me."

"Nothing that wasn't true," I reassure her firmly. "He was using you to get ahead."

Violet visibly flinches, her eyes narrowing as she stares at me. I shouldn't have said that. "And what are *you* doing? Aren't you using me?"

"At least you know I am," I say coolly, my mind scrambling. I need to redirect. I just pissed her off royally. Again.

I seem to have a fucking knack for it.

"I see, then." She sits up straighter and starts moving shit around her desk, trying to look busy. "Three o'clock at the conference room on this floor," she says crisply. "Don't be late."

I know when I've been dismissed. Without another word, I leave her office and head toward the elevators, keeping my head bent, not wanting to look anyone in the eye. One smirk from someone and I might do something I'll regret.

Like smash their face in with my fist.

No one says a word to me and I stop in front of the elevators, pushing the down button as I wait impatiently. I'm watching the numbers light up above the doors, tapping my foot yet again, hoping like hell I don't run into Lawrence since he seems to always be lurking around, when I hear Pilar's familiar voice sound from behind me.

"You are causing quite the ruckus around here," she murmurs.

I barely spare her a glance. "You have zero room to talk."

The doors slide open and she enters the elevator with me, standing so close our arms brush despite there being no one else in the car with us. "At least I make my mess discreetly. You, on the other hand, engage in a fight with your nemesis at a party, tossing insults at each other in front of people."

"I hate that fucker," I mutter as I again resume watching the floor numbers light up.

"He's a rather good fuck. Quite willing to do whatever I ask of him," she purrs, making me grimace. The last thing I want to know is how Lawrence fucks her. I'm afraid that if I open my mouth I'll say something I regret. So I keep quiet.

Pilar hates it when I'm quiet.

She lets out an irritated sound and steps forward, shooting her arm out so she can push the emergency button, and the elevator comes to a jerking halt.

"What the fuck?" I ask, but she's coming at me, shoving at my shoulders, making me falter backward.

"What in the world is wrong with you? You're going to ruin *everything*." She hisses out the last word. "Why did you create such a scene with Zachary last night? You don't even know what I had to do to keep Forrest from hearing about it."

I'm confused. What does Forrest Fowler have to do with any of this? "What are you talking about?"

She wraps her fingers tight around the lapels of my jacket and glares at me, her expression full of menace. "I'm doing everything to keep the old man happy and trying to make him realize how valuable of an asset I am to this company. All while you're out fucking around with his daughter—in *public*, I might remind you—and getting in fights with the very man you want to replace. Did fooling around with Violet Fowler turn you stupid, or what?"

I push her off me, smoothing out the wrinkles her hands left in my jacket. "You have no idea what happened between us last night. The fucker says things to get a reaction out of me. So I'm human. I reacted."

She rolls her eyes and throws her hands up into the air. "You need to learn some control. Haven't I taught you *anything* these last few years?"

Pilar has taught me plenty about the business, but ultimately I'm the con. I'm the one who knows how to bring the hustle. Yet I spend a few stolen moments with Violet here and there and it's like I forget everything I've worked toward. I see her shitty ex-boyfriend and all I want to do is break his fucking nose.

The last thing I need is Pilar irritated with me. Or worse,

dead set on exposing what I'm doing. I need to placate her. Calm her down.

"Listen." I grab hold of her shoulders and give her a gentle shake. "You know as well as I do that Zachary hates me. He hates me as much as I hate him. When he says something, I react. I can't help it."

"Well, learn to control it," she says with a little huff, her eyes softening the slightest bit. "I know I don't help matters, saying such things to you. Like how good in bed he is."

She said that again just to piss me off. I refuse to let her get to me. "You're a bit of a bitch to say things like that, yes," I say, keeping my tone light. Like I'm teasing her. I'm still pissed, but I don't want to deal with her when she's angry. "Bit of a bitch" is an understatement.

Total and complete bitch is more like it.

A little smile curls her lips and relief settles within me. She fell for it. I've got her. I know I do. "You're such a bastard."

"I know. Together, we'll be the ones ruling this company someday, not them," I remind her, hoping like hell she doesn't notice how hollow my words sound. Because . . . I don't mean it. Not anymore. I don't want to rule Fleur with Pilar by my side.

If I get the chance, I want to rule this company on my own.

Her eyes flicker and she looks away from me. "Of course, darling." She looks at me once more, her smile as fake as my earlier words. "The two of us together. Sounds perfect."

She's lying. There's another plan in the works and I'm not a part of it.

No problem. I'm ready to cut her out of my plan, too.

THE THREE O'CLOCK MEETING WITH MY TEAM AND VIOLET GOES relatively smoothly, considering she's quietly furious with me and I'm keeping my distance. Her sister Rose sits in on the meeting, which saves my ass because she's the perfect buffer between us. She approves of every single one of my ideas, much to Violet's disgust.

Not that Violet is going against anything I suggest because she's angry with me. I know the woman has an opinion and has no problem letting it be known. Not everything I've suggested or shown was part of my final plan. I'm testing Violet, testing my team. Hell, I'm even testing Rose.

But Rose is in ready agreement with me to piss off her sister. Fucking unbelievable.

I don't protest, though. It refocuses Violet's anger away from me.

"I thought we were going with peach," Rose says, causing Violet to look up from her iPad. She was typing away, making notes and doing her best to avoid making eye contact with me.

"What do you mean, going with peach?" Violet asks, pursing her lips in an adorable pout.

There goes that word again. *Adorable.* Christ, there has never been one adorable thing in my life, ever. Growing up, I had no siblings, no pets, nothing cute. It was all hard and ugly and noisy. Living in that crap apartment with a father I rarely saw, I was alone. When I was really small, I was scared. Afraid of the dark, afraid of my teachers, afraid of Dad, afraid of random people I walked by on the street. No one cared, though. I felt like nothing.

And I always wanted to be something.

Soon I realized it got me nowhere, being scared. I got tough instead. Life is painful and difficult and a constant struggle, and I fought against my good-for-nothing life. Fought, and eventually I fucking won. I could've ended up like every other loser I grew up with, but no. Look at me now, climbing my way up the corporate ladder. Take-charge. Ruthless.

Definitely not what I would call cute or worse, *adorable.*

Adorable was never even a part of my vocabulary until I started to focus on Violet.

"She's referring to when we were talking about your lips," I add, causing Violet to turn her attention to me, her gaze sharp. "Rather your lip gloss. Peachy Pie, remember?"

"Right." She nods slowly and points toward an image I'd brought her at our what-seems-like-forever-ago dinner. "I prefer this color." She taps the bright orange and black butterfly that's perched on top of a woman's fingertips.

"The orange?" I ask, making a mental note of it. Not a surprise. She's been drawn to that image from the beginning.

"Yes." She nods and tugs the image toward her so she can study it closely. "It's so distinct. And if we make the box glossy . . ."

"Then you'll get your glossy perfection?" I ask with a smile.

"That's too close to Hermès," Rose adds, making us both look at her. "What? It's true," she says directly to Violet. "Orange is their iconic color."

"Orange and brown," I say. "And the orange isn't as bright as this shade."

"It's still orange, though," Violet murmurs, disappointment ringing in her voice.

I can't stand it. I hate hearing her sad or disappointed. I'm a sucker for her. A fucking sucker, when I vowed at a too-young age that I would never be a sucker for any woman. Ever. *Fuck.*

When did this happen?

"How about coral? It's between orange and peach," I suggest. "And it'll go perfectly with the mint-green shade you wanted to incorporate into the packaging."

Violet turns toward me, her eyes meeting mine, dark brown and fathomless. For the first time during this meeting she looks pleased. "That's perfect. You're right. Let's go with coral." She casts her gaze around the table, her smile growing. "What do you all think?"

Murmurs of approval abound, and we call the end of the meeting within a few minutes of her coral-and-mint-green announcement. Rose sneaks out of the room in a blur, complaining of another meeting she needs to get to, and my team empties the conference room one by one, all of them eagerly talking among themselves, plotting and planning the next stage of packaging.

All the while I remain in the background leaning against the wall, my hands stuffed in my pockets. I vacated my chair the moment Violet ended the meeting, hoping she wouldn't notice that we were left alone in the room together until it was too late.

"I feel you lurking behind me," she says, amusement lacing her tone. "Don't think I don't know you're there, Ryder." She turns to face me, her hands resting on her hips. I let my gaze rove over her, taking her in from the top of her head to the tips of her toes . . . which I can't see since they're encased in sexy-as-hell shoes.

"You're mad at me." I don't bother asking because I already know the truth. "I planned on treading lightly where you're concerned."

She ignores my comments. "The meeting went well, don't you think?"

"All that matters is that you're pleased." When she raises her eyebrows, I add, "It's your name that's going on the box, after all. This is your line, Violet. What you say goes."

"I liked your coral suggestion." A little smile plays at the corners of her lush lips. Lips that are slicked in subtle pink lipstick today. "Rose was driving me crazy."

"I know," I say with an answering almost-smile.

"She couldn't stop agreeing with you. I was tempted to tell her to grow a spine and come up with her own opinion."

"She did it to piss you off." I shrug when she gapes at me. "Don't bother denying it—you know it's true."

Violet laughs, the sound soft and sweet in the otherwise quiet of the large room. "People rarely pay attention to the sisterly dynamics between us. I figure most people aren't aware when we're trying to get at each other."

"Oh, I could tell." Mostly because I pride myself on my people-reading skills. That, and Pilar and I have engaged in similar behavior while at work in the past. She's the only person I've ever felt close to . . . though I'm starting to feel that way about Violet.

The realization stuns me.

"Well, you're very perceptive," Violet says, unaware that she's just rocked my world.

I clear my throat and focus on her. "She knows about us, I presume?"

Her cheeks color, and the urge to touch her makes me clench my fingers into a tight fist so I won't. I can't move too fast again. She's like a wounded animal that'll run at first sight of me coming for her. I can't risk it. "It feels like *everyone* knows about us," she says quietly. "After your little fight with Zachary last night."

"I doubt *everyone* knows." I'm such an idiot for letting that asshole get to me. Only a select few saw us arguing last night, but still. "Does that bother you? I know you wanted to keep it secret."

"I did. I still do. It looks . . . bad, that I've fallen out of Zachary's arms and into yours."

That we're compared to each other makes me want to kill him. At the very least, beat the shit out of him. "You haven't necessarily fallen into my arms," I tell her, trying to make light of what's happening between us. "It's no one's business, what we're doing together."

"True."

"And it's all speculation."

"With the exception of you describing to Zachary exactly what you did to me in that closet," she says dryly.

That's right. I did. Don't regret it, either. "Something else will happen in the next day or two to divert their attention. They'll find someone new to talk about," I reassure her. "Don't worry about it."

"I'm not." She studies me, her gaze dropping to my chest as she takes a deep breath. "It made me angry, what you said earlier. That Zachary was using me."

"I know." I'm not going to pretend I'm unaware of her moods. She's like an open book. And a terrible liar.

The complete opposite of me.

"And for whatever reason, it . . . hurt when you said you were using me, too." She rolls her eyes and waves a hand, as if dismissing what she just said. "I know it's stupid. We've said from the get-go that we were using each other. You offered yourself up to me. You wanted to do this to make Zachary mad and I suppose you've done just that, so I'm guessing now that you're . . . through with me."

The disappointment in her voice, that's written all over her, is palpable. "I suppose," I agree, causing her to inhale sharply. *Great,* I've stunned her. But I'm doing it on purpose. Hoping to turn this into exactly what I envisioned.

"All right," she says with that defiant little tilt of her chin. "At least I know where I stand with you."

I push away from the wall and take a step toward her, my gaze intent on her face. "Do you, Violet?"

She backs up a step. "I thought so."

"So where do you stand with me?" I'm toying with her again. Trying to confuse her. It's so easy that I can't help myself.

"What happened between us is . . . done." She's disappointed by the idea and her sadness gives me strength.

"Do you want it to be done?" Every step I take toward her, she steps backward, until her butt hits the edge of the conference table and I have her trapped. I'm all she can see, all she can reach out and touch besides the table, which is cold and hard beneath her ass.

And here I am, cold and hard and standing in front of her. Not much difference, really.

"I . . ." She clears her throat. "What do *you* want?"

"I asked first." Reaching out, I give in to my urges and touch her face. Drift my fingers across her cheek, along her jaw, pressing my thumb into her chin. She parts her lips, a shuddery breath escaping her, and I'm tempted to lean in and kiss her.

But I don't.

"You confuse me," she whispers. "I-I don't like you very much sometimes."

Ouch. "I can't blame you."

"But you look at me and I feel . . . I don't know what I feel. And when you touch me . . ." She closes her eyes as I trace her lower lip with my index finger, then her upper lip. She has the most perfect lips I've ever seen, ever touched, ever tasted. "I want you to keep doing it," she confesses softly.

"Keep doing what?" I step in between her legs and press my body to hers, slipping my arm around her waist. I shouldn't do this. I need to show some restraint. The constant back-and-forth between us is confusing. Both to her and to me.

"Touching me. I want to feel your hands on my skin." She tilts her head back when I bend over her and nuzzle her throat. "You breathe on me and I feel like I could go up in flames."

"Like this?" I say just before I exhale along her neck. The whimper that escapes her makes my dick hard and I chuckle, loving every moment. I wield power over this woman and it's a heady feeling. With Pilar, sex always felt like a battle. With other women, it felt like me using their bodies for my selfish pleasure, and then I'd discard them like yesterday's trash.

But with Violet, it feels like . . . more. Like I want to use and keep and possess and mark and fuck until I can't see straight. She consumes me. Confuses me. Exhilarates me.

I hate it.

I want more of it. More of her.

She settles her hands on my shoulders as if she needs to hold on for fear she'll slip to the floor, her fingers gripping me tight. "Just like that," she whispers as she tilts her head to the side, giving me better access.

"Is that all you want?" I brush my nose against her neck, along her ear. She's wearing her hair down, the long, wavy strands tickling my face, and I breathe deep the scent of her shampoo, soaking it in. "Or do you want more?"

"More," she says without hesitation. "So much more."

"We've hardly done anything," I tell her, which is the truth.

"I know." And I can tell she mourns that fact. "But we can't do anything here. Anyone could find us."

"I doubt that." I kiss her, just behind her ear, letting my lips linger before I dart out my tongue to lick at her skin. A shiver moves through her and she tightens her fingers around my shoulders. "I'd give anything to have you sprawled naked on that table," I whisper. "Your legs spread wide open so I can see just how wet you are for me."

"Oh God." She swallows so hard I hear it, and then her hands are scrambling, shoving my suit jacket off my shoulders, down my arms, so I shake it off my arms and let it drop to the floor. "I want to see you."

I haven't stood naked in front of this woman yet and when I do, she's in for a big surprise. But I'm not going to strip completely now. I'm not going to take that big of a risk. "Not yet," I tell her, stepping away from her eager hands. "Have patience."

She adjusts herself so she's sitting on the edge of the conference table, pushing the chairs on either side of her away before she braces her hands on the edge of the marble tabletop. The lusty glow in her eyes is unmistakable, and I wonder if she gets as overcome as I do every time we're in each other's presence.

I'm going to guess by the way she's behaving that's a yes.

Crossing her legs, the skirt of her dress rides up, offering me a tantalizing glimpse of her slender thighs. She notices where my gaze drops and she hikes up her skirt farther, practically to her hips.

"What are you doing?" I ask amusedly.

"Offering myself to you," she answers with no shame. She is definitely acting like a woman possessed and I fucking love it. "You said you wanted to get me naked on the table . . ."

"Violet." The stern note in my voice makes her pause in her movements, her eyes going wide. "I'm not going to fuck you for the first time in this room, on that table."

She looks downright disappointed, my newfound little hussy. "But I thought . . ."

"I'd love to see you naked on the table, most definitely," I continue, cutting her off. "But I want to watch you while you . . ."

"While I what?" she asks eagerly.

"Touch yourself."

Chapter Seventeen

Violet

HE DID NOT JUST ASK ME TO DO THAT . . . DID HE?

Oh yes. He did.

"Ryder . . ." I shake my head, not sure how I can say this. I have never in my life masturbated in front of a man. Not even Zachary, and he was the man I thought I wanted to marry. It never even crossed my mind to share such an incredibly intimate moment like *that* with someone before.

"Are you too shy, Violet?" The tone of his voice tells me he doubts I can go through with it. "Such a shame. I would've loved to see exactly what you do to yourself to make you come, but I guess I won't be so lucky."

And until I heard that daring tone, his slightly condescending words, I would have said there was no way it could ever happen. Not with what played out between us earlier and how angry he made me. Then with the awful news Father delivered to me, which I still haven't fully absorbed, and the gossip that surrounds me, all of it. I've had an exhausting day. One I'd rather forget about altogether.

"Haven't you ever wanted to just let go?" he asks in that same daring tone.

No. I never have. Not until he suggested it. When I'm with Ryder, it's as if I forget myself. Lose my inhibitions, lose all coherent thought, and all I can do is feel. All I *want* to do is feel. Feel him. His hands all over me, his mouth on mine, his lips wrapped around my nipple, his tongue licking against my . . .

"I'm not going to judge your performance," he says. "Think of this as a gift . . . for yourself."

I frown at him, confused.

"And a gift for me," he adds with a small smile.

His words make me realize that touching myself for Ryder, sharing this very intimate act with him, could bring us closer. Could also bring me strength, something I desperately need right now, what with everything else going on in my life.

I hop off the edge of the table and turn so my back is to him. Holding up my hair away from my neck and back, I ask from over my shoulder, "Unzip, please?"

He doesn't hesitate. He doesn't say anything, either, and I wonder if he's preparing himself to be disappointed in me. That my self-consciousness is still determined to defeat me drives me crazy.

I'm going to relish proving him—and myself—wrong.

His warm fingers tug the zipper of my dress down until it stops just at my lower back and he reaches up, skimming his fingers along my exposed skin. I close my eyes and waver on my feet, letting the overwhelming lust I have for this man take over me. His touch feels so good, his nearness, the sound of his breathing, the scent of his cologne . . . it's all too much.

Yet not even close to being enough.

"Thank you," I whisper as I let my hair fall down my back. I open my eyes and stare straight ahead. A little shocked, but my determination wins out and I'm about to shrug out of my dress when he stops me, pushing my hair to the side so he can press his mouth to the back of my neck. His lips are warm and damp and they move across my nape slowly. Seductively. He licks me with his tongue, bites the side of my neck with his sharp teeth, and a shaky breath leaves me at the sting of pain.

I don't want him to ever stop. I'm addicted to his touch, his mouth, his words. The way he commands me, the demands he makes of me. He makes me feel like I'm someone else. A better, stronger version of myself.

"Take the dress off, Violet," he whispers against my neck and I shrug out of it, letting the sleeves fall from my arms and the top drop to my waist, before I shove it from my hips and the beautiful white dress I wore purposely today falls to the floor in a delicate heap at my feet. I step out of it just as I feel his hands brush against the center of my back, his nimble fingers quickly undoing the clasp of my bra.

The nude lace and satin cups loosen around my breasts and his hands rest on my shoulders for the briefest moment before he's pushing at the lacy straps so they drop halfway down my arms. The bra falls away, fluttering to the floor to join the dress, and when he settles his hands on my hips, I know what he's going to do.

He's undressing me. Slowly. Carefully, with very few words, with hardly a sound. His strong fingers curl into the lace waistband of my panties and he tugs, drawing the silky fabric down, past my backside, exposing me to his gaze.

"Beautiful," he whispers as he bends slightly to tug my underwear down my thighs. His fingers brush against my sensitive skin and a little sigh escapes me when I feel myself go damp and fluttery in anticipation.

I want him. I want him to touch me, want his sure fingers to plunge inside my body, his lips and tongue taking me straight to oblivion. I want his hands to grip my hips so hard he leaves bruises. I want him to make me come so hard I see stars . . .

But he doesn't want that. He's demanding something else from me. Something I want to give.

No matter how much it frightens me.

When there's no more clothing for me to remove from my body he turns me around, his hands firm on my shoulders, his gaze direct on my face. He doesn't look down, as if he's afraid somehow he'll offend me, when I want nothing more than his heated gaze on my skin, on the most intimate parts of me. The parts Zachary and the other men I've been with never really seemed to see.

This man may be using me, but he *sees* me. Every single thing that makes me who I am, he notices. And he wants to see more.

"Take off the shoes," he says, and I kick them off, settling to my rather average height of five-foot-four. He towers over me completely since he's well over six feet, and I keep my eyes trained on his, feeling a calming sense of compliance settle over me. I'm letting him be in control and I like it. Prefer it.

"Now I want you to lie on the table," he says, his voice like velvet as he commands me. "Completely back."

I do as he says as he goes to the door, turning the lock into place with a loud snick. A sharp gasp escapes me when my bare butt makes contact with the marble table and I shiver.

"Tell me what you're feeling," he says as he comes back toward the table.

"It's cold against my skin, the marble," I say as I lie down just as he told me to do, my shoulder blades sharp and awkward against the solid surface. My hair spills out everywhere, the marble uncomfortable beneath my head, and I adjust myself as best I can.

"I'm sure." He sounds amused. Of course, he would be. "Spread your legs, Violet."

I widen them without hesitation, savoring the strangled sound he makes when I do. He must see how wet I am, how much I want him. I can smell myself, the heady scent of my sex filling the room, and my skin tingles in anticipation of what I'm about to do.

"Scoot backward," he urges, getting me into position so he can see me better, I presume. "Bend your legs at the knees."

He settles into a chair right in front of me, and I prop myself on my elbows so I can see him. The lascivious expression on his face as he studies me between my legs fills me with such power I almost feel dizzy. He wants me. He wants to touch me.

But he won't.

"Are you brave enough to do it?" he asks as he leans back in his chair, his startling blue gaze meeting mine. "Or will you chicken out?"

He knows just what to say to both infuriate me and make me want to prove him wrong. "Watch and see," I say, hoping I don't sound as nervous as I feel.

I push the nerves aside and lie completely flat against the table, giving up on getting comfortable. I stare up at the ceiling and blow out a long, steadying breath, close my eyes, and count to five.

Showtime.

Keeping my eyes closed, I touch my breasts, cup their heavy weight in my palms, brushing my thumbs over my nipples. Once, twice, feeling them harden. I don't say a word and neither does he, and I'm fine with that. More than fine with that, because I don't want to say something stupid and ruin the moment.

I pinch one nipple lightly between my thumb and index finger, biting my lip to keep the little moan from escaping me when I feel the pleasurable pain shoot through me, and he notices. He notices everything.

"Don't hold back," he murmurs in encouragement. "I want to hear you."

Ah God, he says things like that and I want to attack him. Demand that he be the one who brings me pleasure, not my own fingers.

But there's pleasure to be found by letting him watch and I remember that, envisioning his handsome face captivated with me touching my breasts, circling my nipples, pinching them both at the same time so that the sharp gasp that fills the room is completely unrestrained.

I run my hands along my waist and hips, across my stomach, the light touch of my fingertips making goose bumps rise. A click sounds and a rush of cool air from the vents in the ceiling bathes my skin, making me shiver, making my nipples harden almost painfully, and I soothe them with my warm palms, clasping my hands over my breasts for a moment.

"Cold?" he asks.

I nod but say nothing, dropping my hands from my breasts and resting them on top of my thighs. My heart is racing so hard I swear he can probably see it pound against my chest, and I press my lips together, searching for the strength to finish this.

Can I do it? Touch myself in front of him, do all the little tricks I know to bring myself to orgasm? It's never as satisfying with my own hand, not usually. More like a quick relief, a way for me to release some tension before I go to sleep. A vibrator brings me the longer, fuller body orgasms, yet compared to Ryder's mouth? His fingers?

They're in a league all their own.

"Touch yourself."

His voice urges me on and I slide my hands to my inner thighs and stroke languidly, teasing myself. That's half the buildup, the tease. The quick, featherlike strokes, the barely there caresses, all of it increases the throb between my legs until it's all I can focus on, and I let my right hand drift until my fingers graze the thin strip of pubic hair that covers my mound.

My body jerks at first touch, and I'm shocked that I can elicit such a reaction out of myself. That usually only happens when someone else touches me, not by my own hand . . .

I'm spread wide open, so there's no being coy here. I touch myself blatantly, streaking my fingers down my wet center, pressing my finger into the middle of my folds. They're slick with my juices, I can hear my fingers as I search myself, circling my fingertips lightly, stroking over my clit.

"Jesus, you're wet," he says, his voice hoarse.

Triumph surges through me and I arch my back, eager to give him more of a show. He sounds as if he's in absolute agony and I love it. Thrive on it. I prop my feet flat on the table and thrust a finger deep inside my body, then two fingers, but that's not what really gets me off. I'm doing this for his benefit. I'm putting on a show just for him.

"Do you like that?" he asks, sounding genuinely curious. "Fucking yourself with your fingers?"

"I'd rather have your fingers inside me," I tell him breathlessly.

"I'm sure." His voice deepens and I hear the chair creak as he shifts. "Show me what you like."

"I am." I press my thumb against my clit, remembering how he did the same to me last night, and a tiny but powerful shudder moves through my body.

"Do you ever touch yourself while you're alone in bed?" he asks, and I nod my answer. "Then show me how you get off, Violet. Make yourself come for me. That's what I want to see."

I withdraw my fingers from my body and slide them up, over my clit. It's swollen and tingly, indicating I'm already close, which is like a miracle. It usually takes me long minutes before I'm even near orgasm, but this moment has everything to do with Ryder watching me and nothing else.

Increasing my pace, I circle my clit again and again, rubbing it faster, feeling the rush rise within me. I squeeze my eyes closed tight and lift my hips, my fingers working furiously over my clit, the sound of my heavy breathing joining with Ryder's, and then I'm coming. The orgasm wracks my body with uncontrollable shaking and I cry out, the throb and pulse of my clit, of my empty inner walls, making me wish I could experience this climax with him inside of me.

But I guess I'll settle for the next best thing. The man himself, sitting in front of me, watching me masturbate.

This is truly by far the craziest thing I've ever done.

I'm lying on the table with one arm draped over my eyes, trying to catch my breath, when I feel his fingers grip my ankles and his breath tickles my sex. And then his mouth is there, licking and sucking, his lips latching onto my clit, driving me into another orgasm that bolts through me like a streak of lightning, hot and quick and a flash of white that sends me spiraling completely out of control.

His mouth leaves my sex and then he's tugging on my hands, pulling me into a sitting position so he can wrap his arms around my waist. I circle his hips with my legs and press against him, feeling his hard, hot length strain against his trousers. He kisses me, his mouth ravaging mine, his lips and tongue tasting like me, and I revel in it. Kiss him hungrily, like I'm starved for him, which I am.

"That was so fucking hot," he breathes against my lips. "I couldn't resist tasting you."

I wrap my arms around his neck, my fingers in his soft, silky hair as I kiss him slowly. Deeply. "I want you," I whisper after I break the kiss.

He moves against me, slow and sensuous, driving me crazy. "How bad?"

"I'll show you."

Ryder thrusts against me again. "Not here. Not now."

I withdraw from him completely at his words, letting him see the pout on my face. Frustration replaces my arousal. I don't want him to deprive me. My body is on fire for him. I just had two orgasms and I still don't feel satisfied. "Then when?"

"Soon. Tonight." He brushes the hair away from my cheek, tucking it behind my ear. His beautiful lips are curved in a slight smile and I drink him in, savoring his every handsome feature. I've never really looked at him this closely before, but now I don't hold back. I reach up and touch his cheek, drift my fingers down until I'm caressing the strong line of his jaw, tracing his lips with my index finger, fascinated with what I see, what I feel. His stubble-roughened cheeks scratch and I lean up the slightest bit, settling my mouth on his.

But he breaks the kiss first, his hands going to my shoulders as if he somehow needs the distance, and I can't help the hurt that I feel.

"Why do you push me away?" I hate hearing the sadness in my voice.

"Because you need to get dressed. What if your father comes looking for you?"

"He won't." I lean in to kiss him again but he presses his fingers against my lips, stopping me.

"What about Zachary?" he asks.

Ugh. He's the last person I want to talk about after what just happened. "What about him?" I ask, hating how snippy I sound.

"Just . . . we need to be careful," he says as he steps away from me to bend down and grab his suit jacket. He shakes it out, then slips it on, and I watch him, admiring the way his biceps strain against his stark white shirt, the width of his shoulders, the breadth of his chest. "I don't need any more run-ins with him."

I don't answer him, embarrassment reminding me that I'm completely naked while Ryder is completely dressed. He hands me my panties and bra and I take them from him, keeping my eyes downcast as I murmur my thanks. Pushing off the table, I slip on my panties and hook my bra on, standing straight to find Ryder holding my dress in his hands, his expression apologetic.

For whatever reason that look on his face makes me angry, and I snatch my dress from his fingers and turn my back on him, pulling the dress on. I reach behind me, trying to zip it up and not able to do it and I let out a low growl of frustration, wondering why the hell I can't do it now when I had no problem earlier this morning. *God.*

Why am I angry? Why do I want him one minute and loathe

him the next? I don't understand. My emotions are so screwed up, I'm half tempted to cry.

And also tempted to yell and scream and kick.

"Let me help," he says, his big hands settling on my lower back, electrifying me even through the fabric of my dress. I remain still as he tugs the zipper up, his fingers blazing a path of heat as he skims them along my bared skin. "There." He shoves my hair aside, flipping it over my shoulder, and pulls the zipper all the way to the top. "You're in."

"Thank you," I murmur, keeping my gaze focused on the floor. I hate how awkward I feel, how unsure. What do I say next? What do I do? What does he want from me? I know what I want from him despite my irritation, but does he want the same?

I turn to face him, see that his lips are parted and he looks like he wants to say something. But my cell rings from where it sits on the conference table, the sound shrill in the stillness of the room and stopping him from speaking. He reaches for my phone and hands it to me, his expression grim.

Zachary's name flashes across the screen.

"Hello." I answer the phone in front of Ryder because I have nothing to hide. I gave up the very last shred of my humiliation when I just fingered myself in front of him, so who am I to be shy any longer?

"Have dinner with me," Zachary says, so loudly I know Ryder can hear him.

He steps away from me, crossing his thick arms in front of his chest, his expression thunderous. Sexy.

"I don't think that would be a good idea," I start, but Zachary cuts me off, his irritation clear.

"I don't want to hear any of your excuses, Violet. This is stupid, us pretending we don't want to be together. I'm in New York for ten more days and then I'm gone. To London." His voice lowers. "I wanted to spend these last days with you."

"You ruined that when you let Pilar suck your dick," I say vehemently, refusing to feel guilty for our breakup. I wasn't the one who destroyed us, he was. "Go find one of your whores to spend your last days with," I retort, angry all over again at the idea of Zachary messing around with other women. How many have there been over the years? Five? Ten? Twenty?

"Are we still talking about that?" He sounds incredulous.

"We will always be talking about that. There's no escaping it, because your other women are a fact. Your wandering eye ruined our relationship."

"No, you fucking around with Ryder McKay is what's ruining our relationship, Violet." He pauses, as if he needed to gather his thoughts. "You win, okay? You got your revenge on me by being with another man. I get why you wanted to do this. The idea of us being together forever . . . I'm sure it's scary. You wanted to make sure you were making the right decision."

The gall of this man is unbelievable. "You think I'm just sampling other goods before I go back to you?" Ryder's dark brows rise at my question.

"You know we belong together." His voice is firm. He thinks I won't argue. He thinks I'll come back to him and eventually become his docile wife.

He's completely delusional.

I can't even bother to argue any longer. I simply hang up the phone and set it on the table, right next to my iPad. I need to gather up my things and go back to my office. Put everything away and go home. I can't take this day any longer.

It's like everyone's trying to break me.

Chapter Eighteen

Ryder

SHE FLED THE CONFERENCE ROOM AFTER HER RIDICULOUS CON-versation with Lawrence, not revealing much, though I could hear him over the phone. Smug bastard thinks he can snap his fingers and she'll come running back to him. That she's just using me as a distraction. *In his dreams.*

I suggested she use me, but I never meant for her to go back to that asshole. He's the worst thing for her.

I'm no better.

I remain in my office though it's past five on a Friday after-noon and everyone's cleared out. The spring weather makes ev-eryone antsy for the weekend and normally I'm just as eager as the rest of them to get the hell out of here, but not today. All I can think about is Violet.

Sprawled naked on top of the black marble table, her skin so pale, watching as she skimmed her curves with trembling hands. The sounds of her creamy pussy as she touched herself, the way she arched her back, how overcome I'd been watching her fall apart that I'd taken over. Making her come again with my tongue and mouth in a matter of seconds.

Christ, I'm hard just remembering it.

The push and pull between us is ridiculous. I infuriate her and ignite her all at once. She's not made me angry once. There's no reason. Frustrated? Yes. She inflames me. Makes me want things I should never, ever consider.

Like her.

Deciding to hell with it, I grab my cell and send her a quick text asking if she's okay, needing to make that contact, hoping she'll answer me. Is she really all right? Or worse . . . is she with Lawrence?

I push my hands through my hair and clutch the back of my head with a growl. *Fuck*. I can't stand the thought of that bastard touching her.

I'm fine. Thank you for your concern.

I stare at her answer, wanting to laugh. Wanting to ask her why the hell she's so damn polite all the time. Instead I type out another text, deciding to cut to the chase.

Are you with your ex?

God no.

Her reply is quick and fills me with relief. I expel a breath, realizing I was holding it, and I grimace, shaking my head at myself. I need to get to the sex part. I don't care about her. Not really. I can't.

I'm still thinking of what happened earlier.

She doesn't respond for so long I become agitated, doubting myself for sending that text. When the hell do I ever second-guess myself? Grabbing a pen, I tap it against the edge of my desk, the rhythmic sound loud and grating on my nerves. I don't stop, though. It's as if I can't.

What exactly are you thinking about?

I drop my pen and pick up the phone with both hands, my thumbs flying over the keys as I answer her.

You. Naked. Spread out on the table. With your fingers in your pussy as you fuck yourself.

Smiling, I set the phone down and wait for her to reply. More than curious to see what she'll say because I've just raised the bar in this text exchange.

Knowing you watched made me hot.

My smile fades. I'm hot right now. Hell, sweat is forming on my skin.

Watching you made me fucking hot.

A minute passes. Then another. The longest two minutes of my life.

I know.

She surprises me. I really didn't think she had it in her. I knew I would have fun playing with Violet, but I didn't think it would be this much fun.

I want to watch you again.

God, I do. So bad it's killing me.

Let's forget about watching and move on to doing.

A chuckle escapes me. Fuck this texting crap. I'm calling her direct.

"You wanted to hear my voice?" she says in answer after picking up on the third ring. Making me wait, smart girl.

Another laugh escapes me. "You're feeling rather bold."

"I'm tired of being meek."

And now I'm intrigued. "How so?"

"Just . . . come over. To my place." She sighs, the sound soft. Wistful. It goes straight to my dick, making me hard. Making me ache. For her. "I need to forget."

"Forget what?" *Forget your troubles? Forget Lawrence? Forget everything but you and me?*

"Just . . . today was awful. But you coming over will make it a lot better." She sounds the slightest bit defeated and I don't like that. Don't want to be the cause of her sadness, either.

"Awful, huh?" I lean back in my chair, picking up the pen again and tapping it against my bent knee. "Even in the conference room?"

Her voice lowers, soft and sweet. "That was my favorite part of the day."

"Mine, too." I lean forward, tossing the pen on my desk so

it rolls away and lands on the floor with a plop. "I can make it better."

"That's what I'm counting on."

"Give me your address."

"I'll text it to you."

"What time should I come over?"

"How soon can you get here?"

No pretense, no bullshit. She wants me. I want her.

And I'm going to have her.

"Give me an hour, tops," I say, then hang up.

I'm gathering up my stuff, shutting down everything, when my cell dings, announcing the text with her address. I turn out the lights and lean against the door frame, letting her know what I want from her when I get there.

Wear something sexy.

Any specific requests?

Surprise me.

THE SECURITY AT HER BUILDING IS LIKE FORT KNOX, AND IT'S touch-and-go for a moment while I endure the doorman's scrutiny. He looks like he wants to frisk me as he puts in a call to Violet, his expression stern, his mouth a thin line as he nods and offers a mumbled, "Yes, ma'am," after everything she says. I wait behind the counter, glancing around the sleek, modern lobby, everything white and chrome and accented with hints of black.

Sterile and cold. So not Violet's style.

"You have permission from Miss Fowler to go up," the doorman says after he hangs up the phone, glaring at me. I love how he says the word *permission*. I wonder if he's a former prison guard. "I need you to fill this out first, though."

He shoves a clipboard toward me with a check-in sheet attached to it. I grab the pen he offers and scribble out my name, impatient that I have to go through so many steps to get to Violet. I'm anxious. Dealing with a grumpy doorman won't spoil my mood, though.

I'm eager to fuck. It's been days. A few weeks, even. I've jacked off countless times. Received a most excellent blow job from Violet. Got her off a few times, but I still haven't fucked her. Still haven't got my cock inside that hot little body.

Un-fucking-believable.

The doorman leads me to the elevator, keying in a pass code with his back to me so I can't see it. *Jackass*. The doors swoosh open and he inclines his head toward me. "Have a nice evening, Mr. McKay."

The moment the doors close I'm texting her. Because it's fun—do I even know how to have fun? Because I can hardly wait to see her, not that I would ever admit that fact to anyone. I feel like a teenage kid, though not the teenager of my past, since I was a holy terror. I didn't anxiously await girls and dates and all that other typical crap.

I fucked. I drank. I stole. I fought. I did drugs. I was awful. A nightmare.

Yet for whatever reason, this perfect, demure, sexy-as-hell woman wants me.

Me.

Your doorman is like a guard dog, I type and then hit SEND.

I pay a lot of money for the added security. And he's very protective of me.

I can see why.

Damn it, I shouldn't have said that. Now she'll think I actually . . . care about her or something. I need to switch gears quick.

I hope you're ready for me.

Ready for what?

My hard cock.

OMG, you're bad.

She has no idea.

You like it.

Smiling, I glance up to see that the elevator has stopped, the *P* button lit. She lives on the top floor, the penthouse level.

Swank.

I exit the elevator and find myself in a short hallway with only one door. I knock on it and wait, my head tilted forward so I can hear her approach. She takes awhile, making me wait, making me yearn, and I can't help but wonder which one of us is getting played here.

Her?

Or me?

The door opens just a sliver and she peeks her head out, a gentle smile curving her naturally pink lips. Her hair is pulled back into a high ponytail, her face is bare, and she's never looked prettier. "Hi," she says shyly.

"Hi." I take a step closer, her floral fragrance hitting me, making me inhale sharply. *Damn,* she smells good. "You going to let me in?"

"Are you ready?"

I cock a brow. "Shouldn't I be asking you that?"

Her smile grows. "I have a surprise for you."

"Really?" The anticipation is killing me. This girl knows how to work it. "Why don't you let me in and show it to me."

"I can show it to you now. If you'd like," she adds, her expression coy. There are so many facets to this woman and I feel like I've only just scratched the surface.

I'm dying to go deeper, in more ways than one.

"Show me," I demand, my voice gruff, my patience thin.

Slowly she opens the door, revealing that she's . . .

Completely naked.

"I took a shower," she explains, her hand still gripping the door handle. Her voice is slightly shaky, revealing her nerves, but her body . . . *Jesus*. She's all tits and legs and curves and almost bare pussy, that thin little strip of pubic hair leading straight to paradise. My skin tightens, my cock grows heavy, and all I can think about is fucking her. Now. "And I figured it would be a waste of time if I got dressed."

"You got that right," I practically growl as I shove my way into her apartment, slamming the door behind me. I grab hold of her waist and turn, taking her with me so I can press her against the door. "Wrap your legs around me," I command, and she does it without hesitation, those long, sexy legs going around my waist at the same time she drapes her arms around my neck. I can feel the scorching heat of her pussy against the front of my jeans and I push my hips forward, indicating just how hard I am for her.

"You feel good," she whispers as I thrust against her again, her eyelids fluttering when I hit her in a particular spot with the seam of my jeans. "You look good, too."

"You don't look so bad yourself," I murmur just before I give her a brief kiss. A torment because all I crave is the taste of her lips, the feel of her tongue. "Tell me you have lots of condoms."

"I have an entire box in my bedroom." She rubs her breasts against my chest and I can feel her hard nipples poke through the thin fabric of my long-sleeved T-shirt. When she presses her face to my neck and kisses me there, I close my eyes. Squeeze her lush ass cheeks in my palms, spreading her wide and making her whimper. "M-maybe I should go grab one now?" she asks shakily.

"I shouldn't fuck you for the first time against the door." She drops one of her hands to my hips, her fingers sliding beneath my T-shirt to touch my stomach. "But I have a condom in my back pocket."

"Always prepared." The devious smile that flashes across her face as she skims her fingers across my abs tells me she's enjoying this. "And maybe I *want* you to fuck me against the door." *Jesus*.

Does she know how much she fascinates me? I'm curious to see how she'll react when I take off my shirt and she sees me for who I really am.

Or was.

No, still am. I may class it up with a suit and tie every day and work an executive position where I make a shit ton of money I never thought I'd see in this lifetime, but I can't forget my roots. No matter how badly I want to.

"Take off your shirt," she whispers, her fingers tugging up on the hem. "I want to feel your skin on mine."

Damn. Her words are driving me wild. "You ready for this?"

"What? How bad can it be? You have a third nipple or something?" She laughs, enjoying the tease, but I remain solemn, pressing my lower body against hers so I can pin her to the door, and slowly, I remove my shirt and toss it to the ground.

Revealing the tattoos that decorate my upper body and the silver rings that pierce my nipples.

Her eyes widen in fascination and they roam all over me, moving fast, as if they don't know where to land first. Other women have reacted this way. Countless times. They proclaim my tattoos are hot and my piercings sexy. That's not what they're about, though. I didn't do any of this for any woman, not even Pilar. The tattoos represent moments in my life, moments I didn't want to forget no matter how difficult they were to endure.

And the piercings? I had those done when I was seventeen and stupid. To prove I could withstand the pain. To show I was some sort of badass, or so I thought.

Only later did they come into play sexually. Sometimes. Pilar has never cared much about them. She prefers I fuck her from behind anyway, so whatever.

"I had no idea you were hiding all this," Violet whispers, her hand going to my shoulder, where a giant blue and red and orange dragon breathes fire across my chest. "It's beautiful. So intricate." Funny how she chose my favorite tattoo, the one that represents me. Breathing fire, destroying my old life, burning it to ashes.

Her fingers flutter up my arm, along my collarbone, over my pec, barely touching my nipple ring. "I just . . ."

"You just what?" If she says she's disgusted by the tattoos, my dick will deflate so fast it'll be some sort of record. That I need her approval is fucking ridiculous. I have never cared before what a woman thought of my body art. I am who I am, and fuck who doesn't get it.

But I can't stand the thought of Violet not liking the tattoos or the piercings. She's as elegant as they come. You look up *class* in the dictionary and you'd probably see a photo of Violet.

If you looked up *trash* in the dictionary, you'd probably find a photo of sixteen-year-old sullen-as-hell me.

"I've never seen so much colorful work up close before." She lifts her gaze to mine, her finger gently tugging on one of my nipple rings. "Does that . . . hurt?"

"It hurt when I got it." Like a motherfucker, though I gritted my teeth and acted like it was no big deal.

"Does it hurt when I pull on it now?" She tugs a little harder, the tip of her finger brushing my nipple.

"It feels good," I whisper just before I kiss her, moaning against her lips when she curls her finger around the ring and pulls. Again. A shock wave of sensation streams through me, straight to my dick, but I keep our kiss languid, searching her mouth with my tongue as if we have all the time in the world, which we do.

And I'm going to savor every fucking second of this night with Violet. Make it good for her.

Make it good for me.

"Later," she murmurs against my lips when I break the kiss, "I'm going to ask for an explanation behind every single tattoo you have."

"And I'll give you one." I kiss her again, my tongue circling hers, teeth nipping at her lower lip. "Much later. But first . . ."

"But first," she agrees, laughing against my lips just before I take hers again in a consuming kiss that goes hot and deep in an instant.

She grinds against me and I slip my hand in between us to find her wet and so fucking ready. I slip a finger deep inside her and pump. Once. Twice. Leaning back so I can watch her. She drops her head back against the door, her eyes closed, her mouth slack. I press her clit and she sinks her teeth into her lower lip, lifting her hips against me, trying to deepen the contact.

"You're getting my jeans wet," I tell her. She's beyond primed, grinding her pussy on my fly, rubbing against my dick like some sort of horny teenager.

I fucking love it.

"Take them off, then," she whispers and I don't hesitate, tearing at the button fly so that the denim sags around my hips.

She opens her eyes, her gaze dropping to my lower body and warming with approval. "You're not wearing any underwear."

"Neither are you." I reach inside the back pocket of my jeans and grab a condom, then shove them so they fall to my feet. I'm so eager to get inside her I don't bother undressing completely. I'm fucking her here. Now. I didn't want to do it like this our first time, but fuck it.

I want her too damn bad.

Violet reaches for the condom wrapper and tears it open, withdrawing the little ring. I watch with fascination as her sure fingers place it at the tip of my dick and she rolls the condom on, her fingers stroking, making my cock twitch. She wraps her hand tightly around my erection and strokes, her gaze lifting to meet mine, and I kiss her again. Devour her.

"Later," she says when she breaks away from my seeking mouth, repeating what she said only a few moments ago, "I'm going to suck your cock until you come down my throat."

Jesus. I never thought I'd hear Violet Fowler say *that.*

"Yeah?" I smash my hips to hers the moment her hand falls away from my cock and I wrap my fingers around the base, guiding it toward her body's entrance. "Later I plan on tasting that sweet pussy again and making you come on my tongue."

"Promise?" she says, a little moan escaping her when I push just the tip of my cock inside her tight, wet heat.

"Fuck yeah," I mutter, breathing deep, trying to control myself so I don't just slam inside of her and take her like I'm some sort of overbearing grunt.

I bet Lawrence did that to her. Probably didn't care about her orgasm, probably didn't think about her pleasure. Jealousy tears at me, making me see red, and I slowly push inside, ready to erase her memory of every single time that asshole had his dick inside of her. Until all she can remember, all she can think about, is me.

Me.

Chapter Nineteen

Violet

HE'S HUGE AND FILLING ME SO COMPLETELY, I HAVE TO TAKE A deep breath and release it slowly for my body to accommodate his thick length. I wrap my arms tight around his neck and press my mouth against his smooth, hard shoulder. Kissing him there. Sinking my teeth into his flesh until I hear him hiss out a harsh breath in response.

I'm completely surrounded by Ryder. He's wrapped all around me, inside me, his mouth at my forehead, his cock throbbing within my body. Cautiously, he starts to move, pulling almost all the way out before he pushes back inside, and I close my eyes, savoring the pleasure of him filling me.

"Feels amazing. Fucking you," he murmurs against my forehead before he slips his fingers beneath my chin and tilts my face up so I have to look at him. "Tell me, Violet. Tell me what you feel."

"Good. You're so big," I say obediently, loving when he commands me. Sex with Zachary was nothing like this. Nothing. Sex with the other men I've been with was nothing like this either. I feel like Ryder casts me under some sort of magical spell where I have no choice but to do as he says.

I'm starting to realize there's nothing wrong with letting a man control me sexually, as long as I demand my satisfaction in return.

"So quiet and proper at the office," he says, his deep voice sending goose bumps scattering all over my skin. I lift away from him, pressing my back against the door, and he touches my throat with his fingers, lightly at first, and then with more pressure. As if he's holding me captive. Fear flutters in my belly as my gaze meets his and I see the lust there. The heat. All of it aimed directly at me. "And such a wicked little tease when you're alone with me."

Should I be insulted by his words? Somehow . . . I'm not. They send a fresh wave of arousal through me, and my inner walls contract around his cock. "Only for you," I whisper.

His eyes flare with an unknown emotion and he leans in, his mouth close to mine, his fingers still locked around my throat. His cock fills me so completely, his hips pressed to mine. We're chest to chest, my legs around his hips, ankles digging into his firm backside. "Really?"

I nod, unsure of how he wants me to respond, what would please him. A shaky breath escapes me and he releases his grip on my throat, his fingers drifting across my sensitive skin, teasing at the spot where my pulse beats rapidly. "No one else," I say, my voice firm, my gaze direct, "makes me feel like you do."

He goes completely still, his eyes hard, his normally full mouth firming into a thin line. He slips his hand around my nape and kisses me, his tongue brutal as he tangles it with mine, his body mimicking the movements of his mouth.

This isn't what I would call gentle lovemaking. Far from it. He fucks me brutally, thrusting into me again and again, so hard my body knocks against the door with his every push. He goes deep. Deeper. I watch with fascination as he takes me, his every muscle strained, his eyes sliding closed, a low grunt leaving him with every twitch of his hips.

I run my hands down his sweat-dampened, thick-muscled chest, absorbing those beautiful, fascinating tattoos. The revelation of his body surprised me. Pleased me. And the nipple rings . . .

They intrigue me.

Smoothing my palms over his pecs, I curl my index fingers into each hoop and pull, causing his eyes to fly open. He stares at me, presses his mouth to mine in a simple kiss before he whispers against my lips, "Harder."

I do as he says, pulling the rings harder, bending toward him so I can run my mouth down the length of his taut neck. He reaches between us and circles my clitoris, making me cry out, the double sensations of him filling my body and playing with my clit driving me wild.

"Ryder." I gasp out his name as he shoves himself deep. I pull at the rings, open my mouth against his neck, and succumb to the orgasm that comes barreling down upon me. I shake in his arms, my mouth still on his neck, my legs quaking around his hips. He thrusts hard and stills, my name falling from his lips as his own climax completely overtakes him.

We stand there, our bodies connected, my back against the door, for long, quiet moments as our breathing evens out and the shudders slowly leave our bodies. My heart races and I take deep, calming breaths. Clinging to him, our sweat-covered bodies sticky, his still hard cock inside my body, pulsing deep within me.

"Are you . . ." He clears his throat and I lift away from him. "Are you okay?"

I nod and smile, reaching up to smooth his damp hair away from his forehead. The swarm of conflicting emotions that washes over me makes me want to be tender with him. Why, I'm not sure. "That was . . ."

"Yeah." He withdraws from me and I disentangle myself from him, wondering at his quiet mood. With care he settles me on my feet, then withdraws quickly, his gaze not meeting mine. As if he can't look at me. "Where's a bathroom?"

I give him directions and he makes his escape, leaving me a jittery mess still leaning against the door. I don't know what to do. Since I answered the door naked, I have no clothes to pick up and throw back on as armor. And with the sudden odd way he's behaving, I'm feeling the need for protection. Should I just go back to my bedroom and tell him to meet me there?

Before I can make a decision, he's back and I figure he disposed of the condom. I admire his perfect masculine body and all the tattoos, drinking him in, imagining all the many ways I could kiss him everywhere. Touch him . . .

Instead I watch in mild horror as he keeps his gaze averted while he grabs his jeans and tugs them back on, then offers me a tight smile. His expression is bland, the cool, mysterious Ryder McKay back in place of the savage, aggressive man who just fucked me senseless with my name falling from his lips only moments ago.

"I, uh, I need to go." He dips down and grabs his shirt and pulls it over his head, all of the colorful artwork disappearing from view. He rakes his fingers through his messy hair, trying to tame it, but there's no use.

There's no use for him. There's no use for us. I don't know how it happened, but I feel the distance grow between us with every second that passes. He's shut himself down completely and I have no idea who or what I'm dealing with.

Blinking, I stare at him as if he's sprouted two heads, because that's how it feels. "You have to go?"

He gives me a look, one that says *stupid, overconfident Violet*. "You thought I would spend the night with you?"

I straighten, insulted at his tone and his words. "Of course not. I just figured it's still early . . ."

"I need to go." He offers no explanation and I know I don't deserve one, but that doesn't mean I don't want one.

I step away from the door as he goes to it, resting his hand on the handle. Slowly he turns to look at me and for a brief moment, I see a flash of regret in his gaze. As if he doesn't want to leave me but he's making himself do it for whatever reason.

I cling to that hint of emotion I see. Probably too tightly, but I can't help myself.

"Have a good weekend," he murmurs, before he opens the door and exits my apartment.

Irritated, I go to the door and wrench the lock into place with a sharp twist of my wrist, letting forth an irritated sound. What the hell was that? He fucks me against the door, makes me come so hard, and then leaves? After all this talk of plenty of condoms and what we're going to do to each other later?

The disappointment that settles over me can't be helped. I feel like I lost this battle. A battle I didn't even realize I was engaged in.

Doesn't mean I've lost the war, though.

"Men." Lily twirls her straw in her Bloody Mary before taking a sip. "I hate them."

I can't stand Bloody Marys because I hate tomato juice, so I can hardly look at my sister as she drinks it. "I agree," I say, lifting my Bellini in agreement before I down it.

We're at Sunday brunch but it's past noon, so I don't know if that's what you call it. Rose is supposed to meet us, but she's running late. Lily looks hung over, and she claims the only cure is a Bloody Mary. I beg to differ but don't protest.

Last night I opened my laptop and tried to do a search on Alan Brown, but that first glimpse of his sneering face sitting at the defense table during his trial made me immediately shut the computer with a sharp snap, chills racing over my skin. I haven't thought of him in so long that seeing him again takes me right back.

I can't even mention any of this to my sisters. I don't want to upset them. Bad enough how upset I am.

"Still mourning the loss of Zachary?" Lily makes a face.

Will I sound like a complete slut if I admit to my sister that I screwed another man only days after breaking up with my long-term boyfriend? And that his seeming rejection after the hottest sex of my life hurts far worse than my breakup with Zachary? My life has turned into a freaking soap opera. I feel like I'm completely unraveling and no one will be able to put me back together.

Save, possibly, for Ryder McKay.

Yeah. I sound like a total slut, wanting a man I barely know, who fucks me until I can't see straight, then leaves with barely a word. But I'd do it all over again in a second.

Seriously. What is wrong with me?

"It's not Zachary," I admit, catching Lily's wholehearted attention. "I . . . I messed around with another guy Friday night and it ended badly."

"What? As in you didn't have an orgasm? Be glad you got rid of him." Lily waves a hand, dismissing him.

"Oh, I had one." My cheeks heat. I don't talk about orgasms with my sisters. I didn't talk about them with anyone until I met Ryder. "But he got weird on me and left."

"One-night stand?" Lily shakes her head and makes a *tsk*ing noise. "Welcome to my world."

I knew I shouldn't have talked about Ryder with her. She wouldn't understand. I don't understand either, so how can I expect her to?

"Work has been stressful, too," I say, gladly changing the subject. "Putting together the packaging for my makeup line has been taking up all of my time."

"Right. Seeing that sexy guy who's heading the project up is such a hardship," Lily says casually, smiling at the waiter as he brings us the shrimp appetizer she ordered.

And we've somehow circled back to Ryder. "He's all right," I say with a shrug, not wanting to give myself away.

"He's more than all right—I think Violet's doing him." Rose appears at our table out of nowhere, wearing a giant grin that I want to smear right off her face. She settles into the chair next to mine and nudges my shoulder with hers. "Tell me you're having a torrid affair with Ryder McKay. Let me live through you."

"Wait a minute." Lily gapes at me. "Is he the guy you were referring to?"

My cheeks feel like they're on fire. "I don't want to talk about it," I mumble.

"We're definitely talking about it. You just got a lot more interesting," Lily says, reminding me yet again that I'm the boring, dutiful sister while she's the wild child constantly in trouble.

"Supposedly Ryder and Zachary are fighting over her," Rose says gleefully. "And at the collaboration party a few nights ago, they messed around in a closet and Zachary caught them. She told me so herself."

Lily reaches across the tiny table and shoves at my shoulder. I flinch away from her with a muttered *"ow,"* rubbing at my arm. I had no idea she's so strong. "Are you freaking serious? I was there with you that night! And you were out getting busy in a closet with some hot guy? Sounds more like something I'd do, not you, Violet."

If I could evaporate into a misty cloud right this minute I would do so, I'm so embarrassed. "It was nothing." Those three words are becoming my standard answer for what's happening between Ryder and me. Especially after Friday night. Talk about nothing. He dismissed me as if I didn't matter.

So why did that moment against the door feel like everything?

My phone sounds from within my purse and I reach for it, pulling it out to check for messages, new emails, whatever. Anything to change the direction of our conversation. But Rose is still chattering on about how hot Ryder is and Lily is eating up every word she says with rapt fascination. I think I've shocked them.

I know I've shocked myself, so I guess I shouldn't be surprised.

What surprises me even more? That I have a text from the very man my sisters are talking about.

I'm an asshole.

He's certainly correct about that.

Yes, I type. You definitely are.

I hit SEND and wait for his answer, which is immediate.

I hate what happened Friday night.

Regret sinks in my stomach like a stone.

I shouldn't have left you like that.

And just like that, a glimmer of hope fills me.

No regrets. We're just using each other, remember?

The words look a lot harsher than they sounded a few days ago.

"Who are you texting?" Lily asks.

"No one important," I mumble, cupping my hands around my phone so Rose can't see. Not that she cares. She's too busy chattering on about Ryder.

It doesn't feel like that anymore. At least to me.

I stare at his words, dumbfounded. How do I reply without having it thrown back in my face? I say or do the wrong thing and he runs. Look at how he reacted after we had sex! He acted like being with me was the absolute last thing he wanted to do. I finally respond.

I don't know what it feels like. All I know is that I'm confused.

Confused about what?

You. And me.

What are you doing right now?

Having lunch with my sisters.

I want to see you.

Now?

Yeah. I need to make up for what I did to you.

And how do you suppose you can do that?

By keeping you naked and satisfied for the rest of
the day and long into the night?

Crossing my legs, I squeeze my thighs together, trying to stave off the need his words light within me.

"I have to go," I say to Rose and Lily, sounding wooden. Like a robot. I've completely disengaged from my sisters. All I can think about is Ryder. Being alone with him. Touching him. Stripping him naked and running my lips all over his skin. Sucking one of those nipple rings into my mouth.

Oh, God. My panties dampen at the image.

"Where are you going?" Rose asks.

"A, uh, work emergency has come up. Some sort of color issue for the new line." The lie comes easily and I'm almost ashamed of it.

Rose studies me, trying to figure out if I'm telling the truth or not. I never lie about stuff like this. But there are a lot of things I never did before, until I became involved with Ryder.

"You didn't even get to eat." Lily pushes the plate of sautéed shrimp toward me. "Have a couple before you leave."

I grab one and pop it into my mouth, chewing quickly before I swallow. *Great.* Now I'll have weird shrimp garlic breath when I see Ryder. I need some gum. Or to make time to brush my teeth before we see each other.

Crap. I'm getting ahead of myself. I never even responded to him. And when I check my phone, I see he kept on texting me.

Violet?

Can you get away from your sisters soon?

I can understand if you don't want to see me.

I fucked up.

I'm sorry.

I stare at the five messages he left me in the time span of about three minutes, and the rush of happiness that threatens to take over me is ridiculous. Those texts make me think he cares.

Foolish. But true.

Meet me at my place in an hour? I say in response.

He waits a few beats before he replies.

I'll be there.

"I gotta go," I repeat, grabbing my purse and slinging it over my shoulder. I ignore my sisters' protests, ignore everything but my intent on getting out of here and catching a cab back to my building.

I feel like I'm walking in a fog as I make my way through the crowded restaurant, my gaze focused on the front doors. They're so far away it'll be an eternity before I make it there and when I feel fingers close around the crook of my elbow, I turn, ready to tell Rose or Lily to let me go.

But it's not one of my sisters holding me back.

It's Zachary.

"Violet." He says my name in this quiet, downright reverent voice, as if he can't believe I'm standing in front of him. I stand up straighter, pissed that I'm dressed so casually in my favorite workout T-shirt and yoga pants. I came straight from the gym to this brunch/lunch date with Rose and Lily, not really caring what I looked like. Still in a funk over Friday night, which was so stupid.

Though maybe my sadness wasn't in vain after all.

"Let go of me," I murmur, and Zachary immediately drops hold of my arm but he doesn't move out of my way. "I'm leaving."

"I can see that." He steps to the side and I start walking, irritated when he falls in beside me. "What a coincidence that I find you here."

"I'm sure." I refuse to look him in the eye. He's dressed in crisp khaki pants and a white cotton button-down shirt, effortless and handsome as always. A few weeks ago I would have stood beside him, wearing one of my more casual dresses, not a hair out of place.

I'm not even wearing makeup today. My sisters weren't either. If Grandma caught us looking like that while out in public, she'd flip.

"Are you really going to let it end like this?" he asks after I push open the double doors with a hard shove, Zachary keeping pace right next to me.

"Like what?" I turn on him, not caring that we're going to fight out in public in front of a popular Manhattan restaurant. I'm over it. Over keeping up the pretense of this falsely perfect life. "Me knowing that you're a cheating bastard? Finding out that you went after that promotion behind my back? That you don't really care about me at all? If so, then yes. That's exactly how we're going to end this."

He takes a step toward me, his expression downright menacing. I won't back down, though. I refuse to. "You never protested."

I frown. "What?"

"You never protested when I was out fucking around. Ever. After awhile I was trying to get caught in the hopes that I would get some sort of reaction out of you, but still . . . nothing." He throws his arms up in the air, frustration in his every move. "All I wanted was for you to care, Violet."

Oh. My. God. He's blaming me for his infidelities. I can't believe it. "Are you serious? Turning this around so your cheating is somehow my fault because I wouldn't react?"

"If you would've put your foot down, I would've stopped," he says simply.

Hate and rage rise within me, an ugly mixture I don't want to deal with. Too late. It's filling my veins, my every pore, climbing up my throat like bile until I can't hold it back any longer.

"Fuck you, Zachary. Fuck you and all your whores. I hope you rot in hell."

I start to leave, but his chilling words stop me.

"He's using you, too, you know." At my frown of confusion he helps me out by saying, "McKay. Don't you think it's strange how all of a sudden he takes an interest in you? And Pilar takes an interest in me? If you don't suspect those two are up to something then you're dumber than I thought."

"Fuck you," I spit out again, his words proving just what Zachary thought of me.

I hate him.

Turning away from him, I make my escape, my head bent, my stride fast. I need to get out of here. Find a taxi and get back home so I can prepare for Ryder. What Zachary said repeats in my head again and again. Words I wish I could forget but I can't.

If you don't suspect those two are up to something . . .

No. He can't be. Ryder wants me. He missed me. Regrets how he treated me. When he looks at me, touches me, kisses me . . . I know he means it. *He. Wants. Me.*

I stop and look out at the street, watching the taxis go by. Rushing to the curb, I hold up my hand and wave, flagging one of them down so that he pulls over to the curb with a squeal. I open the back door, sliding inside so I can collapse against the torn vinyl seat. I offer him my address and close my eyes, hating all the ugly noise carrying on in my head.

The tears that sting my eyes make me angry and I swipe at them with the back of my hand, furious at the weak show of emotion.

They aren't tears over the loss of Zachary. They aren't tears over the confusion with Ryder, either.

They're sad little tears just for me.

Chapter Twenty

Ryder

I'M JUST ABOUT TO LEAVE WHEN A KEY SOUNDS IN THE DEAD-bolt on my front door and the door swings open, revealing Pilar standing there, dressed to kill in a slinky black dress on a sunny spring Sunday afternoon. She looks like she's on her way to a funeral.

Mine, most likely.

I regret not putting the security chain up. I regret more not leaving five minutes earlier. My biggest regret, though? That I gave that bitch a key to my apartment.

"Look at you, freshly showered and eager to leave." She shuts the door behind her and glides into my living room like she hasn't a care in the world, the smile on her face falsely bright and cheery. "Where are you off to?"

"Nowhere special." I can't tell her where I'm going. Where I've wanted to be since I left Violet alone Friday night. The regret that seized me from the moment I fled Violet's apartment has held me paralyzed all weekend.

Now that I finally get my chance, my biggest obstacle comes over like she has some sort of sixth sense. She gets off on screwing me over.

"Well, you look delicious." She pats my chest, her fingers curling, clinging to the fabric of my shirt, and I step back from her touch. A little pout crosses her lips and I'm tempted to tell her that look doesn't work any longer. She's too old for that shit.

But I don't want to start a fight, so I let it pass.

"Did you need something? Because if it can wait . . ." My voice drifts and she sends me a pointed look, one that says she has her suspicions and she doesn't care if I want to get out of here in a hurry or not. She's going to get around to telling me what she wants whenever she feels like saying it.

"It can't wait. And I do need something." The façade drops, revealing just how irritated she really is with me. Her face morphs into a grimace. "You need to end it with Violet."

If she'd come here yesterday, I could have told her I already had. At that precise moment I would have believed every word I said, too.

But now . . . I don't want to end it.

"Says who?" I ask.

"Says me." She taps my shoulder as she walks by and goes to sit on my couch, making herself at home, which irritates me further. "Come sit by me. Let's cuddle like old times."

Cuddle. The word makes me want to puke. "Why aren't you with Lawrence? Isn't he leaving soon? Go cuddle with *him.*" I wish he'd leave tomorrow. Tonight.

"I'm over him." She waves a hand and rolls her eyes. "He's still stuck on Violet. I can't stand listening to him drone on and on about her, so I dumped him."

Jesus. "What do you mean he's still stuck on her?"

"He's madly in love with her, Ryder. They were together for two years. That's a lot of time to invest in someone, you know. And I do know, considering how long we've been together," she says pointedly.

"We're not together," I remind her. And neither are Lawrence and Violet. I need to cling to that. *Fuck,* I need to get to Violet's apartment and make her forget Zachary Lawrence was ever even in her life.

"We will always be together, darling. No matter how much you try and deny it, my claws are so deep in you, you will never be able to escape me." She pats the empty space beside her on the couch. "Sit down."

"No," I bite out, crossing my arms in front of my chest. "I want you to go."

"I'm not leaving until you *really* talk to me. I don't want to fight." She settles even deeper into the couch, looking quite pleased with herself. "Now come here and sit."

"I'm not your fucking dog, Pilar."

She lets out an irritated sound and cocks her head, contemplating me. "No, not a dog. But have you forgotten what you used to be, Ryder? Reckless. A drug addict. A drug dealer. Homeless." She ticks off each item from my painful past like a shopping list. "You were nothing until I took you in. And in thanks, you fucked me relentlessly for providing you with a roof over your head and food in your belly."

Hatred fills me, making my blood boil. I don't say a word, and that just makes her angrier.

She stands, her expression full of fury. "How easily you forget everything I did for you. I cleaned you up. I made you respectable. I got you your start in this business and gave you money. I *made* you."

"Trust me, I know. You won't ever let me forget it, either." I thrust my hands in my hair in frustration. "It's been years, Pilar. You know we've grown apart. Hell, most of the time we go our separate ways. You'll always have a special place in my heart, but what we once shared is over." We stare each other down as we stand on either side of the coffee table, our bodies stiff, our gazes never wavering.

"This one last thing is all I ask from you," she says quietly. "End it with Violet. Do what you're supposed to do. Break her, Ryder. Break her so hard she shatters into a million little pieces, and there will be no one left to put her back together again."

The thought of doing that to Violet makes me sick to my stomach. "She has her sisters," I point out. "Her father."

"Not her father," she says quickly. "And those selfish sisters of hers will pretend to be there for her in her time of need. But then they'll carry on with their lives in their usual vapid ways."

I remain silent, which makes Pilar crazy.

"We agreed," she reminds me, her voice cold, her eyes narrowed as she points her index finger at me. "*You* said you wanted to ruin her. Seduce her and ruin her. Remember that night? When we talked about how much fun it would be? How we could have whatever we wanted if we got Zachary and Violet out of our way? Well, I did my part. Now it's your turn to hold up your end of the bargain."

"What did you do to get rid of Lawrence? He was already gone before you stepped in. And I thought you were going to get me his promotion." I grip the back of my head with both hands, sick that we're talking about this, that I still have to deal with this, with her.

I don't know if I want that London position if it's going to cost me Violet. I don't want to hurt her. Break her into a million little pieces. If I'm the one to blame for her downfall, I definitely won't get on Forrest Fowler's good side.

The man will hate me. Is that Pilar's true plan? Does she want to get rid of . . . all of us?

"He's going to London, but it won't last. He'll come back. Trust me. I've already put the proper bug in someone's ear. You're going to get a chance at that job, too. Just you wait." Pilar smiles, looking quite pleased with herself.

Who is she talking to if not Lawrence? I don't get it. I don't understand how she's able to make these promises when she has nothing to do with them.

Unless there's someone else she's sweet-talking, someone on the executive board, maybe?

"I won't ruin Violet until I have the guarantee that I'm getting that position," I tell Pilar, my voice tight. I'm trying to rein in my anger, but it's so fucking hard. I drop my arms to my sides, my hands clenched into fists, not that I want to take out Pilar or anything.

More like I want to take out myself. I have no one else to blame for how I ended up here.

"You'll do it now. It's the only way I can ensure you'll get what you want at Fleur," Pilar tells me. "It's time, Ryder. Time to put your plan into action and destroy Violet completely."

What if I don't want to? What if I changed my mind? I can't imagine ruining Violet. I . . . I fucking like her. I want to get to know her better.

Deep down inside, I want to make her mine.

"If you don't do it, I'll go to Violet and tell her everything you said, every last little detail, including our plans for them." Her smile is smug. "I'll tell her all your little secrets, too. How you used to eat scraps of food out of the Dumpsters behind restaurants. How I brought you home, cleaned you up, and you became my personal fuck toy. How you used to sell drugs. I'll tell Forrest about you, too. If you won't ruin her, I'll ruin *you*."

Defeat settles over me, heavy and cold. My shoulders sag. She's the one woman who saved me. And now she holds all the power. She's turned into the one woman who will destroy me.

"It's your choice," she finishes with a gleeful smile.

None of this was ever my choice. Not that she'd agree. Not that I can argue, either. I rest my hands on my hips and hang my head, my mind racing to come up with an alternative. Anything so I won't have to do this.

I feel weak and I never do. I'm always in control. No matter what shit life threw at me, I always fought back.

For once in my life, I'm utterly defeated.

"Now let's seal the deal. Come here and give me a kiss," she practically purrs.

Keeping my head bent, I round the coffee table and go to her.

"You're late," Violet greets me as she throws open the door, a mixture of irritation and excitement written all over her pretty face.

A pretty face that I'm so glad to see, I almost sag with relief. *God,* she's gorgeous. I've missed her. It's been less than forty-eight hours since I saw her, but all I can think of is what a waste those last hours were when I could have been with her.

"I'm sorry." I never say I'm sorry. Ever. Yet with Violet it's all I seem to say. "Something came up."

She contemplates me, looking sexy as hell in a pale blue over-sized sweater and black leggings that make her legs look incredibly long. And I know for a fact those legs are long. I can't forget how they wrapped around me while I fucked her against the very door we're standing in front of.

I feel dirty, unworthy of entering her home, as she looks me over. I think of what just happened back at my apartment, the argument with Pilar. How I let her maul me and I placated her so I could get away from her and head over here.

Where I'm now supposed to end it with Violet in the most brutal way possible.

I don't know if I can do it.

You promised.

Pilar's singsong voice haunts me and I rub a hand across the back of my neck, getting irritated that Violet hasn't let me in yet. "Am I forgiven?"

Violet blinks at me. "For what?"

"For being late. Or are we going to have this conversation out in the hallway for the rest of the evening." Not that anyone can hear us, considering she's the only one on the penthouse floor. The grumpy doorman didn't bother calling up to get Violet's permission when I first arrived. He said I was already on the list and escorted me quickly to the elevators.

I'm on the grump's good side, but it won't last for long. Not after what I have to do to her.

"Come in." She opens the door wider and I stride inside, breathing in her delicious scent, glancing around the apartment for the first time. When I came here Friday, I'd been solely focused on Violet and nothing else. Now that I see where she lives . . .

I like it. The walls are white, as are the couches, but the pillows scattered everywhere are a bright mix of colors and the rug beneath the dark coffee table has a cheerful yellow and grayish-blue pattern. Simple and pretty, the décor fits her.

I can't help but wonder if this is the last time I'll be allowed into her apartment.

If you go through with what you planned, that would be a hell yes.

"Nice place," I say as I turn to face her. That sweater she's wearing looks soft. I want to get my hands on it, under it, on her. I need to touch her to get rid of the filth and disgust I feel after being with Pilar.

Fuck. I still can't believe I did that.

"Thank you." She steps closer and sniffs. Her nose wrinkles. "You smell like perfume."

Shit. Pilar douses herself with the strongest stuff possible and it's obnoxious as hell.

Violet moves even closer to me and presses her nose to the front of my shirt. "You've been with another woman," she says dully, starting to back away. I reach out and grab her arms but she jerks out of my hold, her expression fierce. "Don't touch me. God, you're just like him, aren't you? You fuck other women and then come over here believing you can charm your way into my panties? He warned me you were like this."

I should have changed clothes. I'm such an idiot. But hell, my time with Pilar had happened so fast. I got her off on my fucking knee, for Christ's sake. No clothing was removed. She just happened to get her scent all over me when she rode me like a cat in heat. "Who warned you?"

"Zachary. He said you and Pilar together planned something against us both. You smell just like her. You've *been* with her." Her face almost crumples, but then she gets ahold of herself and her expression goes smooth. Blank. I recognize that look. I've used it plenty of times myself. "You fucked her, didn't you?"

"No. Fuck no." Jealousy fills me. I hate that motherfucker Lawrence. "And when did you see Zachary?" I can't believe I just said his pussy-ass name.

"It doesn't matter." She goes to the door and opens it, turning to look at me. Her face may be blank but her eyes are full of fire, and all of it is directed at me. "Get out."

"Violet." I lower my voice. Hell, I'll beg her if I have to. "Let me explain." I have no explanation. I'm flying by the seat of my pants here and I don't know what to say to placate her.

"There's nothing to explain. I've been played left and right for the last few years. For most of my life, really." She laughs, but it's the saddest sound I've ever heard. My fucking heart— which I thought was made of steel and impenetrable—starts to crack the slightest bit in sympathy for her.

No, not sympathy. I don't feel sorry for her. She's hurting and it makes me hurt, too. I want to take on her pain so she doesn't have to feel it.

"I'm not playing you." I pull her fingers off the handle and push the door shut, grabbing both of her hands so I can interlace our fingers together. I need the connection. Need to feel her and remind her that what we're experiencing is real. What Pilar and I have is born of selfishness. It's ugly and unpleasant, just like most of my life. For once, I want something good and clean and pure. I want Violet. "Not in the way that you think."

She stares up at me, those big brown eyes unblinking. Damn it, she looks like she wants to believe me and I'm tempted to tell her she shouldn't. She should run. Get away from me as fast as she can. I'm like a disease that will eat at her welcoming heart until it's completely destroyed. And I won't feel an ounce of remorse for stealing it.

Because I want it. I want her heart. I want her soul. I want her body. I want all of her. Fuck Pilar. Fuck her stupid plans. I deserve one last night.

One last night where I can drown my black soul in the sweetness that is Violet Fowler.

Letting go of her hands, I reach up and cup her face, tilt her head back so her lips are a perfect offering, just for me. "I want you," I whisper. "That's all I know right now, that I fucking want you."

She grabs hold of my wrists, her slender fingers wrapped tight around my flesh. As if I'm her anchor and she's scared to let go. I want to tell her she's safe with me, but it would be a lie. I have no idea how this is all going to turn out. I'm a selfish asshole for wanting this, wanting her.

But I can't be stopped. I won't be.

"Tell me the truth." She takes a deep, shaky breath. "Were you with Pilar?"

"Yes," I whisper, hating the hurt I see race across her face. "Not like you think, though."

"Did you . . . fuck her?" She tenses and closes her eyes, as if prepared for the blow, her fingers clinging to my wrists.

It still startles me to hear her say the word *fuck*. "No."

Those gorgeous eyes pop open and she releases her hold on me, dropping her arms at her sides. "Tell me the truth," she demands.

"I am."

"You didn't fuck her."

"No."

"But you messed around with her."

"She used me." I pause. "And I let her."

"Why?"

I don't have an answer.

"You'll hurt me," she continues, her voice clear and true. "I know you will. This won't end well."

I can't talk about endings or beginnings or any of that shit. All I can focus on is the here and now. With her. "Tonight I just want to make you feel good." And that's the truth. The only bit of truth I can offer her. "Let me, Violet."

She closes her eyes tightly, her thick, dark eyelashes smashed together, and I swear I see a hint of wetness there. I can't take it if she cries. The only one responsible for her tears will be me and I can't face that. "I just want to forget," she murmurs.

"Forget what?" I bend my head and press my lips to her temple, slide them down to her cheek as I push my hands into her silky hair. Her skin is soft and fragrant and I feel the tremor that runs through her. I want to ease her pain. I want to bring her pleasure. I want to put my mouth on her pussy and make her come with my tongue. I want to watch her wrap those pretty lips around my cock and feel her suck me deep.

I want it all. And I don't deserve any of it.

"Everything. My life. Professionally everything's great. But personally, I'm kind of a mess." She parts her lips on a startled sigh when I offer a lingering kiss to the side of her mouth. "I hate that I'm jealous over the fact that you smell like Pilar. I don't own you. I have no right to feel this way."

"I'll take off my clothes," I suggest, and the faintest smile curves her lips, urging me on. "Don't worry about Pilar," I reassure her. "She can't hurt you."

Liar.

Not really, because I'm the one who's going to hurt her. And if I don't, Pilar will hurt me.

Violet cracks her eyes open, staring at me. "I'm more worried about *you*. What you're doing to me."

Again, she's proving just how smart she is. She *should* be worried about me. I will wreck her, there's no doubt about that.

"What am I doing to you now?" I tuck a wavy strand of dark brown hair behind her ear, then trace the delicate shell. I want to spend hours touching her. Kissing her. This is my last chance, and I plan on savoring every little stolen moment.

"You make me feel . . . too much." She turns her head the slightest bit, our lips in alignment, but I don't kiss her. And she doesn't kiss me. It's as if we're both prolonging the anticipation. "It scares me."

"You scare me, too," I whisper before I press my mouth to hers in a chaste kiss. Her lips move beneath mine and I kiss her again. And again. Sweet, sensual kisses, our lips parting with every pass, my tongue darting out to lick at her upper lip before she pulls away.

I stare at her, my heart accelerating, my lips tingling. I don't kiss other women like that. All soft and loving and shit. Not my style.

But with Violet, I . . . want to be soft. And, Christ help me, loving.

Fuck. I'm in way too deep.

"I need you naked," she says, her hands shoving at the hem of my shirt so it rises halfway up my stomach. "I can't . . . you need to get your clothes off."

I understand why she's doing this. I smell like Pilar's perfume and she doesn't like it. I can't blame her. Stepping out of her reach, I tear off my shirt and kick off my shoes at the same time before I undo my jeans, shoving them off my hips along with my underwear so everything ends up in a heap beside me. I hold my arms out to my sides, like an offering to her, and all I can hope is that she'll take me.

That she'll want me.

"This is me," I say solemnly. "This is who I am."

Her gaze drifts all over me, landing on my tattoos, my piercings, then lower, until she's staring at my erect cock. "Who are you really?" she asks as her eyes meet mine once more.

"I'm . . . just a man. A man who fucks up, who makes mistakes and sometimes doesn't think. I'm reckless. I'm arrogant. I've done things I'm not proud of. I grew up fast and didn't have a real childhood." I pause, not sure how much more I should say. I don't want to scare her before I get my one last chance. "I . . . don't know how to love."

She blinks, her gaze never leaving mine. "What do you mean?"

"I didn't have a mother, I don't know who she is. My dad treated me like I was nothing but a burden." And when I grew older, I turned into his drinking and let's-troll-for-hot-chicks buddy. It wasn't a healthy relationship, and that's an understatement. "I've never had a real relationship."

"What about Pilar?"

"It's complicated. Hard to define." Our relationship confuses everyone, including me.

"What about me?" she asks quietly.

"What about you?"

"Do you want me?"

"Yes." I fucking burn for her.

She pulls her sweater up and over her head, revealing she's wearing no bra. She strips her leggings off and she's not wearing any panties, either. In a matter of seconds Violet is as naked and vulnerable as I am, and I have never seen her look more beautiful.

"Then you can have me," she whispers.

Chapter Twenty-one

Violet

I'M GIVING MYSELF TO RYDER LIKE SOME SORT OF OFFERING and he takes it without hesitation, coming for me with a fierce determination I find both terrifying and exciting. He grabs hold of me and sweeps me into his arms like I don't weigh a thing, pausing at the beginning of the short hall that leads to my bedroom.

"Last door on the left," I tell him, linking my hands around the back of his neck. I press my cheek against his chest, feel the thundering of his heart. It beats as fast as mine and the sound reassures me. Fills me with hope that maybe something more could come of this after all.

But deep down inside, I know the truth. We're not meant to be. Not forever. This is temporary, what Ryder and I share. Like a meteor shooting across the sky, bright and hot and thrilling to watch, until it fizzles and burns into nothing.

We enter my bedroom and he looks around, still clutching me close. The windows are open, the gauzy white curtains billowing out with the breeze. There's a candle burning on the bedside table that I lit right before he knocked on my door, and the bedcovers are rumpled since I was too lazy to make the bed when I woke up this morning.

Carefully he sets me on my feet, my body sliding along his

the entire way down. His skin is so hot, his body so hard. I keep my hands around his neck and press my lips to the center of his chest, absorbing the sound of his heart, wondering if it's as dark and broken as he believes. If given the chance, I would work my hardest to heal him. To make him whole.

But I'm pretty sure my chance is already gone.

"Violet." He sifts his fingers through my hair as I run my lips across his chest. I love it when he says my name. I love it more when he touches me. Excitement spirals through me when my lips meet metal and I tongue his nipple ring, teasing it lightly before I draw it into my mouth and suck.

"Jesus," he groans, his fingers going tight in my hair as he holds me to him. I move to his other nipple and tease it with gentle flicks of my tongue, sucking the thin metal ring into my mouth. He pulls my hair, the pain mixing with the pleasure, and I moan, confused by my reaction, by the surge of wetness that floods my sex.

I release his nipple and he grabs me by the waist, pushing me back onto the center of the bed. He follows me down, his big, hot body covering mine completely. He braces his hands on either side of my head and deliberately flexes his hips against mine so I can feel his hard cock rest against my belly, the tip warm and damp. My entire body flutters in anticipation of feeling him move inside me.

"Thank you," he whispers, his gaze dark as it sweeps over my chest. My nipples harden almost painfully and I desperately want his mouth on them.

"For what?" I ask, confused.

"For letting me touch you. For letting me have you tonight." He kisses me, another sweet, sexy kiss. His tongue dances with mine and I push my hands into his hair, clutching him close.

"You don't have to thank me," I murmur when he breaks away from my lips to rain kisses along my neck. "You didn't have to ask for permission, either. You already own me."

He lifts his head to look at me, his expression full of pain. "Don't say that."

I blink at him in surprise. "But it's true."

"No." He shakes his head. "You don't want me to own you. You don't know me. Not really."

"I want to know you better," I admit. "And I know you won't hurt me."

Breathing deep, his chest brushes against mine and he closes his eyes. "I can't make that promise."

I reach up and cup his cheek, his stubble prickling my palm. He turns his head and kisses my hand, his lips branding me, and I want to feel them everywhere. Branding me. Making me his. "I don't care," I whisper. "You don't scare me."

"I should." He moves down my body, kissing me everywhere just as I wished for a moment ago. My shoulders, my collarbone, my breasts; he sucks first one nipple deep into his mouth, then the other, biting it so hard I cry out. "I'll hurt you. Again and again. I don't know how to do it any other way," he murmurs against my skin.

I can't answer him. I don't know how to answer him. Whatever's happening between us isn't normal. It isn't right. It can't be.

But I don't want him to stop.

He kisses a fiery path across my belly, his hands spreading my thighs wide just before his mouth lands on my wet center. He fucks me with his tongue, with his fingers, lapping at my clit, sucking it between his lips, nibbling, biting hard until I scream, coming with an intensity that I've never experienced before.

My body is still convulsing when he moves away from me and slips on a condom before he thrusts deep. So hard he shoves me up the mattress, my head bumping against the headboard with his first powerful push.

"Does it hurt?" he asks with a grunt, his hips slapping against mine, his movements relentless as he fucks me.

I shake my head, my body trembling, fear rising within me

when I see the dark look on his face. I won't let him frighten me. "N-no."

"It should." He reaches beneath me and grabs my butt, his hands squeezing my cheeks so hard I cry out. I can feel every one of his fingers drive into my flesh and I know he's marking me. "That has to hurt, right?"

"No." What is he doing? Is he trying to purposely harm me? Is this some sort of sick reasoning on his part so he can drive me away?

Ryder lifts me, brings my lower body closer to his so his cock slides deep. So deep I swear he's touching my womb, the very deepest, darkest part of me, where no other man has ever been before. He thrusts again. And again. Brutally fucking me, taking me, yes, even . . . making me hurt.

But I won't give up. The pleasure overrides the pain and I cling to him, my legs wrapped tight around his hips, my arms circling around his shoulders. He can't get rid of me that quick.

I won't let him.

"Tell me to stop," he commands as he shoves his cock inside of me, his hands still gripping my ass, his thrusts shallow, then deeper. "Tell me, Violet."

"No." I kiss his neck, lick him, suck his flesh, and finally give in to the urge.

I sink my teeth into his skin, so hard I hear him gasp in surprise, and then he's pulling away from me, withdrawing from my body and flipping me around so I'm on all fours, my ass to him as he slides his cock inside me from behind.

"You think you can hurt me?" he asks, his tone mocking, his balls slapping against my sex with his every vicious thrust. He's trying to break me down and I refuse to let him. I won't run away from him no matter how hard he tries to make me.

"Yes," I hiss in answer because I truly believe I'm hurting him already. Why else would he act this way?

He grips my hips with his big hands and pulls me onto his

cock; back and forth I ride him. He doesn't move, just slides me along his thick, pulsing length, the friction and the heat sparking another orgasm deep within me, one that makes me come apart with a guttural groan as it ripples through my body, my inner walls milking his cock in a rhythmic motion that has him moaning along with me.

"Fuck, you're hot," he whispers, his hands moving to grab at my ass and spread me wide. "Watching your tight pussy take my cock makes me wanna come."

"Do it," I urge him, savoring the words he says to me. I want to feel him lose control. He's been in command this entire time. Trying to push me, hurt me, make me hate him. But I fought back every step of the way.

I refuse to back down.

"No." He slaps my ass so hard it stings and I buck against him, crying out. I hadn't expected *that*. "You're not in control of this, Violet. I am."

What the hell is happening to me? He's being so rough, so horrible, and I . . . I love it. I want more. I want him to break me. I want him to bring me pain and pleasure and every sensation in between.

And when he lifts me up to my knees, his hand wrapped around my throat, his mouth at my ear whispering the filthiest things I've ever heard, I almost come for the third time just at the sound of his voice.

"You enjoy me fucking you like an animal, don't you?" he asks, his voice low and dark. So dark, like his fucked-up heart and lost soul.

"I like fucking you," I tell him, my breath stalling in my throat when his fingers tighten. He wields all the control, his cock buried inside me, his teeth nibbling my earlobe, his fingers pressing into my neck, against my windpipe. I tell myself not to panic. He won't hurt me. He would never hurt me. He's just angry . . . but not at me. I know it's not at me.

So who is his anger aimed at? And why?

"I wanna come all over your pretty tits," he whispers, his other hand grabbing one, sure fingers pinching my nipple until I wince. "I want to mark you with my come. I want you to taste it."

"Please." I reach up and circle his thick wrist with my fingers as best I can. My eyes shutter closed and I lose myself to the sensation of his cock moving inside my aching body, his fingers softening around my throat, his other hand twisting my nipple until the heady burn of pain radiates from my skin. My legs ache, my body aches, and I feel like I'm going to collapse.

"I'm a sick, twisted fuck, Violet," he tells me. "I'm no good. Not good enough for you."

"I don't care." I shake my head and his fingers tighten around my neck once again, making me freeze.

"You should care. You're a good girl. So pure, so sweet. I'll fucking wreck you." He sounds both excited and scared, all at once. He's speaking the truth. I am a good girl. And he's bad. Awful.

Yet I want him.

"I want you to wreck me if it's always going to feel like this." His cock twitches deep within my body and I lean back, my head on his shoulder, his mouth still at my ear, his breathing harsh. He's breaking me down and building me back up and God help me, I love it. I want more of it.

"You don't want to be mine." His voice is firm.

"I do."

"You couldn't handle it."

"I can."

"Swear?"

I nod, his curved fingers bumping into my chin since he hasn't released his grip on my throat. "Make me yours."

"You want to be mine." He doesn't ask, he's telling me, and my brain grows fuzzy at the constant back-and-forth between us. I'm close to coming. Again. His words, his command, his hands, his cock so deep . . . I can't take it. I'm overwhelmed.

"I'm yours," I whisper. "All yours, Ryder. Use me. Fuck me. Hurt me. I don't care. Just make me yours. Own me."

"Fuck." He lifts his hips again and again, his cock pushing, punishing me as the orgasm builds. Reaching higher, higher, until I whisper his name and he's coming and I'm coming, our bodies moving together. He growls my name, making it sound like a curse, his hips brutal against my quivering body, his hand still around my neck, his breath hot against my ear. I slump against him as he braces me from behind and he releases his hold on my throat, his arm moving down to settle over my sex, where his cock is still buried inside me.

"Mine," he whispers possessively, cupping me, his fingers curling around my clit and pinching it.

A shiver moves through me as I nod, turning my face into his so I can nuzzle him. Tears stream down my cheeks, one after the other, but I don't want to tell him. I had no idea I was crying.

It's not from sadness. Not really from happiness, either. It's just . . . another form of release. One that he commanded from me so effortlessly, I didn't even realize it was happening. "Yours," I murmur against his skin, kissing him along his firm jaw. "All yours."

Chapter Twenty-two

Ryder

I TRIED MY BEST TO BREAK HER BUT SHE WOULDN'T BREAK. SHE took everything I gave her. I hurt her. I practically choked her. I told her I was worthless and fucked her so deep she cried out in pain. I pinched and twisted her nipples, I gripped her ass until I'm sure bruises in the shape of my fingers will appear on those pretty, pale cheeks by tomorrow morning.

And still she wouldn't give.

I even made her cry. She said nothing but I felt her tears, tasted them on her lips. Those goddamn tears almost broke *me,* but I kept it together. Said something filthy that made her pussy quiver around my cock and then I rolled her beneath me and pulled out of her body, tossing the used condom on the bedside table like some sort of inconsiderate asshole. I stroked myself, my cock still hard and full of come like I'd never even had that explosive orgasm in the first place.

She's lying beneath me now, watching me with those big brown eyes, her skin covered in sweat, her hair damp and matted against her head. Her lips are puffy and swollen from my brutality and there's a red mark on her left nipple from where I pinched her.

She's fucking beautiful. And mine. I own her. I won't give her up.

Pilar can go fuck herself.

"I want to taste you," Violet says, reaching out to touch my dick, her fingers colliding with mine. I slow my pace, watch in fascination as she props herself up on her elbows and I feed my cock to her parted lips. They close over me, tight and warm, and my eyes shutter closed for the briefest moment as I let myself go and enjoy the sensation of her hot mouth surrounding my hard cock. And when she starts sucking and pulling, her fingers curling around the base, I'm done for.

Fucking done for.

I open my eyes and shove at her shoulder so she releases me from her mouth with a pop. "Lie down," I demand, and she does as I say, always a good girl.

But now she's *my* good girl.

Her eyes widen in fascination as she watches me bring myself to orgasm with my hand. My pace is rapid, my grip tight, and my focus zeroed in on her pretty tits, those puffy pink nipples hard and calling to me. I'm going to decorate them with my come; I'm going to mark her and make her mine in the most primitive way.

I can't wait.

Pleasure races down my spine and settles in my balls. Building up almost painfully, making me wince, making me moan her name as the first spurt flies from the tip of my cock and lands on her chest. Long streams of semen splatter her skin, her breasts, her nipples, and when the last bit of come is wrung out of me I smear my finger through it and bring it up to Violet's mouth.

"Taste me," I tell her and she does, drawing my finger into her mouth eagerly, her eyes closing as she whimpers and sucks. The girl is fucking dirty.

Filthy.

And all mine.

She rubs my come into her skin, licks it from her fingers, and all I can do is watch. I wonder if Lawrence ever did this to her.

I doubt it.

I wonder if any man has ever marked her like this. Fucked her like this. Maybe somehow I'm special. Or maybe I'm a game to her. A chance for the uptown heiress to fuck the tattooed bad boy who's pretending to have his shit together.

The thought alone just about kills me.

Hoping for a distraction, I climb out of bed and walk into the connecting bathroom, hitting the light since the sun has started to go down and it's getting dark. I catch my reflection in the mirror. I look like hell. What she sees in me I have no idea, but I shut my brain off so I won't get all fucked up over it. I spot a stack of perfectly folded white washcloths on a shelf and I grab one, turning on the water so I can wait for it to warm. Once it does, I run the washcloth under the water and then turn it off, squeezing out the water so the cloth is damp but not soaked.

I stare at my reflection again even though I don't mean to. I usually don't like what I see because all I notice are my mistakes. The stains of my past cover me and I can hardly face myself.

I've never done this sort of thing before. Taking care of a girl. Of course, I've never fucked a girl like I just fucked Violet. I hope I don't mess it up.

"Don't mess it up," I tell myself before I hit the lights and go back into the bedroom.

"Are you all right?" I ask her, my voice soft, my thoughts everywhere. If she says no I'll have to leave. And I don't want to.

She nods and shivers, pulling the covers up over her naked body. "Will you close the windows, please?"

I do as she asks, moving about her bedroom and closing the windows one by one. I finally crawl into her bed and lie next to her, pulling the comforter down gently. Taking the cloth, I rest it on her belly, making her jump.

"Are you sore?" I ask, moving the cloth lower.

She doesn't say a word but spreads her legs for me and I

wash her there, rubbing her gently with the cloth, wiping away the sticky come that still covers her.

A sigh escapes her. "That feels nice," she whispers.

My dick twitches in response, though I tell myself to calm down.

I can't help it, though. I want her. Always.

I refold the washcloth and wipe it across her breasts, trying to pick up any last traces of semen I left on her chest. Her nipples are hard and she flinches when I touch the one that has the bright red mark on it. I lean in, dropping a tender kiss on the distended flesh.

Another sigh escapes her, this one deeper, and I draw her nipple into my mouth, sucking her, circling it with my tongue. Her hands sink into my hair, holding me to her as I lavish my attention on her tender nipple. "What are you doing to me?" she says, her voice distant.

I know the question isn't directed at me specifically. She's confused. So am I. I came here tonight to savor her and destroy her all at once.

Instead, I'm the one who's destroyed.

Pulling away from her, I study her pretty face, her sexy body. There are marks all over her normally unblemished flesh, all of them made by me. Bruises are already forming on her hips, her thighs. I should feel terrible. I did that to her.

But I don't.

I roll her over so she's lying on her stomach and I see the bruises on her ass, the red mark where I spanked her. I take the washcloth and wipe it across her cheeks, between her thighs. She spreads her legs, turning her head to the side so our gazes meet, and I stare at her, running my finger along her crack until I dip it in her pussy.

Her lids flutter closed, her lips part, as I continue to touch her there. Tracing her entrance with my index finger, teasing it, teasing her until she's lifting up on her knees, offering herself to me.

"I shouldn't," I say, my voice full of agony even though I don't mean it. I'm dying to fuck her again. "You're sore."

"Please," she whispers. "I want it."

"What do you want?" My voice firms and I discard the washcloth, leaving it on the edge of the mattress as I scoot closer to her. "My fingers or my cock?"

She shudders. "Your cock."

I grab a condom and roll it on, then position myself behind her, my hands at her hips, my cock poised at her entrance. I enter her slowly, keeping my thrusts shallow so I don't hurt her, but she pushes me by begging for it.

"Harder," she demands, and I give her what she wants.

"Faster," she cries, and I increase my pace.

"Deeper," she whispers, and I can't take it anymore. I need to look at her and really see her. I need the connection, and fucking Violet from behind feels cold.

Reminds me of how I used to fuck Pilar.

I pull out of her and turn her around so she's facing me. She's breathless and shaking, her skin damp. I never gave much cred to the missionary position before. I usually found it boring. But fucking Violet this way is . . . perfect. I can look into her eyes, see her responsive face, feel her as she wraps herself around me. I can shift down and kiss her tits, press my mouth to her neck, hold her close to me all while pumping my cock deep inside her.

It's fucking perfect.

She comes quickly and so do I. She falls first, her body tightening around mine, a little "oh" falling from her lips, and I chase after her, pumping my hips until I burst, clinging to her tightly. Probably too tightly. I might be hurting her, but I don't care.

And she never protests.

I withdraw from her body reluctantly, pulling the condom

off and wrapping it in the washcloth before I toss them on the bedside table. She scolds me about warping the wood, asking if I'd throw it on the ground instead because she doesn't want me to leave this bed yet. Neither do I. So I do what she asks.

It's all so normal, so regular, so unlike anything I've ever experienced before. After fucking Pilar I always felt weird, especially when I still lived with her. Like I could never escape her, which I couldn't. Fucking other women was so casual, so meaningless, I was running out the door the minute I got the condom off and in the trash.

Not with Violet, though. I want to comfort her and ensure she still needs me. I gather her in my arms and hold her close, noticing how perfectly her head fits in the crook of my shoulder. Her hair brushes against my face and I push it out of the way, dropping a chaste kiss on her forehead that makes her sigh and wiggle against me.

Wiggling doesn't help my cock whatsoever, but I try to ignore it. I can't fuck her again. Not after what I just did to her. She's gotta be sore.

"Tell me about you," she says quietly. "I want to know."

I stiffen, my voice cautious when I speak. "It's not pleasant."

"I don't care."

"It'll probably shock you."

She props herself on one elbow and peers up at me. "I don't think you can shock me after what just happened between us."

I kiss her because I can't resist and pull her back into my arms, her head on my chest. I need strength to get through this conversation. "My childhood was . . . rough. I practically grew up on the streets."

"What happened to your mom?"

"I don't know." I don't think I want to know. My dad described her as a useless slut who only wanted money.

"And your dad?"

"He's dead." He died when I was sixteen. Overdose. Found in a motel room. One that was notorious for being used by hookers.

Classy way to go.

"I'm sorry," she offers, and I laugh.

"I'm not. He was a prick." Most of the time, I think I'm just like him. The only difference is that I found success, while he never climbed out of the hell he made for himself.

She remains quiet, her fingers stroking over my chest and playing with the rings in my nipples. Her touch feels good. Having her next to me feels amazing, and I don't ever want to let her go.

"After he died, I got kicked out of the shit hole he rented, and so I was homeless," I explain. "I had nowhere to go, so I would crash on random couches. Or sleep outside."

"Outside?" She sounds concerned. Sad. Like she cares. Has anyone ever really cared? Pilar claims she did and she helped me, but it was advantageous for her. "Like where?"

"Park benches. Alleys. Wherever I could sleep for a few hours and not worry about getting jumped."

"That sounds awful." Her voice is small.

"It was." I'm not going to lie. My life was shit.

"How old were you?"

"Sixteen." Young and stupid, and selling drugs was my only source of income. Letting dudes fresh out of prison practice their tattoo artistry on my skin. Getting high. Fucking stupid girls that were younger than me and letting all of it swallow me up and eat me whole.

"Ryder." She kisses my shoulder, her warm lips lingering on my skin. "I'm sorry."

"Don't be sorry," I say, vaguely uncomfortable. "It is what it is."

"That doesn't make it right."

I love that she sounds like she wants to fight for me, even though there's nothing she can do. What's done is done.

"What made you change your life?" she asks. "What turned it around?"

I exhale loudly, unsure of how to tell her. "You don't want to know."

"I do," she says firmly. "Tell me."

"It was Pilar. She found me at a Starbucks and took me back to her place, and . . ." Saved me. Fucked me. Fed me. Cleaned me up. Helped me get my GED and fucked me some more.

Violet remains quiet for so long I grow uncomfortable. Restless. I shift so I can roll on top of her. I need to see her face, look into her eyes, when I ask her this question. "Does that bother you?"

She nods, her gaze skittering away from mine. "A little."

I grab hold of her chin and force her to look at me. "She rescued me then, when I needed it. She helped me, and I repaid my debt to her. I owe her nothing."

"I-I'm glad she rescued you." She reaches up and touches me, her fingers on my jaw. "Thankful."

Jesus. The woman is trying to straight-up kill me with kindness, I swear. "You rescued me, too, Violet." Her gaze softens and I stroke the side of her face, lean into her, and kiss her gently. "I don't want this to end," I murmur against her lips.

"I don't either," she admits.

Her confession fuels me. Makes me feel invincible. We can defy Pilar. We can defy everyone. Fuck them all. If we stand strong beside each other, we can have the world at our feet. I need nothing else but Violet.

Nothing.

I kiss her, then flip over so I'm on my back and she's on top of me. My already hard cock nudges against her ass. "I want you," I whisper.

She rolls her eyes before she admonishes me. "Again?"

"Again." I run my hands over her ass, loving the feel of her soft, plump skin, careful of her bruises. "It's all about you this time, Violet."

"Hmm," she hums, and that sound sends an electric current through my veins, making my dick harder.

I'm starting to think I have a serious problem.

"Come here." I adjust her to my liking, making her move up my body until her hands are gripping the headboard and my head is propped on her pillows, her pussy right above my face. *Fuck*, she's pretty, all pink and glistening. I can't wait to taste her.

"I don't know about this," she says uneasily.

"You're going to love it," I reassure her, my hands going to her hips as I lower her to my mouth. I dart out my tongue, licking her clit, and she jumps in pleasure or pain, I can't tell which.

I'm starting to realize that with us, the line is hard to discern.

I lick her pussy from front to back and everywhere in between. She moves with me, her hips grinding, back and forth against my face as I tongue her, my hands memorizing the smooth skin of her belly and hips and waist. I search her folds with my tongue, teasing her clit, and she reaches out, adjusts my head so I can lick her exactly where she wants it.

Dirty fucking girl. The contradiction of Violet Fowler turns me on like no other woman I've ever been with.

Fucking her deep with my fingers, I suck her clit, lash it with my tongue, gripping her hips tight so she can't move, and I press her pussy directly on my face. Until she's crying out, writhing and coming all over me, her entire body trembling with the force of her orgasm. My name falls from her lips, her fingers wrapped so tight around the railing headboard I'm afraid she'll put a dent in the damn metal.

"I-I can't take it anymore," she says breathlessly after she climbs off of my face, collapsing in a limp heap beside me. "My entire body aches."

"Mmm, come here." I roll on my side and pull her to me, her back to my front, my arm banded across her stomach, her ass nestled against my semi-hard cock. "Go to sleep."

"I don't want to," she protests, but she sounds sleepy and her voice softens. "I don't want this night to end."

I press my face against her hair and close my eyes, inhaling her scent mingled with mine, along with the heady smell of sex. I've done everything I can to destroy her and she wants more. More of me.

I can't believe it.

I don't deserve her.

But she's mine. And no one can take her away from me.

No one.

Chapter Twenty-three

Violet

MY LIFE CAN BE DEFINED BY CERTAIN MOMENTS WHERE EVERY-thing changed. I was almost five when my mother committed suicide and my world tipped on its side, never to be righted again. I became more responsible and took care of Rose like she was *my* baby, not my baby sister. And Lily took care of me.

I was fourteen the first time Lily's face—and naked body covered with black bars across the more intimate parts of her anatomy—appeared on a popular gossip website. That was the jump start to her trying to destroy her life in any way possible. Not only destroy her life, but her relationship with our father, trashing the family name, the family business . . . all of it.

I became the responsible sister. Even more so.

I was nineteen when a man I'd trusted since I was a girl assaulted and tried to rape me. My testimony put him in prison for what I thought would be a long time. That moment became my family's secret shame and in turn, it became my burden to bear. Father couldn't handle any more scandal and though he was thankful and proud I'd fought off my assailant, he didn't want to talk about it.

The incident was swept under the rug. Forgotten by everyone.

Except me.

Every single one of those moments redirected my life, sent it zagging left when it had been zigging right. I went with the zag, changing my direction, adapting to a new plan and always, always pushing forward the best I could.

Sometimes I failed. I backpedaled here and there, but it couldn't be helped. After my testimony during the trial, I fell completely apart. I believed Alan had broken me. He was locked up in a jail cell and I let him haunt me for far too long. I needed to seek outside help in order to realize it wasn't my fault. That the only one who really broke me was . . .

Me.

And when Zachary and I started dating, I finally believed I knew exactly what was going to happen. I had my life planned. I was in control. Marriage. Babies. The two of us together, running Fleur Cosmetics. That would be my future and I was ready for it.

Then Ryder came into my life and . . . rocked it. I broke up with Zachary. I fell into the arms of another man so quickly he helped erase the memory of Zachary altogether. Ryder keeps me off balance. He scares me. Thrills me. Irritates me. Arouses me. And after last night?

I don't even know who I am anymore. All I know is that I crave him. I want him. I'm sitting in my office on a Monday morning, the ache between my legs, the bruises on my ass almost unbearable. My entire body is sore and when he left my apartment early this morning, just before dawn after he fucked me yet again, he smiled and kissed me and said four words that seared themselves into my brain.

Don't forget you're mine.

As if I could. If my brain didn't remind me, my body certainly did. I have never felt so deliciously brutalized after sex before.

I'm supposed to stop by and talk to Father at nine and I'm hiding out in my office until then, scrolling through emails and answering them, adding upcoming items to my calendar. Mindless, tedious work that I hoped would keep my haunting thoughts at bay, but it's no use.

I need to reach out to Ryder.

Opening up a new email, I start composing.

Dearest R —

It's probably best if you destroy this email after you read it. I wanted to let you know that you're in my thoughts. Every time I move, I feel you. What you did to me last night was unlike anything I've experienced before. I can't shake the words you said to me, the way you looked at me, how you touched me.

It was scary.

It was wonderful.

I want more.

You told me this morning not to forget that I'm yours and I won't.

I can't.

Yours,

V

I hit SEND before I can second-guess myself and resume my calendar search, hating the sound of the ticking clock that hangs on my wall. I feel like the quiet tick-tock is somehow sending me to my doom and I don't know why. Unease slithers down my spine and I wish my office didn't have all the windows. I need to find some blinds or curtains so I can close myself off.

I hate being on such blatant display. I'd rather be alone with my thoughts. Reliving what Ryder said to me. What he did to me.

"I'm a sick, twisted fuck, Violet."

"I'm no good. Not good enough for you."

"I don't care."

"You should care. You're a good girl. So pure, so sweet."

"I'll fucking wreck you."

My skin warms at the memory, washing away the unease. He could never wreck me. I won't let him.

And I don't believe he would ever purposely hurt me.

I have a new email and giddiness rises inside me when I see who it's from.

My sexy V,
        You invade my thoughts, too. What happened last night didn't turn out as I originally planned. I thought you would hate me for what I did to you.
        Instead, I think I made you want me more. And you made me realize that . . .
        You're perfect for me.
        All I can think about is having you naked again. Tied up and bared to me. My mouth on your skin. My cock deep inside your body. Today is going to be torture.
        I think we'll need to meet for lunch.
        R.

I press my fist to my mouth to try and conceal the smile that spreads across my face, but it's no use. I hit REPLY and start typing.

        Lunch sounds perfect. And no appetizers, please. I'm extra hungry today.
        Yours,
        V

His response is immediate.

What exactly are you hungry for? Tell me, Violet.

Closing my eyes, I focus on my heartbeat, steady and true. My slow, even breathing, the ache between my legs, the ache all over my body. I know exactly what I want, but I'm a little embarrassed to say it.

He won't let me get away with being evasive, though. He'll want me to be honest. Bold.

Your cock.

I send off my two-word email with a little smile, hoping like crazy we both remember to delete these emails immediately because oh my God, they're awful. Incriminating.

Fun.

Glancing at the clock, I see it's five minutes till nine. I need to get to Father's office but I don't want to leave. I want to be here for Ryder's response. I want to know what he thinks about my request.

Thankfully, Father's office is down the hall and I won't have to go far. I could be a little late even if I had to . . .

My in-box shows a new message and I open it, anticipation curling through me as I wait for it to load.

You're a bad girl.

My belly flutters. *He's* the one who's bad.

Only for you.

I hit SEND.

My phone rings within thirty seconds of my sending that email and I answer it quickly, my skin warm, my body prepared to hear his deep voice sound in my ear.

"Want to do lunch today?" Rose asks.

Disappointment floods me and I slump in my seat. "I can't," I say weakly. "I have plans."

"With who? Break them. I'm your sister. I need counsel."

Responsibility kicks in. I'm always there when Rose needs me. I can't let her down. I never have. That's Lily's job. "What do you need counsel for?"

"All sorts of stuff," Rose says evasively. "Please, Violet? We haven't done lunch in a while and I . . . I need to talk to you."

"Is everything okay?" She sounds sad. I've ignored her lately, chasing after my own wants and needs, and that's not fair. I've always made sure I'm there for my family.

"Well, you bailed out of brunch so fast yesterday because of your so-called color emergency I didn't get a chance to talk to you. And Lily is a terrible listener." I can practically feel Rose roll her eyes over the phone line.

"Okay. We'll have lunch. I'll meet you at your office at noon. Or do you want to go a little later?" If we go later, I could possibly see Ryder for a few minutes. Just take an extended lunch. But it's not like I can have sex with him and then go pick up Rose all rumpled and smelling of him.

God, what's wrong with me?

"Let's do noon. I need to get out of here."

I hang up and shut down my computer, then head out to Father's office. The halls are quiet, normal for an early Monday morning as everyone gets their bearings for the week. His office is at the end of the hall, opposite the small conference room, and I approach his partially open doorway, about to knock when I pause in shock at what I see.

Pilar is perched on my father's desk directly in front of him, her legs spread, her skirt hiked up and revealing her thighs. His hands are splayed on her outer thighs, her fingers are clamped around his tie, and she's lifting away from him as if she just . . .

Kissed him.

Horror and shock collide within me and I turn and run, mak-

ing my quiet escape toward the elevator. Without thought I hit
the button and wait, staring up at the numbers on the wall as
they light up, higher and higher toward my floor . . . until the
ding sounds and the doors swoosh open, revealing an empty car.

I hurry in and press the close door button frantically, releasing a relieved sigh when the doors shut quickly. My mind keeps
replaying what I saw, looking for a mistake. I might have misun-
derstood, right? Was that really Pilar? And did Father really
have his hands on her *thighs*?

Leaning against the wall, I close my eyes and tilt my head
back, forcing myself to face the truth. *Yes.* His hands were most
definitely on her thighs. She was smiling at him in that obvious,
sultry way of hers. She's gone from Ryder to Zachary to my father . . . and who knows how many more.

I think I'm going to be sick.

The elevator takes forever, stopping at practically every floor
so people—every one of them a Fleur employee—can get on and
off. I nod and murmur hello to all of them, irritated when I have
to make small talk, and my responses are brusque. I'm normally
not so rude, but I don't have time for this. I need . . . I don't
know what I need.

Yes, you do. You need Ryder.

When the elevator stops on his floor I shove my way through
the small crowd and make my hurried exit, heading toward his
office without saying anything to the receptionist who calls out
a greeting as I pass by her desk. His door is partially open, just
like my father's, and I pause, fear making my heart race.

What if . . . what if he's not alone either?

But when I peek inside, I see that he's sitting behind his desk,
leaning back in his chair and talking on the phone. He looks
gorgeous. Wearing a perfectly tailored dark blue suit and crisp
white shirt, a pale yellow tie knotted around his neck. He is the
epitome of the sexy businessman.

And just beneath, he's also the epitome of the pierced and

tattooed bad boy. I love that he's both. I still know so little about him, but I'm dying to find out more.

Cautiously I knock on the door and walk into his office. His startled gaze meets mine and he leans forward in his chair, ending the call with a made-up excuse and hanging up within seconds of my entering the room.

"Are you okay?" He gets out of his chair and rounds his desk, coming for me.

Zachary would never have done that. He would have held up his finger like I'm the one interrupting something important, versus me being the important one.

I wave a hand toward the door, pleased that he sees I'm upset. "Shut it. Please."

"What's wrong?"

"I'll tell you when you shut the door. It's, um, a private matter." I offer him a shaky smile, which makes him frown, and he goes to his door, shutting and locking it before he returns to me.

"Tell me," he demands as he pulls me into his arms. I go willingly, circling his waist, pressing my face against his chest, his scent, his warmth, invading me. Comforting me. I hold on to him for long, quiet moments, savoring the feeling of being in his strong arms until finally he withdraws from me, his hands grasping my shoulders, his expression serious as he studies me. "You're worrying me, Violet."

Is it wrong that I love that he's worried? "I went to my father's office. He asked that I stop by so we can discuss a few things." I take a deep breath, not exactly sure how I should say this. "When I peeked through his open door I saw him inside with . . . Pilar."

Ryder frowns and pulls away from me slightly. "So?"

"She was sitting on his desk directly in front of him and he had his hands on her . . . on her thighs. I think they'd just kissed or something."

"*What?*" Ryder sounds as incredulous as I feel. "Did you see them actually kiss?"

I shake my head. "They appeared to be in a very . . . intimate position, though."

He releases his hold on me and starts to pace, his expression determined, his body rigid. I don't know what he's thinking and it scares me. At least with Zachary, I knew where I stood. After being with him for two years, I sometimes felt like I could read his mind.

But with Ryder, it's still too new and I know hardly anything about him. He's so mysterious, revealing bits and pieces of himself that don't always make sense. He's completely closed off, and I wish he were more open to me.

"We need to be careful," he finally says, his voice low, his expression distant. I can tell his mind is still churning, with what I'm not sure.

"What do you mean?"

"I don't want people to suspect that we're—together." He almost seems to stumble on the last word and that irritates me. After everything we shared, everything that happened last night, there is no doubt in my mind that we're together.

"Well, you blew that by getting into a fight with Zachary at that stupid party," I remind him. I'm not taking responsibility for exposing what I wanted to be a secret affair from the beginning. That's all on him.

"I know. *Fuck*." He thrusts his hands into his hair, messing it up completely. I want to go to him and push his thick hair back into place, but I remain where I stand. Unsure of where I stand with him, really.

I hate that.

He comes to me, takes my hands and holds them loosely in his. "I'm going to ask you to do something that you won't like."

Frowning, I stare up at him. "What?"

"I want you to go back to Zachary." He grimaces the second he says his name.

"Are you serious? No." I jerk my hands from his and wrap my arms around myself to ward off the sudden cold that washes over me. "Why would I do that? Especially after . . ."

"Last night? I know." He pulls me to him and wraps me in his arms, his mouth at my forehead, his hand possessively resting on my backside. "I can't stop thinking about it, what happened last night between us, Violet. I need you to know that. But I also need you to do this. It'll be temporary. We just need to create a cover while I figure out exactly what Pilar's doing."

"Why do we need a-a cover?" My voice hitches when Ryder runs his hand slowly up and down my ass. His caress lights me up from within, makes my body yearn for what only he can give me. I should hate him for making these suggestions, but it's as though he's putting me in a trance with his touch while asking me to do something I normally would never do.

I almost feel . . . manipulated.

"I don't want Pilar knowing that we suspect she's with your father," he says as he nuzzles my face with his. "Christ, you smell good."

"Ryder . . ." I protest just as he cups my face and tilts my mouth up to his. He takes my lips in a savage kiss that has me turning more fully into him, my arms going around his neck, my tongue tangling with his.

"You are too much of a distraction." He pushes me away, his hands gripping my shoulders, arms extended so there's plenty of distance between us. "This afternoon I want you to go to Zachary's office and tell him you miss him. That you regret you're not spending his last days in New York with him. It won't take much to convince that asshole you want him still."

My skin crawls at the thought. "I don't want to do this," I admit softly.

"Baby." He cups my cheeks, drifts his thumbs across my skin

so gently I close my eyes, savoring his touch. Nerves ravage at my stomach. It almost feels like this will be the last time we're together. Dramatic but true. "I know you don't. But do this for me. For us. I promise it will all work out in the end."

"And what will you be doing while I'm pretending to be with Zachary?" Disgust roils through me, upsetting my stomach. What if he goes back to Pilar? I can hardly stand the thought. Just the idea of Pilar having her hands all over him makes me want to hurt her.

And I never want to hurt anyone.

"Investigating. Questioning Pilar. Questioning your father."

Of course, he mentions Pilar. I hate that. And what he wants us to do . . . it sounds risky. I don't understand why we have to turn this into such a covert operation. "I won't have sex with him, Ryder. He'll want to, but I won't do it."

"The last fucking thing I want you to do is have sex with him. If you did, I'd have to kill him." He kisses me again, savagely sweet, his hands pressing into the bruised flesh of my backside so hard I cry out against his mouth. He immediately relaxes his hold, looking contrite. "Just tell him you're considering giving him another chance but you want to go slow."

I nod, taking in his words. I could do that. And Zachary would believe it, too. He's so arrogant he probably believes he's pushed me into a corner. He'll be so excited that I'm willing to give him yet another chance, he'll probably agree with my stipulations. He'll also continue to do whatever he wants anyway.

Not that I care anymore.

"I understand, though, if you have to . . . let him touch you. Kiss you." The flash of anger on his handsome face almost scares me. "Avoid it if you can."

His words make my heart hurt, which is stupid. But I thought our relationship shifted since what happened last night. I don't want to be just a game to Ryder McKay.

But what if this is some sort of game? What if he's using me to get back at Zachary and Pilar somehow? For all I know, I could be walking into a trap.

"Exactly how long do you expect me to pretend?" I ask warily. No way do I want Zachary to kiss me. It would feel like I was cheating. I don't want anyone's hands or lips on me unless they're Ryder's.

"However long it takes. Hopefully before Zachary leaves for London," Ryder answers. He withdraws from me, lost in thought, and I watch him pace, admiring his fine masculine form. He looks like he could have stepped right out of a magazine, he's so immaculately dressed. Even his messy hair is artfully arranged and incredibly sexy. My panties dampen just looking at him.

Which makes me remember that I have to cancel our lunch date.

"My sister asked if I'd go to lunch with her," I say hesitatingly.

He stops his pacing and turns to look at me. "You told her you had plans, right?"

I slowly shake my head, nervousness filling me when his eyes go dark with anger. "I told her I would meet her. She said she needed me."

"Violet." He sounds angry and I back up a step when he approaches me. That long-legged stride brings him to me in seconds and he slips his hand around my neck, his long fingers gripping my hair tight. "I need you, too. This might be our last chance to be together for a while."

"I-I know." I nod my head quickly, my entire body shaking when he tightens his fingers in my hair. It hurts. It feels good. Why do I like his show of aggression? Why do I want him to wield such power over me?

"You chose your sister over me," he murmurs, his voice tight, his eyes lit with fire.

"She's family," I argue.

"Don't I matter, too?" He pulls me so close his face is in mine and my legs wobble.

"I . . ." Pausing, I contemplate him. Does he? Yes. But do I matter to him?

I thought I did. Maybe I was wrong.

Memories of last night come back at me, one after another. He was so rough, yet gentle, too. I want that again. I want what only he can give me.

I don't know if he's willing to give me what I want. If he even wants to.

And that scares me the most.

Chapter Twenty-four

Ryder

I'M BEING AN ASSHOLE AND I KNOW IT, BUT I CAN'T HELP IT. I'M hurt that she'd rather have lunch with Rose than with me. That she'd prefer to sit at some crowded restaurant listening to her sister complain about whatever when she could have been with me here in my office, naked and gasping and coming again and again.

The truth? I'm jealous. Jealous that Violet has these other relationships that mean something to her and I have no one save for Pilar, and that bitch doesn't count. Violet's family comes before all others for her and I have no freaking idea what that's like. None. My mother was never in my life. My dad was a selfish bastard who didn't want to deal with me. I had no real friends. No other family.

It doesn't help that I'm sending her back to Zachary for . . . what? To protect her from Pilar while I figure out what she's trying to do with Forrest? And is that shit even for real, her involvement with the old man? The woman is conniving, I'll give her that, but would she take it that far?

Yes. Looks like she would.

"Do I matter to you?" she finally asks, her voice low and husky and sexy as hell. She chews on her lower lip, obviously nervous about my answer.

And just like that, I'm nervous, too.

"Yes," I murmur, not sure what else I should say. I've never done this sort of thing before. Embarking on a normal relationship with a woman is foreign to me and I feel like a complete idiot. More than anything, I feel completely out of control, and I hate it.

"Really, Ryder? Because if I *did* matter to you, I'm thinking my going back to Zachary, even if it's pretend, wouldn't be easy for you to deal with. I know I can't stand the thought of you being near Pilar." She purses her lips, looking so damn prim and proper in her cream-colored button-up blouse and slim black skirt. Simple and elegant, with her hair pulled into a low ponytail and those damn diamonds sparkling in her ears. I hope to hell Lawrence didn't give them to her or I'm going to have to flush them down the toilet.

She's right. I'm the asshole who's pushing her back into his arms. It's fake, but still. I'm taking a huge risk. What if she's not over him? What if she goes back to him and realizes she wants to . . . stay?

It's a chance I'll have to take to find out exactly what Pilar is up to.

"I care. More than you know." I take a deep breath, hating how vulnerable I feel.

"That's all I can ask for." Violet comes toward me, reaching out to touch the side of my face. We stare at each other quietly and I close my eyes for a brief moment, taking a deep breath. She overwhelms me. I want her. Always. If I could, I'd throw her on top of my desk and take her, not caring if anyone caught us.

But I won't. I let the memories of this morning float through my mind. How I fucked her before I left her apartment. Stood at the end of the bed while she lay sprawled, my hands at her hips, my cock powering inside of her gorgeous and well-used body. Her breasts jiggled, her eyes glowed, and when I pulled out and came all over her stomach, she ran her fingers through the spots of creamy white and then licked them clean with a satisfied smile on her face.

Yeah, I've got it bad. It's like she was made for me. Never before have I acted this way with a woman. I like to boss them around in bed, but that's only because I know what I want. But there's something about Violet that makes me want to command her. Mark her.

Own her.

"You make me fucking crazy," I growl as I pull her into my arms, my mouth locking with hers. She moans and holds me close, her tongue sliding against mine, her breasts smashed against my chest. I'm instantly hard. Again I'm tempted. I could tug her skirt up and fuck her right here. Right now.

But I won't. I need to get her out of my office so we can start putting our plan into action. I'll trick Pilar. And Violet will trick Zachary.

Hopefully, we'll get to the bottom of this and get what we want.

"You should go," I whisper against her lips after I break our frantic kiss. She pulls away from me, her eyes on mine, full of hurt at what I just said.

Doesn't she realize that all I want is to protect her?

"Okay." She takes a deep breath and nods, trying to withdraw from my hold, but I don't let her go. Not yet.

It's as if I can't.

Reaching out, I carefully cradle the side of her head so I don't mess up her hair. I rub my finger over the diamond stud in her ear. "Who gave you these?"

Her eyes dim and her expression is somber. "They were my mother's."

Ah Christ. I don't know much about her mother's death, but I know it happened a long time ago. I don't want to upset her. "They're beautiful."

"*She* was beautiful." A little smile curls her lips. "People say I look a lot like her."

"Then I know she was definitely beautiful." I lean in and press a soft kiss to her mouth. She tilts her head, her lips clinging, prolonging the connection, and I sweep my tongue into her mouth, deepening the kiss . . .

Damn it. I need to stop.

Breaking away from her, I drop my hand. She looks up at me once more, those soulful brown eyes making me wonder what other secrets she keeps hidden. Because she's got them. Everyone does.

"I don't know if I can do this," she whispers.

My fingers pause at the front of her shirt. "Do what?"

"Pretend I want Zachary. That I want my old life with him." She shakes her head and closes her eyes, her mouth crumpling as if she might cry. "I don't want him. I only want you."

"Hey." I draw her close and kiss her trembling lips softly, keeping them there as I murmur reassurances. "It's okay. It won't last for long. I promise."

She nods once, her eyes shining with tears, and I clasp her cheeks with both hands, bringing her in so I can kiss her forehead, her nose, her lips once more. "Don't cry, baby. Seeing your tears kills me." They tear at my heart and make my head swim. I can't fucking take it, seeing her so sad.

I may want to own Violet, but I'm afraid she might already own me.

"I'm sorry," she whispers. "Just . . . tell me you'll come over tonight. Tell me I get to see you."

"I'll come over." I hadn't planned on it. I planned on staying away so this looks real. I can't tell her everything yet. I don't even know if I can one hundred percent trust her.

But I know one thing: I can't stay away from her. I'm addicted. To her scent, her smile, her brain, her lips, her tongue, her pussy . . . every single piece of her.

I want to protect her. From Pilar and Zachary and the rumors, and hell, I even want to protect her from . . . me.

I'm afraid I'll hurt her. The very last thing I want to do.

"Help me understand why I'm doing this. Why I'm pretending with Zachary," she says.

"I need to figure out what's going on with Pilar and your father, and the only way I can do that is with Zachary occupied. If he's too focused on you, he won't think about Pilar," I explain. And with Pilar believing I've ended it with Violet, she'll open up to me and let me back in.

"Right." Pressing her lips together, she nods, her lids lifting so she can meet my gaze once more. Tears linger in her eyelashes, stream down her cheeks, and I kiss them away from her skin, rub my thumbs underneath her eyes to catch the ones still clinging there.

"Don't cry, baby. Everything will work out just the way you want it to. I know it will." I kiss her sweet lips, fighting against the surge of protectiveness I feel for her, but it's no use.

It's there. I need to face it. Face exactly what I feel for this woman.

If only I could figure that out.

"And if I don't know exactly how I want this to work out?" she asks cautiously.

Damn this girl. She is so perceptive. "Then we'll figure it out day by day."

"I DID IT."

I slam the door of Pilar's office behind me as I stride toward her desk, stopping just in front of it. She frowns at me, looking completely irritated that I'm standing in her office, bugging her. A far cry from the crazy woman who gyrated on my knee yesterday afternoon like some sort of highly skilled stripper and brought herself to orgasm in a matter of minutes.

"You did what?" she asks, sounding bored.

"Violet Fowler is officially broken." I smile and settle into the chair across from her desk, getting comfortable. I figure she'll have a lot of questions to ask and I've spent the last hour in my office alone, trying to figure out exactly what she would want to know.

I'm as prepared for this interrogation as any proper Boy Scout would be.

"Broken how?" Her gaze flicks to mine for the briefest moment before she returns her attention to her laptop. "I have a meeting in thirty. I don't have time for petty bullshit."

I stand and slam my hands on her desk, leaning down so I lurk over her like some sort of starving vulture looking for a meal. "I said that I broke Violet. Just as you asked. I dumped her this morning. I have no doubt she'll be back in Lawrence's arms by the early evening."

She studies me, looking for a slip, looking for the lie. I keep my expression impassive, my demeanor calm. Any cracks in the façade and she'll jump all over them. She's particular like that. It's a skill that's worked well for her through the years.

"God, I knew if given the chance she'd probably return to Zachary. So dreadfully boring." Pilar rolls her eyes, then slams her laptop shut. I have her complete attention now. "Tell me what happened. I want every detail."

Here come the lies. The chance I have to slip up and fuck up is at hand. I need to keep my facts straight and give Pilar exactly what she wants. I sit back down in the chair. "I went over to her place. We'd agreed to meet there."

"What? To fuck?" She snickers, and I send her a hard glare that shuts her up.

"I strip her naked. We start going at it. In the middle of the sex I tell her she's awful. A bad lay. I'd been saying all sorts of things throughout the entire act. Little things that probably made her question whether it was an insult or not. I'm breaking her down, fucking with her head, fucking with her body until she can't see straight, let alone think straight, and she starts crying."

Pilar's eyes light with pleasure and she props her elbow on the edge of her desk, leaning her chin onto her curled fist. "Crying? My, my, Ryder. Have you ever made a girl cry in bed before?"

"No. She's my first." We both laugh, and I ignore the sick feeling in my gut. I hate doing this. Making fun of Violet, making her look weak and pitiful when she's far from that. "Right after I fucked her, I left. She texted me but I didn't respond. Left me a voicemail but I deleted it. When she showed up in my office this morning, I told her I didn't think we were a good idea anymore."

"You were never a good idea, my darling," Pilar says snidely and I glare at her.

Bitch. I can't wait to fuck her over.

"She cried and raged on over what an asshole she thought I was. Then she stormed out." I pause. Making up these lies is harder than I thought it would be. "So it's over. Done. I did what you asked. Now it's your turn to deliver." I lean back in the chair and cross my arms over my chest, my fingers linked. "Tell me. Who have you been talking to?"

She purses her lips. "I can't reveal all my secrets."

"Not even to me?"

"Especially not to you. You'll run right over me and cut me out. I prefer to be the middleman." Her smile grows. "Or middlewoman. You know, that reminds me, I've never participated in a threesome. Have you?"

She turns everything back to sex. And that is the last thing I want to think about when it comes to Pilar. "No. Too much work, not enough return."

A laugh escapes her. "Hmm. Selfish as usual, Ryder. I wouldn't mind giving it a try." She taps her finger against her lips, her usual look when she's contemplating something. If she suggests getting it on with her, me, and old man Fowler? Fuck that noise. No way, no how.

"Yeah, well why don't you plan your threesome later and focus." Her laughter dies when she realizes I'm serious. "I'm done."

Pilar gives me a blank look. "Done with what?"

"I'm done playing this game with you. We've done what each of us said we would do. There's no need to take it any further." I can't keep up this pretense any longer. I don't want to. It's painful, spending time with Pilar. I can hardly stand her. Plus, I'm trying my best to protect Violet.

She's becoming my weakness, as much as I don't want to admit it. If Pilar knew this, she'd know just how to get to me.

By hurting Violet.

"So you just want it to . . . end." Pilar sounds surprised, which she probably is.

"It's time to sever our ties, don't you think?" I scrub a hand along my jaw, frustration making it tight. This is harder than I thought, ending everything with Pilar. I need to do what's right. And what's right is for me to stand by Violet. Without Pilar knowing, of course.

She laughs and shakes her head. "You're so funny, darling. Like I'd cut you loose. You can't get away from me that fast."

"Yeah, I think I can."

"No. I think you can't." The thin smile on her face tells me I've irritated her. She won't let me dismiss her. I don't understand why. "You really believe I'll let you cut and run? You could use this against me somehow."

"What? And throw myself under the bus, too? I'm not that stupid." I'm almost insulted that she'd think so.

"Men do strange things when under Violet Fowler's spell." She arches one perfectly sculpted brow. "I wouldn't expect you to be any different."

"I dumped her. Or did you forget?" My voice is tight. My blood is boiling. I'm tempted to walk out before I say something stupid and ruin everything.

"I haven't forgotten. And I thank you for it. Truly I do." The serene expression on her face is a total ruse. "I need you to do more."

Unease causes my stomach to pitch. "There's nothing more I can do." The possibilities don't settle right. I don't know what she wants, but I know it can't be good.

"Liar. You could do plenty more. Didn't you take any dirty pictures of her naked? We could make it look like Zachary took them and send them out via the company email. Something that scandalous could make Violet leave Fleur for good and never, ever come back," Pilar murmurs, her eyes flashing with pure hatred.

"What the hell did she ever do to you?" I ask incredulously. Her unwarranted anger takes me aback. I don't get it.

"She was born with the last name Fowler." She tilts her head, a smug look on her face. "Isn't that enough?"

"She can't help who her family is. And why do you think getting rid of her will help you get ahead here? There's still Rose to contend with. And you never know, Lily could straighten up and come work here someday," I point out. Pilar is downright vicious when it comes to Violet and I don't get why.

"Violet is her daddy's favorite," she practically spits out, the disgust written all over her pretty face, making her look rather . . . ugly. "He never stops praising her. She can do no wrong in his eyes. With her out of the way, he'll need to focus on someone else. Rose doesn't have the chops. Lily is a fucking mess who will never work a day in her life. Violet's the only one with true focus. The one the fucking grandma believes in."

"The fucking grandma? You mean the woman who founded this company?" That she speaks of Dahlia Fowler with such disrespect when she's revered by everyone at Fleur surprises me.

And that she speaks of having conversations about Violet with Forrest Fowler so casually surprises me as well.

"Whatever. I'm sick of all the nepotism that goes on around here. I deserve a fair shake." She slams her fist on her desk. "I'm damn good at what I do and it's about time someone recognized it."

"Christ, Pilar." I say her name softly, startling her. She's ruthless. One has to be to get as far as she has in this business. She's determined and a hard worker and she's never backed down from a challenge. Hell, I think she relishes them.

She's also a troublemaker and she'd fully admit that. She has no problem having a tantrum, either, kicking and screaming and making unreasonable demands until she gets what she wants.

I wonder if that's worked for her on someone else lately. Like Zachary. Or . . .

Forrest Fowler.

"What? You act like this is a big surprise. You know I should run Fleur someday, and the only way it won't happen is if Forrest hands over the reins to Violet. So I'll get rid of her and the obstacle is out of my way. It'll be easy, especially with your help. When she realizes that we've been working together against her all along . . ."

Fear races through me. I'm trying to trick a tricky bitch. Everything is riding on how I handle it.

And how Violet handles it, too.

Chapter Twenty-five

Violet

"YOU DON'T KNOW HOW HAPPY YOU'VE MADE ME."

I offer Zachary a tight smile but say nothing. I'm afraid if I talk too much I'll blow my cover. Or worse, accuse him of being an asshole cheater, then run out of the restaurant.

Ryder would be disappointed in me. And that is the last thing I want.

Well. Besides Zachary.

"How's your salad?" he asks. He's on his best behavior, taking me to my favorite Italian restaurant, buying the most expensive wine on the menu in honor of our celebration—his words. The celebration of my giving our relationship another go after all—he's positively thrilled.

I feel one part glad that I'm getting some sort of revenge against Zachary, and two parts completely awful for doing this to him.

"It's delicious." I stare down at my Caprese salad, admiring the perfectly sliced tomatoes and mozzarella, the vibrant leaves of basil and the drizzle of balsamic vinegar. This is my favorite salad, my go-to when nothing else sounds good on the menu.

But my appetite is gone. Being with Zachary feels wrong.

Dreadfully, horribly wrong.

"Not hungry?" He sends me a soulful look. One that I used

to fall for. "You usually devour that salad like a starving woman."

His remark sets my teeth on edge. Is he somehow implying that I eat too much? I'm making a big deal out of nothing, I'm sure. But I can't help but feel defensive every time I'm with him. "I had a late lunch," I lie.

I had lunch with Rose and listened to her talk about an ex-boyfriend who's giving her trouble, how Father seems to be ignoring her, and that the brunch with Lily drove her nuts. I'm the one who normally gets them to play fair and talk nice when we're all together. It's the middle child in me. So without me there, Lily got snarky, Rose got defensive, and they ended up arguing.

Again, I feel responsible, since I left them to meet with Ryder. He called me a distraction earlier in his office. I have to confess he's a distraction for me as well. A sexy, delicious one, but a distraction nonetheless.

And he makes me do things . . . things I could never imagine contemplating, let alone actually *doing*, before. I've been an achy mess all day just thinking about him.

I'm still an achy mess. I miss him. I want him. And I'm stuck with Zachary.

"A meeting?"

"No, lunch with my sister." Let's see if he asks which one. If he asks how she's doing. If he asks anything personal. Most of the time he's so full of himself, he doesn't give others much consideration.

So again, why was I with him for so long?

"How was that?" he asks sarcastically. "Lily complaining how Daddy cut her off yet again?"

"No, it was with Rose." *Hmm.* He's making conversation like his old self. Making snide remarks, but I guess I can let them slide. Talk about being on his best behavior. "We haven't talked much lately, so we were catching up."

"Uh-huh." I've lost his interest. I can tell by the way he watches the pretty waitress pass us by, his gaze glued to her swishing backside. Guess he hasn't changed much after all.

"Are you excited about leaving?" I ask brightly. When he looks at me strangely I add, "For London."

"Oh. Yes. Of course." He busies himself by drinking from his water glass, wiping his mouth with his cloth napkin, then pulling another piece of bread from the basket that rests in the center of the table. "You sure you want to talk about this?"

He's nervous? How very strange—and it's somewhat refreshing. I'm the one who's usually walking on eggshells. "If we're going to work on our relationship, we need to be completely upfront." I wince the moment the words leave me. I'm a liar. And I never lie. I hate what Ryder's making me do.

"You're right." He visibly relaxes. "I just . . . I need to know something first. Before I say anything else."

"What?"

"Are you still speaking to McKay?" The scowl on Zachary's attractive face is nothing short of furious.

"No." I slowly shake my head and press my lips together. I hate denying it. Denying Ryder. I want to talk to him. I need to see him. He promised he would come over tonight, but what if he doesn't show? What if he falls back into Pilar's trap and I'm left with Zachary?

I'd deserve it for being deceitful. It doesn't matter if Zachary's deceitful, too. A lie for a lie isn't right, no matter how much I can justify it.

"Good." His features even out and he's once more attractive, charming Zachary. "Trade secrets, you know. I don't want that asshole finding out any details about my promotion."

Now I'm really curious. And willing to test the waters. "You know . . . my father mentioned the position to me."

"He did? What did he say? Anything about me?"

Such an egomaniac. "Well . . . yes. But he also said that he believed I would do well in London."

"You?" He sounds shocked. And even mildly disgusted. "You're not interested in anything like that."

"How do you know?" I ask indignantly. I'm about to give him a piece of my mind when the cute waitress appears with our dinners. She sets the plate of chicken Marsala in front of me as I push aside my salad, then settles a plate of lasagna in front of Zachary. He smiles at the waitress as she flirts with him while I watch them both, silently steaming.

I hate this. I want to grab the back of Zachary's head and smash his face in that steaming-hot lasagna. I want to hear him scream and feel him struggle. I want to call him out on his sexist ways and bullying approach.

But I do none of that. I smile at the waitress even when she glares at me and I push my chicken around on the plate like I haven't a care in the world, while I watch Zachary shovel giant forkfuls of lasagna into his mouth.

Ugh. He's repulsive.

"You'll come visit me soon, right?" he asks after five minutes of long, almost painful silence.

"Oh, yes," I say, setting my fork down on my plate. I'm giving up. I'm just not hungry. "It's been years since I've been to London."

"We'll check out the sights together. And go to Paris." He smiles, knowing that's exactly what I want. He's just trying to please me. Trying to suck me into his web until I'm trapped and back in the same position I was in before.

Stuck and miserable.

My cell buzzes and I check it discreetly, my heart pounding when I see it's a text from Ryder. I read his words slowly, savoring them, trying to repress the smile that wants to break free.

I miss you.

He confuses me. He's cold. He's hot. I can't figure him out.

I'm with Zachary, I tell him to see if I get a rise out of him. It works.

Tell that asshole you need to go home and I'll meet you at your place.

I can practically hear his growling, sexy voice. A shiver moves through me as I hurriedly peck out my response.

I can't leave yet. We're eating dinner.

Fuck dinner.

But I'm hungry.

Come fuck me instead.

"Who are you texting?"

"Oh." I glance up, clutching my phone tight, covering the screen. It's in my lap, so Zachary can't see anything, but still. "It's, um, Lily. She wants to meet for breakfast this weekend."

"Tell her you have plans this weekend with me." He flashes me a smug smile.

"I can't ignore my sisters, Zachary. You know how important they are to me," I reprimand him.

"And I'm not important? I know I need to prove myself to you, Violet. I should consider myself damn lucky you're giving me this chance, and I do. But I'm leaving in a few days and I'd really like to spend any free time I have with you." The sincerity glowing in his eyes is hard to ignore, but is it for real? This is such a turn-around from the man who announced he was leaving and that he didn't have much time for me, what with all his preparations.

My phone buzzes in my palm and I glance down, Ryder's impatience blatant in his one-worded text.

Well?

Lifting my head, I offer Zachary an apologetic smile as I stand, still clutching the phone. "Do you mind if I call her real quick? I won't be long."

"Go." He waves me away with an irritated glare and I flee,

finding a secluded spot near the bathrooms so I can make my call.

"Tell me you've left," Ryder answers, all growly and sexy.

"I haven't. I snuck away from him to call you," I say, glancing around to make sure no one is paying attention to me lurking in the dark near the restrooms.

"Tell him an emergency came up and you need to leave."

"What sort of emergency?"

"I don't know. That you need to get fucked and the only one that can do it for you is me?"

"Ryder." I close my eyes and lean against the wall. "You told me we needed to be discreet."

"I didn't think it would bother me so much that you're with him," he says, sounding as confused as I feel.

"You think I like it that you're spending time with Pilar?" I throw back at him.

He remains quiet. His usual mode when he doesn't know what to say.

"We're almost finished," I say quietly. "I'll beg off and tell him I have a headache. I'll text you when I'm on my way."

"Ten minutes," he says tightly. "If you don't text me in ten minutes, there will be hell to pay."

Everything inside of me goes liquid. "What do you mean?"

"Test me and find out." And then he's gone.

Releasing a shuddering sigh, I go into the women's bathroom and wash my hands, then splash cool water on my heated cheeks. I tear off a paper towel and stare at my reflection as I dry my hands and pat at my cheeks.

Who am I? What has happened to me since Ryder so casually walked into my life and turned it upside down? I'm pretending to want to be with my ex-boyfriend while texting my lover on the side. The very man who demands that I meet him at my place or there will be hell to pay.

I remember what he did to me last night. His hand around my throat as he fucked me . . . when he spanked me . . .

God. That had been so shocking. Yet I want more. I *crave* more.

On shaky legs, I return to my table with Zachary and settle in, grabbing my glass of water and gulping it all down in a few swallows.

"You all right?" he asks, concern lacing his voice.

"I have a terrible headache. All the stress I've been dealing with lately . . ." I offer him a trembling smile, hoping my subtle guilt trip works. "I'm afraid I need to cut this short."

"I understand." He leaps to his feet and helps me out of my chair as if I'm fragile. I let him escort me out of the restaurant, regret filling me that I didn't enjoy my meal. My nerves are frazzled, my mind is fuzzy, and between my legs I'm wet and throbbing.

Because I know soon I'll be with Ryder. And I'm almost hoping there will be hell to pay.

How sick am I?

THE MOMENT I ENTER THE LOBBY OF MY BUILDING I SEE HIM. Pacing near the bank of elevators, the expression on his face fierce. He doesn't even notice me at first, what with the way he's scowling and staring at the ground, and I watch him for one unguarded moment, loving the way he checks his cell. In the hopes he has a message from me, perhaps?

I clear my throat and he whirls around, his expression softening in an instant. But he remains coolly impassive, keeping his distance as I approach him and reach out, pressing the button for the penthouse floor.

"Hi," I murmur, stepping back.

"Hello," he greets in return, shoving his hands into the front pockets of his dark-rinse jeans. He looks amazing. The spring night has turned cool and he's wearing a black Henley shirt that hugs his torso, his biceps straining against the sleeves. I always see him in suits—or naked—and I savor these moments when I get to admire him in such casual clothing.

He looks good no matter what he wears.

"Having a nice evening?" he asks as if he's a complete stranger making polite conversation.

"Not really," I admit truthfully.

He raises a single brow, the subtle move so sexy it takes my breath away. "And why's that?"

"I was with a man I don't . . . like very much."

"That's a shame."

"I know." I pause, deciding whether I should say what I want or not. I go for it. "I'd much rather spend my time with someone else."

"Really?" The elevator dings and the doors slide open. Ryder holds out his arm, indicating I should enter the car first. He follows in after me and leans against the wall opposite of where I stand. "Sometimes we have to do things we don't like in order to get what we want."

I press my lips together and employ one of his tricks by saying nothing.

The doors close and the elevator starts to rise. I remain where I stand and so does he, but the palpable tension between us grows with every second that passes, with every floor we climb.

"So. Was I late?" I ask, my voice small, my insides quaking with anticipation.

"Did you want to be?" he asks.

"You said there would be hell to pay if I was."

A smile curls his beautiful lips. "Are you telling me you're in the mood to pay, Violet? Or should I say . . . play?"

Oh, God. He's so bad. "Is that what we're doing? Playing?"

He stares at me, his hands gripping the rail behind him. His stance is casual, but I can feel the tension in him. He's coiled tight, ready to pounce, and I can only hope he's ready to unleash all of that built-up sexual tension all over me.

The elevator chimes and the doors slide open. I exit without looking back, feeling his magnetic presence as he falls into step behind me. I stop to unlock my door, stiffening when he presses close, my breath catching as he trails a finger across the exposed skin along my shoulder and the back of my neck.

"Did he touch you?" he asks, his voice low, rumbling from deep within his chest. He doesn't have to say Zachary's name. I know exactly who he's talking about.

I shake my head, my fingers fumbling with the lock. "N-no."

"Good." He steps even closer, his entire body pressed against mine, and I close my eyes, savoring the hard, delicious feel of him. "Open the door, Violet."

My fingers falter again and he reaches out, pushing them away so he can take over. I feel the hard length of his erect cock nudging against my ass and my breath catches in my throat. He's surrounding me. Taking over. And he makes me so weak I don't want him to stop.

The door somehow opens and we both rush inside, Ryder slamming and locking the door before turning to me, his hands cupping my face as he kisses me. I kiss him back with everything I have, dropping my purse to the floor before I reach for the waistband of his jeans and undo the button fly with surprising efficiency.

He breaks the kiss for a quick second to tear off his shirt before he's going back in, his tongue and lips working their usual magic over me. I shove his jeans down his hips and he kicks them as well as his shoes off, revealing that he's not wearing underwear. My eyes are closed but I know this because when I reach for him, my hand comes in contact with his very erect, very thick cock.

I stroke him, grip him tight, and he groans in agony. The

sound fuels me and I suck his tongue deep into my mouth, my entire body clenching with anticipation.

"I can't figure out how to get this damn dress off of you," he mutters as he pushes me away. I turn my back toward him and he undoes the zipper, shoving at my dress so it practically falls off me. I step out of it and turn to face him once more, standing in my virginal white lacy bra and matching panties, feeling not so virginal as I see the way he studies me.

As if he wants to swallow me whole.

He licks his lips as if anticipating a particularly delicious meal and he slowly approaches me. "How do you want me tonight?"

I frown. "What do you mean?"

"Do you want me to go slow?" He drifts his fingers across my cheek, then down my neck, toying with my bra strap. My breath quickens at his touch. "Or fast?"

Oh, God. I don't know what sounds better. "Wh-what do you want?"

He hums and tilts his head. His gaze lingers on my face before it dips low, landing on my breasts. My nipples harden at his blatant contemplation and I fidget, wishing he would say something. "Both have their merits," he finally says as he reaches out and runs his finger along the lacy trim of one bra cup, then the other.

Gooseflesh rises at his touch and I sway on my feet. "Yes."

"I think I'd rather take my time." His gaze returns to mine. "And savor you."

That sounds absolutely perfect.

Chapter Twenty-six

Ryder

I'M MINDING MY OWN DAMN BUSINESS IN YET ANOTHER PACKAGing meeting when I see her walk by, sexy as fuck. As usual. She stops in the doorway of the conference room I'm sitting in, giving me a perfect view of her, and I almost feel like she does it on purpose.

She may act sweet and innocent, but she's devious—at least when it comes to tempting me.

Violet is wearing her hair up, revealing that elegant, kissable neck. Pearl studs are in her ears and the dress she wears is a deep shade of purple. It fits her body to perfection, accenting every dip and curve.

But it's her legs that do me in. Usually they're bare—which is a temptation I fight against since that first moment she let me touch her. Today, though, she has on black, diamond-patterned stockings and the highest, shiniest black shoes I've ever seen her wear.

Instantly my brain goes to Violet sprawled across my desk, her skirt hiked up to her waist, those patterned legs splayed in the air while I stand between them, fucking her until she screams.

Yeah. I'm a twisted mess over this woman. I can't get enough of her. I stayed the night at her place last night and kept her up.

Alternating between talking, kissing, and fucking, there wasn't much time to sleep.

I wonder if she's up for a repeat performance tonight.

"Ryder. Did you hear me?"

I jerk my attention away from Violet standing in the doorway to smile at Luann, one of the smartest members on my team. "Sorry. Repeat that?"

We're talking about finalizing the packaging for the holiday sets and she asks if I prefer gold or silver trim.

I go with gold.

The meeting is over and Violet is still standing there, talking with someone. I can't tell who. Anticipation fills me as I get up from my chair and start for the doorway. I keep my steps measured, not wanting to look too eager.

The woman makes me fucking eager. She's all I think about. All I want. I care about her. Worry about her when I don't know where she is. It's confusing as hell.

I draw closer. I'm about to say something when I see exactly whom she's talking to.

Zachary motherfucking Lawrence.

"Violet." I murmur her name as I stride by her, not stopping, not even looking in Lawrence's direction. I can sense his smug arrogance, the triumph he feels radiating off him. The asshole thinks he's won.

But he's not the one sleeping in Violet's bed at night. He's not the one with his face buried between Violet's legs, tonguing her until she comes. And he's definitely not the one sinking his cock deep inside her welcoming body.

Yeah. That honor would go to me.

She doesn't say hello, but I can't blame her. I feel her eyes on me, though, as I walk away, and I smile. We've gone full incognito with this . . . affair we're having, and I'm enjoying the hell out of it.

I take that back. I don't like her spending time with Lawrence, even though I told her to do it. I don't like pretending I'm on good terms with Pilar, either, because I don't trust her. That bitch is trying to cross me and fuck over Violet. She is hell-bent on getting whatever she wants, and it doesn't matter who gets hurt in the process.

Oh, and I'm this close to having confirmation that she's fucking around with Forrest Fowler.

The woman has balls of steel, I gotta give her that.

Deciding I may as well go see her and get it over with, I make my way to Pilar's office, knocking on her open door before I enter. She's on the phone and she turns away from me, murmuring something quick before she hangs up and turns on the charm.

"Darling. A visit from you is always a lovely surprise. Especially since I feel such a . . . distance between us lately." She leaps up from her chair and comes to me, clasping her arms around my waist and pressing her lips to mine.

I lean away from her mouth, startled that she would try and kiss me at work. Shocked that she would kiss me at all. "What's gotten into you?"

"Oh, wouldn't you like to know," she trills, as she releases her hold on me and does a little dance around her office. "It's a good day, you know? The sun is shining, the weather is warm. I had words with Violet this morning and I think I upset her. Life doesn't get much better than this."

I'm stunned. "Words? What are you talking about?"

Why didn't Violet tell me? What the fuck is going on?

Pilar *tsk*s and settles back in her chair. "I paid her a visit in her palace, otherwise known as her office." She rolls her eyes. "Nothing like *this* dump."

She has a corner office with an amazing view of the city. It's far from a dump. "Hell, Pilar, are you ever happy?"

"Today I am." She laughs. "You should've seen her. I got her riled up. Trembling so hard her voice shook as she tried to defend herself."

"What exactly did you say?" I feel fucking awful. I wish I had been there so I could defend Violet, but . . .

Yeah. That would've blown our cover for sure.

"I heard her complaining to her sister that she was worried her line wouldn't be ready in time for its set debut date. The moment Rose left her office, I went in for the kill." Pilar smirks. "I tried for the innocent act, feigning concern for her line, then implied that maybe she wasn't cut out for heading such a large, demanding project after all."

"And what did she say?"

"Nothing! Well, she told me she had it under control, and there was hardly any fight in her. God, she's boring. I don't understand why you're all fascinated with her. You. Zachary. Forrest." She shakes her head. "She's a little nothing."

Jealous. Pilar is so jealous she can hardly see straight.

"Sounds like you got your digs in." It grates that I have to play along. "I notice you keep mentioning our fearless leader's name so casually," I drawl, hoping she thinks I'm teasing her and not fishing for information.

But I am fishing.

"I've spent an awful lot of time with Forrest lately," she says coyly. "He's a lovely man."

"I'm sure." Old enough to be her father, too, but that's not stopping her. "Sleeping with him to climb your way to the very top?"

"Oh, stop." She laughs a little too loudly, her discomfort a little too obvious. "I would never do that."

"Uh-huh." I approach her desk, my gaze never leaving hers. "Tell me the truth, Pilar. Are you fucking Fowler?"

Her eyes widen and she rests her hand at the center of her chest. "Are you accusing me of having an affair with Forrest?"

"I am."

She bursts out laughing. "I can neither confirm nor deny your suspicion."

"Give me a break."

"I can't give up all my secrets, you know."

"You used to," I remind her.

"So did you," she throws back in my face. "But that's all changed, hasn't it? Now you've cut all ties between us and walked away. If you can't help me, then I need to help myself, right?"

I can't even deal with this woman. I decide to change the subject, throw her off. "What about Lawrence?"

Her brows rise. "What about him?"

"Why did you fuck around with him?"

"He was nothing. A distraction." She waves a hand, dismissing him. "You said you wanted to seduce Violet and I wanted in on the action. I couldn't let you have all the fun."

I ignore her teasing tone. I don't find anything about this funny. "Were you already fucking Forrest when we had that conversation?"

She doesn't say anything, but she doesn't have to. The coy smile that curls her lips is my answer.

"You never told me," I say stiffly. I'm shocked—and surprisingly hurt, which I know is stupid, but I can't help it. We've shared so many things, so many ups and downs, that the fact that she deliberately chose not to tell me that she was having an affair with Forrest Fowler bothers me.

Yet I'm lying to her about Violet, so I have no room to judge.

"There's nothing to tell." She's holding it all in, I can tell. She's not going to give me anything, not that I can blame her. We're lying to each other. I may have called off this game, but we're still playing and it's getting dirty.

When I don't say anything she starts to laugh. "Darling, are you jealous?" She looks thrilled at the possibility.

Fuck no. Irritated, yes. "If you'd told me what you were up to all along, I might've done things differently."

But then I might not have gone after Violet so hotly. I can't regret that.

"Everything is falling into place perfectly. Don't second-guess your choices. And don't question mine." She beams at me. "I'll get what I want and you'll get what you want. Trust me."

I don't trust her. And I'm worried that she *won't* get what she wants.

Not sure if I will, either.

MINUTES AFTER I RETURN TO MY OFFICE, VIOLET IS STRIDING IN, her expression fierce. Sexy. She stops in the middle of my office, her hands on her hips, her head tilted to the side. She looks like she wants to tear me apart. "Why the hell were you in Pilar's office?"

I lean back in my chair, startled. Irritated. "Why the hell didn't you tell me you got into an argument with Pilar?"

"When was I supposed to tell you that?"

"Oh, come on." I sit forward, resting my forearms on the edge of my desk. "You have no problem emailing me that you want me at any given time of the day."

Her cheeks redden and her stance wilts a bit. "Keep your voice down," she practically hisses.

I smile. "You started it." Arguing with her is going to lead to sex. I can feel it.

Then again, everything Violet and I seem to do leads to sex.

With a huff, she turns and goes to the door and for the briefest, scariest moment, I think she's going to walk out and never look back. Ever again.

But she doesn't. She goes to the door and shuts it, then carefully turns the lock before she faces me once more.

"She came into my office this morning after she *spied* on my conversation with my sister." Violet lifts her chin. "Then she tried to imply that I can't handle the responsibilities I've been given."

Nervy bitch. "What did you tell her?"

She shrugs. "I didn't really say anything except that I have it handled, and I asked her to leave my office. I wasn't going to lower myself to her level and sling insults. My father raised me right."

Huh. Not going to touch that one, considering Pilar is possibly messing around with Violet's "raise her right" father.

"Why were you in her office?" she asks when I don't say anything.

I don't want to talk about Pilar. "Come here," I say softly.

"No." She stands her ground. "Tell me, Ryder."

"Are you defying me?" I ask, irritated that she won't do what I say. That I always feel the need to command her and possess her like some sort of warrior set out to conquer.

"Yes. I am." She stares me down but she doesn't scare me. And I don't think I scare her, either. She knows how much I want her. Is she aware of how much I need her? "Tell me what you two talked about."

"It was nothing, Violet," I finally confess with a gentle sigh. "I tried to ask her a few questions about your father, but she dodged them all."

"Really." She sounds skeptical and I can't blame her.

"Really," I answer firmly. "Now come. Here."

Reluctantly she approaches me, her teeth sunk into her lower lip. As she draws closer, I can smell her and I inhale discreetly, a surge of lust bolting through me. *Fuck,* I want her. Always.

"Sit down." I turn my chair toward her and pat my thigh in invitation. She tentatively settles her ass on my leg, keeping her head bent. I lean in and smell her neck, nuzzling the soft, sensitive skin behind her ear. "Feeling a little defiant today, aren't you?"

She keeps her head bent but doesn't move away from me. Not that she can, with my arm wrapped firmly around her waist. "I don't like you spending time with Pilar."

"I don't like it when you chat up your ex right in front of me," I return.

"I didn't know you were in the conference room," she says in her defense, but her voice is weak.

Leaning in, I place my mouth at her ear and whisper, "Liar."

She doesn't look at me, doesn't deny what I said, either. Proving she knew I was in that conference room the entire time she was talking to that asshole.

"You're a bad girl, Violet. Lying to me. Trying to make me jealous." I touch her hair, skim my finger over the shell of her ear. Her breathing shallows and finally she lifts her head, her gaze meeting mine.

"Are you?"

I frown. "Am I what?"

"Jealous?"

I scowl. She's trying to drive me crazy and it's working. "Do you want me to be?"

"I don't know what I want from you," She shrugs.

"Ah, but I think you do. And for your information, I was." I kiss her neck, let my lips linger on her soft skin. Emotions swirl within me at having her so close. "Extremely jealous."

"Then let's give up this stupid charade and be done with it," she suggests hopefully.

Sweeter words were never spoken. "Sounds good to me." I rest my hand on her knee and give it a gentle squeeze. "Nice stockings."

"You like them?" She sounds hopeful, and I wonder if she wore them just for me.

"Not your usual style. I thought I preferred your legs bare. Easy access, you know." I slip my hand up her thigh, the silky feel of her stockings adding a sensual friction I can definitely appreciate. Her breath catches, making me smile. "But these are very interesting."

"I'm glad you approve," she says as my hand slips beneath her skirt, feeling the bare skin of her naked upper thigh.

"Thigh highs?" I push her skirt up to reveal that indeed, she's wearing thigh-high stockings. I trace the wide band of lace, my finger coming perilously close to the front of her black panties. "Little hooks and a garter belt probably would've done me in, though."

Her cheeks flush pink. "I'll remember that for next time."

She fidgets on my lap, making me fucking hard, and I clamp my arm tight around her waist, trying to keep her in place. "That I can still make you blush after everything we've done together blows my mind." I slide my hand over the front of her panties and discover they're soaked. No surprise.

Her hips lift, a subtle indication that she wants more, and I oblige, slipping my fingers beneath her panties and rubbing against her. "You like that?"

She nods and sinks her teeth into her lower lip again.

I shift lower, plunging into her drenched folds, inserting my index finger inside her body. "Feels so good you can't speak?"

She nods again, her eyes sliding closed when I start to fuck her with my finger in earnest. I press my forehead to the side of her head, my mouth at her ear, and I watch my hand move beneath the black lace of her panties. It looks hot. Forbidden. The way she's moving with me, the sound of my fingers working her creamy pussy, her quickening breaths . . .

"You're close, aren't you." I bite her earlobe and she squeals. "Say it."

"I-I'm close."

"Beg me to make you come." I stop moving my hand.

"Please." She whimpers when I flick her clit with my thumb. She's a pro at this now. I've made her beg me to let her come time and again. "Please, Ryder. I need you. Make me come."

"I'm going to fuck you on my desk," I whisper in her ear as I slowly, deliberately start to thrust my fingers within her body again. "Would you like that?"

"Yesss," she hisses.

"I don't have any condoms, though." My hand stills and so does she as her gaze meets mine. "Are you . . ."

"On the pill?" She nods. "Yes."

"I'm clean." Excitement builds within me. I've never had sex without a condom. I may have been a dumb kid, but I never forgot to suit up. A big mistake like that could screw you up forever.

"So am I," she whispers as I start to stroke her again. She closes her eyes, seemingly overcome. "I want to know what it feels like. With no barriers."

Christ. So do I.

She turns her head toward mine, her cheek resting against my hair, and we remain like that, my hand furiously working her pussy, our accelerated breaths mingling. She's trembling on my lap, my cock is poking against her ass, and when I whisper in her ear, "Come," she shatters, my name falling from her lips accompanied by a sob.

I wonder not for the first time if this woman was made for me. She's so responsive. Feisty. Smart as hell. Sweet. Sexy. Filthy when I demand her to be.

I'm an addict, but she's the only one that I crave. The only thing that makes me feel good. That makes me feel whole and like I have a purpose in life. The scary thing about addiction, though?

It takes over your life. Becomes the only thing you can focus on, the only thing that takes the pain away. If I keep this up, it'll become more and more difficult for me to walk away.

And I should walk away.

She knows it.

I know it.

Doesn't mean I'll do it, though.

Chapter Twenty-seven

Violet

I'M LYING ON TOP OF RYDER'S DESK, MY DRESS HIKED UP TO MY waist, my panties lying on the floor, my legs spread wide with Ryder standing in between them while he pushes his thick cock inside of me again and again. He grips my ankles, his fingers curved tight, thumbs skimming over the patterned stockings I wore just for him.

I knew he'd like them.

In a daze, I watch him. Admire him. His dark hair is a riotous mess from me running my fingers through it only minutes ago. He shed his jacket but he's wearing one of his usual crisp white shirts and a black silk tie, everything perfectly in place above the waist. His pants are bunched around his knees along with his charcoal boxer briefs, but that doesn't hinder him in his ability to fuck me into oblivion.

Nothing keeps my man down.

I close my eyes and savor the thrust of his cock inside my body. In. Out. Faster. Deeper. His hands move away from my ankles and he's gripping my hips, holding me in place as he increases his thrusts even faster. I wrap my legs around his waist, moaning with every slap of his balls against my ass. Reach out and grip his wrists to ground me as I feel the orgasm build and sway. It teases me, offering me a glimpse of its intensity, and I chase after it, close my eyes tight, concentrate on reaching that pinnacle. If I could just grasp hold of it and not let go . . .

The rippling sensation washes over me and I cry out, my eyes popping open to take him in as he stills, his expression one of shocked, blissful agony. One hard buck of his hips and his semen fills me as he comes, his entire body wracked with shudders.

Feeling his flesh sink into mine with no latex barriers . . . *my God*. It makes everything that much better. Like, mind-bogglingly better.

"Fuck, that was unbelievable," he mutters, sounding overcome. He grabs hold of my hands and pulls me into a sitting position, his cock still imbedded in my body. I tilt my head back just as he kisses me, his lips soft and damp, his tongue teasing against my lower lip. I part my lips on a sigh and slide my tongue against his, and the kiss turns lazy and sweet. I tighten my grip on his hands, our fingers intertwined, and I realize I've never felt so content.

Ridiculous. Most of the time he confuses me. My feelings for him confuse me. He can be so indifferent sometimes. Mysterious. Standoffish. And other times, he's passionate and all-consuming. Intense, and even a little . . . cruel. But a delicious sort of cruel that makes me want more.

Then he looks at me in a certain way and says something dirty while he touches me like I'm a possession and he owns me. And all I want to do is fall into his arms and let him do whatever he wants to me.

I'm giving him too much power. I've been in this position before and I've always felt held back, especially with Zachary. There's something about handing the power over to Ryder, though, that's different. I feel both cherished and liberated. Taken care of yet free.

"I should go," I whisper against his lips, reluctant to break the spell he's woven over me.

"Why?" He runs his fingers over my hair, pushing it back into place.

This entire charade we're participating in is beyond frustrating. "If I stay locked up in your office for too long, people will get suspicious."

"We're in a meeting." He kisses me again. Softly. Sweetly. I could kiss him all day. All night. "Discussing packaging for your cosmetics line."

"That excuse will hold up for only so long." I touch his face, feeling closer to him now than I ever have. It's so silly. We just had sex on his desk, but it felt . . . different somehow.

"Mmm." His low hum vibrates through me, making me warm, and then he's gone. As he withdraws from my body, I feel his semen drip out of me and I frown. He bends down and snatches my panties off the floor, pressing them against my sex so he can clean me up as best he can. "Sorry," he whispers as he crumples up my panties in his fist and strides around his desk to shove them in his top drawer.

"Don't forget those," I tell him. I'd be mortified if he opened his drawer one day in front of someone and there lay my panties. Not that anyone would know they're mine, but still . . .

I slide off the desk and tug my skirt back into place, feeling awkward as usual. It's always this way after we mess around in his office or some other clandestine location. Usually I become nervous, he becomes brusque, and I scurry away like an insecure little girl, hoping he doesn't hate me.

"Hey."

Turning, I find him watching me, his gaze soft, his smile warm. He's looking at me as if he might actually care, and my heart swells with hope. "Yes?" I ask, hoping I don't sound too nervous.

He approaches me, drops a kiss to my lips. "I'll see you tonight, yes?"

I nod. "Of course."

"Good." He traces my lips with his index finger. "I'll come over after work?"

"Maybe we could grab dinner," I suggest, loving the idea of actually going out with him.

"How about takeout?"

Disappointment crashes within me. "All right." I step around him and start toward the door when he comes up behind me and rests his hands on my hips, twirling me around so I'm facing him.

"Where do you think you're going?"

"I should go." I frown up at him, reaching out to straighten his tie.

"With no kiss goodbye?"

Standing on tiptoe, I press my mouth to his in a chaste kiss. "Goodbye," I murmur, hating how final that word sounds.

"Violet. What's wrong?"

I shake my head. I can't tell him that I'm worried about all of this. About him. About us. I'm falling for him. And I think he's falling for me, but what if . . .

What if this is all a lie?

He slips his fingers beneath my chin, forcing me to meet his gaze once again. "Tell me."

"I'm fine. Just worried. About . . . everything." I sound silly. Like I'm making up an excuse.

"You worry too much." He drops a kiss on the tip of my nose and then reaches out to unlock and open the door for me. "It's been a pleasure, as usual, to discuss packaging details with you, Miss Fowler," he says loudly in case anyone is passing by.

No one is, of course. I want to laugh, but I don't. "Thank you, Mr. McKay. Your advice, as usual, is spot on."

"That's what I hoped." He smacks me on the ass and shoves me into the hall with a wink and a smile before he walks back to his desk.

I return to my office in a dreamlike state, hardly remembering taking the elevator to get there. There's a bright pink Post-it note stuck to the middle of my monitor and I snatch it off, reading the familiar handwriting of my father's assistant, Joy.

Your father would like to speak with you at your earliest convenience.

Settling behind my desk, I dial her extension.

"Is he busy?" I ask in greeting when she answers.

"Not at the moment. If you come now, you'll probably be able to squeeze in a few minutes before his next appointment."

"I'll be right there." I hang up and head down the hall toward Father's office, wondering what he could want to talk about. Nothing unusual is going on that I know of. I've been lying low, especially after my fake tentative reconciliation with Zachary. I haven't mentioned it to Rose or Lily, and I'm hoping I'll never have to mention it because everything will come together perfectly. They will *kill* me if they think I'm back with him.

But I have my doubts about this plan. How can it come together when Ryder is being so secretive? I don't even fully understand what's going on.

"Ah, there you are." Father smiles when he spots me standing in the open doorway. He looks genuinely happy to see me. *Weird.* "I was hoping to talk to you. Sit."

I do as he asks, straightening my skirt, ignoring the ache between my legs and the fact that I'm not wearing any panties. I don't even recognize who I am anymore. "What's going on?" I ask politely.

"First, I want you to know that Alan Brown has been released from prison." He lifts his hand when I open my mouth, silencing me. "He's in upstate New York and can't leave the county. He has to check in with his parole officer on a regular basis."

I release a shuddering breath. "Do you think that will stop him?"

"Violet." He levels his gaze on me. "He's not going to come after you. You're worrying about nothing."

Leave it to him to dismiss my fears. He's been doing that in regard to Alan Brown since the incident happened. "I can't help it," I admit softly. "You didn't see his face when I testified against him, how angry he was. I could see the rage he felt toward me, but you don't know. You weren't there." He was at work. Grandma came with me, sitting discreetly in the courtroom, hiding in the back row. She's such a recognizable icon that she couldn't risk being seen by any of the media.

She had no problem coming with me, being there for me. Lily wanted to come, too, but she was even more recognizable than our grandmother, especially back then, since that was at the height of her notoriety.

Father acted like it was nothing. A blip in my existence. Nothing more.

"Of course, you can't help it. It was a traumatic experience, but you can't let it control your life." His voice is firm, his expression pleasant. Telling me that I'm just wasting my time.

So I do as he asks and move on. "Is there anything else?"

"Yes. As you know, Zachary is leaving us. Temporarily of course," he adds hastily. "But it's happening, and I'm not sure when his short tenure is up in London if he'll be returning here," Father explains.

I frown. "What do you mean?"

"Well, we're opening up a small office in Japan. I believe that would be a better fit for him. We want to tap into the edgy Tokyo market and I think he would do well leading the team there." He leans forward, his voice lowering. "We both know it wasn't working between the two of you."

I can't believe he just said that. "So he won't be coming

back?" I ask, my words slow and careful. I want to make sure I completely understand what he's implying.

"No. I have no plans for his return." He gives me a look, one that says he knows everything. "He's disruptive, Violet, and you know it. I let him stick around this long because of your relationship with him, but now that's in complete shambles . . ."

"I'm still talking to him," I say, interrupting him.

"Don't waste your time." The way Father says it, it's as if there's no argument necessary. We're done. "He's no good for you, Violet. His philandering has hurt you terribly."

I'm shocked. I didn't realize he even noticed. "What about his current position?"

"His second in command will take his place," Father says smoothly, without a care. "I'd like to talk to you about taking on the London position. Permanently."

My mouth drops open. "I haven't thought much about it." All lies. From the moment he mentioned the possibility, the idea has lingered in my mind. Going to London would be a terrific opportunity. I could learn a lot there. The only thing I fear is leaving New York, my family, my friends.

Ryder.

"Really? It's the perfect opportunity. And it wouldn't be forever. You can assist with foreign production, catch a glimpse of the sales side and the marketing side. All of it excellent information you can add to your résumé when you take over the company for me after I retire."

I'm gaping at him like some sort of dying fish. What he's saying is blowing my mind. "What about everything I do here?"

"Rose can help. And Lily . . ." His voice drifts and his gaze turns sad. "I have high hopes I can convince her to come back and work with me. Maybe with you gone she'll understand how much we need her."

I can't help but want to be here when that moment happens because it will be a miracle. "It sounds wonderful," I say, excite-

ment rising within me. This is a chance I can't let slip by. And if
Lily came back to Fleur to take my place, then I wouldn't feel so
guilty for leaving.

"Think on it," he tells me, his voice gentle, as is his expression. "You have time. Zachary will be in the London office for
the next four to six weeks. Perhaps you could have a decision
within the next two weeks?"

"That sounds fine." He smiles at me and I know the conversation is done.

"Perfect. Now. I know you just told me you're talking to
Zachary and I'm irritated by the way he treated you all of these
years, but I still would like to give the worthless ass a quick
going-away party. Will you help with that?"

Did my father just use the word *ass* in front of me? What in
the world is happening to everyone? "Help as in coordinate it
completely?" Dread threatens, but I push it aside. If we have a
going-away party for Zachary, I know he'll want me by his side
the entire evening. And if Rose or Lily discovers this while at the
party, seeing me playing the sweet stupid girl while he's off doing
whatever he wants, I'll never hear the end of it.

"Yes, exactly," he says with a contrite laugh. "Does that
sound all right to you?"

"Sounds fine," I say nervously. This will be my last official
duty as Zachary's supposed girlfriend, I swear. "You're in a good
mood."

His smile softens, as do his eyes. He looks so happy . . . almost carefree. "That's because I've met a woman."

My breath freezes in my lungs. No way could he be referring
to . . .

"So you're seeing someone?"

"I am." He nods.

"And is it serious?" I ask casually, clutching my shaking
hands together in my lap.

"It's turning that way." His smile fades. "I hope you don't

think I was hiding her from you. It's just that . . . I wanted to make sure of our feelings for each other before I introduced her as my girlfriend to you and your sisters."

"I understand," I lie. He was totally hiding her if he's referring to Pilar.

Rose is going to flip. So will Lily. I'm ready to lose it right now, but I keep my cool.

"Good." His smile returns, bigger this time. "She keeps me young. I haven't been this happy in a long time."

I wonder if he knows that Pilar has cheated on him—with my ex. I wonder if there have been others. I can't help but wonder when was the last time Ryder and Pilar had sex.

I think I'm going to be sick to my stomach.

"Thank you, my dear." He stands, and I do so as well. "I appreciate you coming by." Slipping back into his formal ways. I see where I get it from.

"And I appreciate the offer you've made. You've given me a lot to consider." More than I ever imagined, both about my professional life and his personal.

"Good." He smiles with approval. "I can't wait to hear your answer."

I walk out of Father's office in a daze, this one different from the sexual stupor Ryder put me in before. This time, I'm amazed and confused by Father's offer and his subtle revelation. He wants to keep Zachary away from me. He has a girlfriend who keeps him young. He wants to give me an opportunity to prove that I'm capable of running Fleur Cosmetics someday.

If Father makes Pilar a more integral part of Fleur, I don't know if I want to remain in New York after all.

His offer for me to work in London is looking more and more like a positive change.

A fresh start. And the opportunity I've been waiting for.

Chapter Twenty-eight

Ryder

I'm worried.

I sit at my desk and stare at the text Violet just sent me, wondering what she's referring to. There are all sorts of things that should be worrying Violet.

And me.

We've snuck around for days. Pretending we don't care about each other at work beyond that we're business associates working on a project together. At night, I go to her place, where we talk. Eat. Have sex. Lots and lots of sex.

Plenty of talking, too. The woman's mind fascinates me. She's so smart, she's done so much, seen so much in her life, and I can only hope to do and see as much as she has. I learn something from her every time we have a conversation. I learned plenty from Pilar, too, but this is different. Deeper.

I feel connected to Violet.

She seems as fascinated by me as I am with her. I don't feel like I'm being used or have to throw up all my defenses in case she's trying to trick me. What I share with Violet is as genuine as it gets.

Well. I still haven't told her how this all started, plotting with Pilar. I'm too freaked out to confess. That admission could ruin everything.

And I'm not ready to take that risk yet.

My phone buzzes again and I focus on the most recent message from Violet.

I'm really stressed out.

About what?

Everything. What's happening between me and you. What's happening with Zachary. And Pilar. And my father.

There's a lineup that's causing me nothing but grief.

What's going on with your father?

Remember when I talked to him a few days ago? I never told you, but . . . he confessed that he's in a relationship.

Shit. Why did she keep that from me?

Like I have any room to talk.

Did he say it was with Pilar?

No, there were no names mentioned, but I have a strong feeling he's referring to her.

Fuck this texting thing. I call her.

"What exactly did he say?" I growl into the phone the minute she answers.

"He spoke in vague terms. Said he kept it quiet because he wanted to ensure it was turning into something serious before he mentioned it to me and my sisters." Her voice lowers. "I don't want it to be her, but I'm sure it is. She'll hurt him, Ryder. I know she will."

Violet's right. If things don't go her way, Pilar will have no qualms about wreaking as much damage as possible. "Could he be with someone else?" I suggest, wishing it were so. That would simplify everything.

But the way I feel about Violet, what's happening between us . . . is not so simple. I don't want to hurt her. I care for her. Want to protect her. Lies always hurt, and I'm keeping a big one. She'll hate me when she finds out I was dishonest.

That's the last thing I want, though I know it's best.

I'm starting to think *fuck what's best* and chase after what I really want.

"It's not someone else. Who else can it be? I saw them together, Ryder. They weren't acting like two business associates having a chat. They weren't behaving like two old friends hanging out, either. The way he touched her, the way she looked at him, they were like . . . lovers," Violet argues. "He doesn't want to reveal who he's seeing not just because of me and my sisters, but because he works with the woman."

"Well, you really shouldn't fuck where you work," I say, a reminder for us as well as anyone else.

She remains quiet, pulling one of my tactics. *Damn,* I really like this girl. The way she thinks, the things she says, the things she doesn't say. How responsive she is to my touch. The connection we have is unlike anything I've experienced before. I'm not only attracted to her body; I appreciate her mind. I value her opinion. She's thoughtful and beautiful. So beautiful. We could go far, Violet and me.

But I'm lying to her. Tricking her. Our entire so-called relationship is based on a lie. She's too good for me. She deserves a man who'll treat her like a princess. Not a man who pushes his girl too far and lies.

Violet may like it when I push her too far, but it's a cheap thrill. One that won't last. She needs a man like Lawrence, minus his asshole tendencies. A man who works hard, is honest, comes from a good family, and can provide for her what I never, ever can.

I'm a mess. And most of the time, I revel in my mess. Not now, though. I want to change for Violet. I want to be a better man, but is it possible? I am who I am and sometimes, when I'm particularly low, I feel like no one can fix me.

No one.

Not even her.

"Very true," she finally murmurs. "Such wise words, Ryder. I suppose you're referring to us?"

Now it's my turn to remain silent.

"If you want to end it, just say so." Her voice is tight. She sounds furious. "I'm tired of the back and forth, Ryder. What we're doing, it always feels like a game, and I'm the loser every single time. I try to be real with you. I try to give you everything you want and you're still not happy."

Her words claw at my useless heart, tearing it to shreds. She's one hundred percent right and I can't disagree. "I'm a user, Violet. You know this." Why am I saying this? It's as though I purposely want to sabotage what we have.

But really, all we have is smoke and mirrors. None of this is real.

"So you're just using me."

"Isn't that what we established from the get-go?"

She's quiet again. I hear her breathing. I swear I can hear the slow, steady beat of her heart. The fine little crack I just struck through it with my callous words. "I really hate you sometimes, Ryder," she whispers just before she ends the call.

I dump the phone on my desk and run my hands through my hair, sliding them down until they cover my face.

Sometimes, I really hate myself, too.

I FEEL LIKE I'VE BEEN SUMMONED TO THE GREAT AND POWERFUL Oz's lair. Or the gallows where I'll get my head chopped off, take your pick.

The voicemail was waiting for me when I returned to my office after lunch. A solo lunch I spent at an extremely crowded hole-in-the-wall sandwich shop. I ate a roast beef with Swiss on sourdough at a table so tiny my knees kept bumping into it. I stared out the window, sipping on my extra-large Dr. Pepper, and watched the people pass by, filled with regret. And I never have regret. Life throws shit at me and I just move on. When opportunity knocks on my door, I take it. Run with it.

I look at my time with Violet as an opportunity to get ahead in this company, so why the hell can't I run with it?

Because you feel guilty.

I'm taking. Taking and taking from Violet and enjoying every fucking minute of it, too. Slowly but surely, I've been giving, too. I want to take care of her, not ruin her. I want to spend my days and nights with her, not use her, toss her aside, and move on to my next opportunity.

I think the very opportunity I want is a relationship with Violet. But I've already fucked that up.

The voicemail waiting for me had been from Forrest Fowler's assistant, Joy, asking me to meet with him at three o'clock on the dot. I returned the call, confirming I would be there, then sat in my office until two forty-five, my brain on speed mode as I thought of the many things Forrest Fowler might want to discuss with me.

Hardly any of them good.

I'm in his office now, sitting in a plush, oversized chair, watching as the president and CEO of Fleur Cosmetics reigns behind his desk, trying his best to wrap up what appears to be an extra-long phone call all while sending me apologetic glances and holding up his finger, gesturing it won't be much longer.

No big deal. I have all the time in the world. My schedule is slow this afternoon and I'm still grouchy as hell after the way I treated Violet. She didn't call me, she didn't text, she didn't email, and usually she'll reach out to me somehow. Some way. I know she's pissed. I wonder if she told her daddy just how pissed she was.

If this conversation has anything to do with his daughter, I will lose it. Swear to God.

He finally hangs up the phone and reaches beneath his desk, hitting some secret button that shuts his office door with a quiet efficiency that only the very wealthy can afford. "How are you doing, Ryder?" He smiles benignly, and the sight of it puts me on edge.

I sit up straight. Something about this man commands my absolute attention. I don't want to disappoint. I don't want to look like a slacker. I want this man's respect, and the only way I'll receive it is if I give him the respect he deserves in return.

He also just so happens to be the father of the woman I'm fucking, and I can't lie—being in his presence makes me extremely nervous.

"I'm very well, sir. And you?" I sound like a putz. But *shit*, what else can I say? Definitely not the truth.

It's been insane these last few weeks, old man. I'm jealous every time I see Violet with her smarmy asshole ex. Jesus, that guy is a prick. By the way, I think I know who you're banging, so I guess it's not such a secret anymore. And I've also been fucking your daughter all over the building. As a matter of fact, I really pissed her off when I reiterated—yet again—that I'm just using her.

Other than all that crazy nonsense, I've been most excellent, sir.

"I hear you've been busy lately, working on Violet's new project."

His casual mention of Violet makes my heart drop. Here it comes. He's going to demote me. Fire me. Whatever. "We're in the process of having the package prototypes put together. By next week they should be available. I know . . . I know Violet is extremely excited." Not a lie. She's very protective of this project and I can't blame her, considering her name is appearing on everything.

"Violet says they're going to be beautiful." He looks at me pointedly. "She told me you've been a big help with the line, even suggesting marketing ideas when that's not necessarily your area of expertise. She says that you really know your stuff."

"Uh, thank you." I'm shocked. When did he talk to her about me? And why would she heap so much praise on me? I thought she hated me.

"I'm sure you know about Zachary Lawrence's temporary promotion," he says, changing the subject completely.

I try my best to remain neutral, but my lips curl into a sneer for about two seconds. Long enough for the very astute Forrest to notice. "Of course," I say stiffly.

He laughs and shakes his head. "You don't have a very high opinion of him?"

"Not in the least, sir." I say nothing else. He can't hold it against me if I remain fairly neutral.

"I understand, son. I'm not too fond of him myself." His use of the word *son* startles me. No one calls me that. My own father called me a no-good, money-sucking bastard. I have no idea how to let an older man care about me in a fatherly manner. I didn't think it was possible.

Not to mention the fact that he just revealed he doesn't like Zachary Lawrence. *Interesting*.

"International positions are opening up within Fleur," Forrest continues when I don't say anything. "Not just the one Zachary is filling. Temporarily, I might add," he says, making me like him even more. "I wanted to see if you were interested."

"Interested in taking a position overseas?"

"Yes. More opportunities are set to open within the next few months." He studies me, his gaze never wavering. "I think you would be a most excellent candidate."

Triumph surges through me. This is exactly what I want. What I've been working toward over the last few years, ever since I came to Fleur. Recognition from Forrest Fowler accompanied by promotions and opportunities that'll bring me the money and prestige I fucking deserve.

"I'm honored, sir," I say with all honesty. "Your consideration means a lot to me."

He smiles. "Not that I haven't noticed your hard work, McKay, because I have, but you need to thank Violet. She's really been championing your work."

I frown. Really? What about Pilar? She's the one who's supposed to be working Forrest over to get me a promotion. "Violet?"

"Yes. We had a meeting a few days ago with the board, discussing who we thought would be a good fit for the international positions. Your name was brought up by Violet. If I didn't know any better, I'd think she has a crush on you." He winks at me.

A crush. That's a funny way to describe what Violet and I are doing. How I feel about her.

And just how do you feel about her, asshole?

I ignore the bitchy voice still lingering inside my head.

"I really doubt that," I tell him, earning a chuckle. "Seriously, Violet has been a joy to work with. She's very smart."

"I know." Forrest beams with pride.

"Her cosmetics line will bring in tremendous business to Fleur. It'll appeal to the younger set and attract an entire new customer base," I say.

"That's the plan."

"You know . . ." I lean forward and brace my elbows on my knees, cupping my hands together. While I have his attention, I'm going to take a chance. The worst he could say is no. "I have this idea . . . but I probably shouldn't bother you with it."

"You absolutely *should* bother me with it," Forrest encourages. "I love an idea man. Not enough of them here if you ask me. Just a bunch of sheep, always nodding in agreement with whatever's said."

Interesting. I'll have to remember this for future use. "All right. Here's what I was thinking." I've had this idea since I started working for Fleur, but I'd never had the balls to mention it to anyone. Now that Forrest Fowler is my captive audience . . .

"Perfume."

Forrest tilts his head, not looking impressed. "We have a few of those already, son. That's nothing new."

"I know, you're right. But it's been a while since Fleur has introduced a new scent. And I was thinking it would be smart on Fleur's behalf to roll out three," I explain.

"Three?" He frowns. "All at once, or every six months . . ."

"All at once. Each one of the scents will be distinctly different yet somehow still cohesive. They'll go together, complement each other. We would sell all three as a set—and separately—and they would be aimed at the woman on the go. The girl in her early twenties who's graduated college and is just starting out on her career, savoring her independence and attempting new things."

"Interesting. Go on." Forrest nods.

"And we would call the perfumes . . ." I go for the dramatic pause because holy hell, I have nothing to lose. "Lily. Rose. And Violet."

The room is silent. I swear he can hear my thunderous heartbeat. I put it all on the line and if he says no, I'll be all right. At least I made a suggestion, which is a lot more than I can say for the rest of the chumps that work at Fleur.

Forrest grins slowly and he keeps nodding his head. "I like it. I like it a lot. Hell, why did I never think of it? We have a Dahlia scent, Fleur's very first perfume. Why wouldn't I think of my own daughters?"

Relief floods through me and I almost slump in my chair. But I keep my shit together and act like this is a normal experience. "I'm glad you like it," I say tentatively.

"Brilliant is what it is. I want you to write me up a more detailed proposal and then email it to me. CC my assistant Joy, too."

"Thank you, sir." Excitement builds within me. This little meeting is turning out better than I thought. He actually listened to me. And even better, he likes my idea, which he should because it's a hell of an idea. One I never shared with anyone, not even Pilar.

That bitch would steal it from me and take all the credit. I knew this, and that's why I chose to remain silent. We do nothing but keep secrets from each other. That's all we've ever done throughout our entire, strange relationship.

No wonder I have no idea how to love a woman. I'm so fucked up, I trust no one. Don't want to get too close. Don't want to reveal my vulnerabilities, my fears, my weaknesses. The only person I've gotten close to doing that with is . . .

Violet. And I hardly know her.

"I have a call to make." He stands and rounds his desk, holding out his hand toward mine. I stand and shake it, giving it an extra pump, which makes him smile. "I'm impressed, son. Keep this up and you'll go far at Fleur."

"That's my plan, sir." I release his hand and take a step back, needing the space. Needing to make sure this is real and I'm not dreaming.

"Stop calling me 'sir.'" He grins as he falls into step beside me and escorts me out of his office. "It's Forrest."

"Thank you, Forrest," I say with utter sincerity as he pauses in front of his assistant's desk. She's typing away on her keyboard, not paying attention to us in the slightest. "I'll do my best to prove to you this idea is worth it."

"Oh, I'm not worried about that. I have a feeling you'll come through and impress the hell out of me." He claps me on the back with his palm, nearly sending me staggering forward. "I have all the faith in the world in you, son. All of it."

Chapter Twenty-nine

Violet

THE DELIVERY COMES NEAR THE END OF THE DAY, AFTER I GIVE up pretending I can concentrate and actually get any work done. The argument with Ryder threw me.

What else is new? He's constantly throwing me. I feel like I've been on a roller-coaster ride these last few days, torn between my work here in New York and the opportunity London could offer me. Torn between Ryder wanting to keep our relationship secret and announcing it to everyone, including Zachary.

Especially Zachary.

I'm cleaning off my desk and preparing to go home when someone from reception walks into my office carrying a beautiful, heavy silver flowerpot filled with delicate purple and yellow flowers.

Violets.

I smile as I tease the velvety petals with my fingertip, looking for a card, but there isn't one. The flowers brighten what ended up being a completely horrible day. Starting with the argument I got into with Ryder and the conversation I suffered through with Zachary not even an hour ago. The man is persistent. I've put him off for days, but he cornered me. Kept trying to convince me to come back to his place so we could reunite like old times, he said with a suggestive leer that wasn't one bit sexy.

A firm no was my answer and he didn't like that at all. Did he really believe I would fall into his bed as if nothing had ever happened? I suppose, considering I'd done it before. But I was a different person then. I'm stronger now.

My smile fades and I wonder if Zachary sent the flowers. I can't keep them if he did. I don't need any more unnecessary reminders of him in my life. I spent twenty minutes after lunch trying to put together a small going-away party for him, much to my irritation. My heart simply wasn't into it. Though I should view this dinner as a celebratory, "yay, he's out of my life" type of party.

I'm awful.

I turn to my computer, ready to shut it down for the evening, when I see the new email in my in-box. From Ryder. The subject line reads, "I'm sorry." I click on it and read:

My sexy V,

I'm an asshole. I know I've said this to you before and you've agreed readily. I can't blame you for agreeing because we know the truth.

I'm not good enough for you. I never will be. But I want you. I can't let you go. Not yet. I'm a selfish motherfucker but trust me, you benefit from this arrangement just as much as I do.

At least I hope you think so.

I'm sorry. I'm sorry for the horrible things I say. I'm sorry for the horrible things I do.

But I'm not sorry for the things we've done together. Or for the way you've made me feel. What we share means . . . so much. Too much.

I hope you like the gift I sent you. If I had my choice, I would scatter the violet petals all over your

naked skin. But you might think that's a waste of a
good flower. I'm not sure.
Yours,
R.

Stinging, sweet pleasure blooms in my chest as I read his
email over and over again. He still wants me. He's the one who
sent me violets. No man has ever done that before. You'd think
they would; given my name it's an easy choice.

But I guess no one is as thoughtful as Ryder.

If he knew I believed he was thoughtful he'd probably flip.

I hit REPLY and start typing.

Dearest R –
    Thank you for the violets. They're beautiful. And
thank you for the apology. It was beautiful, too.
    You say you're not worthy of me but I think you're
wrong. I love the idea of you scattering violet petals
all over my naked body. But only if I can do the same
to you.
Yours,
V

I hit SEND before I can second-guess myself or add more. My
gaze snags on the flowers and I stare at them, reaching out to
rub my finger over each individual petal. I'm torn between wanting to leave the pot on my desk or take it home. Maybe I can do
both?

My cell beeps and I grab it, smiling when I see Ryder's name.

I see you.

Glancing up, I find him leaning his shoulder against the door
frame, gazing at his cell phone. He slowly lifts his head, those
beautiful blue eyes locking with mine, and I remain still in my
chair, waiting for his next move.

"Come home with me," he says, his voice low, his gaze heavy.

Everything within me goes hot and fluttery at his request. His demand. I'm scared to say yes. Going home with him is a risk. I could lose my head. My body. My heart. My soul.

But I'm more scared to say no.

"Violet," he starts, but I cut him off.

"Yes." I stand, pressing my fingers against the edge of my desk, as if that can brace me somehow. "I will."

WE LEFT THE OFFICE AND HAVE BEEN RIDING TO HIS APARTMENT building mostly in silence, sitting in the back of a taxicab while the driver listens to a baseball game on the radio, turned up at maximum volume. The crowd cheering with every play grates on my nerves and I tap my fingers on the empty space between us, tracing the cracks in the vinyl seat.

I'm desperate to reach out and touch him, but I don't.

Keeping my gaze affixed to the window, I watch the city pass us by as we head downtown. I have no clue where we're going. I know nothing of Ryder's personal life besides what he shows me.

And he doesn't reveal much.

Another ball is hit and the crowd roars, the sound coming from the tinny speakers within the car deafening. I wince and close my eyes, hating how nervous I feel. Hating more that Ryder won't talk to me.

Maybe he doesn't know what to say either.

I feel something brush against my pinky and I still my fingers, almost afraid to look. But I know it can only be Ryder touching me. His finger strokes over mine tentatively. Like a test. I keep my hand steady, pressing my lips together when each of his fingertips settles over the length of my pinky. Stroking up and down in the softest, most sensual touch I've ever experienced.

Goose bumps form on my skin and a shiver steals through

me. My nipples harden beneath my bra. I grow damp between my legs. I feel restless. Uneasy.

Aroused.

His hand slips over my fingers achingly slowly, almost as if he's afraid I'll push him away. Deny him. I keep my gaze averted, not wanting to look at him, scared of what I might see. Or what I might not see.

I'd rather savor the way he's touching me and pretend it means something to him.

His hand covers mine completely and he curls my fingers into his grip. He runs his thumb across the back of my hand, along my knuckles, and then releases me, his hand sliding almost completely away before it comes back and covers mine. His warm, wide palm over the back of my hand, his fingers over the top of mine, he threads our fingers together, interlacing them, connecting us.

My heart is pounding an incessant beat. My body is on fire. All because of his hand linked with mine.

"Violet." He says my name reverently and I close my eyes. "Look at me."

I turn my head, my gaze meeting his, and I see so much yet not enough in his eyes. I don't say anything. I can't. My throat is clogged with emotion and I'm scared I might burst out crying if I open my mouth and try to speak.

So I don't.

"You said you hate me." When I frown, he continues. "Earlier. On the phone."

I let my gaze drop, ashamed that he's confronting me with my words, but he squeezes my hand tight, forcing me to look back up at him.

"I can't blame you. You *should* hate me." His eyes close and he leans his head back against the seat. "Having you near . . . all I can think about are the filthy things I want to do to you."

Heat sizzles through me, settling in between my legs. I want that, too, but I also need more. I feel so close to him, that we've experienced so much together in such a short amount of time. Does he feel the same? I want that connection. I want truth and loyalty and, dare I think it . . . love.

I'm just afraid to ask for it. Afraid he'll deny me. He can't stop reminding me that what we share is temporary. It hurts, even though I know it's most likely the truth.

I want to share my most innermost secrets with him, but will he push me away? I'm reminded of the night he kept trying to push me physically. That's not what hurts.

No, what hurts are his words. They tear me apart inside.

"I don't deserve you being with me tonight," he whispers, his eyes opening to stare into mine. "You should tell me to fuck off."

A little sigh escapes me and I shake my head. I still don't say a word, employing his favorite tactic. He brings our linked hands up to his mouth and brushes a kiss to my knuckles. My eyelids flutter at first contact and I release a shuddering breath. His mouth feels so good on my skin.

"What if I confess something important to you?" I ask, my voice shaking. I'm nervous. I want to admit my darkest secret to him. Am I doing it as some sort of test?

Probably. Is that fair?

Not really. But the way he treats me and the things he says are sometimes not fair. If he really cares, if he really wants to pursue a relationship with me, then he won't turn me away. He'll listen, he'll understand, and he'll want to take care of me.

That I'm about to confess all in a taxicab is crazy. But I'm feeling a little on edge tonight.

"What do you want to confess?" There's a wariness in his gaze that wasn't there before.

"Something happened to me a long time ago, when I was in

college." I pause, swallowing hard before I forge on. "I was attacked."

His eyes narrow and he shifts away from me, as if he needs the distance. "What do you mean, you were attacked?"

I drop my head, my hair falling forward so I can't see him. "He was an old family friend, I grew up with him, and when I first got to the university he was the only person I knew."

"And he *raped* you?" He sounds incredulous and as ridiculous as it sounds, I love that sign of worry and anger that I hear in his voice.

"No." I lift my head and stare at him, wishing I could reassure him. Wishing he would reassure me. "No, I was able to stop him before it went too far. It turned into a physical fight and I . . . he hurt me, but I hurt him worse. I got away and reported it to the police." I remember how terrified I was. How it felt like such a betrayal, that Alan would try to hurt me when he was supposed to be my friend.

What hurt worse is how angry Father was after he learned that I'd reported the attack to the police, that I made it public. Heaven forbid I tarnish the Fowler reputation, even though I did nothing wrong.

Ryder moves in close to me, grabbing my shoulders so he can pull me into his arms. I feel safe there. Protected. Cared for.

"Alan was so *angry* when he came after me. Completely unhinged," I admit, my voice muffled against his chest. "And when I testified against him, he yelled at me in the courtroom, and the look on his face was pure evil."

"He yelled at you in court?"

"He didn't like it, when I described how I fought him off on the stand. It made him mad, that a female bested him."

"He sounds like a real piece of shit."

"He is." I pause again. "He's also just been released from prison."

"*What?*" Ryder shoves me away from him, his hands still gripping my shoulders, a worried expression on his face. "You've got to be kidding me."

"His sentence was reduced and they let him out early. Or was it on a technicality? I don't know." I shrug, trying my best to act nonchalant, but I'm trembling inside. "He's in upstate New York. Father says I shouldn't worry."

"Do you think . . . he'll come after you?" His brows furrow in concern.

"No. I don't know. It's so hard to explain. You see . . ." I pause again and close my eyes briefly, struggling to find the right words. "Father didn't want me to testify. My grandmother didn't want me to at first either, but I was determined. Alan scared me. I was afraid he'd do this again and again, and keep hurting innocent girls. I couldn't be responsible for that."

"Of course. Jesus, Violet." He pulls me to him and holds me so tight, I almost can't breathe. But I like it. Being in his arms makes me feel safe. "You did the right thing, baby. Know that."

His words are ringing in my head when the cab finally stops and we climb out. They still echo as we enter the modest building and ride the elevator up to his floor. There's no doorman at Ryder's building, no opulent lobby, and the elevator is old and rickety. When we exit from it, the hallway is dark and dim, not all of the lights are lit, and I glance around, surprised that he lives in such a place.

He's always dressed impeccably. His suits are expensive, his watch pricey. I figured he'd live in a palace, an apartment as showy as Zachary's because everyone knows Zachary loves to show off his wealth, even though he obtained plenty of it via credit.

Ryder stops in front of a door with the number 426 on it and pulls a key out of his pocket. I watch his nimble fingers as he unlocks the door and then holds it open for me so I can enter. I do so, my eyes widening when he flicks on the light switch close to the door, illuminating everything within.

"Home sweet home," he says sardonically as he closes and locks the door.

It's simple. The living area is small and the kitchen is galley style. There's a black leather couch and love seat with a coffee table in front of it and a flat-screen TV on the wall. Typical for a bachelor pad. There's not one single picture anywhere. Not a photo or a painting or a sketch. The walls are blank and white; the entire apartment has a blank quality to it, and seeing it makes my heart hurt.

This apartment isn't a home. It's just a place for him to rest his head, shower, and keep his things.

"It's not as nice as your place," he says as he approaches me from behind, his hands settling on my shoulders. "But it works."

I don't tell him that I think it's awful. I don't want to insult him.

Instead I turn and loop my arms around his neck, smiling up at him. "Take me to your bedroom." I need to feel his hands on my naked body. I need his mouth and his words to cleanse me.

More than anything, I crave the connection only he can give.

He grabs my hand and leads me down a very short hallway, reaching into a dark room and flicking on the light so I see the giant bed that dominates the room. I walk inside, noting yet again that there are no photos, no anything covering the walls.

"What do you think?"

"It's very . . . efficient," I say for lack of a better term.

He chuckles. "You hate it."

"It needs some prettying up. But I'm a girl. That's what we're supposed to say about bachelor pads."

"Are you okay with this?" His expression turns solemn, and fear rushes through me that he'll think I'm too delicate, too frayed after what I confessed.

But I feel clean. Free. All I want is him.

Just him.

"I'm perfectly okay with this." I go to him and wrap my arms around his neck. "I want you, Ryder. Please?"

"How can I resist when you say please?" The relief in his gaze is obvious and the smile on his face wicked. "Did you see what's hanging above you?"

I tilt my head back, a gasp escaping me when I stare at my reflection. "You have a mirror above your bed?"

He shrugs. "Yeah. Don't know why, though, since I never bring any women back here."

So silly, but this admission pleases me. Not even Pilar? I'm not brave enough to ask because I'm afraid of his answer. "Then why do you have it?"

"I don't know." He glances up at the mirror again. "I watch myself sometimes when I jack off."

My cheeks warm. He says it so casually, like it's no big deal. "You don't bring women back to your place at all?"

His gaze meets mine once more, intensely dark. "You're the first."

I wonder if he's telling me the truth. He's had plenty of experience. "Really?"

"Yes. Really." He drops a kiss on the tip of my nose.

"I just find it so . . . strange."

"You know what I'd like to see?" he asks, changing the subject.

"What?"

"You. Naked. On my bed." He disentangles my arms from around his neck and steps away so he can study me, his gaze unwavering. "Strip, Violet."

I turn my back to him and he undoes the zipper for me. I let the dress fall off my body then step out of it, wearing only my heels and my bra. I step out of the shoes and shed the bra, getting naked quickly before I crawl to the center of the surprisingly firm bed. Rolling over onto my back, I spread my legs and stretch out my arms, staring up at my reflection, startled by what I see.

Me. Completely naked. Completely open. I reach behind me and pull the band out of my hair, letting it fan across his stark white pillow. My breasts rise when I reach and I touch them. Cup them in both hands, play with my nipples with my thumbs.

"Having fun?" he asks amusedly.

I laugh and shake my head, closing my eyes against my image before I turn my head to look at him. "I've never watched myself like this before."

"Overcome by your own beauty?"

"You make me sound incredibly vain," I admonish, embarrassment surging through me. "Besides, I'm not the prettiest one."

"Prettiest one what?" he asks, looking genuinely confused.

I turn away from him and stare at my reflection once more. I assess myself as objectively as possible. Boring brown hair. Dark brown eyes. Average nose, too-large mouth that kids made fun of when I was in school. Decent body. I'm no great beauty like Rose. I'm not an outrageously sexy bombshell with a body that makes men drool like Lily, either.

I'm just . . . me.

"The prettiest Fowler sister," I finally say with a sigh. "When you compare me to Rose and Lily, I'm definitely lacking."

I barely get the words out before he's right on top of me, his bent legs on either side of my hips, his hands going to my wrists and hauling them up above my head, his face in mine. He looks . . . angry. "Are you serious?" he asks incredulously.

"Wh-what do you mean?" His ferocious expression, the sound of his voice—he's scaring me.

I can't ignore the trickle of arousal that runs through me at the way he holds me down, his fingers tight around my wrists. That he makes me fear him and want him all at once is so confusing.

But I feel safe with him. Always, always safe.

"You think you're lacking?" He slowly dips his head until his mouth brushes against mine and he breathes, "You're the most beautiful woman I've ever seen."

I don't close my eyes. I can't. It's fascinating, looking at him like this as he holds me down. I'm helpless, at his mercy. He could hurt me so easily. He even said he *would* hurt me, but he doesn't. He never has.

More than anything, Ryder has shown me how to let myself go and be free.

"You have the prettiest, darkest eyes," he says when I don't say anything. "All that long hair I like to pull." He releases one of my wrists to thread his fingers through the ends of my hair and gives it a tug, making me wince. "And your mouth . . ." His voice trails off and I blink up at him in confusion.

"What about my mouth?" I gave up long ago trying to hide my too-big lips. I wear both the brightest and the darkest lipstick colors as much as possible. I may as well play up the asset that will help sell Fleur lipsticks.

"I like kissing it," he whispers and does just that, pressing his lips to mine in a sweet, lingering kiss before he adds, "I love kissing you."

Oh, God. A tremble moves through me and I close my eyes against the onslaught of emotions that bombard me.

I open my eyes to find him staring at me, his face so close I can make out the stubble covering his cheeks and chin. I love it, too, when he rubs his rough face against my sensitive skin, making me shiver. Leaving red marks all over my body, imprinting himself on me in all the various ways he has. "I love kissing you, too," I whisper.

He smiles and releases his hold on me, pressing his face against my neck so he can deliver a kiss there. Slowly he slides down my body, running his mouth across my chest, over my breasts, his tongue teasing each of my nipples quickly—too quickly—before he moves on.

I sink my hands in his hair, trying to hold him to me, but he keeps going, his warm, damp mouth drifting along my stomach, his tongue circling the dip of my navel. My skin heats from his attention and I grow wet and achy between my legs. Anxious. Needy.

Always needy.

He knows. He knows exactly how to elicit a reaction from me, how to make me want him so bad I lose control. He's using it against me, driving me purposely crazy as he pulls away and starts to slowly unbutton his shirt, his legs straddling my hips once more as he looms above me.

"Fuck, you're beautiful." He tears off his tie viciously and tosses it to the floor, then finishes unbuttoning his shirt, shrugging out of it, revealing all that smooth, muscular skin.

I let my gaze wander, taking in the colorful tattoos that cover his upper body. His abdominal muscles ripple as he moves and I want to lick them. The dark hair that starts just below his navel and trails beneath the waistband of his pants, God, I want to lick that, too. The silver rings in his nipples glint from the dim light in the room and I want to suck them into my mouth, tongue his nipples, hear him moan and tell me to stop.

My gaze drops. His cock strains against the front of his pants and I want to free him so I can draw his erection between my lips, just like he wants. Unable to help myself, I reach out and touch him, drifting my fingertips along his turgid length. He tenses, doesn't move as I curl my fingers around him and grip him tight. I prop myself up on my elbows and move my head closer, pressing open-mouthed kisses along his covered cock, exhaling hotly against him, my gaze never leaving his.

"Jesus," he mutters, shoving at my shoulder so I fall back against the pillows. I wait breathlessly as he undoes his belt buckle and pulls it from the belt loops, dropping it so it lands on the floor with a clank. I'm transfixed as he unbuttons and unzips his pants, tugging them and his boxer briefs down his muscular thighs so his cock thrusts out, toward me.

My mouth waters and I part my lips, whimpering when he wraps his hand around the base of his cock and starts stroking.

"Fucking little tease. You want this?" he asks, his voice deep and so very, very dark. He's shifted into that edgy mood that takes over whenever we have sex. That dark, scary place that I love to experience with him.

"Yes," I whisper, inhaling sharply when he scoots closer, and I lift my arms, my hands resting on the sides of his thighs, his erect cock directly in my face, in front of my mouth.

"Open those pretty lips," he croons and I do, the heavy weight of his cock parting my lips farther. I suck him in, surrounding just the head, my tongue teasing at the flared edge. "Just like that," he moans.

Lavishing all of my attention on just the tip, I wrap my fingers around his thick length as I withdraw him from my mouth. I lick my lips and then trail my tongue across the tip, back and forth, curling it around and putting on a show just for him since he's watching me so avidly.

A thrill moves through me and his hot gaze burns into mine. I want to make this good for him. The position is so intimate, our bodies so close together, his gaze tracking my every move, his breathing heavy as I slowly draw his cock deeper into my mouth.

"Fuck," he murmurs as he reaches out and touches the side of my face. He plays with the corner of my mouth, touching it, touching his cock, and I withdraw my lips, taking his index finger between them instead, sucking deep.

Ryder pulls his finger from my mouth and traces my lips, his mouth curved into this half-smile that I rarely see but like so much. "Enough playtime, Violet."

I nod and try my best to relax, breathing deep to expand my lungs, my throat.

"Watch."

Glancing up, I see us in the mirror. Me sprawled across the bed, Ryder on top of me, his cock in my face, his head bent as he watches me. Slowly he looks up, his gaze meeting mine in the mirror as he aims his cock at my lips. I part them, lost to the image of him pushing his cock into my mouth, encouraging me with rough words that send a thrill buzzing straight through my body and landing between my thighs.

"Deeper, baby. Let me fuck your mouth," he urges, his gaze still on mine in the mirror above us.

I take him deeper, trying my best to open up my throat and coax him in. He fills my mouth so completely I almost choke and my eyes water. But I don't stop.

It's as if I can't stop.

He's fucking my mouth and I don't fight him. I give in to the sensation of him using me, dominating me—and witnessing it as everything unfolds in the mirror. My skin burns, my lips hurt, and my vision goes hazy as he thrusts and holds his cock in my mouth so deep, I'm afraid I'll gag.

But I don't. He withdraws and fists his cock, drawing the tip back and forth across my parted lips, coating them with a mixture of my own saliva and pre-come. "So beautiful," he whispers, his eyes on me once again. I tear my attention away from the mirror and watch him. "What you do for me. What you do *to* me. You take whatever I give you and never complain."

I lick at the head of his cock, wanting more, craving the taste of him. He strokes himself as I suck him between my lips. Fast. Faster. Until I'm whimpering and he's groaning and he stiffens as come spurts into my mouth. It happens so fast I barely have time to register it.

I don't move away, don't even blink as I eagerly swallow every drop, licking my lips and savoring the salty-musky taste.

He watches me with amazement, his chest heaving from the intensity of his orgasm, and pleasure races through me, knowing I did that to him. I feel powerful in this moment. I'm the one who gave him so much pleasure. No one else.

Only me.

Exhaling loudly, I close my eyes, feel him lift off of me and get off the bed, and I immediately mourn the loss of him.

My heart aches. My entire body aches. I've thought it again and again, but now I know. I'm in too deep.

And I don't want to find my way out.

Chapter Thirty

Ryder

I DIDN'T MEAN TO COME DOWN HER THROAT BUT IT COULDN'T be helped. She knows just what to do to send me over the edge, and watching us together in the mirror . . . *fuck me*, that was hot. Those plump lips wrapped tight around my cock, her tongue working the length, the look of complete submission on her beautiful face as she took me deeper and deeper, again and again . . .

Yeah. I lost all control. I used to be able to hold out forever. I've had women begging for me to just finish already and come. I'd wear their pussies out with all the fucking and I thought it was perfect. Exactly what I was supposed to do. I was in control. No one demanded an orgasm from me. I gave them their pleasure and finally, when I felt like I'd had enough, I'd come and be done with it.

Not with Violet. I see her naked and want to come in my pants. Hell, I see her walk around the fucking office fully dressed and wearing patterned stockings and I'm eager to fuck. Eager to come—in her, on her, near her, whatever. And when I'm finished, I'm ready to do it all over again.

I'm all urges when it comes to Violet. Working off basic instinct, one scent of her and I'm raring to go like I'm an animal.

But it's more than that with her. Yeah, she makes my natural urges go haywire, but she also makes my protective instincts kick in. I want to take care of her. And after what she just confessed in the cab of all places . . . all I can think about is how I want to watch over her.

For the rest of my life.

The thought of a scumbag—worse, a trusted family friend—trying to harm a hair on her head makes me want to kill him.

Violet gives so selflessly and I'm not used to that. I'm a selfish asshole. And pretty much every woman I've been with was selfish, too, especially Pilar. She may have helped me find a new direction but ultimately, it was all for her own selfish gains. I was her little puppet to create and mold into exactly what she wanted. For a while, I let her, I was so grateful to be saved.

I'm over that shit. I'm over other women, period. I just want Violet. No one else. She's mine.

All mine.

The realization makes me freeze. I stare out the window, the cracked blinds offering me a glimpse of dimly lit buildings and the dark night sky. *Fuck*. It's hard to believe still.

That I only want . . .

Violet.

"Ryder." Her sweet voice draws my attention and I turn to look at her, letting my pants drop and kicking them along with my underwear off. Naked, I go back to the bed and crawl over her, hands braced on either side of her head, my still hard cock resting against her soft belly.

"Yeah, baby?" I kiss her neck, lick her skin, taste the faint salt of her sweat. *Fuck*, I could eat her up I want her so much.

"I want to be on top," she whispers, her voice soft, her hands sliding up to my shoulders and giving them a squeeze. "Please?"

Without warning, I roll over so I'm lying on my back and she's sprawled on top of me, a little smile curving her lips. I run my hand down the slope of her back, over the curve of her ass.

Her skin is so soft and smooth and she feels so damn good on top of me. I could stay like this for . . .

Don't even go there, jackass. Forever *isn't possible in your world.*

The negative voice in my head can fuck off.

"Lift up," I tell her, not able to shake giving up complete control. She does as I demand, sitting up so her hot, wet pussy rests against my abs, her hands braced on my chest. My cock hardens, brushing against her ass and she gives a little shudder. "Take me inside you. I want to watch."

She rises up on her knees and grabs hold of my cock, guiding it inside of her body. I watch, fascinated, as she slides down my dick, taking all of me in one slow glide. Watching and feeling it all at once makes everything inside me tense up and I close my eyes, trying my damnedest to fight off the urge to pound inside of her until I'm coming with a shout.

"You feel so good," she murmurs as she slowly starts to ride me. "You're so big and thick."

I grip hold of her ass and guide her movements, my fingers pressing so hard into her skin I'm sure I'll bruise her.

I don't really fucking care. I don't think she does, either.

"Oh, God." She sounds like she's in pain and my eyes fly open to find her riding me with her head thrown back, her gaze locked on the image playing out in the mirror above us.

It's amazingly hot, watching Violet and me together. Why haven't I thought of bringing her here before? The way her breasts bounce, her long hair dangling so far down her back it almost touches her ass. She lifts her arms over her head, gathering her hair in her hands, and I tear my gaze away from the mirror to actually watch her.

Damn, she's gorgeous. Eyes closed, teeth nibbling on the corner of her bottom lip. She's riding me, her knees braced on either side of my hips as she slides up and down my cock in this amazing rhythm that is bound to make me come soon if I don't do something about it . . .

I grip her hips and try to slow her down, lifting my hips and sending my cock deep inside her body. She stills and releases her lip from her teeth, moaning as I circle my hips and try my best to send my cock as deep as she can take it.

"You're so fucking tight," I whisper. "Wet and hot, baby. I love fucking you." She gets off on this type of talk. Sweet, quiet Violet Fowler, the ice queen, as Pilar called her.

Not even close to the truth. She's fucking wild, this girl. She takes it any way I can give it to her and loves every second of it.

I reach out and brush my thumb over her clit, making her gasp. I tease her, not giving her the pressure she needs to come but just enough to push her to the edge. Her movements become jerky and she throws her head back again, her eyes closed, lips parted as she pants, lost in her own little blissed-out world.

"Come here," I tell her as I remove my hand from her pussy, needing her closer. Needing to feel her skin on mine.

She opens her eyes and falls over me, her face in mine, her hands on my shoulders, her hips working up and down my cock. I keep my hands on the globes of her ass, pushing and pulling, sending my cock deep, savoring the sounds of her moans as we increase our pace.

Together. Always together. We're so in sync it's almost scary.

"I-I'm going to come," she whispers and I lift my hips, working her on my dick, wanting to watch that inevitable moment when she falls apart all over me.

"Come for me, baby," I encourage as I thrust balls deep. "Come all over my cock."

She does as I command, her body stiffening, her lips parted on a silent cry as the tremors take over her completely. Her inner walls grip my cock like a vise, the rhythmic contractions sending me spiraling over the edge as well, and I come for the second time in freaking ten minutes.

"Oh, my God." She collapses on top of me, all smooth, soft limbs covered in sweat, my cock still buried inside her body. "You're going to kill me."

"Not if you kill me first," I mutter, caressing her ass until she starts wiggling against me. "Stop squirming, or I'll spank you."

"Ooh, promise?" Her gaze meets mine and I see the arousal and amusement lit within her gaze.

"You'd like it if I did, wouldn't you?"

"Maybe." She wiggles against me again and I grab hold of her ass, gripping it tight.

"Stop." I smooth my hand over one cheek, then give it a solid slap. She jolts, her legs going wide, and just like that my cock is hard.

Yet again.

"I'm hungry," she whispers into my ear, her stomach growling as if punctuating her statement, and we both laugh.

That we can take it from outrageous orgasms to me spanking her ass to the both of us laughing because we're hungry . . .

I don't even know what to call what's happening between Violet and me anymore. All I know is that it scares the hell out of me because it can't last, but I want it to. We shouldn't make sense together. She's sweet and good and I'm mean and awful. She cares too much and I have zero fucks to give. A woman like Violet deserves to be worshipped and loved. She's powerful and smart and gorgeous and sexy and . . .

Fuck. I want to be the one who worships her and loves her and tells her just how smart and sexy she is every day. For the rest of her life.

The thought terrifies me.

Much later, after we've had Thai food delivered and we've taken a shower together—where I fucked her from behind, her breasts pressed against the cold tile with the warm water raining down on us—we fall into bed, wrapped all around each other, her ass nestled against my dick, my arm tight across her breasts.

Her breathing is evening out and so is mine. I'm ready to fall asleep. Beyond ready. We still have to go to work tomorrow . . .

When her phone buzzes, indicating she has a text.

Violet reaches over and grabs the phone off the bedside table. She looks at the screen, the light from it casting her face in shadow and letting me see the frown on her pretty face. "It's Pilar." She glances up, her angry gaze meeting mine. "Asking if you've told me the truth yet."

My heart sinks to my fucking toes and I hold out my hand, needing that damn phone now. "Let me see it."

"No." She holds her hand away from me, the phone out of my reach. "What is she talking about?"

"It's nothing. I swear." How do I get out of this? Fucking Pilar, does she know Violet is with me? How could she know?

"It certainly sounds like something. Her message says, 'Has Ryder told you the truth about us?'" She stares at me, her gaze cold, the screen going dark. "What's the truth, Ryder?"

I'm quiet, my mind scrambling to come up with something, anything. More lies? That would be stupid. I need to be honest.

For once in my fucking no-good life, I need to tell someone I care about the honest-to-God truth.

"The night I saw you and Zachary at dinner. When I was with Pilar . . ." I clear my throat, wondering how I'm going to be able to see the pain cross her face when I tell her. She's going to hate my guts.

"Yes?" she prompts me, sounding irritated.

"I told Pilar I wanted to seduce you. That I wanted . . . everything Lawrence had. His job, his promotion, and . . ."

"Me." She takes a deep, shaky breath. "You wanted to take me away from Zachary."

"Yeah. I decided right then that I was going to fuck you, and I was hell-bent on making it happen. You were such an easy mark." It sounds worse than I thought. *Fuck.*

"An easy mark." Her voice is flat.

"That's . . . yeah. That's how it started." I run my hands through my hair and clutch the back of my head, watching as she carefully deposits her cell on the bedside table and then crawls out of my bed without a word, refusing to look at me. Beautiful and naked, her creamy skin flushed with anger. I know she's leaving me and I deserve it. "Where are you going?" I ask dumbly.

"I can't stay here with you." She flicks on the lamp and I wince against the harsh light. She's standing there naked and beautiful and so heartbreakingly vulnerable. I see the pain in her eyes, etched across her face, and I feel like a complete asshole.

But maybe this is better, her knowing the truth. Knowing what she's dealing with. I'm reminded yet again that I don't deserve her.

I still want a chance, though.

"It all changed for me." I lean forward, watching as she grabs at her clothes and starts pulling them on, her back turned to me. "The more I got to know you, the more I liked you."

"Liked me." She snorts, a sound I never thought I'd hear come out of Violet Fowler. "How sweet, that you liked me."

"You're right. I screwed up. I thought by getting close to you, it would help me advance at Fleur. I'll admit it. Hell, it worked for Lawrence, so I assumed it could work for me, too." I climb out of bed and go toward her as she slips on her dress, taking advantage of her not seeing me. The second she tugs the dress over her head, she turns to glare at me and takes a step back. "Instead, getting close to you made me realize how much I care for you, Violet. I can't let you walk out of my life like this, baby."

"Stop with the 'baby' crap." She steps around me and I grab her arm to stop her, but she shakes out of my grip. "You used me. Just like you always told me. I should've known better than to fall for your lies. I knew I would get hurt. I knew it."

"Please, Violet . . ." She's slipping on her shoes and she's going to walk right out of my life. I can't fucking stand it.

"Did Pilar put you up to this? Does she get a little thrill out of watching her little boyfriend fuck around with the boss's daughter while she's screwing the boss? What the hell is wrong with you two and your games? You two are so twisted, you deserve each other." She stalks out of my bedroom and I chase after her, ignoring the hurt that courses through me at her words, ignoring the fact that I'm naked and chasing a woman as she tries to make her escape.

I have never in my life done something like this. *Ever.* Only for Violet would I make such an ass of myself. The realization that I would do anything to protect this woman steals the very breath from me.

She handed me her body. Her trust. Soon it would be her heart and I would break that into tiny little shards. I don't think I could love. I have sex. I use women. I enjoy them. But love? Not a part of my personality. Not a remote possibility until I met her.

I'm destroying her. All starting with a cruelly intentional text from Pilar.

"Don't leave like this." I stop in the living room, watching as she gathers her purse. My heart pounds so hard I can feel the erratic throb in my throat, and I swallow past the fear and fury that rises within me.

Though I'm not furious at her—I'm furious at myself over how this is going down. Maybe I shouldn't have let this thing between us go on this long. What started out as a trick, as a way to get revenge against Lawrence, turned into something more.

Turned into something . . . real.

"You really expect me to stay?" she asks incredulously. "I've been used enough by Zachary. I'm not going to let you do the same."

"It's not like that anymore . . ."

She laughs, but the sound is harsh. Hard. "It's never been real, what's happening between us, right? Isn't that what you really mean? You used me and I used you. You were the distraction I needed to help me get over Zachary." She pauses, and I hate that she brought that fucker's name up. "You can't go any deeper with me. You've told me over and over you're incapable of it. Scratch your surface and I'll find you're hollow inside. Heartless."

The truth fucking hurts, so I say nothing. There's no point in arguing.

"You're not going to say anything?" she asks.

I remain silent, standing in my living room naked with my heart in my hands. Hell, my heart is in *her* hands and she's stomping all over it. I deserve it.

Her gaze meets mine, never wavering once. "Who *are* you? Did I ever know the real you, Ryder?"

Yes. You're the only one I was ever real with. But I fucked it up. Fucked it up royally and now you're gone. You may be standing in front of me, but you're long, long gone.

I shrug in answer.

She storms toward me, her gorgeous face screwed up in anger, disbelief, and pain. So much damn pain. "Fuck you," she whispers just before she rears back and slaps me across the face. The sound of her palm when it meets my cheek is like a loud crack in the silence of the room.

I rest my hand against my stinging cheek and watch her go to the door. Swear I hear a sob, the sound faint but filled with so much hurt my chest aches. She opens the door and slams it so hard everything seems to reverberate within my shitty apartment.

Violet's gone. She exited my life as fast as she entered it.

And I'm forever changed because of her.

Chapter Thirty-one

Violet

TONIGHT, MY LIFE IS GOING TO CHANGE.

I had this thought once before, that fateful evening when I went to dinner with Zachary expecting one thing and received something else instead. At first, I'd been devastated by Zachary's news that he was leaving me. Disturbed by Ryder's sudden interest in me and irritated by Pilar's overbearing interest in Zachary.

It's all come full circle. I'm back at square one. Zachary and I broke up and somehow I'm back with him. Sort of.

Not really.

Ryder entered my life like a tornado, destroying everything within me in a matter of days, weeks, before he spun right out like it was nothing. Like he was nothing.

More like I was nothing to him.

But he was everything, at least to me. He used me to get back at Zachary, and the idea of it still stings tremendously. I thought he'd started to care . . . but he was still in contact with Pilar. Still wanting to be with her for whatever sick, twisted reason.

Ryder tricked me. He didn't go after me because he was attracted to me. He wanted to hurt me. Use me. And he did, most thoroughly. Worse, I wanted to be used by him. I miss him, which is so incredibly dumb, but . . .

I can't help it.

Now he's gone. I banished him from my life. I walked out of his apartment that horrible night and never once looked back. He left for London the next evening on a red-eye flight after being called to a very important—and secretive—meeting. A three-day meeting that also involved my father at one point. Zachary is sure there's some sort of sabotage going on in England despite my constant reassurances that he's overreacting, because yes, I'm still talking to him even though I shouldn't be.

Deep down inside, I'm sure he's probably right.

It's so silly, after everything he did to me, but I miss the connection Ryder and I shared. One look from him and my knees weakened. He made me laugh. He made me moan. He made me think. We worked well together. We made love well together, too . . .

He'd touch me and I'd grow dizzy. He has a magical hold on me that I can't deny, that I don't want to deny.

More than once I told Ryder that he owns me. And I thought . . . I thought he felt the same way. That he somehow owned me and I owned a little piece of him, too. He commanded me like no other man ever has. He understands me. My needs and wants. All of those wickedly sexual things we indulged in never once felt wrong with him. He consumed me. And scared me.

I'm still scared, more over the fact that I'm alone again. I'm mourning the loss of Ryder, which is stupid. I've never felt more alone in all my life.

I assume Pilar is having an affair with my father, though that hasn't been confirmed. He hasn't shared much information beyond that one time, telling me there's a woman in his life. And Pilar doesn't talk, especially to me. We're unspoken enemies. She's never liked me, even before what happened between all of us.

For all I know she's seeing Ryder on the side as well, and that thought . . .

I can't even go there.

Imagining her with Father, though—I don't like it. I don't trust her. She's only using him, the way she used Zachary. The way Ryder used me, and I don't want to see my father hurt. But I can't stop my father from doing what he wants, so I can only wait this out and hope for the best.

And prepare for the worst.

"Lovely spot," Father says, suddenly standing at my side. It's as if he knew I was thinking about him and magically appeared. "Zachary will be pleased, I'm sure."

I make a face. I don't really care if Zachary's pleased with the restaurant I chose for his going-away party. I just want him gone. "I'm sure he will be." But by the end of the evening, he'll no longer be my problem.

Ever again.

"Thank you for planning it," he says. "I know it wasn't easy."

"Of course." I'm doing what any good ex-girlfriend would do.

Good and *crazy* ex-girlfriend. *God,* who am I? Didn't I ask Ryder that very question? I don't even recognize myself anymore.

"Please don't make a fuss over this but, I have a date that will be accompanying me tonight," Father informs me, his voice low, as if he wants no one else to hear.

"A fuss?" I ask.

He waves a hand. "Don't mention it to your sister. She's been badgering me lately and I've been evasive."

I glance around, panic flaring within me, but I don't see Pilar anywhere. "Is your date here?"

"She's meeting me in a bit." He exhales loudly and shakes his head. My heart freezes. "Violet, I need to tell you—"

"Forrest! Glad to see you, old man." Zachary approaches us with a giant smile on his face, slipping his arm around Father's shoulders and slapping him on the back like they're dear friends. I watch in disgust, shocked at Zachary's behavior, surprised that he has the nerve to call my father "old man."

Is he drunk already? I'm in trouble if he is. The night has barely begun.

"Good to see you, Zachary." Father smiles, completely unfazed by Zachary's overly friendly ways. "Seems that Violet has put together a fine celebration for you tonight."

"Yes, she has." Zachary's eyes alight on me, heating in that way of his that tells me he's pleased to see me. His gaze scans down the length of my body and I suppress the disgusted shiver that wants to steal over me. I'm wearing a pale yellow chiffon dress that's sleeveless and hits mid-thigh. It looked bright and cheery when I slipped it on, the exact opposite of what I'm feeling. "She's too good to me," Zachary murmurs.

"More like too good *for* you." It's Father's turn to slap him on the back, so hard Zachary coughs. "I need a drink." Father nods at me. "We'll talk later."

I watch him head for the bar, barely paying attention to what Zachary's doing until he slips an arm around my shoulders and tries to press his mouth to my cheek. "Stop," I admonish him, shoving him so he staggers backward. "We're not together anymore, remember?"

He shoots me an irritated glare. "Please. It's my last night in this country. I'm leaving, Violet. For *months*. If I want to kiss my girlfriend, I will."

"You keep forgetting I'm your *ex*-girlfriend." I pull my arm out of his hold when he tries to grab me again. "Please, Zachary. Stop."

If Ryder saw Zachary do this to me . . . would he have stopped him? Not that he's been around to notice, even though I hear he's just back from London. The last packaging meeting we had, his assistant Luann led the entire thing—rather efficiently I might add, but still.

My connection to Ryder McKay has been effectively severed. Funny, how having Ryder out of my life, the façade became easier to maintain. I segued right back into quiet Violet mode. Working diligently in the office all day, attending meetings, making decisions, taking conference calls. Going home to no one, ignoring my sisters' calls, not wanting to see anyone and face too many questions.

It hurts to realize I meant nothing to Ryder. I was just a game, a silly, stupid girl who fell for his game and ended up . . .

Hurt. A robot. Unfeeling.

Destroyed.

"Just for tonight can you act like you like me? Come on, Vi," Zachary pleads, his voice rising, drawing the attention of a few people as they enter the private room I booked for tonight.

"Hey." Fingers curl around my arm and I turn to find Rose standing before me, a brittle smile on her face. "Help me out for a minute, will you?"

I nod, releasing a shuddering breath. "Of course. Excuse us please, Zachary?"

He glares but doesn't say a word, and I hurry away with my sister before he starts in again.

"What the hell is going on?" Rose asks me the moment she finds a private corner so we can talk. "Why are you letting him treat you like that? I thought you two broke up."

God. I haven't spoken to my sisters. I haven't told them anything, and now I'm embarrassed to say a word. I'll look like such a fool. "I—I don't know."

Rose frowns. "You don't know? Come on, Violet. Be honest. I know you were messing around with Ryder. What happened to him? He's way more exciting than that boring stiff you've been with for far too long."

I can't hold back any longer. I tell her everything. Well, as much as I can tell her in a two-minute span. She stares at me in disbelief, her arms wrapped around herself, her mouth hanging open when I wrap my story up.

"And I think Father is . . ." I sigh. This is harder to say than I thought. "I think he's, um, dating Pilar."

"*Ew.*" Rose rears back with a grimace. "I hate that bitch."

I burst out laughing. "I hate her, too." We both start laughing and it feels so good. Almost like a relief, to confess everything, to get it off my chest.

"Listen." Rose grabs my hand and gives it a squeeze. "Get through tonight. Stand by that dick's side and smile and make nice. He's gone tomorrow morning, bright and early. You can endure a few more hours with that ass, can't you?"

"Yes." I nod firmly. "I think I can." If I've endured the last two years of my life with him, I can handle tonight. "What if . . ." My voice trails off and I shake my head. "Never mind."

"What if what? I've got you, no matter what. Don't forget that," Rose says firmly.

My love and appreciation for my sister nearly overwhelms me. She's going to back me unconditionally. I needed to hear that. Badly. "What if Ryder shows up tonight?" I ask, my voice small. This is a celebration for Zachary, after all, so I doubt that will happen, but . . .

"You really think he would show his face here tonight? If he does, I'll kick him in the balls. No, scratch that. I'll *stomp* him in the balls with my stiletto heel." She kicks out her foot, admiring her newfound four-inch weapon. "I'll have him howling in pain, no problem."

Is it wrong that I want to see him suffer just a little bit? I feel so brittle, like the littlest thing will cause me to shatter.

And he's off advancing his career, after having a great time in London. Probably going after the job Father offered *me*. I hate him.

I miss him.

I've fallen in love with him.

"And if Pilar shows up, that should be really interesting," Rose continues, clearly on a roll. One I sort of wish she would stop. "I don't know what I'll do if Daddy introduces her to us as his girlfriend. Slap her in the face?"

I roll my eyes. Now, that sounds amazing. "I wish."

"Kick her out of the restaurant, then?" Rose asks hopefully. "You could totally do that, you know. Since you planned it."

"No, technically it's Zachary's party and considering she was fucking around with him not that long ago, he probably still wants her here. Hoping for another chance, maybe?" I shudder at the thought.

"So gross." It's Rose's turn to roll her eyes. "And *fucking* around? God, Violet, you really have changed. Let's go grab a drink. I think we're going to need it."

Being the good sister that she is, she keeps the drinks coming. All through dinner as I sit next to Zachary, enduring his droning on and on about the opportunities that await him in London. The changes he wants to make.

I want to snort, but I keep it in check. Worse, I'm tempted to toss my drink in his face. But I restrain myself. Looking to my baby sister for guidance because for once, I need her.

Desperately.

Father sits at the table with us but he's distracted. His date hasn't shown and I know he's disappointed. Rose and I aren't. More like we're thankful that skank Pilar didn't make an appearance.

"Think I should give a speech?" Zachary asks as the wait staff clears our plates. "I think they want me to."

I glance around and notice that no one's paying much attention to Zachary. They're all talking among themselves. I don't know where he's getting the idea that people want to hear a speech from him, but I decide to indulge his ego. "I'm sure they'd love to hear a few last words from you," I say warmly. Rose slams her knee against mine, but I don't miss a beat. "Go for it, honey."

"I'll do it now, before dessert is served." He leans in and drops a surprise kiss on my cheek before he stands and heads for the other side of the room, stopping in front of the wall of windows that overlook the city.

"What's wrong with you? Why are you being so nice?" Rose whisper hisses.

I shrug. "You told me to keep up the pretense. That's what I'm doing."

"You called him *honey*." Rose makes a gagging motion with her finger toward her mouth.

A little giggle escapes me and I realize I'm buzzed. *Good.* I need the alcohol to help me forget. I've been depending on it too much lately, but I don't even care. "So? I want him to make an ass of himself. It'll be fun to watch."

"I guess," Rose mutters. "More like torture for us forced to listen to him."

Zachary starts speaking and I straighten my shoulders, assuming the perfect supportive position. Rose keeps poking at my side, like the annoying little sister she used to be, and I hardly move save to jab my elbow in her direction every time she tries to touch me.

"I want to thank everyone who came to celebrate with me during my last night here in New York," Zachary starts, a perfect smile on his perfect face. He's a little drunk, too, talking as if he's really got this job in London when he doesn't.

But that's okay. We can let him pretend.

He goes on and on, reminiscing over when he first started working at Fleur, the guidance Father gave him. He seems to acknowledge every single person in the room who is listening to him with rapt attention, who laugh and cheer along with him, and I wonder how he can still charm everyone else but not me.

Not Rose, either, who keeps making these rude snoring

sounds. I send her dirty looks and she shuts up, but within minutes she's doing them again. Not that I can blame her. This is the Zachary show and we're all here just to watch and indulge him.

This night, everything about it, feels surreal. I'm me but I'm not. My body is here but my mind wanders. I think of Ryder. I don't want to, but I do. I can't help it. What is he doing? Where is he? Will he avoid me forever? Do I want to see him? Can I ever forgive him for what he did?

I want to. It hurts too much, being away from him. It might have started out as a trick, but our relationship turned into something so much more . . .

"And finally, I want to thank Violet, who changed my life in so many ways, all for the better. I'm a lucky man to know her, to have her in my life." He pauses and sends me a loving smile. "Come up here, Violet, please? Join me."

I stiffen at Zachary's words, at all the sincerity I hear in his voice. At his request for me to stand by him and fake being happy for him.

I can't do it.

Rose quits jabbing me and instead rests a reassuring hand on my arm. Father is looking at me oddly, as if he's questioning whether I should go up there at all. And all I can do is stare at the open doorway. At who I see standing there.

Ryder.

With Pilar standing next to him.

My heart cracks in two. He brought her. I could kill him. Or hug him. I don't know which one would come first.

I stand, Rose's hand falling away from me, Father's gaze tracking my every move. With a forced smile I make my way through the tables, nodding at those I know, praying my nerves won't betray me. Zachary greets me with a smile as I approach him, taking my hand and pulling me to his side. He kisses my cheek, then turns to everyone watching us.

"I plan on making this woman my wife someday," he says

assuredly, and I don't protest. Just smile as everyone claps, with the exception of my sister and father.

Oh—and Ryder and Pilar.

I can't believe he brought her. I can't believe he had the nerve to show up.

I hate him.

I miss him.

I can hardly stand to look at him.

But my gaze goes straight to him. I see the hatred he has for Zachary in his gaze, the sneer on his gorgeous face. A face that haunts my dreams, that makes me want to weep and smile all at once.

"Finally!" someone shouts at us, making Zachary laugh and tug me closer. I play along. All while my gaze stays on Ryder's. He doesn't look away either and I can feel his anger, though the chemistry between us is still there, too.

He hates me.

He misses me.

He wants me.

I know it.

Pulling myself out of Zachary's hold, I make my way back through the room, heading straight toward Ryder and Pilar. She leaves, going where I don't know, and I don't care. All I want is to see Ryder. Tell him I hate him.

Tell him I miss him.

The wait staff enters the room, bringing with them our dessert on large trays. Beautiful slices of chocolate cake sit on the little white china plates, but I'm not interested. I'm the farthest thing from hungry.

"Hello." I stop just in front of him. His scent reaches me. Deliciously male and all Ryder. His hair is a catastrophe. He needs a haircut in the worst way. There's stubble on his cheeks and jaw and there are dark circles under his eyes. He looks terrible.

He looks amazing.

And as usual, he doesn't say a word. Merely dips his head toward me in greeting.

I clench my hands into fists, wishing I'd brought Rose's shoe with me so I could stab him with it. Talk about shocking. That would be quite the way to end Zachary's going-away party, wouldn't it?

"You shouldn't be here," I tell him. He needs to know he's not welcome. The moment Zachary spots him, all hell could break loose. "Zachary doesn't want you at his party."

Hatred flickers in his eyes at the mention of Zachary's name. "I'm not here for him."

Hope fills my heart and I immediately tell it to go to hell. He didn't come for me. He's a heartless user. "Then why are you here?"

His gaze never leaves mine. "You know why," he says, his voice low.

"No. I really don't." I shake my head, hating the confusion that haunts me.

"I want to win you back."

His words are devastating. I can't believe him. I won't. "No, you don't. Go back to your date." I turn to walk away from him but he stops me, his hand going around my upper arm so I can't get away. Electricity crackles where he touches me and I try to jerk out of his hold, but he won't let me. He tightens his grip, almost to the point of pain, and I swear I feel faint.

"She's not my date."

"You came together."

"No. We showed up at the same time. Unfortunate coincidence. She's with your father," he murmurs, flicking his head toward the table I vacated only moments ago.

Glancing over my shoulder, I see Father standing, Pilar beside him. Rose staring at them both like they'd mutated into soul-sucking aliens right before her. She lifts her head, her gaze meeting mine, and mouths "what are you doing?" very clearly.

I don't know, I want to tell her, but I don't.

I turn back to face Ryder to find him studying me. "I don't want you here," I tell him very clearly, aware that his grip has softened. His thumb is stroking the inside of my arm and causing all sorts of flutters to start low in my belly.

"Liar," he murmurs. "Come with me."

"No."

"Violet."

"No." I shake my head. "I won't."

"Are you defying me?"

"You have no right to ask me that question. You gave up that right when you confessed that you just used me." I take a step closer, my face in his. I want him to see how angry I am. How hurt. I want him to feel it.

I want him to hurt, too.

"I made a mistake. I didn't want to end it, but you were so mad," he admits, his gaze dropping to my mouth, looking at it like he wants to kiss me. My lips ache to feel his mouth on mine.

"Of course, I was mad. Please." I roll my eyes, snarky laughter starting to form when he slips his hand around my nape, holding me still.

"Don't," he whispers fiercely.

"Don't what?"

"Make a mockery of this. Of us. I fucked up, Violet. But I still want you. Need you. Care for you." He presses his forehead against mine and closes his eyes. He's so close. So deliciously, wonderfully close I want to kiss him. Forgive him and accept him back into my life for good.

But I don't. I shouldn't. No matter how badly I want to.

"Don't tease me, Ryder. I mean it." I rest my hands on his chest, my fingers curling into the fabric of his shirt.

"I'm not teasing you. I think . . . I know that I'm falling in love with you." His fingers tighten on my nape and he pulls away slightly. I tilt my head up at the exact moment his mouth crashes on mine and he's kissing me. Claiming me. Making me his.

Just.
Like.
That.

Chapter Thirty-two

Ryder

I SHOULDN'T HAVE COME TO THIS FUCKED-UP PARTY FOR A MAN I hate. But knowing Violet would be there, I reluctantly made a late appearance, running into Pilar through some sort of dumb shitty luck. I've been back in the city not even forty-eight hours and I wanted to see Violet. *Needed* to see her.

The moment I caught a glimpse of her, I felt like I'd been struck in the heart, punched in the balls. She was wearing a yellow dress that floated around her legs. All I saw was skin. Her bare arms, her long legs, her hair up, revealing her neck, the very neck I want to touch and kiss and lick and bite.

I should have turned around and walked out. Instead I watched as Lawrence had her come up to stand beside him, declaring he was going to make her his wife someday.

He's not going to make her do shit. That is going to be my privilege and mine only.

She stood next to him like some sort of show pony, smiling politely, putting on that act she's so good at. I saw the dead look in her eyes, the hollowness there. Saw, too, the way her eyes lit with fire every time they met mine.

She *is* mine. I'm making my claim right now. Right here. I was an idiot, letting her walk away from me like that. I should have fought for her. I would have come for her sooner, but I got called away to London. An opportunity I couldn't pass up, an opportunity that she put in my lap. *Not* Pilar.

Violet.

I break the kiss first, needing to catch my breath. Needing to see her and make sure she's real. Her swollen lips are parted and damp, those beautiful, velvety brown eyes staring at me like I've both lost my mind and I'm the best thing she's ever seen.

"Ryder . . ." she starts, but I place my finger over her mouth, silencing her.

"Don't fight it," I whisper. "Don't argue, don't tell me what I did was wrong. You're right. I handled it all wrong. I fucked up. Letting you walk out of my life was a huge mistake."

She blinks but doesn't say a word. I trace her lips, a surge of emotion pulsing through me when she draws my finger into her mouth and sucks just the tip. Watching her do that takes me to a place I can't go yet. A place where I take her somewhere private so I can tell her—more like show her—how I really feel.

I remove my finger from her mouth, not wanting this moment to be about lust and sex. I need her to see what she really means to me.

"Forgive me." The words rasp from the depths of my chest and my throat is scratchy. I'm laying everything on the line. Every fucking thing. "Please."

"I want to." She closes her eyes and a tear escapes, sliding down her cheek. I stop its progress with my thumb, my heart cracking in two at the sight of her pain. "I want to so badly. I miss you, Ryder."

"I miss you, too, baby. Being in London without you just about killed me. I wanted you there."

She opens her eyes, staring at me. "Really?"

I nod, caressing her cheek, thankful she's not pushing me away. She's my woman. Mine. I own her. She fucking owns me.

I'm in love with her. The moment she walked out of my apartment I knew it. Knew that I couldn't live without her. This was my chance and I couldn't fuck it up. Never again. I needed to play right by her. Show her just how much she means to me.

"It was so awful, listening to your confession that night. I've never been so hurt. I was—" She presses her lips together and sighs heavily. "I was falling for you, Ryder. So hard. And you stomped all over me like I didn't matter. You broke my heart."

Without a word, I grab hold of her arm and pull her along with me as we exit the room. She protests mildly as we hurry down a darkened hallway toward the back door of the restaurant, saying she forgot her purse, her phone. I glance over my shoulder, seeing everything she's feeling shining in her still tear-filled eyes. Stopping, I run my thumbs across her cheeks, catching as many falling tears as I can, then I lean in and kiss her forehead. "Your sister will get your purse and phone. Just . . . come with me."

"Where are we going?" she asks softly.

"I don't know. All I know is . . . I need you." I close my eyes against the swell of emotions that threaten. I won't fuck this up. I refuse to ruin this. We can start fresh, Violet and I. That's all I want. All I need.

Violet.

WE ENTER HER DARKENED APARTMENT AFTER HER DOORMAN let us in and I grab hold of her before she starts toward the lamp that sits nearby, needing the darkness. "Are you really okay with me being here?"

She steps close to me, leaning her forehead against my chin. "Yes," she whispers. "Everywhere I look, you're here. Even when you're not."

I slip my arms around her waist and pull her close, relishing the feel of her body against mine. It's only been days. A week. And I feel like it's been months. Years since I've seen her. Held her. Touched her. Kissed her.

"Will you forgive me, Violet? For what I did?" I ask.

Reaching for her face, I cup her cheeks and tilt her head up so I can look at her, barely making out her beautiful features in the dim light the cracked blinds let in. "Tell me, baby. I need your forgiveness."

She presses her lips together and slowly nods. "Y-yes."

I hold her more firmly, my fingers pressing into her scalp. "I'm falling in love with you. You'll probably tell me I'm not because I don't know how to love, but I'm one hundred percent positive that's what I feel for you."

"Oh, my God." She closes her eyes, her entire body seeming to sag. She said I broke her heart. Seeing her like this is breaking mine, slowly but surely, into a million tiny pieces. All I want to do is put her back together again. Let her put me back together again. "You don't mean it. Do you?"

"I fucking mean it. Don't ever doubt me again. I swear I'll be nothing but truthful with you for the rest of our lives." I give her head a little shake and she opens her eyes, staring at me. "I'm in love with you, Violet."

Violet presses her trembling lips together and swallows. I see the gentle movement of her throat. Leaning in, I press my lips to the spot where her pulse throbs and I whisper against her skin, "Tell me. It's okay if you don't feel the same . . ."

She grabs hold of my wrists and clings to me, reminding me of the first night I took her against the door. How I fucked her and left her like a coward immediately afterward.

This woman makes me feel too much. Makes me soft when I've been nothing but hard. Unfeeling. I didn't like it then. I hated it.

Now, I crave it. Need it. Need her.

I brace myself for her answer.

"You broke me, Ryder. You were the first man I felt truly safe with and then you hurt me so bad with your words, with the truth. I didn't know . . ."

She pauses, and I smooth my thumbs across her cheeks, wanting her to know I need to hear the rest. No matter how much she's torturing me, I have to know. "You didn't know what?"

"After I left your apartment, I didn't know if I could ever forgive you for what you did." A choked sob escapes her and I release my grip on her face to pull her into my arms, running my hand up and down her back as she cries against my shirt, her tears soaking the fabric.

"Don't cry," I whisper against her hair. "I'm not worth your tears."

"Yes, you are. You're worth all I have to give. Don't you see that?" She lifts her head and I push the hair away from her forehead, my gaze roaming over her every sweet feature. I can't believe she's back in my arms. I'm never going to let her go. "I hate when you say you're not worthy of me."

"I'm not," I say firmly.

"Yes, you are," she says just as firmly.

"Can you forgive me, Violet?" I pause, running my index finger across each of her eyebrows, down the slope of her nose. I want to memorize everything about her. "For breaking your heart?"

She stares me straight in the eyes, her gaze unwavering. "As long as you promise never to do it again."

I kiss her forehead, her cheek, along her jaw. The sharp intake of her breath encourages me and I kiss the tip of her nose, either side of her lush mouth. Teasing her, teasing myself. "I promise," I whisper against her lips just before I take them.

Violet melts into me, sliding her arms around my neck, her body pressed firmly to mine, her full breasts crushed against my chest. I slide my hand down, over her backside, devouring her mouth with my lips and tongue and teeth as I slip beneath the hem of her dress and touch the bare skin of her ass. My fingers toy with the lace of her thong and she moans, her lips falling away from mine.

"I missed you," she whispers as I trace the crack of her ass with the very tip of my finger, making her shiver. Her mouth is at my neck and I'm hard in a second. "So much."

"Never again will I let you go." I grip her ass, my touch possessive, my emotions all over the fucking place. This woman belongs to me and no one else. "You're mine."

I mean it. For once in my life, I fucking mean it. Something—someone—is more valuable to me than any possession. *She* is my possession. An obsession.

One I revel in gladly.

"Yes," she murmurs against my throat, licking and sucking at my skin. "I love you, Ryder."

I close my eyes, trying my best to keep my shit under control. But her words nearly bring me to my knees. She's pushing me. Prodding. She makes me want to give in to my baser needs and take her like the animal she turns me into every single time we're together. "Violet."

"Hmm?" The sexy hum against my neck makes my eyes cross. Her hands sliding down my chest and slipping under my shirt to touch my stomach make my muscles tense. This is happening too damn fast, when I want to savor her. Linger over every inch of her fragrant skin. Absorb her into my body so she'll never, ever leave me again.

"You're driving me fucking crazy," I mutter, grabbing hold of her shoulders so I can wrench her away from me. I need the distance to gain some control before I rush this and fuck her where she stands.

The wicked smile that curves her lips surprises me. "Good."

"Good?" I frown, realizing she's putting up a fight. That she wants to cross me.

And my girl gets off on this.

"Remember when you told me you would wreck me?" she asks.

My frown deepens. I don't like having my words tossed back

at me, especially when I said them in a moment of anger. I'd been furious that night. Furious that she wanted me despite all my threats, the awful way I treated her, until my fury morphed into something else. Something that scared the hell out of me.

I'd found the woman who seemed made for me. Just for me.

"You don't really wreck me, not in a bad way. I'm broken without you. I . . . I need what you do to me, what you do *for* me. The things you say, how you touch me. I crave it." She closes her eyes and I bet if it were brighter, I'd see the familiar blush steal across her cheeks. "Wreck me, Ryder. Tear me apart and put me back together again in the way only you know how. Make me feel safe."

I stare at her, shocked at her words, at the request she's making. She's giving herself to me. She wants what only I do to her, what only I can make her feel.

When I don't say anything she touches my cheek, her fingers tentative against my skin. "Please?"

I can't resist. I've never been able to resist. And now that she's given me permission . . .

Stepping away from her, I watch as confusion flashes across her face, along with fear. She's afraid I'm rejecting her.

She has no fucking idea how wrong she is.

"Take off your clothes," I demand, loving how pretty she looks in the pale yellow dress but more determined to see her out of it. "Now, Violet," I tack on when she doesn't move.

My voice, my demand, pushes her into action and she reaches to her side, undoing the zipper near her waist, just under her arm. The dress loosens, revealing the pale lacy straps of her bra, and then she's tugging it off completely, pulling it up and over her head and tossing it to the ground with an eagerness I can practically feel. She stands before me in blush pink lace and nude-colored heels. Mouthwateringly beautiful and all mine, ripe for the plucking.

Her nipples are hard little points, poking against the thin lace of her bra, and her skin is flushed with arousal. I've never seen a prettier sight.

"Take it all off," I say, my voice low, my thoughts dark and sinister. I would never, ever hurt her and she knows this, but I can't deny I like it rough. I like seeing the flash of fear in her eyes just before the pleasure comes. I love hearing her sharp gasps and harsh cries.

If this makes me a sick, twisted fuck, then she's just as bad.

And I love her that way. Need her that way.

Chapter Thirty-three

Violet

I'm naked and trembling, save for my shoes, which Ryder demanded I keep on. Draped over the giant overstuffed chair that matches my couch, my legs spread over the arms, my feet dangling, my body on complete display for his perusal. I'm at his mercy, and I can't ignore the trickle of fear that pools in my belly.

The arousal wins over the fear, though. I want this. Need this from him so badly my entire body shakes. He hasn't even touched me yet and I'm afraid I'll come if he so much as grazes my skin with his fingers.

I want to let go and let him take over my body, my pleasure, completely. Take me to where I can let all the pretense fall away and become who I really am, who I am only with this man who's shown me how to fly.

Tonight my life did change in ways I never thought possible. I'd dismissed any thoughts of another chance with Ryder. I believed it truly over. I was fully prepared to be alone, thinking I would be fine with that. Knowing deep down inside that was the farthest thing from the truth.

And then he saved me. He said the exact words I needed to hear, showed me just how much he wanted me—how much he loved me—and I left with him. He fought for me.

I needed that. Needed him. I have what I want. Who I love. There's no looking back now.

We're in this together.

I'm greedily watching him as he strips out of his clothes until he's completely naked, his thick cock rock hard and curving up toward his washboard belly. My mouth waters and I wish I could lick his skin. I love his beautiful body, the way he looks at me with those heated blue eyes, his hair a disaster created by my hands, the tattoos that decorate his upper body . . . everything about him, I love. Want. Need.

"Beautiful," he whispers as he drops to his knees reverently and runs his hands from my knees up, palms coasting along my inner thighs, making me shudder. Making me weak. His thumbs barely brush against my hot, wet center and I bite my lip, releasing a quiet moan. "All pretty and pink and glistening."

I lean back against the chair, holding my breath when his face comes closer to the place I want him most. He'd turned on the lamps earlier, the living room glowing brightly enough that we can see every single detail of each other's bodies and normally, I would be mortified. Embarrassed.

But I'm not. I want him to see me. I want him to know what he does to me. How much I want him. I can't control my body's reaction to him and I don't want to.

"You want my mouth on your pussy?" he asks roughly, his thumb tweaking my clit almost painfully.

I nod, unable to find my voice.

"Say it." He leans in close, his mouth almost grazing my folds. I can feel his hot breath against my vibrating skin, and my lids flutter as I fight to keep my eyes open. I don't want to miss a thing. "I need to hear you say it, Violet."

"Touch me," I whisper, purposely not saying what he wants. I'm drawing this out and when I see the irritation flare in his gaze, I know he realizes it.

"Not good enough." He backs away, taking with him his

heat and scent and touch, and I whimper, needing him close. Needing his mouth on me. "Say exactly what you want from me. I won't give it to you until I hear the words."

A trickle of moisture slides across sensitive skin and I clench my inner muscles to stave off the need that's ratcheting up inside of me. But it's no use. I want him so badly. I need to feel his hands and mouth and tongue on me. In me.

Now.

"Touch my pussy," I whisper, pleasure bolting through me when I see approval fill his gaze. "Lick it. Suck my clit. Make me come, Ryder. Please. I need you."

"Perfect." He's back where I want him, where I need him, his hands gripping my thighs and holding them open, his fingers digging into my skin roughly. I hope he bruises me. Marks me. Making it known that I'm his.

His mouth nuzzles my pussy, his tongue darting out for a lick. All the while he never looks away, his gaze remaining locked on mine, and I stare at him, my chest tight, my body tense, as he tongues my pussy with expert precision. Playing with my clit, searching my folds, circling my entry. He slips a finger slowly inside me and I groan, wanting more, wanting his cock but not wanting this moment to end, either.

"Like that, baby?" he whispers. "You taste so fucking good. I could do this for hours."

I don't know if I could handle him doing this for hours. I'd probably faint. Or die from too many orgasms.

"Don't stop," I whisper, my eyes sliding closed, concentrating on the way his mouth moves over my skin, his lapping tongue, his finger sliding inside of my welcoming body. And then he's gone, his mouth and finger leaving me, frustrating me. I open my eyes, glaring at him to find him glaring at me in return.

"Watch me," he demands. "Keep your eyes on me."

I do as he asks, already fighting against the orgasm that wants to sweep through me. It's like a slow summer storm forming in the pit of my belly, warm and dark and almost scary. I'm shivering, a moan escapes me when he pulls my clit between his lips and sucks hard. My lids flutter and it's such a struggle. I want to close my eyes and fall under the spell his mouth is working over my body, but I don't for fear he'll stop what he's started.

And the very last thing I want is for him to stop.

"Close?" he whispers against my flesh. He circles my clit slowly, the feeling so exquisite a long, shuddery moan escapes me, and he smiles. *Wicked, terrible man.* He knows what he's doing is exquisite torture. "Ask for it, Violet."

"Make me come." The words fall out of me in a rush, my belly quivering, my legs trembling from the awkward position I'm in. I feel like I could shatter at any given moment. I *want* to shatter.

Fall completely apart so only Ryder can put me back together again.

The orgasm explodes within me in mere seconds, making me cry out, my hips bucking of their own accord against his face as wave after wave of sensation washes over me, draining me completely.

"Beautiful," he whispers as he moves up my body to kiss me, his lips covered with my juices. "Taste yourself. See why you drive me wild."

I lick and suck his tongue, do the same to his lips, and then he's pushing away from me, reaching out to pull me into a new position. He eases my legs off the arms of the chair until I'm sitting, docile and perfect, perched on the edge. My thighs shake, I feel dizzy, completely overcome, and he reaches beneath my chin to tilt my face up, forcing me to look at him.

"I don't know how long I can hold out until I have to fuck you," he murmurs, stroking my chin with his thumb.

Staring at him, I say nothing. I know we should probably talk more. We're too caught up in the sexual haze that overcomes us every time we're together, but things need to be said. Exposed.

Confessed.

"Fuck, you're so beautiful, Violet. I'm sorry," he whispers, his fingers gentle as they brush through my hair.

I move so I can sling my arms around his shoulders. "Sorry for what?" I ask as I run my fingers through his soft hair, stroke the back of his neck. I never want to stop touching him. Never want to let him go. He's become . . . everything to me.

Everything.

"For hurting you. Saying what I said pushed you away and I did it to protect you, which is fucking stupid." His hands run down my back, making me shiver.

"Protect me from what?" I ask.

"Me." He tilts his head back, his unwavering gaze meeting mine. "I can't help but wonder what you're doing, wanting to be with a man like me."

I smile as I trace the line of his jaw. "You make me feel. You challenge me and you care about me more than any other man I know. You've shown me so many things in such little time and I can't wait to see where you'll lead me next. I'm in love with you, Ryder."

"I love you, too, Violet. I know . . . I know it's all happened so fast, but . . ." He pauses, his expression going serious, his entire body still. "Your father wants me to go to London."

Pressing my mouth to his, I whisper against his lips, "He wants me to go to London, too."

"Really?" He sounds surprised, but not irritated like Zachary had when I mentioned it to him. I love that about Ryder. To him, I'm an equal. "Doing what?"

"Whatever I want. It would be an executive-at-large position." I dip my head, kiss his neck, lick at his salty skin. I can't get enough of him. "What about you?"

"International brand marketing." He sounds so proud and I squeeze him close, simply enjoying the feeling of his hot, damp skin on mine. "Sounds pretty fucking impressive, doesn't it?"

"It sounds amazing," I whisper against his neck.

"He offered me the job. Told me more than once that you praised my abilities."

I lift my head to smile at him. "I did."

"As long as they were my professional abilities." He chuckles and my heart soars. The mood between us has changed. What I thought would be another filthy endeavor of long, hard fucking has turned . . . sweet. Tender.

Loving.

"Always." I shift and press my chest to his, enjoying the closeness, the sound of his heart, the sensation of his chest rising and falling with his every breath. I close my eyes and savor just sitting with him. Absorbing him.

"Come with me," he whispers, his hands going to my hips, tickling my skin. "Let's go to London together."

"Do you mean it?" I lift my head, breathless at the words he's saying. He wants me to go with him. "We haven't known each other very long . . ."

His fingers press into my flesh so hard I gasp. I lift my head to see his eyes are blazing with heat and aimed right at me. "When you know, you know. I was stupid, trying to deny this, but I can't any longer. You're mine, remember?"

I stare at him, overwhelmed by what this means. "Yes," I whisper. "I remember."

"Come with me, Violet," he demands. "I don't ever want to be apart from you again."

I nod, too overcome to speak. More tears come, filling my eyes, spilling down my cheeks, but they're not sad tears. I'm happy. Happy that he would want to make such a commitment to me, thrilled that we're together. That he wants me just as bad as I want him.

He brushes the tears away, catching them with his thumb, his lips. "Don't cry," he whispers. "You're killing me, baby. All I ever want to do is make you happy."

"I'll go with you," I finally say, gasping when he grabs me tight and falls against the back of the chair, taking me with him. He clutches me close, kissing me as he lifts his hips, thrusting his cock deep inside me again and again. I'm his captive; I can't move as our bodies slap together, damp with sweat, skin on skin, his cock hitting just right deep inside my body until I'm crying out and he's shouting my name, the two of us coming together, like some sort of miracle.

But that's what we are, Ryder and I. What we share is like a miracle. Our strange little relationship that should never have worked, that makes no sense . . .

It makes absolute, perfect sense after all.

At least to us.

And that's all that matters.

Epilogue

Violet

Six months later

THE PARTY IS IN FULL SWING. EVERYONE WHO IS ANYONE IN London high society is here tonight, ready for the launch of the Violet Fowler Collection for Fleur Cosmetics.

And here I hide away in the bathroom, chewing on my nails nervously, not wanting to face them.

What if they hate it? We postponed the launch once already, due to our move to London. Pilar took great delight in that, complaining to Father that I wasn't prepared, but he shut her down, defending me like a good father should.

That they're still . . . lovers baffles me, but I can't tell him what to do. Just like he can't tell me what to do. We've come to a peaceful understanding that we don't talk about Pilar. Ever.

Rose, though? She's furious. She even quit Fleur for a while, going on a sabbatical. Sounds better than her leaving in a huff because she's upset about her father's romantic choices, which is the real reason she's gone.

I miss her. I miss Lily, too. And Father. But I'm not alone here in London. I have my biggest support, my man. My lover. My Ryder.

Rising from the overstuffed couch in the powder room, I go to the mirror and study my reflection. I'm wearing makeup from my collection. From the special gold eye shadow created for the upcoming holidays to the deep red lipstick, everything on my face is by me. Early reviews have already come in and they're full of praise, which reassures me, but still.

This party feels like everything. As if the success of the collection depends on their reception, which is ridiculous, but I can't help myself.

I've never been so nervous over a work project in my life.

Someone knocks on the door I purposely locked and I turn to look at it, watching as whoever it is turns the handle but can't get in.

"Sorry, occupied!" I yell, wishing whoever it is would just go away and leave me alone. I need five more minutes to gain my composure before I go out there and face the slaughter.

"Violet," Ryder's voice hisses from the other side. "Damn it, open the door."

Rising from the couch, I rush to the door and undo the lock, letting him in. He strides inside, turning to face me as I relock the door, and I can see the irritation written all over his handsome face, the stiffness in his posture that indicates he's frustrated.

"What the hell are you doing hiding out in here?"

I shrug, unable to answer. I don't have a good enough explanation. "I'm scared."

"Of what?" he asks incredulously. "Of impressing them so much you won't be able to fill all the orders that will pour in come Monday?"

I roll my eyes, suppressing the urge to laugh. He's my biggest champion and I adore him for it. "They might hate it, you know. Some of the biggest names in fashion and beauty are out there just waiting to skewer me and my collection."

"Who fucking cares? For every one who hates it, there will

be fifty who love it." He holds out his hand and waves his fingers. "Come here."

I go to him without protest, letting him wrap me up in his arms. I rest my head against his chest, breathe in his delicious scent, as I close my eyes and absorb the comfort he offers me.

"What the hell are you wearing?" He pushes me away from him, his hands gripping my shoulders as he rakes his gaze over my body. My dress is blood-red lace, a sleeveless column of fabric that skims my body to my ankles. The bodice is open and plunges deep, all the way to my navel, exposing plenty of skin in what I hope isn't in an obscene way.

Judging how Ryder is looking at me, it might be borderline obscene after all.

"You don't like it?"

"I fucking love it, but my God, Violet. You're completely exposed." He sounds . . . horrified. Like he's my father or something, which I find so infinitely amusing I start to laugh.

This only makes him scowl.

"You're not wearing a bra, are you?"

I glance down at my exposed chest. The lace perfectly covers up my breasts, thanks to body tape. "How can I? You'd see it."

"Right," he says tightly, his nostrils flaring.

I decide to goad him. Something I've become quite skilled at. "Let me tell you a little secret—I'm not wearing any panties, either."

His shoulders fall the slightest bit. "Fucking great." He looks so handsome tonight in his black suit and the tie I bought him to replace the one I ruined so long ago. I told him to wear it, and now we match perfectly.

"Easy access for later?" I step into him and kiss him, then wipe away the smudge my lipstick left on his mouth. "I marked you."

"Good." He slings his arm around my waist and holds me close. "I love it when you mark me."

"I never do."

"That's why I love it. It's such a rare occasion. I, on the other hand, mark you all the time." He runs light, sucking kisses along the length of my neck and I bat him away, but it's no use. Not that I want him to stop.

"Save that for later," I murmur, tilting my head to give him better access. "We should get out there."

He lifts his head. "Are you ready?"

I nod, ignoring the nervous trembling that threatens to overtake me. I can do this. I've made plenty of public appearances before. I'll be fine. Really.

"Then let's go, baby." He releases his hold on me but takes my hand, entwining our fingers and bringing our linked hands up to his mouth. He presses a kiss to my knuckles, his gaze hot, his voice deep, as he whispers, "I love you."

My heart aches at his words; they mean so much to me. Words he's never uttered to anyone else, ever.

"I love you, too," I whisper, leaning in to give him a kiss. "Let's do this."

"I'm right beside you," he says as he leads me to the bathroom door and unlocks it, the roar of the crowd in the ballroom almost deafening even from all the way over here.

"I know," I murmur with a nod, trying my best to exude confidence. I've got this.

"I'll never leave your side tonight." He's trying to reassure me but I can't answer, too wrapped up in my own fear to focus on how hard he's working to help me. To ease my worry.

"Thank you." I offer him a tremulous smile.

"Your dad is here. And so is Lily."

I gape at him, happiness filling me. "Are you serious?"

"They wouldn't miss your big debut."

"What about Rose?"

He slowly shakes his head and I fight off the twinge of disappointment that threatens. I need to focus on the positives tonight.

And all those positives came true because of this man. His guidance, encouragement, and faith in me fuels me like nothing else.

"Thank you." I wrap my arms around him again and hold him close, right before we enter the noisy ballroom. "For everything."

"Anything for you," he tells me, his lips against my hair, his hand on my backside because hello, it's Ryder. It's as if he can't keep his hands off my ass.

"Anything?" I ask, pulling away slightly so I can meet his gaze.

He nods solemnly, every emotion and feeling he has for me shining in his gaze. "Everything."

The moment we walk through the door, all worry, all nervousness lifts away, and I smile, glancing about the room at all the smiling faces. Seeing a few friends, fellow employees, some even from Fleur in New York. My father is standing close by, Lily by his side, the two of them wearing such huge grins I can't help but smile in return.

Ryder slips his arm around my waist and guides me through the room, guiding me through life. Leading me and being the partner I needed so desperately but never knew . . . until I met him.

Now I have him. He's mine.

And I'm his.

Acknowledgments

The idea behind this book/series started as a tiny seed in my brain many years ago. I wanted to write a book about sisters with flower names and I wanted it to be a paranormal story (they were going to be nymphs).

Clearly, the original idea has changed. A lot.

I'm so thankful to Bantam/Random House for publishing *Owning Violet*. A huge thank you to my editor, Shauna Summers, for encouraging me, for believing in Ryder and Violet's story and for helping me make it stronger. Also a big thanks to Sarah Murphy for pointing out that Ryder acted like a "horny manservant" in the first, very rough version. I secretly wish for a horny manservant, just sayin'.

Bantam's art department rocks my socks off because the covers for all three books in the Fowler Sisters series are gorgeous. Thank you, thank you, for blessing me with such beautiful covers that take my breath away. To the entire team at Bantam, especially Gina Watchel, it's been an amazing experience working with you and I'm thankful for all that you do. And to Jin Yu for your enthusiasm behind *Owning Violet*. I feel as though you're their personal cheerleader and I appreciate all of your ideas to help spread the word.

And to all the readers—I wouldn't be here without you. Thank you for all your support. I hope you love Ryder and Violet as much as I do.

Playlist Note

I had the *Great Gatsby* soundtrack on repeat while writing *Owning Violet*, especially the last half. Specifically the songs:

"Back to Black" by Beyoncé and André 3000
"Over the Love" by Florence + The Machine
"Hearts a Mess" by Gotye

The words from all three of those songs reflect Violet and Ryder's story so strongly. I hope you check them out if they're unfamiliar to you.

The Fowler sisters may share a last name, but they couldn't be more different. The next novel in *New York Times* bestselling author Monica Murphy's scintillating new series is all about the youngest sister, Rose, and the gorgeous, but dangerous, man who steals her heart.

STEALING ROSE

Available soon from Bantam Books

Turn the page for a sneak peek!

Chapter One

Rose

WHAT DO YOU DO WHEN YOU DISCOVER SOMETHING ABOUT your family that you never wanted to know?

You pretend it doesn't exist. That your perfect little family is precisely that—untouched. Pristine. No amount of tragedy has ever put its fingers upon us. At least, that's what we want you to believe. There are books out there, unauthorized biographies about my grandmother and her legacy, Fleur Cosmetics. How my father and my sisters and I have continued on with that legacy as best we can, referencing us as if we're somehow insufficient. Daddy is the one who made it flourish, though he gives all credit to Grandma and she takes it, the greedy old lady that she is.

I love that greedy old lady to bits. I really do.

My oldest sister, Lily, has done a piss-poor job of carrying on the legacy, and she'd be the first to admit it. Her brutal honesty is one of the things I love best about her, though most of the time I resent her actions and the attention they receive. She is all about the spotlight and when it doesn't shine on her, she will do whatever it takes to snatch back that light so she can revel in it.

Then there's Violet, the middle sister. The quiet one. The secretly strong one. Oh my God, is she strong. She's been through so much. Tragedy has placed its greedy hands all over her, yet somehow she's always risen above it. Now she's so happy with her man, Ryder, and I can't begrudge her that. He's so intense sometimes it's almost scary, but then he sees Violet and his eyes get this dreamy sort of haze to them . . . he's a total goner for her.

It's sweet. *Too* sweet. My jealous side can hardly take it.

Me? I'm the Fowler sister everyone believes is normal, with a bit of a fighter streak in me. Grandma says I'm closest to her personality-wise and I want to believe her, but I don't know. Do I really want to be like her? Like any of them? My disillusion with the Fowler image is firmly secure on the worst night possible.

I don't know what to believe anymore, after what I just found out about our mother. The tragedy that no one ever, ever talks about—even those unauthorized, horribly scandalous family biographies gloss over the death of Victoria Fowler. I don't remember much about her, and what I do recall is fuzzy at best. Those memories are fueled by my sisters, though, since they actually do remember Mom, especially Lily. The loss was especially hard on her. Hence Lily's outrageous behavior from the age of about fourteen until now.

At least, that's what we all blame it on, including Lily. I'd like for once to see her take full responsibility for her actions, but I doubt that will ever happen.

There is more to our mother's death than I ever knew. I wonder if Lily or Violet knows. It's such a touchy subject, one I don't broach with them . . . ever. As for Daddy, I never talk about Mom with him. He swept our mother's death under the rug, something he's so good at doing. Threw himself into his work instead of focusing on his daughters, though he wasn't a bad father per se. A tad neglectful sometimes?

Yes. Most definitely.

We strive for perfection, yet every last one of us is far from perfect. When I was little, I was protected in this silvery, pillow-soft cocoon where nothing ever touched me, or the people I loved. Not even my mother's tragic death brought by her own doing could bother me. How could it, when no one ever talked about it?

But I want to talk about her now, after reading her last diary. The one I discovered when I was given a box of her old things by Daddy. He finally cleaned out our mother's rooms and closet. He'd kept them preserved for so long, but now that his new . . . girlfriend is in the picture, he's banished all reminders of our mother from his home.

Forever.

I couldn't even look at the contents of that box without nerves eating me up and feeling nauseated. I kept what was in there a secret from myself for months. Until a few nights ago, when I finally opened the box and found her diary filled with passages she wrote up until she took her own life.

Fascinating reading. And sad.

So incredibly sad.

What's happening tonight . . . things could be revealed. Moments from our family history are going on blatant display. All of it controlled by my grandmother, which means . . .

It will all be glossed over—become glossy perfection. Isn't that the term Violet used for her collection when they discussed packaging? That could be the Fowler family theme.

I watch as Grandma approaches me, a fond smile on her face, her eyes misty with memories.

"I want you to wear this tonight." Grandma Dahlia presents the large, square box to me, her frail hands shaking the slightest bit, causing light to glint off the diamond rings on her fingers. "It hasn't been worn by anyone in ages."

We're in my hotel room, my grandmother having knocked on the door only minutes before as I was getting ready. We were all supposed to meet later but here she is, resplendent in her gorgeous black lace dress, a sweet smile on her face as she studies me.

I have no idea why she's doing this and I don't like the uneasiness that settles over me as I take the box from her, my fingers smoothing over the black velvet. It's old, the color slightly faded, and it's heavy. Slowly I open the box, anticipation and fear curling through me, and I gasp at what I see lying inside.

A necklace. But not just any necklace—the stones alternate between a brilliant white and a soft, blush pink, and each one is perfectly cut, perfectly matched. "It's beautiful," I murmur, surprised at the size of the stones. I've never seen this necklace before in my life, and I thought my sisters and I had all played with or worn every piece of fine jewelry there is in the family. "What are the pink stones?" I ask as I drift my fingers across the necklace almost reverently.

"Why, they're diamonds of course, some of the rarest in existence. Your grandfather gave this necklace to me long, long ago." Grandma sounds at once both proud and sad. "A present for when your aunt Poppy was born." A wistful sigh escapes her and she looks away, her mouth turned down, her eyes shining with unshed tears. "You remind me of her. So much."

"I do?" I purposely keep my voice soft, not wanting to upset her. I didn't know my aunt Poppy, though I wish I had. She died in a horrible car accident before I was born. I've seen photos and yes, there's a resemblance, but I never thought I looked much like her.

More tragedy. More death. Another family member we lost that we rarely mention. It's frustrating, how easy we forget what happened to those who are gone. If I disappeared, would everyone eventually forget me too?

I don't want to forget anyone. Not my mother. Not my aunt Poppy. I want to know more. But tonight is supposed to be special, so I should let it go. This night is for my grandma, for the family, for Fleur.

I will myself to let it all go.

"Oh, yes." Grandma turns to face me once more, the tears

gone, the familiar determined look back in place. She rarely shows any signs of weakness and I love that about her. She's such a strong influence on all of us, and right now I'm in need of some of that strength. "There's some similarity in your looks, but really it's your attitude. The way you speak, the way you behave, how you think. It's just like my Poppy. She was so vibrant, so full of life, and she was never afraid to back down from something she believed in. Just like you." She reaches out and clasps my face in her wrinkled hands, her fingers cold against my skin. I smile at her but it feels fake, and I let it fade. The velvet box is clutched in my hands, my fingers digging into the stones. "Wear this tonight and think of Poppy. Think of Fleur."

"But Grandma, tonight is all about *you*." We're in Cannes for the movie festival, here to watch the premiere of a documentary about Grandmother and how she started Fleur. She monitored every step of this documentary and claims it is a collaboration of love between her and the director and producers of the piece.

More like my grandmother dictated to them exactly what she wanted mentioned. Again, no one crosses Dahlia Fowler. To do so would be taking an extreme risk. The woman has no problem making claims of ruining people.

She *has* ruined people. Time and again.

"*You* should wear this necklace. Not me," I say when she still hasn't said anything. She's staring at me as if she can look right through me and I blink, hard. Blocking my thoughts, my anger, my frustration. But she can probably see it.

Grandma just chooses not to talk about it.

"No." She shakes her head and drops her hands from my face. "You should wear it. It's yours for tonight. Violet has her young man and Lily has . . . whatever it is she thinks she wants. Such a disappointment that she's not here." Her mouth screws up into this bitter line and I want to smack my sister for yet again letting everyone down. "You . . . you deserve this. Wear it proudly. It's your legacy too, my love. Never forget it."

My legacy. Most of the time, I don't feel like it's mine. It's Daddy's and Violet's. It's slowly becoming Ryder's. Lily's? Not so much. She loves to wear Fleur cosmetics and spend the Fleur money, but that's about it. She has no desire to be a part of the family business. She's allergic to work.

Lucky bitch gets away with it, too.

I work like crazy and no one notices. I'm tired of putting the time in. I'm tired of dealing with Daddy and his horrific relationship with that slut Pilar Vasquez. The woman is scheming to become a permanent part of Fleur Cosmetics—by nabbing the last name Fowler—pure and simple. Does she really care for him? Doubtful. But my father is so blinded by lust he can't see beyond her big tits and her supposed great ideas.

"My legacy," I murmur as I withdraw the necklace from the velvet casing and hold it up to the light. It sparkles, the blush-colored stones even more dazzling when they shine. I vaguely remember hearing of the Poppy Necklace and I'm pretty sure I'm holding it in my hands at this very moment.

The necklace will look amazing with the white dress I'm wearing tonight. White may signify virginity and purity and all that other nonsense, but wait until everyone sees *this* dress. It'll blow their minds.

And I'm in the mood to shock this evening. This is my last hurrah before I give notice to my father next week. Yes, I'm quitting Fleur. I can't imagine staying there now. I made my escape for a short period of time after it came out that Daddy was dating one of the most conniving employees Fleur Cosmetics has ever had under its roof. Pilar rubs it in our faces as much as possible that she has our father wrapped around her little finger.

I hate her. I refuse to work with her, especially now that I've heard rumors that Daddy is promoting her. Not that he'd ever come to me and tell me about it. No one tells me anything. I'm ignored at Fleur. So much so that I don't think it's even worth continuing to work there . . .

Considering this evening will most likely be the last I'm representing the Fowler family for a long time—I know Daddy is going to be furious over my giving notice—I'm going all out. Besides, I've never been to the Festival de Cannes before. The necklace will only add to the effect.

Our family has been on public display our entire lives and most of the time, I don't mind, though I prefer to be in the background, much like Violet. Leave it to Lily to be our public representative. Not that Lily makes Daddy happy with her antics. Or Grandma, considering how scandalous my oldest sister is. She's tamed down somewhat, but she still has a flair for the outrageous.

I'm stealing that flair for the outrageous from her tonight, though. Since arriving in France, the energy surrounding the festivities has renewed me. Inspired me to take a chance and do something daring. Wild.

Like wearing a dress that might cause a scandal. Like mentally preparing the speech I'm going to give my father when I turn in my two weeks' notice once we're back home.

"Yes," Grandma says firmly. "Your legacy. And Violet's. Even Lily's. I'm proud of what I've accomplished, but I'm even more excited to see what you and Violet do with Fleur. Perhaps even Lily, if she ever gets her head out of her ass."

"Grandma!" I shouldn't be shocked at what she says, but every once in a while she does surprise me.

"What? It's true." Grandma shrugs. "Besides, someday I'll be gone, you know."

"But . . ." I start to protest and she shushes me in an instant.

"Hush, you know it's true. I'm eighty-three years old. I can't live forever, as much as I'd like to." She waves a hand at the necklace I'm still clutching in one hand, the velvet box in the other. "Turn around, my child, and let me put that on you. Why are you still in your robe? Shouldn't you be dressed already? The premiere is going to start soon."

"I'm almost done." Nerves suddenly eat at my stomach and I turn around at Grandma's direction, setting the box on the dresser beside me and handing the necklace to her so she can help put it around my neck. I'm taller than her, so I bend at the knees, making it easier for her to slip the necklace on. "Hair and makeup is finished. I just need to put on my dress and shoes."

"You'd best hurry, then." She slips the necklace around my neck and hooks the clasp before stepping away from me. "There. Let's see how it looks."

I turn to face her once more, my chin lifted, the weight of the diamonds heavy against my chest. I can't believe she's letting me wear it. From the few stories I've heard about it, the necklace rarely if ever makes public appearances. "What do you think?" I ask.

She contemplates me, her expression serious, eyes narrowed. "It's beautiful. Originally I thought I wanted Lily to wear it since she's the oldest, but she's not here. And the more I thought about it, the more I realized you're a better fit since you're so much like Poppy."

Guilt assaults me and I fight it down. I refuse to feel bad for what I'm about to do. I can't help it if Daddy chooses his conniving girlfriend over me. And I won't let him run right over me without a care. I need to stand up for what I believe in.

And what I believe in means never letting Pilar Vasquez have any sort of authority over me. That bitch can die before I ever let her tell me what to do.

"You didn't want Violet to wear it, hmm?" I touch the necklace, turning toward the mirror to my right. The necklace is stunning, even against the white silk robe I have on, and I stare at my reflection, overwhelmed at what the necklace represents.

Grandma's right. Fleur is my legacy too. I need to remember that. Not get caught up in the mess that's been created by Violet and Ryder against Daddy and . . . Pilar.

Ew. Just thinking about that bitch makes me want to puke.

But I can't stand by and let everything happen *to* me. I need to make a stand. I need to let Father know that I don't approve of his tactics. Something needs to be done. Someone needs to say something.

If that has to be me, then so be it.

"Please. Violet has that lovely diamond on her finger. She doesn't need any other piece of jewelry right now." Grandma waves a dismissive hand at my suggestion. She's right. Ryder asked Violet to marry him only a few days ago and my sister is positively giddy over it.

For so long I'd been afraid she'd saddle herself to that idiot Zachary Lawrence, but thankfully she saw the light and found a man who cherishes her. Understands her. Respects her. That he's gorgeous and sexy as hell doesn't hurt matters.

I'm a little envious of my sister's happiness, but I can't begrudge her finally finding joy. She's had so many challenges and she's fought every single one of them. I'm proud of her. Happy for her.

Truly.

"Enjoy that necklace. There's a segment in the documentary about it." Grandma winks and starts toward the door. "We'll meet in your father's suite in twenty minutes. Don't be late, you hear me?"

"I hear you," I call to her, shaking my head as she exits my room with a loud slam of the door.

I turn to face the mirror once again, my hands going to the belt of my robe and untying it, letting the white silk part before I shrug it from my shoulders. The fabric falls to the floor in a crumpled heap around my feet and I kick it away, then stand tall.

The necklace looks good against my skin and I take a deep breath, watching my naked breasts rise and fall. I might need to have a drink or two before I don the dress. I'll need the liquid courage to face my family later.

Daddy will probably hate the dress. Violet will be scandalized. Grandma will laugh and silently cheer me on. And Pilar? She's accompanying us tonight, which I hate. I don't give two shits what she thinks about the dress. Or me. Or any of us.

Sighing, I go to the closet and pull the dress out, smoothing my hands over the layers of white, frothy chiffon that make up the skirt. Considering it's strapless, the necklace will be showcased perfectly. I wonder what sort of story surrounds the piece of jewelry?

I'll find out soon enough.

"NICE DRESS."

A shiver moves down my spine at the sound of the warm, inviting tone. I glance over my shoulder to find a very handsome man standing there, an arrogant smirk on his face as he blatantly scans me from head to toe.

My smile falls and I straighten my spine. I was tricked by his voice. He sounded flirty and fun, but really he's just a creeper. Not bothering to say anything, I turn my back to him but he halts my progress, his hand going around the crook of my elbow.

I glance down at his offending hand on my arm before I lift my head and send him a withering stare. He doesn't even flinch. He doesn't let me go, either. "Aren't you Rose Fowler?"

He has an accent, but I can't tell from where. The room is filled with a variety of accents and languages; people from all over the world are at this party tonight. "I am," I say, trying to discreetly pull out of his hold. But his fingers tighten not so discreetly on my flesh and I feel like I'm trapped.

"I thought so." He flashes me a smile but it doesn't quite meet his dark eyes. Everything about him is dark. His hair, his swarthy complexion, the way he's looking at me. A ripple of unease washes over me and I glance around, looking for my father, my sister, or preferably Ryder, who'd tell this asshole where to go if I asked him to. "Interesting documentary on your family."

"Thank you." I'm trying to be polite but he's making it so hard. He pulls me a little closer to him and I'm assaulted by the scent of his strong cologne, put off by the way his fingers smooth over my skin in a seeming caress. "If you could let me go, please. I have someone waiting for me."

"Who?" He smiles, his teeth overly white, especially against his dark skin.

He's making me angry. "Um, that's none of your business."

"You're here alone tonight, aren't you? I saw you on the red carpet." He tugs so hard on my arm my footsteps falter and I nearly fall into him. "Let's go have a drink."

Politeness flies out the window as I rest my hand against his chest and give him a push. But he doesn't budge. His fingers are so tight they're pinching my flesh, and he'll probably leave a mark. "Let. Me. Go," I say through clenched teeth, fighting the panic flaring deep within me.

"You heard the lady," another man practically growls from behind me, his deep, very pissed-off voice setting every hair on my body on end. "Get your fucking hands off her. Now."

The man's fingers spring away from my arm like someone turned a key and unlocked his hold on me. Backing away with his hands in front of him as if he's pleading for mercy, he laughs nervously. "Didn't know she was with you," he says shakily just before he turns and practically sprints away from us.

Rubbing my arm, I turn to thank my savior, but the words die on my lips. Dark brown eyes watch me, the man's demeanor still and silent, his full mouth pulled into a straight line. He's wearing a black suit, not a tuxedo, and it appears a little frayed around the edges. As if he's had it for a while and it's been to the dry cleaner one too many times. Despite the aged suit, he has an elegant yet rough air about him. As if he doesn't quite belong among this glittering, powerful, and extremely rich crowd.

"Thank you," I croak, clearing my throat and feeling like an idiot.

"Are you all right?" He steps closer, but his presence doesn't feel threatening. More like protective, what with the look of concern marring his handsome features. His brows are drawn downward and a lock of golden-brown hair hangs over his forehead.

That I have the sudden urge to push the hair away from his face and test its softness is . . . crazy.

"I'm fine." I offer him a shaky smile, which only makes him frown deeper. "Did you know him?"

"Never seen him before in my life. But a lot of assholes come to these parties. Cannes is full of them," he says, sounding disgusted.

I want to laugh. My savior has no problem being crude and I can appreciate it. At least what he says is real. Most of the people I encounter speak carefully, as if they're afraid they'll somehow offend me.

"Thank you for scaring him away." I absently rub at my arm, glancing down to see the imprint of the man's fingers glaring red on my skin.

"He marked you." He grabs hold of me, his large hand engulfing mine as he holds my arm out to inspect it. His jaw goes tight and he lifts his head, scanning the room with ruthless efficiency. "I should kick the shit out of him."

"It's no big deal." My heart is all fluttery at the protective streak this man is displaying and I tell myself to get over it. "It's already starting to fade. See?"

Slowly he tilts his head down, his lips parting as he examines my arm. He releases my hand, his thumb smoothing lightly over the imprints, causing gooseflesh to follow in the wake of his touch. "Does it hurt?"

"No." I shake my head, watching in fascination as he continues to touch me. His hand is so large, his skin tanned and the pad of his thumb rough. I can't help but wonder at the difference between the two men. Both of them strangers, yet my reaction to each is so completely different.

"Good," he says gruffly, though I can tell he's not satisfied with my answer. His hand drops away from my arm and I wonder for a moment if he's going to take off after my so-called assailant, but he remains rooted in place, standing next to me as if he was put on this earth to be my protector for the evening. "Want a drink?"

"Oh, please." Before I can tell him what I want, he walks away without another word, his broad-shouldered body cutting a swath through the crowd, and they all part for him obediently. He's a head taller than the majority of the people in the room, so it's not difficult to keep tabs on him as he strides toward the bar across the way.

He doesn't smile at a soul, doesn't stop to make pleasant conversation with anyone either.

I'm completely fascinated.

"Who's the guy?" Violet magically appears at my side, her gaze dropping to my dress, pointedly taking in the slits in my skirt, my thighs playing peek-a-boo whenever I move. "Did you draw him in with the dress or what?"

"Not everyone is as scandalized with the dress as you are," I mutter, irritated that she's ruining my mood. Violet and I are usually on the same side about everything, but the moment I made my appearance at Daddy's suite before we all went to the premiere together, I knew she wasn't happy with my choice of attire.

And that hurt, despite my brave face and carefree attitude. I blame it on the fact that she's always had a motherly, almost protective attitude toward me. Daddy didn't like the dress either, but that's no surprise. Ryder gave me a high-five with a wicked grin on his face before we left the suite, and I appreciated that. Clung to his approval like some sort of anchor that was saving me from drowning. I needed any show of support to get through tonight.

You did this to yourself. The only one you have to blame is . . . you.

That naggy little voice inside my head needs to shut up.

"Can I be honest with you?" Violet turns to face me, her expression somber, warning me I'm not going to want to hear what she has to say.

I barely withhold the sigh that wants to escape when I answer, "Go for it."

"You're reminding me of Lily." She wrinkles her nose, looking both cute and disgusted. That's the ultimate low blow, saying I remind her of *Lily*. I feel like she stabbed me right in the heart. "The flashy outfit, the necklace. Did you know Grandma was going to let you wear it tonight?"

Ah, is that what this is about? That Grandma let me wear the necklace and not her? Maybe it was stupid, wearing such a dress. The press had shouted at me continuously as we posed on the red carpet. Asking me who designed it, where was Lily, since when did I get so bold. Hardly any of them asked about the necklace.

I wonder if that made Grandma mad.

"No, I didn't," I answer. "She brought it to me about a half hour before we all met. I had no idea she had it with her."

"She mentioned to me she was going to bring it to Cannes a while ago. But I figured she would want Lily to wear it. Since she's not here . . ." Violet's voice trails off.

"You're right, she did want Lily to wear it. She also said I reminded her most of Poppy." I absently drift my fingers across the stones, my thumb smoothing over the largest one set in the center. "So she let me wear it tonight. Said you didn't need to because you already have your big diamond on your finger."

Violet immediately holds her hand out, the diamond catching the light just right and making it sparkle. A little smile curls her lips as she stares at it. "She's probably right."

"I know," I say dryly, my gaze snagging on my savior, who's still waiting in line at the bar. His shoulders are terribly broad and he's so tall. His hair is longish in the back, in dire need of a trim, and he reaches back at the exact moment the thought passes through my mind, scratching at his nape absently before he turns, his gaze meeting mine all the way across the room.

The look in his eyes renders me completely still. Even my breath stalls in my lungs. I part my lips, the low roar in my ears growing louder, drowning out what Violet's saying to me, blocking out every little sound until all I can focus on is him.

He doesn't look away. Doesn't smile or lift a brow or wave a hand, no acknowledgment that we're watching each other. Slowly, the movement so subtle I almost don't notice it, he works his square jaw, his lips pressing together, his chest rising with his deep inhale. Squinting his eyes, one side of his mouth goes up slightly, the lopsided ghost of a smile appearing before it's gone.

In a snap.

The man turns, his back facing me once more, and I wonder if I imagined it all. Blinking, I tear my gaze from him and turn to my sister, who hasn't stopped talking. I have no idea what she just said. None.

All I can think about is the man who saved me.

And I don't even know his name.

PHOTO: COLBY RAIMER

New York Times and *USA Today* bestselling author MONICA MURPHY is a native Californian who lives in the foothills of Yosemite. A wife and mother of three, she writes new adult contemporary romance and is the author of the One Week Girlfriend series and the tie-in novella, *Drew + Fable Forever,* as well as the Fowler Sisters series.

monicamurphy.com
missmonicamurphy@gmail.com
Facebook.com/MonicaMurphyauthor
Facebook.com/DrewAndFableOfficial
@MsMonicaMurphy

About the Type

This book was set in Sabon, a typeface designed by the well-known German typographer Jan Tschichold (1902–74). Sabon's design is based upon the original letter forms of sixteenth-century French type designer Claude Garamond and was created specifically to be used for three sources: foundry type for hand composition, Linotype, and Monotype. Tschichold named his typeface for the famous Frankfurt typefounder Jacques Sabon (c. 1520–80).